CLEARWATER SUMMER

CLEARWATER SUMMER

John E. Keegan

AN AUTHORS GUILD BACKINPRINT.COM EDITION

Clearwater Summer

All Rights Reserved © 1994, 2000 by John E. Keegan

AN AUTHORS GUILD BACKINPRINT.COM EDITION

Published by iUniverse.com, Inc.

For information address:
iUniverse.com, Inc.
620 North 48th Street, Suite 201
Lincoln, NE 68504-3467
www.iuniverse.com

Originally published by Carroll and Graf

ISBN: 0-595-00784-8

Printed in the United States of America

For Macaela, Carla, and David.

———

In memory of Burchard Ross and Hazel Keegan.

I thank the many people who helped me before, during, and after the story's conception, including Rebecca Brown, Neil G. McCluskey, Bruce Wexler, fellow writers at the University of Washington, and especially, my parents, brothers, children, Shanti, and Macaela.

I cannot say what loves have come and gone,
I only know that summer sang in me
A little while, that in me sings no more.

—*Edna St. Vincent Millay*

They wouldn't let me see the body. But I couldn't accept the death until I'd seen some evidence. So I made a solo journey to the A&M Wrecking yard.

People in town tried to explain it away with bromides. Car accidents were the leading cause of death in the county for minors. Youthful carelessness. A neat package.

But there was nothing conventional about the death weapon or the victim. A hundred-ton Great Northern locomotive pulling forty-five boxcars had hurtled through town in the blizzard, unaware of a stalled car at the State Route 16 crossing. It wasn't the first time someone had died there. The train ran through that gully like a swollen river. It owned the channel. This was the chute where the train had to build speed before climbing out of the valley and onto the plains.

The yard, on the outskirts of Clearwater, was fenced off on the highway side to screen the wreckage. I must have looked lost when I pushed the door open and stuck my head inside the windowless wooden shed just inside the gate.

"In or out but don't just hold the door open!" The man behind the desk in the shack was Shorty, the operator of A&M. "Can't you see it's snowing?" The coils of a space heater next to his swivel chair glowed fire-log red. The room smelled like burning dust. A&M Wrecking calendars with bosomy farm girls covered the wall. They sat on fenders, roofs, and running boards of cars and pickups, wearing short pants and men's shirts parted generously down the front.

"Do you have the car from Friday's wreck at the crossing?" If it had really happened, he didn't need more details than that. If the whole thing was a conspiracy, fabricated in the four months I'd been away at college, I doubted they would have thought to include Shorty in it. Judging from the cigarette butts floating in the half-drunk bottles of cream soda on his desk, there was no pretense in this man.

He moved a plug of chew from one cheek to the other and spat into the galvanized mop bucket on the backseat that served as an office couch. The juice was forced through the gap in his teeth like milk from a cow's udder. It sang against the metal. "I'm the undertaker, who else do you think scrapes 'em up?" His voice was bitter as if he'd been sentenced to this job. "Who are you?"

"Will Bradford. Do you mind if I have a look at it?"

"If you're claiming ownership, you can have it," he said. "Usually, I get one or two good tires, maybe a speaker. This sucker's pure scrap." He shuffled through the mess of invoices and notes on his desk. A bottle tipped over. "Holy Christ!" Cream soda gurgled onto the papers before he could grab the bottle and put it upright.

"I don't want it, I just want to see it."

"You an adjustor or something? Believe me, it's totaled." He searched the mess on his desk for a rag. Finding none, he pulled open a drawer and retrieved two bent slices of white bread and dropped them onto the pool of soda.

"No, I'm just a friend."

"Your friend's been spooned out of there." He flipped the bread slices over and scrubbed them across the top of his pile.

"I know. I just want to see the car."

He studied me carefully as he wiped up the rest of the soda and tossed the soaked bread into his spittoon. "You some kind of masochist?"

I had to see how it happened, hoping the remains would explain something. "Just point me to it, you don't need to leave the hut."

"Didn't intend to, buster." He stuck his arm out, pointing past the 1959 calendar with a Daisy Mae blonde looking under the hood. "Follow the tracks, it's on the far side of the yard, the heap with the least amount of snow on it." He rang the bucket again and I imagined the bread on the bottom sopping up his spit.

As I wedged the door closed against the warped frame, the shack trembled. I immediately felt the sting of the snow blowing into my face. The thick flurries darkened the sky, creating a premature dusk. What a godforsaken piece of town this was.

The snow gave way, letting my shoes bog down in the brown mud underneath. Each rising step pulled against the suction of the junkyard. Wind whipped through missing slats in the fence. The tracks from Shorty's truck led me down an aisle bordered by damaged automobiles, derelicts draped white like ghosts, with dark cavities where windows or radiators had been bashed in. On the other side of the fence, I heard the rhythmic clank of a loose chain against the inside of someone's fender.

Where the tracks turned sharply left and then backed into the row on my right, I saw it. And gulped. The middle of the car was caved in like a beer can someone had stamped on. I recognized the twisted grill that had sprung free of the frame. If Shorty towed this, it must have been as a mangled sled because the wheels slanted inward perpendicular to each other.

I inched my way toward the driver's side. The window opening had been flattened to the size of a mail slot. I brushed snow off the roof, uncovering a patch of black, an appropriate color for a coffin I thought. Then I pricked my finger on something sharp and realized someone must have opened what remained of the roof with a pair of heavy tin snips. The jagged triangular hole was just large enough to pull a corpse through.

The car rolled when it was hit. They said they found it in the ditch several hundred yards past the crossing. That's how far the locomotive pushed it along the rails, the car a mere tumbleweed in the sweep of the cowcatcher. Everyone said it was a bad crossing, the railroad should have installed drop gates. In a blizzard, the train could spring on you out of nowhere.

The steering wheel had been squeezed oblong. I recognized the pearly knob. The knob was a way to make one-handed turns with the other arm draped over your date or carelessly flung out the open window on a hot summer day. Something to hold onto. Watching the snowflakes float through the hole in the roof and light on the hunks of seat cushion, I tried to imagine the explosion when it hit.

I couldn't accept that it was just an accident. That would excuse all of us. The pieces fit too well for coincidence. It was more as if people in Clearwater had willed this, as a way to clear the record, a way to bury what had surfaced the summer before the three of us started high school.

1

From the top of the diving rock, the sun made the river shimmer and flash like an unrolling ribbon of aluminum foil. The Clearwater River murmured as if all three thousand three hundred and fourteen people counted on the city limits sign were talking at once. Their conversations merged into a liquid hum.

Two days had passed since our eighth-grade graduation party in the school basement. But this was our first trip to Devil's Elbow and, for me, the official start of summer.

I knew that once Dad discovered school was out he'd suddenly have the need for more chores at the hardware store. Last summer, it was sorting wood screws that had become mixed from people picking up 1″ screws and dropping them back into the 2″ bin. When that was done, he noticed the whitewash was flaking off the concrete blocks and taught me how to operate a roller with an eight-foot extension handle. Working every second or third day, I had the whole outside repainted by the end of July and spent August scraping paint flecks off the show windows with a razor blade.

Wellesley Baker, Taylor Clark, and I took turns diving into the still spot, a deep pool protected by the bend in the river. The dark green water circled slowly in a whirl below the diving rock, a stone platform big enough to sunbathe the three of us. Wellesley and Taylor dove headfirst, seeing who could make the least splash. They teased me for doing cannonballs and lifesaving dives. I preferred head in last. Too close to the wall, you'd scrape the skin off; too far away, you'd break your neck in shallow water.

Fishing near this spot once, Grandpa Blane told me about his high school friend who'd dove outside the pool. Many times I'd studied that seam between the slow-circling water, which was safe, and the fast-passing water which bubbled and broke over the main bed of the river. When they pulled him out, Grandpa said his friend's mouth was bloody and his neck as limp as a jellyfish. The kid's dad had a bad heart and collapsed when he learned what happened. They started school late so everyone could attend the double funeral.

I quit jumping to referee. Wellesley's slender build gave her an advantage. She entered the water like a sharp pencil. The only points of friction were her kinky brown hair and the belt end that flapped loose from her cut-off jeans.

Taylor's skin was smooth enough, even with the dimples in his cheeks. He was a half inch higher on the kitchen door than me and, like everything else about him, his body was well proportioned. But he couldn't keep his feet together.

"You're a fricking liar, Wellesley!" Taylor's hands stripped the water off his stomach like a window squeegee.

Wellesley sat shivering on the rock with her arms wrapped around her knees. "Really, you looked like a pair of scissors opening." The sun sparkled off her glasses as she looked up at Taylor.

"Easy, you guys," I said. "Who cares how big the splash is? Let's talk about something else." I always ended up in the middle of Wellesley and Taylor's little tiffs. They were the boxers and I was the man in the black slacks who tiptoed in circles around them, slicing in to break up the clinches when things got too rough. They depended on it. Someday, I was just going to step out of the ring and see what happened.

"Yeah," Taylor said. He ruffled his hair and showered raindrops onto Wellesley. "Let's talk about stock . . . cars!" He let his tongue stick in the roof of his mouth on "stock," so it spit at Wellesley. "Is your old man going to chicken out of tomorrow night's races?"

"Eat shit, Clark!" Wellesley pushed against the side of Taylor's knee, knocking him off balance. "You're jealous because your dad's a refrigerator repairman."

Taylor faced her on all fours. "You're stuck-up! My dollar

bill says the Pink Lady gets skunked tomorrow!" His thick eyebrows raised a notch.

Wellesley moved her face closer to his. "The Pink Lady will wipe your ass with that dollar bill." She angled her head and snarled.

"Ding!" I stepped between them. "End of the round."

Taylor tried to push his head through my legs to get at Wellesley. I squeezed him off. "The Pink Lady's a loser!" he yelled.

"Taylor, come on," I said. It was obvious he was still mad about losing the diving. I knew he felt the same way about Wellesley's dad I did. When Wellesley wasn't around, he bragged about Mr. Baker and the "Lady." When you were fourteen and hadn't accomplished much, it mattered what your parents did. Telling people your dad ran a hardware store didn't get you very far. But it was another thing if your friend's dad drove the Pink Lady.

Taylor scowled.

I changed the subject. "Wellesley, you've got to take me horseback riding." My plans for the summer were simple— play golf, learn more about girls, and ride in the Junior Rodeo. I counted on Grandpa Blane for the golfing. Girl information was harder to find. Neither Taylor nor I had a sister and Wellesley was just a pal, not the type interested in dating. Horses were something else; Wellesley had connections. Her cousin owned two.

"I'll take you riding, Will," she said, "if you can beat me arm wrestling." Her thick brown hair had dried in a matted helmet.

"You're on," I said. Wiry as a monkey, Wellesley was too skinny to beat me. Standing on the unabridged version of *Webster's Dictionary* in my living room once, she easily touched the floor without bending her knees. But she didn't show a trace of muscle.

Of course, there were lots of things about Wellesley that didn't show right off. She didn't talk much about her family, except her dad. Everyone bragged about him. There wasn't a better stock car driver in the whole state of Washington. Her older sister Tiffany was a mystery. She was never around. I hadn't seen her since she graduated from high school a year ago. For that matter, I hardly ever saw her mom either. When we went to Wellesley's house, we hung around in her backyard.

"Taylor, hold my glasses." She dangled the glasses she'd worn since third grade by the strut.

Taylor put out his hand, avoiding her look.

Wellesley and I locked hands and chanted, "One—two—three—go!" We squirmed on our bellies. I could feel a sharp pebble digging into my elbow. Wellesley's puffed red cheeks and bulging eyes were inches from mine. I tried to think of the patron saint of strength and the only name that came to mind was Charles Atlas.

As she pushed my arm backwards, I thanked God this wasn't the school cafeteria. The back of my hand hit the ground and I let loose the air in my lungs. Wellesley rolled over and smiled up at me. Taylor hooted with glee.

I didn't know where she hid her strength. Maybe it came from her dad. His Paul Bunyan build carried enough strength for a squadron. I figured even in a daughter, his manliness was bound to show through. It was hard to be mad at her with that grin though. One half of her upper lip raised farther than the other, as if a string held one side down. I'd seen that smile survive bike wrecks, falls off fences, and hailstorms hard enough to tear holes in your clothes.

The three of us wandered over to Beller's house after dinner. Some nights there was nothing to do. Grandpa Blane said monotony was one of the benefits of peace. That's why the country had elected Eisenhower to a second term. When we arrived, Beller and Woody were sitting on the curb. Wellesley suggested swimming at the river again and Taylor nixed it.

"How about kick the can?" I asked.

Taylor poked me in the ribs. "Goo goo, Bradford," he said in baby talk, wobbling his head, "isn't that a little grade schoolish?"

"Yeah, how about Mother May I?" Everyone laughed with me.

"Taylor's scared of the dark, Taylor's scared of the dark,"

Woody said in a mocking, falsetto voice and the rest of us joined him.

Taylor knew he was beaten. "Okay, we'll kick the stupid can!"

Everyone yelled, "Not it!"

Taylor covered his ears. Slowly, he lowered his cupped hands, staring into each one as if something had leaked out. When I squinted to look, he boxed my cheeks and jumped into the air laughing, "Okay, I'm counting to fifty. Stay in this block!"

The four of us scattered as Taylor put his head against the weeping willow in Beller's front yard. When you stood next to the trunk, you had to look out through green tears on stringy branches that drooped almost to the ground. All of us had carved our initials on it at one time or another. We'd never played kick the can anywhere else.

Taylor's words ran together like an auctioneer, ". . . one thousand nine one thousand ten one thousand eleven one thousand twelve . . ." He kept his voice loud to prove he wasn't cheating.

Cutting between Beller's and Durgan's, I vaulted over the picket fence into the backyard. When the dog barked, I changed course, heading directly through the garden for the rear gate. The compost pile smelled of warm garbage. I'd lost count in my head but it felt like more than fifty.

Standing on the trash can, I could just reach the lasso hooked with bent-over nails to the tar-paper roof of my garage. I hiked up, pulling myself by the rope, and stepped into the maple tree that had worked its way into the eaves of the garage like an ingrown toenail.

My hand was on someone's jeans. "Who is it?"

"Me!" Somehow, Wellesley had beaten me into my own tree.

"How'd you get up here?"

"Same way you did," she whispered, "with your rope. I saw you do it once."

I straddled the branch and sat. Although we faced each other, the tree trunk blocked my view of her face. There was a silver dollar moon behind her in a sky dusted with cigarette smoke clouds.

"Do you think he'll find us here?" she asked.

"I don't think so, but I didn't think I'd find you!"

"Are you mad at me for being here?"

"No, I just can't believe you knew about my tree." Neither of us said anything for a while. The leaves swept the shingles. There was no sign of Taylor on the section of street visible between the houses. Wellesley shifted position every few minutes. So did I, to keep my legs from going numb.

"Does your dad talk much about his races?" I asked.

She hesitated. "Sure."

"God, you're lucky! I'd love to drive a race car someday, wouldn't you?"

"Sure, but not here. I'd want to run at Indianapolis or set a speed record in the Utah Salt Flats." The moonlight illuminated the right side of her face. She looked proud.

"Yeah, but you could start here, maybe race against your dad?" I couldn't think of a bigger thrill than beating Mr. Baker.

"My dad says this is small town stuff. People here don't know what racing is. When he gets a better car, he'll join the circuit."

I didn't exactly know what the "circuit" was. Wellesley had a great advantage being in a racing family, probably talked about it at dinner. Just once, I'd like to be the mutt under their table and listen. "Are you going with him?"

"If he goes, I go," she said. "He said he'll make me the first female NASCAR driver in the country. Baker and Baker. How does that sound?"

"Pretty cool."

"When he moves up, he says he'll give me the Pink Lady."

"You're kidding?" I said. "Hey. When you move up, can you give the Lady to me?"

"If I don't drive the heart out of her first."

I laughed and waited for her to say more. "Wellesley, can we go to the races with you tomorrow?"

"Who's 'we'?"

I knew she knew, that's why she asked. "Taylor," I said, "you, me, and Taylor."

She stared off toward the street. Wellesley sometimes annoyed me the way she went at Taylor and then afterwards only seemed to remember what he'd done. By now, she should have been used to his carping whenever he lost at something. It was obvious his cracks about the Pink Lady were sour grapes. Maybe there was another reason for her reticence.

"Are you going with your mom?"

"She never goes."

"I can't believe that. Your dad's a modern Ben Hur! How can she stay away?"

No answer. I wondered if she'd heard. With my fingertips, I grazed the tops of the goose bumps that had grown on my arms from thinking about the races. The rubbing made them bigger. Wellesley had wrapped herself around the trunk in a bear hug.

"Wellesley . . ."

She interrupted. "Don't you sometimes wonder what it would be like to just live in a tree like this . . . away from everyone else . . . come and go when you please. . . ." Something about being in the dark must have loosened her tongue. Maybe it was the distance from the bottle caps, bugs, and baseball cards that were the props of our real world. "Do you ever wish you were somebody else, Will?"

"When I was young," I said, "I wanted to be a cowboy with leathery skin and a gravelly voice." The bright side of her face smiled at me. "Then I was going to be a milkman driving standing up from house to house with the van door open."

She laughed. "Those are things you want to be, Will. I mean have you ever wanted to be in someone else's skin?"

I'd missed her point. Somehow she always seemed to look at things a little harder. "You mean like me being Taylor?"

"Bad choice, but yeah, that's what I mean."

If I was Taylor, I wouldn't have freckles. I could trade my nondescript hazel eyes for his steely blue ones that girls drooled over. If I had his parents, maybe I'd get his allowance. And his mom was beautiful. "I guess I haven't." I tried to sound philosophical. "It's a neat idea."

We continued talking in the tree, telling each other dark secrets. Beller kicked the Folger's coffee can and made it home free. My crotch was aching to be walking again.

Taylor yelled from the street. "Woody, you're dead as a doornail! I see you on top of Nelson's car."

No one answered.

"Let's try and make it into home," I whispered. "Everyone will be getting ants in their pants wondering where we are."

"Let 'em itch. It's Taylor's problem, not ours. He hasn't even set his rabbit feet in your backyard yet." She hitched her leg over the branch and started down.

We split up once we reached the ground, to make it harder for Taylor to catch both of us I said. The truth was I didn't want Taylor to think we were operating as a team.

Crawling on my hands and knees between the blackberry bushes and the foundation of Beller's house, I parted spider webs with my face. From my spot next to the front porch, I could see the coffee can. This was the closest place to home base. My palms were wet with squished berries that smelled like marmalade when I tried to wipe the stickiness off my face. Taylor paced in the street, turning his head like a periscope.

Taylor about peed in his pants when Wellesley and I reached the tree free. Spread flat as a coat of paint on top of the car, Woody was "it."

When we split up after the game, I took the alley home and stopped under the maple tree where Wellesley and I had talked. The dining room drapes were still open. I could see Dad's head sticking up over the back of his chair where he read the newspaper, watched TV and wrote checks. Mom was probably already in bed reading.

Wellesley's talking had stirred up thoughts of some of the other things I didn't understand about her. She once told me her favorite animal was the wolf. Her sister Tiffany had been kicked out of school for drinking and ran away from home three times. Her grandpa shot her dad's dog when he was a kid and left him bleeding to death on their porch. For as much as she told me though, I had the feeling there was something else bothering her.

2

By the time we reached our seats at the fairgrounds, a cloud of exhaust hung over the arena. We sat on a two-by-ten plank about eight rows up. I sucked it in. "I love that smell!"

"Car farts, Bradford," Taylor said, "miles and miles of car farts."

"Spoken like an expert," Wellesley said.

Even Taylor laughed as he pulled his sweatshirt off. When his head reappeared, the part was mussed and he immediately combed it out with his fingers and looked around. Taylor lived for the glance of a pretty girl, but the stock-car crowd was mostly men, some with their kids. The only girl I knew who gave a hang about racing was Wellesley. But that was because of her dad.

With the brilliance from the racks of tilted spotlights, it seemed warm enough for short sleeves. Taylor wore a Hawaiian print, Wellesley her pink T-shirt (she was superstitious), and I had on a golf shirt Grandpa Blane had given me. We sat high enough up to see over the wire and post fence that circled the track. The fence was designed to hold rodeo horses. For the stock races, they reinforced it with bales of hay and stacks of old tires in the turns. Plastic banners blocked people from sitting in the first two rows of seats.

Stock cars from all over northern Idaho and eastern Washington were parked in the infield like colored dominoes. The infield was also the pit for tire changes, engine repairs, and first aid. In between races, the drivers and mechanics hammered fenders away from tires, revved engines, and smoked cigarettes.

"There he is," I said to Wellesley as soon as I'd spotted

her dad. He was wearing a pair of blue denim mechanic's overalls and was smoking. One foot rested on someone else's running board, a squarish jalopy with a wrinkled roof. On the door, it said "Little Brown Jug." The sponsor was Shirtcliff Oil Company. As Mr. Baker pumped his leg, the jalopy rocked back and forth and Mr. Baker laughed at the man in the driver's seat.

"Maybe your dad's trying to hitch a ride with that little turd-colored car," Taylor said. "The Pink Lady's in the toilet."

Wellesley just grinned over the top of her glasses at Taylor. She wasn't going to take the bait.

"It's the other guy who's going to need the life raft," I said, unable to restrain myself from siding with Mr. Baker.

"It looks like your dad is trying to capsize him," Taylor said.

"That's the way stock car guys talk to each other," she said.

After each race, the man in front of us with a pack of Camels rolled into his sleeve turned to tell stock car stories. They sounded like they were straight out of *True Life.* "Did you see last year's Memorial Day races?" He didn't wait for anyone to answer. "I think it was the first heat. That sonofabitch Baker"—he twisted his mouth and blew the smoke away from us—"his car was flaming like some kamikaze pilot. Flames shooting out of the hood vents, smoke pouring from the cab. I thought he was going to explode." His gut shook gently as he laughed. "A couple of mechanics tried to wave him into the pits with their fire extinguishers, but that bastard drove a lap and a half that way. Won the heat!" He took a long drag on his cigarette and turned to watch the action.

I'd seen the same race and thought Mr. Baker was going to burn himself to death. Anyone else would have bailed out. I jabbed Taylor, who was still staring at the back of the Camel man's shirt with his mouth open. "Taylor, you're going to be a driver. What would you have done?"

"Started spitting on it." He laughed.

Taylor was soon on a first-name basis with Bill, the Camels man, and he won Cokes for us from Bill in a bet on the third heat. But Taylor had to pay him back when he lost in the fourth.

The announcer named the entrants in the A-Main, the eight cars with the most points from the earlier heats. They were the hot ones. With each car, the announcer named the sponsors: Hanson Jewelers, Popeye's Galley, Trueblood Real Estate, Mountain View Funeral Home, Hometown Insurance Center, Polar Storage, and Shirtcliff Oil. I'd been in all those places except the funeral home. The Pink Lady, sponsored by the Arctic Cafe, had pole position in the third row.

I watched Mr. Baker drop his cigarette into the dirt, twist the heel of his boot into it and exhale. Then he slapped the top of the other guy's car and wove through the jumble of vehicles with stripes and bull's-eyes on the roofs until he reached his own car. Gripping the top of his helmet like a basketball player palming the ball, he crammed it over his ears. The chin strap dangled. He grabbed the post between the welded doors and tipped the car to make it easier to reach the window with his beefy leg. Swinging his other foot in, he lowered himself through the window and into the bucket seat behind the wheel.

One by one, the engines ignited. It was a marching band of flywheels, each engine blaring like a trumpet as the drivers pushed down on the gas. Occasional backfires punctuated the music. The conductor ushered them onto the track with the yellow caution flag as they filed into a moving formation, rumbling by us in a ragged military formation. The Pink Lady had a modified Ford coupe body that Wellesley said had been chopped and channeled. It was dented as badly as the skin on a golf ball. Behind the reinforcing bars across the radiator was the biggest Cadillac engine made. Wellesley said it was rebuilt for racing, whatever that meant. Mr. Baker's helmeted head filled the window.

"Your dad looks ready," I yelled over the roar of the engines.

Wellesley gave an okay sign with her fingers and smiled confidently. Taylor stared with his mouth open as wide as a drainpipe. This was the real thing and he knew it. Mr.

Baker's entrance had pretty well shut up any thought of another one of Taylor's Pink Lady jokes.

The crowd rose to its feet. People around us talked excitedly as if the whiff of the exhaust was some kind of quickener. The noise smothered the words, so everyone used gestures to help communicate, pointing to the cars moving slowly around the track, illustrating their predictions with one flat hand sliding in front of the other. The names of the drivers and the cars popped out of the racket—Beesley, Bomber, Baker and the Lady.

When the starter showed the green flag he'd been holding behind his back and frantically waved it at the lead car, the decibel level suddenly raised from target practice to a full-scale assault.

I yelled into the scream of the engines and the shrieks of the crowd, "Go Lady!"

Wellesley threw her fist into the air. Taylor put his fingers against the tip of his tongue and whistled. The cars chased each other into the critical first turn. Wellesley called it the "blood and guts" turn. This was where the cars were most congested and most apt to crack up. In a four-lap race, whoever emerged in the lead had a big advantage.

I screamed in Wellesley's ear, "Your dad's making a move!" Instead of hugging the red-and-white striped barrels filled with concrete which marked the inside of the course, the Pink Lady veered to the outside. She forced the brown jalopy driver Mr. Baker had been talking to before the race to slam into a stack of hay bales against the fence. The bales broke apart, scattering hay all over the hood as it skidded sideways out of control. Then Mr. Baker moved even with the outside driver in row two and passed him as they entered the far straightaway. He was in third place.

"Go gettum, Lady!"

Taylor leaned toward Wellesley. "Is this still just drivers' talk?" He hooted and slapped his thigh.

The starter grabbed the yellow flag and started fluttering it. This meant everyone had to slow down until the track was clear. In the first turn, three men had already run onto the track and were shoving the brown car into the infield and spreading around the stuffing from the stray bale of hay that had fallen onto the track. Meantime the cars entered the second turn. Mr. Baker wedged inside, so close to the Blue Torpedo they seemed locked together. As they exited, he shook off the Torpedo to take over second. The drivers decelerated as they moved into the straightaway and saw the caution signal.

My muscles relaxed. "One more to go, Wellesley!"

"Not bad, huh?" Wellesley said. Her eyes beamed through her glasses.

"He cheated," Taylor yelled. "The Pink Lady cheated!"

The man in front of us turned around and scowled at Taylor. An inky blue and red mermaid showed on the ball of his shoulder just below the cigarette pack. "Says who?"

Taylor took a big swallow and looked over at Wellesley and me. He was momentarily flustered. "You can't pass"—Taylor cleared his throat—"when the caution flag's out."

"First you have to be able to see the caution flag," Wellesley said.

Taylor started to point to the first turn to explain.

"That's just good driving, pardner," the Camels man said. "That ain't no Bible school out here. The lady's right. Baker had no way of seeing that piss-colored handkerchief waving until he'd already made his move in the south turn. In stocks, you take what you can get. That's why Baker's the class of the field!" Then he looked directly at Wellesley. "This tenderfoot has any more ethical questions, let me know."

"Thank you, sir," she said, smiling at Taylor, "I don't think he will. Just joking anyway, weren't you, Taylor?"

I was holding my teeth together to keep from laughing. Taylor's eyes rolled to the top of his head as if to say he didn't need that little lecture. We both knew Wellesley didn't need an ex-Marine, or whatever he was, to sit on Taylor. She could hold her own with anyone. If Wellesley had told the Camels guy that she was Mr. Baker's daughter, I had the feeling he would have bowed down to her right there.

When the guy in front had turned around and tucked his T-shirt over the spare tire above his belt, Taylor flipped him a finger. Wellesley put her hand up to tap the man on the shoulder and Taylor grabbed it and kissed it front and back to make amends.

The flagman let the cars circle one lap on caution. The trailing cars used the opportunity to close the gap with the car in front of them as much as they could without actually passing, this way abiding technically, if not in spirit, with the requirement to hold positions during caution. He turned them loose again at the original starting line and the drivers accelerated.

Mr. Baker chased first place Polar Storage through laps two and three, trying to take bites out of the lead car's back tires with jabs and pokes of the Pink Lady's bumper. The pink on the outside of the car misrepresented the personality of its driver. Mr. Baker used his vehicle as a weapon.

I poked Wellesley and showed her two fistfuls of crossed fingers as the dueling front-runners howled past us heading into the final lap. The Camels man pounded his fist into his palm. The outcome of the race wasn't going to cheer Taylor either way. If Mr. Baker lost, he'd have to hold his tongue; if Mr. Baker won, he'd have to bite it. So Taylor just stood there while everyone around him jumped and shouted.

Just as Polar Storage and the Pink Lady steadied themselves coming out of the last turn and pointed their hoods toward the finish line, a cocker spaniel ran from the infield onto the track. Maybe someone had called him from the stands. When he reached the fence he was confused and started zigzagging along the track looking for a way to get through. I heard the thunder of the approaching cars. The noise was so loud the dog couldn't distinguish background from immediate danger.

Polar Storage backed off; Mr. Baker did not.

The cocker was still rolling in the dirt like a bag of dirty laundry as the Pink Lady took the checkered flag.

"Oh, God!" I put my hand over my mouth.

The dog was motionless. The Camels man raised his fists over his head, exposing his fleshy spare tire again. People screamed as the rest of the field crossed the line. I wondered if I was the only one who saw it. Wellesley must have noticed my hands not clapping because she looked at me and frowned. She'd seen it too.

"Hot damn!" The Camels man turned to Taylor, shaking his head in admiration. "Did you see my man bust that puppy in the chops? Jeesuz, shit, Christ! He's something slick, isn't he. Takes more'n a mongrel to slow Baker down."

Taylor wasted no time choosing sides. "Nobody's gonna mess with the Lady," he said, imitating the man in front of us. "Hot damn, huh?" Taylor extended his hand like he'd just won the race himself and the Camels man shook it enthusiastically. When he took his cigarettes out, the man offered Taylor one too. Taking no chances on blowing his cover by choking into the guy's ear, Taylor declined.

Clearwater only had three stock car races a year and whenever they did, Miss Clearwater or the Queen of the Labor Day Festival presented the trophy to the winner. This year, there must have been a shortage of pretty girls the right age because Rebecca Amberly was both. I knew her younger sister, Monica, who was even prettier.

Taylor leaned in front of Wellesley and tugged at my arm, "Will, look at that!" He acted as if Wellesley wouldn't be interested in the girl stepping out of the convertible. The white sash said, "Miss Labor Day Festival." Her dress had so many silver sequins it made you squint.

Nobody was going to stop the festivities for a funeral. Miss Labor Day stood on the tiptoes of her high-heel shoes and planted a kiss on Mr. Baker's cheek. Near the fence, someone shoveled the buff-colored cocker spaniel into a gunny sack. The photographer's flashbulb didn't go and they made her do it again, this time her smile a notch less perky. Mr. Baker leaned over and wrapped one arm around the girl; with the other, he squeezed the gold trophy by the stem and held it high. Next to him, Miss Labor Day looked as pale as pearls. When he dropped her back to the flats of her feet, I strained to see if he'd left a grimy handprint across the sequins on her waist.

"Now, that's why I'm going to race someday," said Taylor.

"They'd have to hire a donkey to kiss you," said Wellesley.

Taylor thrust his butt toward Wellesley. "Kiss me, sweetie!" He laughed, going along with the joke, probably not sure yet whether the guy in front had figured out yet that his hero was Wellesley's dad.

My eyes kept returning to that mangled mess next to the fence post. I thought how sick Mr. Baker must have felt when he discovered what his dad had done to his own dog. Wellesley had said he was only eight years old. That's probably why he'd refused to let Wellesley have one. Bad memories.

"Let's go down to the pits," Taylor said.

Wellesley got a gleam in her eye and we charged toward the arena.

A uniformed policeman guarded the hole in the fence on the south turn where they'd pulled the wire open wide enough to let the cars out. "Nobody allowed in without a pass," he said. We stood there refiguring our options while trucks with trailer hitches paraded through the gate to pick up what remained of the cars in the arena. Without mufflers, lights, or license plates, those monsters weren't permitted to drive on ordinary streets.

Then Wellesley had an idea. She stopped the owner of the Polar Storage as he was heading toward the gate to tow his car out. He pushed the door of his pickup open without even answering. Wellesley crammed Taylor and me against the floorboard with her feet. Then she put on the grease monkey's hat and sat in the seat proud as a tomcat with her elbow hanging out the window as we drove into the brightness of the arena. We were stowaways.

The pits looked like the end of the circus, everyone putting tools in boxes and hitching up cars. The smell of burnt oil and hot metal filled the air. We found Mr. Baker leaning over the hood of the Pink Lady talking to another driver with goggles pushed over his forehead. Wellesley slowed down when she saw they were trading swigs out of a tan whiskey bottle resting on the hood.

"Come on, Wellesley," Taylor said, nudging her with the side of his arm, "don't be a candy-ass."

Wellesley ignored him.

Mr. Baker stood with his boots wide apart and his belly anchoring the front end of the Lady. This close, he looked too big to fit through the window. His laugh shook the car.

The racing had sweated up his bristly hair and the night air had dried it the way the ear covers raked it when he pulled the helmet off. I knew we were seeing the drivers the way they really were. When people talked tomorrow about the races, I'd be able to say I met with Mr. Baker in the pits afterward. As the three of us stood to the side waiting for a break in the drivers' conversation, Taylor pushed against Wellesley to get us closer.

"What are you doing back here with those kids?" Mr. Baker's voice boomed so loud I stumbled backwards a step bumping against Taylor.

Wellesley stood firm, her voice matter-of-fact. "We came in with Mr. Shoudy." I liked the way she brought another race car figure into the picture to take the focus off Taylor and me.

Mr. Baker's stare drilled through my golf shirt. His overalls were unbuttoned to the tops of his yellow boxer shorts. He held the bottle neck full-fisted the same way he'd gripped the stem of the trophy when he posed with the queen.

"Ah, hell, they ain't going to hurt anything," the driver in the green nylon jacket said.

"You know the rules and so does she," he bellowed. "Out!" Mr. Baker gestured in the general direction of the south turn.

"Let's go, you guys." Wellesley shrugged. "I guess this isn't a good time."

Taylor didn't get it. "Ask him if we can look in the car," he whispered.

Wellesley kept walking.

"How come he's kicking us out?"

"I'll explain when you grow up," she said, not breaking stride.

Taylor gave me a quizzical look. I watched Wellesley grinding her jaw bones and knew we'd gotten as close to the Pink Lady as we were going to get that night.

I couldn't blame Wellesley for being p-o'd. If she'd gone in without Taylor and me, her dad wouldn't have cared. He acted the same way my dad would have if I brought friends around to his office when he was counting money for the bank deposit after closing the hardware store. That was the private part of the business.

As I was lying in bed with the lights off that night, I could still hear the ringing of the stock cars in my ears. I was glad Mr. Baker won but I wondered why he hadn't slowed down for the dog the way the other driver had.

3

Mom's voice calling downstairs woke me up. "Will, your grandpa's here!" I'd forgotten about my golfing date with Grandpa Blane.

A car door slammed out front. I sprang to my feet and pulled aside the towels hanging across the basement window. His '54 cream Chevrolet was parked out front and Grandpa was charging up the path. He wore the same thing golfing as he did for Christmas dinner—beige baggy cotton pants with no crease. The cuffs were turned up in case of wet grass. The collar of a faded, Scottish plaid shirt stuck out the neck hole of his navy blue pullover with leather elbows. He looked down as he walked, probably muttering something. The brim of his crumpled fisherman's hat shaded his glasses.

I pulled on my jeans, kept on the same golf shirt with Coke stains I'd slept in, and ran up the stairs.

"Hi, Daddy!" Mom said as she opened the front door.

"Hi, Grandpa," I called from the kitchen, extra loud. He didn't hear me.

"Where's my golf partner?" His voice was bigger than his five-foot-four frame.

"He's right here, Daddy." Mom stayed close to his ear, raised her voice like a long distance phone call, and pointed. He'd damaged his hearing when he was a boy by sticking a pencil in his eardrum. Mom didn't say where it had happened but I was sure it had to be in a social studies or math class, when he was bored stiff and didn't care whether he heard what the teacher said or not. The hole in his ear had saved him from listening to a lot of blather since.

We turned north on Sawyer Street. It had just been sprayed with that reddish-brown oil that Taylor said smelled like piss and vinegar. I looked down Taylor's street. All I saw were some little kids jumping over a swinging rope that had one end tied to a tree in the parking strip. He was probably still drooling into his pillow.

Each time Grandpa popped the clutch, the extra putter and nine iron on the backseat clattered together. I think he thought it was hard on the transmission to hold the pedal down too long. With less than two years to go for my license, I'd started asking Dad a lot of questions about driving and soaking up all the tips I could. Grandpa had been driving longer than Mr. Baker but he sure didn't have Mr. Baker's touch.

"When's our tee-off time?" I asked.

He didn't hear me. "Damn women drivers," he cursed, as we tailgated a blue Oldsmobile Cutlass. "They have no business driving." I looked at him in surprise. There was no use explaining that the person braking for each cross street in front of us was a man in a straw hat.

In person, Grandpa always tipped his hat and seemed on his best behavior around women. Only on highways and fairways did he have any trouble with them. He'd helped raise three daughters and a son. All except Mom had moved out of Clearwater.

We parked in his regular space, closer to the trout pool than the clubhouse, even though there were empty stalls in the first row. It was habit. The weathered shingles and yellow trim on the clubhouse reminded me of the lodge where our family stayed in Yellowstone Park two summers ago. Whizzing down the highway on the way home, Dad had vowed to visit one national park each year until we'd seen every one west of the Rockies. I knew it was a boast even then. Last year we couldn't take a vacation because of the remodeling at the store. This year it was because he chaired the Fair Committee. I didn't care. Taylor had already invited me to spend a week with his family at Spirit Lake.

Grandpa bought my ticket in the pro shop and met me at the first tee. The morning sunshine baked the smell of fresh-cut grass right out of the ground. The first hole started from the top of a hill and the fairway was a long valley of green that narrowed like spilled paint as it got closer to the pin.

"Are you giving me strokes today, Will?" He spoke so loud two pimply boys on the practice putting green looked up to watch us.

"I'm just learning this game, Grandpa," I said. This was part of Grandpa's pregame ritual.

"You know, I'm going to shoot my age someday," he said, pulling the cellophane off his Roi Tan cigar. Grandpa didn't cuss or drink. He'd be a total stranger in a place like the Drift Inn tavern where the stock-car drivers hung out. But he sure was partial to his cigars.

"I think you'll do it today, Grandpa. I just have that feeling." He didn't answer, as he burrowed into the side pouch of his bag to retrieve a handful of broken tees.

None of my friends ever talked about their grandfathers. It was another way I felt different. Everyone else acted as if they'd outgrown their relatives. Golfing wasn't exactly the ticket to popularity either. None of my friends golfed, although Taylor had tried it a few times with me and Grandpa. Taylor couldn't get down in less than a dozen strokes and finally dismissed it as a sissy's game. Maybe his razzing was one of the reasons I'd decided to turn out for freshman football even though he'd finked out.

"We're up next," Grandpa said, motioning toward the tee with the back of his hand. "You've got the honors, Scott," he said, mistakenly calling me by his son's name. I didn't correct him. Uncle Scott shot the best golf in the family and had played first man on Clearwater's varsity.

Scott's moving to Sacramento and getting married had hurt Grandpa most of all. That didn't mean he disliked Mom and her sisters, but Scott was his only son. And a golfer. Maybe that was why he was so patient with me.

I didn't understand why so many good people left Clearwater. Like Grandpa said, there was no crime here and the taxes were low. He'd already targeted me to take over Western Hardware when Dad retired. I went along with his idea, he meant it as a compliment, but the truth was I wanted something bigger. Maybe I'd be a judge or a state senator, something you had to wear a suit and tie for.

"There's no water on this hole, you know." He laughed as I bent over to balance a Maxfli on its tee. He probably remembered the last time we played here when I scuffed three shots into the creek. This time I cleared it.

So did he.

As we crossed the wooden trestle, I asked Grandpa about politics, something I'd seen in the headlines of the *Chronicle.*

"They'll settle it on the golf course," he said, his teeth clenched on the cigar. I knew Grandpa wasn't teasing. He was a staunch Republican who felt safer knowing Dwight Eisenhower could hit his way out of a sand trap.

He shifted hands on his golf cart to drag it up the hill on the fairway side of the bridge. "Your folks have done a pretty decent job." I didn't know what exactly he was referring to. Grandpa had a special respect for my dad. He always seemed to hear whatever Dad said. Probably because Dad was in business. Grandpa Blane volunteered compliments as rarely as he polished his cracked leather golf shoes. They curled at the toes from drying in front of the heat register.

At the turn, he had a 45 to my 58. We passed the threesome ahead of us when they went into the clubhouse. He never stopped between nines, always in a hurry to finish the game he loved the most.

From the ball pocket in his khaki canvas bag, he pulled out two bent candy bars with faded wrappers. "This is better than what they're serving!" He hated to pay clubhouse prices. "Take your pick." I chose the Snickers. He peeled away the paper and licked his melted Baby Ruth from the paper just like a kid.

Mom told me once that Grandpa had lived his life backwards. When he was a kid, he was a fuddy-duddy who everyone teased because he wouldn't kiss girls or skip school. He had a full-time job and married Grandma by the time he was seventeen. So that I wouldn't get any wrong ideas, she explained that people married "much younger" in those days. Since retiring from the postal service though, Grandpa had turned boy. He'd skip dental appointments, come late to family dinners, and ignore mowing the grass just so he could play a round of golf.

Number 10 was a par 3, within reach of his sixty-nine-year-old swing. "Say, did I tell you how lucky I was on this hole one time," he said, smothering a cackle. "I made my first hole in one here. Really slick." I'd heard the story plenty of times before.

"You've got the tee again, Grandpa."

Lining up the club face behind the ball, he rocked his elflike body and twisted his shoes deeper into the grass to find equilibrium. Thumping the bottom of his brassy against the turf, he drew a stunted backswing and exploded in a chopping motion against the ball. Crack! He squinted down the fairway until the ball settled, using his left hand as a visor. Then he bent over and retrieved his smoldering cigar from the grass by the tee markers.

"You're pin high, Grandpa. Birdie putt!" His ball was a pearl six feet from the flag.

"Oh shucks, it was easy." He burst into his wheezy laugh. A smudge of chocolate showed over his upper lip.

We used our golfing as an opportunity to talk finances as well as politics. The Great Depression haunted him. He blamed it on the business shysters back East. That's why government bonds made sense. He still had the War Bonds he'd purchased in the forties, a nest egg for his retirement.

On the ride home, he hummed bars from waltzes while the disc jockey played "Poison Ivy" on the vibrating dashboard speaker. I thought of telling him about the stock car races, but Grandpa had never shown much interest in them. The noise probably caused an earthquake in his hearing aid. The accident with the dog would have turned him against the races even more. He had an affection for animals. I felt a twinge of jealousy knowing that Wellesley's dad could win the A-Main and get his picture in the paper and Grandpa hit a hole in one and nobody even cared.

I decided Grandpa Blane liked golf because it was reliable. It didn't talk to you but it wouldn't up and leave you when you weren't expecting, like Grandma Blane had. She'd passed away when I was in first grade. I remembered Mom sitting on the edge of my bed telling me she was the only woman Grandpa ever loved. She said his heart broke in pieces when Grandma died.

The first house I lived in was across the street from

Grandpa. After Grandma Blane died, Grandpa's mother moved in and made a small apartment out of the back bedroom. Then his sister Ruth lived there. Everyone thought of Grandpa as helpless.

I wanted to ask what he was thinking. Maybe he was remembering his old golfing partners who had dubbed him Barney. He'd buried most of them. Maybe he was wondering why he'd never been invited to join the Sylvanus Country Club. It was supposed to be the best manicured course in the state. But they didn't put mail train clerks high on their invitation list. If love for the game counted, they'd have made him their Grand Master.

Grandpa Blane sat tall on his checkered red and black pad and fingered the steering wheel with quarter notes as he crooned. Maybe he was singing to his bride, taken from him by cancer in the prime of her life.

4

The first thing I did when I got to Wellesley's was check the backyard. That's where they kept the Pink Lady between races. The car was a monument to Mr. Baker. Kids who Wellesley let touch it treated the experience as more sacred than church.·

She must have seen me in the yard and came out. We inspected the car from front to back, looking for new dents and scratches from Saturday night's races. On the right front fender, we were sure the new smudge of brown had been scraped off the Little Brown Jug when Mr. Baker shoved it into the hay bales. There were no signs of dog hair or blood on the front bumper or tires and I wondered again if I'd really seen it.

"You want to take her for a spin?" Wellesley asked.

I glanced at the house. "Are you sure it's okay with your dad?"

"He's at the plant." She hadn't exactly answered my question but I wanted to get inside so badly I didn't care. Besides, after seeing what Mr. Baker put the car through, there was hardly any way I could hurt it. "What are you waiting for?"

"Have you been in her since the race?" I asked.

She gave me her crooked smile. "Nope. She's been waiting for you."

I lowered myself feet first through the front window into the driver's seat. The spiral springs that pushed straw through the bucket seat dug into my back pockets. I tensed waiting for Wellesley to give me the green flag. When she said go, I felt Mr. Baker's energy arcing through me from the steering wheel to the pedals as I pretended to run away from the Polar Storage. The round of golf must have cleared the fumes from my lungs. The uneasiness I'd felt since the end of the races was momentarily gone. I was ready to see Mr. Baker bombs away at the track again.

Later, Wellesley pulled her own racing bug out of the garage, a two-by-four frame that looked like a church steeple laid sideways. The hood was an oil drum her dad had blowtorched in half. Split black garden hose covered the jagged edges. The rear wheels from a fertilizer spreader, larger than the wagon wheels on the front, gave the rig a forward bias. She steered it with a loop of manila rope tied to each end of the front axle like the reins of a horse.

While Wellesley was painting a name on her hood, she had a flash. "Let's set up a neighborhood bug race. Taylor has a car, so does Woody."

"I don't."

"No sweat, I'll help you."

When Taylor wandered into the yard, Wellesley told him about the race.

" 'Dragon Lady,' that's a good one," Taylor said, looking over her shoulder. "You might as well call it the 'Dragging Behind Lady' because you'll be sucking my exhaust pipe, Wellesley!"

"You're a turd, Taylor," she said.

"Just try me, you'll like the taste," Taylor said, licking his tongue around his lips.

"You don't know the difference between shit and a popsicle," she said, wiping the brush with a rag.

They were flint and steel. Wellesley didn't know how to back away from a taunt and Taylor couldn't help making them.

A few days later, we pulled our cars to the top of Cemetery Hill. I had scrounged whatever I could find in the basement and garage to build my own jalopy. It ended up as an ironing board that Wellesley's mom donated, with steel lawnmower wheels. In the tradition of racing, I gave my pointyheaded creation a female name, "Cinderella."

The highest point in Sylvanus County was inside the cemetery fence, somewhere between the graves of Mayor Tubbs' family and the Lutheran plot for dead ministers. As far as I

knew, there weren't any Catholic priests buried there. We
had St. Paul's, a Spanish stucco church that looked like a
mission, but the closest parochial school was in Coles Corner. Mom said she didn't want me taking the bus that far so
I went to Adams Elementary like almost everyone else.
Maybe it was because she grew up Presbyterian before Dad
converted her.

We had to start the race just outside the chained entry
gates so we probably lost twenty feet of vertical drop. It was
still higher than the crop dusters flew. I could see the bend
in the Clearwater where it finally turned south and headed
for the Snake. North of town, a row of freight cars waited
patiently on the siding in the rail yard.

Making like the electronic mike at the Indianapolis
Speedway, Johnny Wizer bellowed between cupped hands,
"Racers, start your engines!" Taylor was in lane 1, Woody in
2, Wellesley 3, and me on the outside. We climbed in, keeping our feet flat on the gravel to keep the cars from rolling.

"Ladies and gentlemen, the first running of the Annual
Suicide Race, the most dangerous test of the internal com-
bustion engine known to man!" As Wizer raised his hand,
we revved our throats and backfired with puffs of our
cheeks.

Taylor razzed Wellesley, who hunched in her cockpit,
weight forward over the shiny pink enamel of her hood.
"Get ready to eat my dust, Weller!"

"On your marks . . . get set . . . go!"

I pushed down on the rear wheels to build momentum.
Four abreast, we aimed down the one-lane serpentine
course. The iron wheels turning against rocks made Cinderella a vibrator sander. My vision blurred like winter breath
on a windshield. I could smell the oil they sprayed on the
road to hold the dust down.

"Wahooo!" Wellesley yelled. Her rear wheels passed my
needle nose as she veered to the middle of the road, gripping her steering rope and pumping it up and down like a
jockey. Wellesley made me seem rooted to the road.

I made it past the Ewins' mailbox still in second place.
The only thing I could see of Wellesley was her dust. But as
I coaxed my car into the curve, the tires lost their grip.

Spinning counterclockwise, I faced Woody's broomstick-handle grill straight on. He swerved and went into his own spin in the opposite direction. Then Taylor's apple crate special bulldozed me sideways into the drainage ditch like a snowplow.

Taylor jumped out of his car and slapped the bottom of my ironing board. "Dammit, Bradford, I could have caught her! Where'd you learn to drive?" He still had his green swimming goggles on. They pinched the top of his nose and made him talk like a pig.

High centered on the other side of the road, with the front of his car pointing uphill, Woody laughed and laughed. "That was a hoot! Let's go again."

Trouble was, the only car still in condition to race was Wellesley's. She produced, directed, and starred in her own spectacle. Taylor had to drag the carcass of his crate home with two wheels wedged under his armpits. I stacked mine on top of Woody's and we each took an end. The Suicide Race was a one-woman show.

I never understood why Wellesley didn't blab this catastrophe all over town. Taylor would have pressed the *Clearwater Chronicle* to run something on the sports page if he'd won.

If her silence was an experiment in diplomacy, it failed. Taylor and Wellesley were not speaking again after the race. Taylor couldn't stomach the idea of losing to a girl at a man's sport.

"Heredity," Taylor said. "She didn't beat us, we lost to heredity."

Taylor stayed in hiding the day after the race, probably waiting for me to find him. Maybe he thought I'd gone over to Wellesley's side. After I figured he'd stewed long enough, I went over there.

Even though he lived in the next block, I took my bike out of habit. The fastest way to get there was through the alley, a dirt lane lined with pairs of rumpled garbage cans, trash-burning barrels, and sunflowers as high as the Moshers' garage. I cut across the vacant lot between the Georges' and the Whittakers'. We'd worn a bike path in a diagonal over the mounds of fill dirt that someone had dumped there years ago. The rumor was that someone rich was going to build a house with a swimming pool there.

Taylor's parents and his older brother, Dan, worked, so his house was available during the day. His dad owned Clark's Refrigerators. Mr. Clark doodled with anything that plugged into a socket—toasters that popped too early, irons that wouldn't heat. Mrs. Clark was the receptionist at Mary of the Angels Hospital. She was the first person you saw when you walked through the double doors under the brass crucifix. My friends thought Mrs. Clark was the prettiest mom in Clearwater. Her orange hair looked so smooth you wanted to rub your face against it like a cat on a pant cuff. Her voice was strawberry syrup. Wizer told me Taylor didn't deserve her, but he never had the guts to say it to his face.

I wondered if the Clarks had adopted Taylor. His wavy black hair looked more like the Durgans' sheepdog than Mr. or Mrs. Clark. None of his mom's polish showed in Taylor's manners, nor any of his dad's respect for equipment. Instead of cursed with freckles and hair verging on reddish like mine, Taylor had a creamy complexion with a permanent hint of pink in the cheeks like he'd just blown a bugle. The girls thought he was cute, probably because of his deep blue eyes and the dimples.

Taylor was a human joke book. He laughed at everything. When Mr. Wiskit came into class with toilet paper dragging from his shoe once, everyone ignored it except Taylor; he guffawed like a donkey. Sometimes I came up with good ideas, but Taylor made them happen.

The Clarks lived in a comfortable two-story house made of fancy brick, jagged on the edges. Everything worked in their house, light switches, cupboard door catches, toilet balls. Although we owned Western Hardware, Mom kidded Dad saying we were as shoeless as the shoemaker's children. Our faucets dripped and the bathroom doorknob came off in your hand unless you held it just right. The Clarks put up storm glass in the winter instead of tacking plastic to the outside of the windows like we did. Thick navy blue carpet covered Taylor's room upstairs; it was better than our living room. Pennants from places he'd visited on family vacations hung from a clothesline stretched across his bedroom. He'd seen the national parks Dad had promised.

The front door was open and I went right in. Taylor lay on the floor in his room, reading one of the dirty magazines he kept between the mattress and box springs. Because he was Protestant he could read them without worrying. For Catholics, it wasn't so simple. I timed my looking to days I already had "impure thoughts" to confess, on the theory my soul couldn't get any blacker.

"They're just pictures," he said. "Wait 'til you touch the real thing."

"You're lying, Taylor."

"Betcha I'm not."

"Prove it and I'll lick your butt."

"You know Monica Amberly?" he said. Of course I did, she was the most beautiful and womanly girl in our class. "You know how big her tits are? Well, she let me put my hand on one. Under the sweater." Taylor milked his breasts with both hands inside his T-shirt.

"When? I don't believe you!" I imagined Monica at school and wondered which side Taylor had touched. Why would one of the smartest kids in our class let Taylor feel her up?

"Just ask her. And ask who she wants to get laid by when she's seventeen." Taylor rolled on his back and pointed an index finger at each side of his head, grinning like Howdy Doody. When he loosened his belt buckle to drop his pants, I beat it down the stairs before he could make me pay the bet.

We had work to do anyway. That summer, Taylor and I had formed a business partnership: lawn mowing with an old Toro that Mr. Clark fixed up. It was a chance to branch out from hardware, get out from under my dad's shadow. We rang doorbells for jobs. Dad supported the idea; he called it good experience. "If you can sell, you can do anything," he said.

When Taylor finally ambled downstairs, we got ready to do the Ewins' lawn. They were retired farmers and liked to have things done on a schedule. Taylor filled the Toro. Then while I screwed the lid back on the tank, he poured gas on the floor.

"What are you doing that for, Taylor?"

"I'm making Apache war dance!" He pranced on his toes, bringing his knees above his belt, as he splashed gas in a circle around me. We'd seen *Cochise* together. He'd come out of the Orpheum dancing like this.

"You're wasting gas, that's what you're doing."

"I won't waste it, give me a match."

"Don't be stupid, Taylor!"

"Don't be such a pucker-ass!"

I stood in the circle thinking that even Taylor wouldn't kill his partner. Whoosh! Suddenly, a wall of flames separated me from him. It was hard to breathe. Taylor yelled, "Dance, paleface! Dance!" The heat in the air made it look like I was in the fireplace and he was on the hearth.

By the time Mr. Clark pulled into the driveway, we had sprayed the garage inside and out with the garden hose. We couldn't wash the blisters off the drawers of Mr. Clark's tool cabinet; we hadn't even noticed the film of soot on the bottom of the unfinished doors resting on the ceiling cross beams.

Dad went crazy when Mr. Clark called him. When I was seven and poked the top of each chocolate in Mom's Mother's Day box, looking for the caramels, Dad had made me eat the whole box in one sitting. Would he make me drink the gas? Dad's eyes enlarged and the veins in his neck stood out like mower starter cord as he yelled at me. "If you don't know how to handle gasoline, you sure don't know how to handle a car. You can forget about ever studying for a driver's license."

Dad suggested Mr. Clark make us pay for sandpaper, brushes, and paint to refinish the outside of the garage, which the flames hadn't even touched. This took all of our lawn profits and then some. In the instant it took for Taylor's match to drop from his hand to the pool of gasoline, we'd become bankrupt.

When Wellesley heard about the gasoline caper, she didn't believe anyone could be so stupid as to stand there and discuss it with Taylor while he pulled out a matchbook.

"Taylor's got dead grass for brains, but I thought you knew better, Will."

"It wasn't that obvious at the time," I said. "You had to be there." As usual, I covered for Taylor.

When Taylor told the story later to the punks who hung around the park though, I forgave him. The way he reported it made me sound like a martyr. Everyone just stared with their mouths hanging open as Taylor emptied the make-believe gas can around my feet.

5

In summer, the weather imitated Clearwater's name. Some days the sky was so blue you'd lose your balance if you looked at it too long. Any cloud that dared to appear seemed to dissolve from the heat. The wheat farmers loved the heat because it thickened the crops for the August harvest. The smell in the air made you hungry.

Ever since the fire in the Clarks' garage, we'd had the other kind of day, cloudbursts so hard they knocked the petals off the roses and flattened the grass like the hair on a wet collie. I figured God was dampening things in case Taylor experimented anymore with his pyromania. On these days, Dad said customers became water conscious and bought chains and ballcocks to stop the runs in their toilets and putty for the leaks in their windows.

Wellesley and I thought of rain as a good excuse to take Taylor for a cherry Coke. I'd already done my chores at the hardware. We debated under the awning in front of the Rexall.

"Who's paying?" Taylor asked, looking at me. I had a part-time job and Taylor had his allowance; Wellesley had neither even though her dad made her get up at five-thirty and clean their house and do chores before school every day.

"I haven't been paid yet," I said. My excuse sounded trumped-up but for some reason Dad hadn't paid me since Easter. He said to keep track of what he owed me in a Western Hardware invoice pad. Each time I filled up a page, I gave the carbon copy to him and he stuck it in a drawer in his office. Dad said it was a forced savings plan.

"Lame, Bradford," Taylor said. "You're probably squirreling it away in mining stocks or something. When I'm pan-

handling for pennies with a tin cup on street corners someday, you'll be smoking cigars in a corner office in Chicago
counting the money you saved from my cherry Cokes."

"What else would you spend it on, Taylor?" Wellesley
asked.

"Hah! I've got plans, like buying a car . . ."

"Your parents will give you Dan's," Wellesley interrupted.
Taylor's brother had a cherry '49 Ford his parents had
bought him for high school graduation.

"And college . . ."

"You won't make it out of high school," she said.

"And Christmas presents for my family . . ."

"Last year, you gave your mom a stolen potholder," she
said. Taylor had lifted it from the Sprouse Reitz store in
Union Gap.

"I paid them back later! Besides, I'm trying to reform,"
Taylor said, faking a hurt look. "If you take my money, I'll
have to steal."

"I'll pay you back," I said, "as soon as I get paid."

"I'm not that thirsty," Wellesley said. "It'll spoil my dinner. I'll just watch you two rot your guts out with that stuff."

"Don't you go holy on me like Bradford," Taylor said. "By
the way, if your old man's got enough to blow on stock cars,
why don't you hit him up for an allowance?"

"My Dad grew up in Philadelphia," she said. "The kids
stupid enough to have allowances got their arms bent off if
they didn't fork it over to someone tougher."

We sat on the stools at Martin's soda fountain in the Rexall
and watched the rain drizzle down the windows. Taylor ordered a round for three and took back four dollars and forty
cents change from the five dollar bill he'd tried to hide. I
wished my parents shared some of the Clarks' philosophy.
The Clarks managed to give their sons a sense of handling
money without violating the child labor laws. Dad didn't
believe in giving away something for nothing.

Wellesley's sister, Tiffany, strolled into the Rexall with her
arm on a guy. She wore a nice white cotton dress with a sash
around the waist. She had a fuller shape than Wellesley and
wasn't bad looking. Now that she'd finished school, Welles-

ley told me Tiffany hardly ever came around the house. She said her dad considered graduation from high school emancipation into the real world. I'd never totally bought that excuse because Tiffany left home before her graduation. She was supposed to be living with a cousin in Olalla but Wellesley said she was shacking up with a car mechanic.

The guy with her, in low slung pants held up by a pink suede belt, looked too anemic to grip an end wrench. I doubted Mr. Baker would approve of someone so puny. He'd want a weightlifter or a fullback, someone who'd crush your knuckles when he shook hands. The guy's hair was greased into a ducktail. I could smell the Brylcream. They shared drags on his cigarette.

Tiffany acted surprised to see Wellesley and pulled her hand away from her friend. "Isn't it about dinnertime for you kids?" She spoke in a sarcastic voice that I could tell grated on Wellesley.

"What are you doing here?" Wellesley asked.

Tiffany looked at her friend as if to say isn't it obvious. Her ninety-pound weakling was trying to read the price on the sunglasses in the rack next to him. A pair of those horned-rim ones would just about complete the picture, I thought.

"Have you seen Mom?" Wellesley asked.

Tiffany looked at her friend again, who was ignoring the discussion at the stools. "No, but Dad's over at the Drift Inn. I saw the car." The Drift Inn was one of those places I'd been warned to stay away from. People said men from the rendering plant stopped there to drink their paychecks and brawl. "How's Mom doing?" Tiffany's question seemed an afterthought.

Wellesley ignored her. "I've got to go, you guys." She took one more suck of her cherry Coke to get the ice water that had melted and then spun off her chair. Maybe she couldn't afford much, but Wellesley never wasted anything she got her hands on.

As soon as Wellesley reached the door, Tiffany turned to the rack and stuck a pair of white plastic glasses on her friend. He slipped into an Elvis Presley pose with his hands ready to strum a guitar. Tiffany tittered.

"There's a pair," Taylor whispered to me.

Tiffany never bothered to introduce her greasy friend. Afterwards, Taylor wished he'd asked some motor questions to see if he was the car mechanic Tiffany was living with.

After dinner, the rain let up and Taylor and I thought of spying on Wellesley as a joke.

Wellesley lived about eight blocks from our house in a neighborhood without paved streets or sidewalks. It used to be the site of Clearwater's lumber mill. The mill burned down before World War II. Now it was just a poor part of town with a wrecking yard. People in Clearwater called the area "Milltown" and the people "Millers." "Mill" was a shorthand way of describing what they wore and what they thought—an ugly pair of cords were millpants and a dull person was mill-brained.

Wellesley's house had asphalt shingles coated with red-colored sand to imitate bricks. Where shingles had fallen off, patches of yellowed siding showed through like a knee through a hole in your jeans.

Every light in her house must have been on when we got there. We saw Wellesley in the kitchen, her back to us, washing dishes. Mrs. Baker fidgeted in a chair across the table from her husband. He shoveled food into his mouth from the plate he held up to his chin. We kept our faces far enough from the window so no one would see us.

Then Mr. Baker set his plate down and planted his fist and the handle end of his fork on the table. The plate rattled. "This tastes like horseshit! When are you going to cook something edible?" His bass voice vibrated the half-open window.

Taylor and I looked at each other. I knew we shouldn't be doing this.

"Look at me when I'm talking to you! Do you hear me?"

Mrs. Baker slowly raised her head, holding it sideways to protect herself.

He sloshed his drink in her face. "Wake up! You act like you're dead!"

Wellesley ran to the table and patted her mom with the

dish towel. Then Wellesley hugged her as if she was the mother and her mom the hurt child.

In Taylor's eyes, I could see the reflection of the Baker family in the kitchen. He seemed mesmerized. Then the chair scraped against the floor.

Mr. Baker rose from his seat, one hand on the table for balance, and started toward Mrs. Baker.

Wellesley stood tall between her mom and dad.

He slapped Wellesley's face. "Let her fight her own goddamn battles."

Wellesley raised her eyes, but didn't move her head. She looked so defenseless next to her dad, like the performer in the rodeo who runs into the ring to distract the Brahma bull from the fallen rider.

I felt like I'd swallowed one of the Coke glasses at the Rexall and it had choked off my air supply. I couldn't believe the town's stock car champion was slapping his daughter around.

Mr. Baker grabbed Wellesley by the jaw and bent her neck back. "You don't like it here, go live with your whore sister!" Then he flicked her head, knocking her off balance, and turned toward the window.

We ducked. Taylor's face was panicked. Mr. Baker would pound us if he knew we'd seen him. I held my breath and pressed against the side of the house. Nothing moved inside. Then Mr. Baker belched. A cupboard door opened, slammed shut, then another. His shadow moved across the rectangle of light cast onto the dead grass next to us.

Taylor offered no resistance when I tugged on his sleeve to leave. Nobody followed us.

Even though it had started to pour again, we walked home slowly, hands in our pockets. Jags of lightning exposed the cardboard-looking fronts of the cracker-box houses in Milltown, followed by angry thunderclaps. Cold water ran down the back of my neck and under my shirt. Neither of us said anything.

In my darkest fantasies, I couldn't imagine my dad doing what I'd seen in that kitchen. He'd yelled at me plenty. I'd seen him mad enough to break the guts of my tennis racket over the bedpost. But he'd never lay a hand on a woman.

I was still wide awake at midnight when the train came through town. I thought of Wellesley and me in the tree over the garage that time, the way she'd hugged the trunk like it was a friend. The wail of the train whistle hung in the air. It sounded sad, like it was lost in some faraway place.

6

Laddie Tilford was a gray-haired man who only traveled by bicycle. He rocked his shoulders front and back as he pedaled to make it go faster. Then, when his balloon-tire Raleigh reached cruising speed, he coasted. He wore rubber bands around his pants cuffs to keep them out of the chain. His vest sweater with large diamond prints and blue cap made him look like a Western Union delivery boy. He was always on a mission.

Most people just ignored him. Laddie was part of the landscape.

Laddie came by once after school when Johnny Wizer and I were patrolling the crosswalk in front of Adams Elementary. Wizer called him a "spastic." He said he'd heard his dad call him that. When Laddie came close, Wizer threw his patrol flag to spear his spokes. The flag missed and Laddie raised off his seat and pumped like he was running up stairs. Wizer and I got in a fistfight right there on the corner. When Mom asked what happened to my face, I told her I slipped climbing Grandpa Blane's apple tree. She said to stay out of the tree because Grandpa didn't want kids playing in his yard. She overlooked the scratches from Wizer's fingernails on my cheek.

Laddie's main route went by our house and then straight down Willow Street to the Rexall. Martin told me I drank more cherry Cokes than anyone in town, thanks in part to Taylor's generosity. "You're going to rot your insides out if you drink one more glass of this battery acid," he'd say and then give me a wink that bent his bushy white eyebrow. From my bar stool, I could watch Laddie drive by on the sidewalk. Sometimes he looked in at me through the window with the hanging neon "Prescription" sign. But he never stopped.

He wasn't sneaky about where he went. I could hear Laddie's bell ringing before I saw him. He had one of those bells on the handlebars you worked by pushing your thumb against the paddle. I had one just like it until Mom and Dad gave me a horn with a voice as deep as a goose. You were supposed to ring the bell at street crossings or to make animals get out of your way. Laddie rang it often, like he saw dangers invisible to others.

Whenever there was a fire or an accident in town, Laddie was there. Wellesley said he must have radio contact with the police department.

When that soldier smacked into a Nash last summer, his car jumped the curb and pushed the Nelsons' porch steps against Mrs. Crumbacher's clothesline pole. Mrs. Crumbacher brought out the quilt she kept on her couch and handed it to the ambulance driver to put around the soldier lying on the grass. His face was covered with a sheet of blood from the slice on his forehead. He reminded me of the kid at the park who was hit in the face with a flying horseshoe. Laddie straddled his bike behind the drooping sheets on the line and watched through the spaces. Everyone else huddled around the soldier. Laddie chewed on his lower lip with his buck teeth. I could see stubble patches of beard he'd missed shaving. His eyes darted from one person to the next.

Afterward, when I was holding the ladder for Mom while she scrubbed the kitchen ceiling, I asked her what was really wrong with Laddie. She said he was an "innocent." The mind of a child in a man's body. She told me Laddie's mother was housebound with polio and got around in a wheelchair. If she needed something, she called the order in and Laddie delivered it.

Nobody I knew had ever been inside the Tilfords' house. From the street, you could hardly see it because of the maple trees and the blackberry vines that swarmed over the trestles and arches in what used to be a garden. A cracked cement walk wove a lazy "S" to the porch.

* * *

Wellesley didn't show up in the usual places the day after the fight in her kitchen. I checked the park, the Rexall, downtown. I didn't dare go to her house. What if Mr. Baker had seen us?

When Taylor and Wizer asked me to go swimming at the public pool, I said okay.

On our way, we saw Laddie swerve to miss a jaywalking dalmatian. His bike landed sideways on the gravel. Laddie slid headfirst like he was coming into home plate. The paper grocery bag in the wire carrier behind the seat split, spilling spuds and soup cans everywhere. I ran over to Laddie while Taylor and Wizer picked up the food and set it in a pile on the grass.

"Are you okay?" I didn't feel comfortable using his name.

He mumbled something through twisted lips, pulling his arms against his chest like he was trying to cover himself.

"I'll help you," I said, petting his shoulder lightly to stop him from shaking.

Wizer and Taylor wanted to go on to the pool. They seemed anxious to get away.

I helped Laddie home. He could walk but I didn't think he should ride his bike. The handlebars were wrenched sideways like he was in the middle of a left turn. The basket was deep enough to hold the soup cans. I took off my T-shirt, tied it into a knot at the neck end and filled it with the knicked-up potatoes. As we walked together, little kids stopped playing and watched us pass. I guessed this was the first time any of them had ever seen Laddie just walking.

I had a hundred questions but I couldn't think of a good way to ask them. I didn't know if he would understand me and I didn't want to fluster him. Laddie looked at his feet and shuffled along, trying to hold his knees together. My hands hurt just looking at the gravel ground into his palms. I wondered if his mother could help him get the dirt out from under the torn flaps of skin.

Laddie kept looking at his damaged bike like he was going to cry. I thought he cared more about the rip on the side of the leather bike seat than he did about his own wounds. When I tested the bell, his eyes opened wide like he'd just seen a grasshopper jump.

He guided me down the dirt alley to a garage with a sagging roof. He motioned me to lean the bike against the gate while he pushed on the sliding door with two broken windows. Disconnected from its railing at the top, the door moved in a ditch along the ground. He wheeled his bike into the only clear space amid apple crates, fruit jars, and dusty cardboard boxes. Cobwebs seemed to hold the stacks from toppling.

I think he wanted to carry everything to the house himself but he didn't know how to explain. He shaped his mouth in different positions like he was going to start a sentence but then just bit his lip and nodded. I smiled and nodded back to show that I understood. Finally, he reached down and loaded five cans against his vest, securing them with his chin on the top of the pyramid. We were both going in the house. Twice he stopped and looked over his shoulder to see if I was still coming.

The back porch slanted like a ramp and the rotting slats swayed and creaked as we stepped on them. He set the cans down on the lid of the abandoned Maytag and opened the door with the key from the black shoestring around his neck. I thought he didn't want me to watch.

I wondered if I was violating a secret that Laddie wanted to keep. If I went in there with him, I was worried that Laddie might not ever want to come out again.

When he pushed the door, it scraped on the linoleum and shook like it was going to break. After regathering his load, he walked on tiptoes into the house. I took a deep breath and followed. The house smelled like Grandpa's root cellar where he kept sacks of onions and the fruit that Aunt Ruth had canned. I imagined angle worms and beetles crawling in the cupboards.

"Don't bring anyone in the house!" The voice from the next room trembled like Laddie's hands. The frayed shades rolled down over the sink made the kitchen seem gloomy. "Do you hear me, Laddie?"

We looked at each other.

I emptied my shirt onto the card table between the dirty dishes, guarding the edges of the table with my bare arms to hold the potatoes. Laddie retrieved one that rolled off and, instead of adding it to the pile, he held it out to me.

Our hands met in the column of daylight coming through the open door. His fingers were ice.

"Good-bye, Laddie."

Though he'd never said a word I could understand, I felt like we knew each other. He was the innocent cocker spaniel who was deaf to the roar of Mr. Baker's car. As quietly as I could, I walked backwards out the door. Laddie just stood there by the table watching me, his empty hand still cradled in the shape of a potato.

7

I was ecstatic when Wellesley called asking me to ride horses at her cousin Annie's. Maybe things were better at her house. It also meant she'd forgotten about beating me in arm wrestling at the swimming hole.

Wellesley and I had started trading stories about horses the day she saw a blank newspaper form fall out of my pocket. It was one of those contests to say in twenty-five words or less why you wanted a horse. I entered every cereal box and newspaper horse contest I could find. She told me she'd done the same thing thinking that if she ever won she could keep it with Annie's two quarter horses.

Mom agreed to give us a ride over if Annie's mom would bring us back. The Currans' farm was about twenty miles west of Clearwater on a route that crossed the river, then gradually rose out of the valley onto a plateau of rolling wheat, pea, and alfalfa fields. Clusters of sycamore and pine trees shaded each farmhouse.

Although I'd always wanted a horse, I never liked the idea of living on a farm. You had to pedal or walk a couple of miles just to have someone to play cards with. Things you needed, like magazines and Cokes, were so remote. Taylor was even more adamant on the subject. "Farm kids are hicks," he said, "hayseeds, Herkimer Jerkimers." I needed a horse I could keep in the garage or lean against the house under the eaves like a bike.

While Annie was helping me put the bit in Apache's mouth, Roland Bushner showed up. Wellesley had warned me he was putting the make on Annie. Bushner was two grades ahead of us in school and someone with a bad reputation. I once saw him coldcock Larry Sodorff from behind with a rock. Sodorff had just been accepted at Washington

State University to study business. The good ones always seemed to leave Clearwater.

Bushner walked through the barn door with thumbs in his pockets and a piece of straw hanging out of his mouth. His snake eyes glared at Annie like she'd stood him up and he was coming by to find out why. He just muttered when Annie introduced me, acting as if I was trying to move in on his girl or something. When Annie stretched to throw the saddle on top of Dolly, he put his hands on her butt.

Annie and Roland rode Apache. Wellesley and I took Dolly. From behind, I didn't know whether to hold onto the curve of the saddle back or Wellesley's waist. It felt awkward. Wellesley knew her horses though. Once we were out of sight of the Currans' gabled house, she put Dolly into high gear.

"He yaa! Come on, Dolly!" Wellesley whipped Dolly with the loose ends of the leather reins, one side then the other. Her heels planted into Dolly's belly just under my own dangling legs.

"This is great!" I yelled in her ear, my arms wrapped around her middle to keep from falling.

Bushner reined Apache off the road ahead of us, crossing the creek bed. Annie, in the backseat like me, pressed against him. Suddenly, Dolly drew up like she'd seen a ghost step out of Apache's dust. As Dolly pulled left, the saddle, Wellesley, and I shifted right. When she finally stopped, we hung like window washers against Dolly's torso.

"Goddammit to Christ almighty, horse, what are you doing?" Wellesley's voice strained as she struggled to hold onto the saddle horn and pull her foot from the stirrup.

I dismounted in a handstand when Dolly stilled. "She must have seen something in the creek," I said, refusing to believe that Dolly would do anything to hurt us.

Wellesley kicked a dirt clod, spraying Dolly's front legs. "Probably her own goddamned shadow."

Dolly's big brown eyes blinked at me, as if I should help her.

"We were going too fast to make the turn and she knew it," I said. I stroked Dolly's mane to clear the hair from her face. Her neck glistened with sweat. "She probably needs to be worked more often. If she were mine, I'd ride her every day." My resolve to stay off the farm was weakening.

Wellesley recinched the girth with a vicious downward tug. "When I'm in the saddle, I'm the boss! Now we've lost Annie and Roland."

I didn't tell her that suited me better. In the short meeting at the barn, I'd decided Bushner had the personality of a badger. We hadn't traded a single sentence and I'd bet he didn't even remember my name.

Once we were back on Dolly, Wellesley walked her across the stream and up the draw. The rich topsoil, furrowed with rows of young wheat stalks, formed a thick carpet for Dolly's shod feet. The saddle leather squeaked as Dolly lumbered up the slope, shifting her weight from side to side, exhaling with a force that vibrated her nostrils.

Suddenly Wellesley pulled Dolly to a stop, "Hey, I know where they went! They're at the Berringer homestead."

"What's that?"

"An abandoned farmhouse. It's still got some furniture in it. Annie took me there once. Out in the middle of nowhere."

We cut a diagonal over the hill into the next draw. Wellesley galloped Dolly until the homestead came into view.

The Berringer place looked haunted. Wind and rain had scrubbed it paintless. Moss grew on the scattered patches of shingles; shutters hung askew by their corners. The whole house tilted left, resembling a man standing with his weight on one leg. In the front yard, the remains of a two-wheel tractor and a combine rose from the stinkweeds and cheat grass like rusted sculptures. Two paddles hanging from the windmill wheel behind the house rocked back and forth, destined never to make another full circle.

Apache was tied to the porch railing.

"Let's sneak up on them," I said. "Leave Dolly out here. We can tie her to one of these tire rims."

Wellesley said they wouldn't see us if we approached from the bunkhouse in back. We made a big loop, hunching over to make ourselves less obvious. Closer to the house, we went to our hands and knees to stay below the windowsill.

When we heard Bushner's voice, we ducked.

"Come on, take 'em off! Isn't this what you wanted?"

I swallowed the air in my throat. Wellesley put her hand on my shoulder to keep me down while she positioned her head in the corner of the window.

"Not like this." It was Annie's voice. "Let's just go back, Roland." She was pleading. I watched Wellesley's eyes. They showed the same kind of fear I saw in Dolly after she threw us.

"Listen, bitch, don't go hot and cold on me! You wanted this."

"Not like this, Roland, please. Let's go back."

Wellesley poked me with her finger and wiggled it in the direction of the window. She wanted a second opinion. I lifted myself up.

"Let's see those hungry tits you were rubbing against me on the way over." Bushner popped the buttons on Annie's blouse and pushed his palms against her bra.

Annie gripped his arms. "Leave me alone!"

When he clawed the bra down over her breasts, I lowered myself to the ground.

Wellesley chewed on her finger, studying something in the space between her boots.

"What should we do?" I whispered.

I knew something was building in Wellesley. She was going to explode. I felt like a coward, strapped to the ground. Everything in that room was foreign to me.

In the dust, Wellesley drew a quick sketch of the homestead and the path she wanted us to take. The argument inside the house continued. Annie was bawling. Bushner kept calling her an "iceberg."

Wellesley crawled over to the bunkhouse on her stomach and dragged back a two-by-four the length of a baseball bat. I found a rock about the size of a hardball that had fallen out of the crumbling foundation. She gave the advance sign and we duck-walked to the backdoor. From there, we could see the open door to the bedroom about halfway down the hall. Each time Bushner raised his voice, we moved closer.

From the bedroom door, I could see him straddled over Annie, holding her wrists against the black-and-white striped mattress. She was naked. He still had on his faded denim shirt.

Wellesley signaled. We sprang into the room.

Bushner grabbed for his pants and scurried to the foot of the bed, bracing his back against the metal railing. Wellesley took a level swing, hitting him across the ribs with her two-by-four.

"Get out of the way, Annie!" Wellesley jumped onto the bed ready to take her next cut. I dropped my rock and grabbed Bushner around the neck from the back, holding him tight against the bed frame.

"Stop! I give!" His voice gurgled from the pressure of my forearm on his throat.

"You shit-eating bastard, let's see you try something now!" Wellesley's eyes flared. She held the board over her head like an ax. Bushner coiled his legs to his chest in a fetal position.

Annie huddled on the floor, shivering, holding her torn blouse against her front.

"Are you okay, Annie?" I asked.

"Yeah . . . yeah," she whispered in a defeated voice. She looked ashamed. I wanted her to feel saved.

Bushner trembled in my grip. He seemed smaller than I remembered him in the barn.

Wellesley tried to poke the board between his legs. "I'd like to beat your balls to mush."

Annie and I convinced her to just leave him be.

It was the second time this summer I'd found myself looking in a window, seeing what I wished I hadn't. Wellesley didn't know about the first time. I wondered what I would have done to help Annie without Wellesley. Her boldness embarrassed me. It was as if she'd trained for this. She seemed so natural in the role of rescuer.

We left Bushner at the homestead. Annie and Wellesley took Apache. I rode back on Dolly alone.

8

I was waiting on the front porch steps with my duffel bag when Mr. Clark drove up. Taylor popped out of the backseat and bounded up the walk. The week for Spirit Lake had finally arrived.

Taylor sat between me and his brother, Dan. They elbowed each other for space in the backseat. Dan's voice was deeper than Taylor's. He was eighteen and I could tell he had to shave every day. "Don't start wising off, Taylor," Dan said, loud enough so that Mrs. Clark turned around.

The sun coming through the windshield made her orange hair glow. "This is no way to treat our guest," she said, looking at me as if to apologize. I should have volunteered that I was used to this kind of stuff. Wellesley and Taylor did it all the time.

"It's Dan's fault, Mom. He's taking half the seat."

"You think Mom's blind, stupid? She can see for herself you're lying."

"That's enough, both of you." Mr. Clark tilted the rear-view mirror so he could see the three of us.

I hoped Taylor would just drop it. The Clarks would regret they let him bring someone. Mr. Clark made a face in the mirror, trying to look as tough as one of the waffle irons he repaired. Mrs. Clark smiled triumphantly at Taylor and Dan. The incident was closed.

Arrowhead Resort was a small village, with a general store for groceries, fishing tackle, bait, and tools. One gas pump with a hand crank served boats and cars. Mr. Arnold, the manager of the store, gave us a candy bar or popsicle if we'd carry gas cans and supplies to the dock for customers.

All the units were white with forest green trim. Our cottage had a bedroom for Taylor's parents and one for Dan. The bulk of the space was a big room which served as the kitchen, living, and dining area combined. A cast-iron stove and kindling box sat in the center of the big room. The walls stopped where most houses had a ceiling, exposing the ridgepole and rafters. Instead of a bathroom, there was an outhouse.

Taylor and I slept in an olive drab, Army surplus tent pitched next to the path that ran from our cabin to the beach. We shared our quarters with black ants, mosquitoes, and slugs as big as hot dogs.

The first night we played poker for pennies with a flashlight. When it flickered out, we slid into our sleeping bags and talked about Mr. Baker.

"He's just a little pissed at the world," Taylor said. "The guy's a talent. He could be driving in the big time and he's holed up in Milltown."

"So is that Wellesley's fault?"

"It doesn't matter. When you're pissed off you swing at whoever's closest."

"I think it stinks."

"So does shit, but we still have to eat," he said.

Taylor's philosophy didn't satisfy me. But I wasn't bothered enough to lose any sleep over it, despite the fact that the ground felt like petrified scrambled eggs.

On the second day, we discovered some familiar faces. While we were sunning on the swimming dock, Monica Amberly and Marilyn Tubbs rowed up in one of the wooden dinghies with "Arrowhead—Rental" stenciled on the bow. In her raven black swimsuit that matched her silky hair, Monica was even prettier than she looked in school clothes. On the other hand, Marilyn had suffered from the transition. Stomach rolls showed through the tight orange skin of her one piece bathing suit. Her legs looked as if they'd never seen sunshine.

In between doses of Coppertone, Monica read *Crime and Punishment* and Marilyn *Lord of the Flies*. Besides sandwiches in tin foil, chips, fig newton cookies, and a thermos of juice, their wicker basket had several personal letters, a writing tablet, pens, *The Scarlet Letter*, and *Advanced Algebra*. We didn't belong on the same dock with these two. Besides Taylor's dirty magazines, I couldn't think of anything else we both liked to read.

Monica's voice matched her skin—soft, smooth, and lightly basted. I tried to avoid her noticing my stare at her cleavage by frequently shifting my sunning positions. Monica was an hourglass with winking eyes. Marilyn was a barrel.

Taylor chose the hourglass. "I started your book once," he said, practically putting his face between Monica and the page.

Monica smiled kindly on Taylor at this revelation. "How far did you get?"

About as far as he was going to get with Monica I thought. For someone who was supposed to be expert at getting girls, he should have known better than to start down this path. But Taylor didn't flinch. "To the first love scene," he said.

Monica and Marilyn giggled. "The one with Raskolnikov and the pawnbroker, you mean?" Monica asked.

"Yeah. Some sizzler, huh?"

Monica carefully folded the corner of the page and closed the book. "I'm curious, what made you put it down?" She was enjoying this but I suspected it was at Taylor's expense.

Taylor adjusted his lips and frowned like he was trying to find the words to explain. "Just something rang false to me, I guess."

"You mean when Raskolnikov hit her on the head with the hatchet," Marilyn said, the flesh of her legs shaking with the laughter she was holding back.

Taylor snapped around to get a good look at her. "What do you mean?"

"I mean the jig's up, Taylor," Marilyn said.

Taylor looked at Monica for assistance. She raised up on one elbow and pulled her suit to reclaim the white tops of her breasts. "I think Taylor's confusing this with *Lady Chatterley*," she said. "They're both long."

That night in the tent, I told Taylor I thought Marilyn and Monica were unlikely companions.

He said it always happened that way. "The pretty-faced, movie-star types always keep a plain jane around who adores them. Marilyn's the protector."

The truth was I just wanted to talk about Monica. It wasn't anything sexual. After seeing what Bushner had tried to do with Annie Curran, I'd made up my mind never to try it with a girl unless we were married. But my adoration of Monica seemed unstoppable. I thought about her all week. The way she handled herself was so smooth.

When Taylor wanted to go squirrel hunting with sling-shots, I voted for the swimming dock. When Taylor wanted to put honey in Monica's swimsuit on the clothesline, I distracted him. I tried to squelch my feelings for Monica, to hide them from Taylor.

He encouraged me to chase Marilyn. "We're at the lake. Nobody at school needs to even know about it."

Taylor was probably right. I wasn't in Monica's league. With someone like Marilyn, I had a chance. But I couldn't stop thinking of Monica. I had never seen beauty and wisdom so plentiful in the same person. When Taylor bragged about Monica, I bit my lip and offered up assets in Marilyn that tied her to Monica. She read the same books. Their parents were friends. They were both rich.

My experience seemed so limited. I probably came off as a fuddy-duddy the way Grandpa Blane did. The only female friend I'd ever had was Wellesley. But she was a friend who happened to be a girl, not someone you dreamed about.

Taylor and I blew tunes into empty Coke bottles in the tent that night. We hung our flashlight in a makeshift T-shirt hammock hooked to the ribs in the top. Taylor told me a Mr. Baker story I'd never heard, how he'd been chased by the State Patrol from Clearwater to Coles Corner.

"They clocked him at a hundred miles an hour," Taylor said.

"No way, the turns are too sharp."

"That's not the best part," Taylor said, as he worked his finger in the bottle, making a pop sound each time he pulled it out. "When the cop squeezed him off the road, Mr. Baker got out and pinned the guy against the patrol car. He was pissed as hell at the cop."

"What did the cop say?"

"As soon as he recognized who it was, the cop laughed and let him go. Said he felt damn proud just to have kept up with Baker."

On Sunday, our last day, Taylor wanted to go fishing. So we rented one of the rowboats and borrowed Mr. Clark's tackle box. He fixed up two rods and reels, with a cherry wobbler on one and a speckled yellow and black flatfish on the other. The salmon eggs which he gave us for bait looked like a jar of pink eyeballs. Taylor also snuck a warm bottle of Budweiser into the fish basket. He said we could put it in the net and dangle it in the water to cool off once we got out there.

As we passed the swimming dock, I pulled down the bill of my baseball cap. Monica was laughing with a muscular blond guy who'd arrived Saturday. In my swimming suit, I had a habit of crossing my arms so my ribs wouldn't show. This guy shamelessly thrust his chest at her. He was out of my league too.

The Amberlys were staying a second week. By the time she returned to town, she'd be as brown as cocoa, going steady, and have forgotten the winks I thought she gave me on the dock. I'd been widowed just like Grandpa Blane.

As I fixed my line, my insides felt like the salmon eggs must have felt as I ran them through with the barbed hooks on our lures. I couldn't laugh at any of Taylor's jokes. I told him it must have been something I'd eaten.

9

I found Wellesley in front of the candy counter at the Rexall. In the dark walnut counter with beveled glass there were penny candies on the bottom shelf: Lick 'm Ade, wax whistles filled with fruit syrup, jaw breakers, and bubble gum. For a nickel, you could choose between Sugar Daddies, Baby Ruth, Snickers, and other candy bars from the top shelf.

"How was the lake, you lucky stiff?"

For an instant I thought of telling her about Monica and me but realized she might slip and tell Taylor. Besides, what was there to say? The history of our relationship was a shooting star in my own imagination. I was the only one who'd seen it. "The lake was great, swam every day, slept in the sun, even went fishing."

"How was Taylor?" she asked.

"You know Taylor, he mostly read books in the cabin, helped his mom." We both laughed. Wellesley would have loved to see Taylor get caught trying to fake his way through *Crime and Punishment*. I checked to make sure no one was near us. "How's Annie?"

Wellesley's face was determined. "It took her about six showers to wash away the smell of that slimeball. She's fine. But I don't think you'll see her with Bushner again."

"She should have called the police."

Wellesley leaned against the counter, one elbow on top, as she spoke. "I wish she had, but Annie doesn't want anyone to know about it. Besides, Annie thinks he'd get off because he didn't go all the way." I could feel Wellesley getting worked up again. "They should cut his dicky off before he tries it on someone else."

Martin, the soda jerk and owner, stepped next to the

counter, ready to drop a ball of chocolate ice cream from his scoop into the tall aluminum milkshake container he was holding. "Good afternoon, chums! I haven't seen you two for a while. Thought somebody opened another soda fountain in town."

We laughed. Wellesley took a step back from the counter, "Hi, Martin."

"Hi, Martin," I said.

"What can I get for you?" he said, as he squeezed the tab and dropped the chocolate into the canister.

"Just window shopping," Wellesley said.

"Pick something off the top shelf," he said. "It's on the house. Both of you."

"Martin, you don't have to give anything away," I said, "we're not kids."

"I'd make you pay for it if you were." I wondered if Martin was thinking of Wellesley's sister, Tiffany. He caught her with four packs of Chesterfield longs in her blouse last summer. She apparently took them out of the rack on the counter while Martin was in the storage room trying to find birthday candles for her. He became suspicious when Tiffany changed her mind about the candles. Anyone else would have turned her in for shoplifting, but Martin just put the cigarettes back in the rack and gave her a talking to. Wellesley was furious at Tiffany when she found out.

"Speaking of free ones, here comes Taylor," Wellesley said. "Don't worry, Martin, we won't spread your offer."

Taylor's rubber thongs flip-flopped as he marched to the marble-topped bar and plopped down a twelve-box package of Diamond wooden matches. "Hello, Martin."

"What on earth are you going to use those for?" Martin inspected the package with a "tsk, tsk" clicking of his tongue. I had the same question. He almost burned his garage down the last time he struck a match.

"Don't worry, I'm not taking up smoking." Taylor laughed, pulling a folded dollar bill from his front pocket and sliding it across the marble.

"You can put two Mountain bars with that," Wellesley said, pointing to Taylor's matches.

"No way," Taylor said, putting his forearm between his matches and us.

"Just testing, Taylor," Wellesley said. Then she winked at Martin. "Give this kid a Sugar Daddy and put it on my bill. I'm too full to eat mine."

"Me too, Martin," I said, going along with Wellesley's joke.

Taylor looked at each of us trying to figure out what was going on. Then his face softened. "You missed me, I'm touched, Wellesley."

"We've known that all along, Taylor." Even Martin laughed.

"I'll get your change, Mr. Clark," Martin said, returning to finish the milkshake.

Taylor, still not sure what had happened, changed the subject. "Hey, I've got a plan! What are you guys doing tomorrow?"

"Nothing," Wellesley said.

"Do you have to work, Bradford?"

"Probably, but I can do it anytime."

Taylor's eyes brightened. "Good, meet me at the dump tomorrow morning at nine."

Wellesley and I biked to the Sylvanus County dump, three miles north of Clearwater on Indian Trail Road. Taylor was waiting for us in the shade near the turnoff. When he had our full attention, he pulled three clothespin contraptions out of a stiff canvas pouch snapped to his Army ammunition belt.

"What the hell are those?" Wellesley asked.

"Rat guns," Taylor beamed. He explained how he reversed the direction of one leg of the clothespin and taped it to the top of a short dowel to make a gun that shot wooden matches fifteen to twenty feet. The spring ignited each match as it exited the chamber. From the drawstring bag over his shoulder, he handed Wellesley and me one box each of the Diamond matches he'd bought at Martin's.

I started to say something.

"Don't panic, Bradford, there's no gas this time."

"This is great, Taylor." Wellesley was already emptying

the matches into the front pockets of her shorts which were held together with patches of curtain fabric on the butt. "How we going to catch them?"

"Hey, I'm not trying to catch 'em, just have a little fun."

"What about Webster, he'll call the cops," I said. Unless he was sleeping off a hangover, I knew the caretaker would make trouble.

"He's dead to the world in the hut," Taylor said. "I already checked. He'll never know we're here. Besides, he could give a rat's ass." Wellesley and Taylor laughed. Despite their rivalry, they shared a craving for recklessness I didn't have. Sometimes their hunger for wildness intimidated me. With Taylor, I could understand it. He had a pushover of a dad to fall back on if he got in trouble. With Wellesley, it was just the opposite.

For a couple hours, we stalked rats in the dump, imitating our prey on all fours. The trick was to find a likely nest, surround it and then move closer until they made their run. The rats darted one way then another each time we fired a match. Then they scampered over the refuse out of range while we reloaded and looked for more.

The smoke, decomposing food, and mold blended into a sour gas that made my eyes water and nose run. The place was how I imagined Purgatory. Stripes and dabs of rust, tar, and garbage slime smeared my tennis shoes and jeans. The black streaks on Wellesley's face made her look like a chimney sweep. Taylor gashed the inside of his right arm on a piece of barbed wire.

When we reached our bikes at the end of the hunt, we rested in the scrub grass to count our "hits." I had three and Wellesley seven. Taylor said he had ten.

"Bullshit, Taylor!" Wellesley threw her gun down. "You couldn't hit ten rats if they stood on their heads!"

"Oh yeah, Baker, you better start praying you're right." Taylor fired his rat gun at her crotch. Their fight caught the dry grass on fire. We stomped it out and covered it with handfuls of dirt.

Before leaving, Taylor divided another box of matches between us to top off our pockets.

On the way home, we looked for targets to hit on the run

—road signs, telephone poles, parked cars. Taylor called it plinking. In a game of rolling follow-the-leader, we shot whenever Taylor did. He swung wide at the turn for the county fairgrounds, ignoring the stop sign. We followed.

The fairgrounds were deserted. We leaned our bikes against the cyclone fence and squeezed through an opening allowed by the slack in the chain holding the gate. From the top row of the bleachers, we stared at the weeds in the arena. Instead of stripped-down, banged out stock cars, there were just beer bottles, pieces of cardboard, and rags. The place where Mr. Baker drank whiskey from the hood of the Pink Lady that night was marked by a dark stain of oil the size of a manhole cover. Behind us, the rows of plywood carnival shacks were plastered with peeling clown posters, advertising last year's Labor Day Fair. Paper cups, crumpled napkins, and cigarette wrappers had blown up against the fences. There was a lot of cleaning to do before the Junior Rodeo.

Wellesley seemed to stare at that same oil spot I saw. I wondered if her dad being so popular made what happened in the kitchen easier, averaging the good with the bad. Maybe it hurt more, seeing other people cheer for someone who had hit you. Since the fight in the kitchen, I hadn't even mentioned his name.

Taylor made a fart sound with his hand cupped in his armpit. "Excuse me, madam," he said, "enjoying the races?" It sounded so real I took a whiff to be sure. All I could smell was the garbage that had rubbed off on us in the dump.

"Sometimes, your IQ doesn't make room temperature," Wellesley said, smiling for the first time since we'd sat down.

He farted again, in a series of blasts from his armpit. "Begging my pardon . . ." fart-fart, "I'm a bit gassy this . . ." fart, "morning . . . oh, thank you." His face relaxed.

"Faker," Wellesley said.

Taylor lifted his buttocks off the bleacher and let go a real one. "Say what, ma'am?"

Everyone laughed.

"What if I had . . . pork 'n beans before the Trophy Dash," Taylor said, struggling to get the words out over his laughter, "and I ripped my crotch out . . . with a zinger . . . just as the Queen was kissing me?" His eyes watered and he doubled up, rolling down to the next row of the bleachers. He must have been feeling full of himself because the match guns had worked so well.

Wellesley and I just looked at each other. It was hard to imagine Monica letting this guy touch her the way Taylor said he had.

I spotted someone on the opposite side of the fairgrounds standing at the base of the Ferris wheel. The merry-go-round and Ferris wheel were permanent parts of the fairgrounds. At the Labor Day Fair, additional rides were hauled in by trailer and set up to make a regular midway.

"Hey, let's see what's cooking," Taylor said. He jumped from one row of the bleachers to the next.

Wellesley and I followed. We climbed over the fence, sprinted across the arena and climbed out the other side into the corral. The ground stunk. We kicked dried horse pies like they were hockey pucks. The Ferris wheel was just beyond.

A husky man with no shirt sat on the operator's platform next to the motor. His hands were holding the greasy innards of the gears for the Ferris wheel like he'd just performed surgery. "How'd you guys get in here?" He spit something to the ground.

"Through the gate," Wellesley said.

"You can turn your skinny asses and go right back outta here, you're trespassing." He twisted to face us. One leg was in the engine well and the other stretched along the planks parallel to the ground like a runner going over a hurdle. His chest was covered with swirls of black hair. On his bicep was a tattooed heart with a long-handled knife through the middle.

"You think you own this place? Your truck says you don't even come from here." Wellesley moved to the front, like she was speaking for the three of us. I hadn't noticed until she said it that the sign on the panel of his dilapidated truck read "Cirro's Road Shows—Missoula, Montana."

"You have a pretty shitty tongue for a girl. What's the matter with the boys in this backwater town, can't they speak for themselves?" Holding a gigantic wrench in his hand like a hatchet, he stood up, probably six-foot four in his logging boots.

"Let's get out of here," I said, "this guy isn't worth wasting our time on." I pulled on Taylor's arm.

"Get the fuck out of here before I ream your asses," he shouted. "I mean now!" His muscles rippled as he twisted the wrench. He was coming at us.

Wellesley and Taylor fired their rat guns at him. He dodged, then charged.

We ran. He chased us all the way around the outside of the arena. The narrow opening in the locked gate acted as a sieve, letting us pass but catching him. While he unfastened the padlock, we mounted the bikes and kicked up gravel with our tires.

Taylor and I zigzagged the side roads on the race back to town. My fender was rubbing against the front tire. It sounded like a dull siren. But there was no way I was going to stop and fix it. I pulled matches out of my pocket as I drove, littering the road with them, then turned both pockets inside out to make sure there was no more evidence.

We shoved our bikes into the racks at the Rexall, tore through the alleys to my garage, and hiked ourselves onto the lumber Dad was storing on the cross beams. This was the leftovers from remodeling the hardware, triangular pieces of plywood, mahogany veneer that matched the cash register, and strips of molding. Dad would have croaked if he knew he'd built me a place to hide from the police.

"What happened to Wellesley," I asked, still panting. My head rested on a sheet of dusty plywood inches away from Taylor's face. I could still smell the root beer he'd drunk from the bottle he found at the dump.

"She probably took her own way back, it's smart to split up," Taylor said.

"What if he caught her?"

"Not Wellesley," Taylor said.

My mind kept returning to the chase, trying to get to our

bikes before he got us. "That guy's in a class with Wellesley's dad," I said, still unable to say Mr. Baker's name.

We lay motionless in the hideout for what seemed like
hours, listening to every voice and car door slam from the
street. I imagined the carnival repair man engaged in a
door-to-door search of the neighborhood.

There was no sign of the panel truck when we crawled
down. I headed home, scared something had happened to
Wellesley. And mad at myself for not staying with her.
Wellesley would have never ditched us.

10

At dinner, Dad said Sergeant Payne had stopped in the hardware to pick up some floor wax on his way home from day shift. The sergeant told him about booking the "Baker girl" for an incident at the fairgrounds.

I stopped chewing.

"Meantime, he says they've released her. I hope she gets jail time," Dad said, enjoying the opportunity to make a point about the decline in my generation's respect for authority. "A kid like that needs to get hit over the head to knock some sense into her." The whole subject seemed to increase Dad's appetite, as he sawed his meat with a steak knife.

"Dad, how do you know she's guilty?"

"You think Officer Payne made this up?" Dad pointed his fork at me. A double bite of round steak was skewered on the prongs. "Besides, the man saw the whole thing, said she cussed at him and then threw a match at the machinery. Just about caused an explosion."

I wanted to change the subject. What if Wellesley was forced to name Taylor and me?

My silence didn't discourage Dad. "Will, you'd be smart to stay away from her. Kids like that don't know where the line is. They push and push until they find themselves on the outside looking in. Pretty soon, they're outlaws!" Dad should have been a priest instead of a hardware man. He loved to preach, especially to me. Of course, if he'd gone to the priesthood, he couldn't have had a kid and I wouldn't have had to listen to him.

I wanted to push the table over and explode. Dad, leave her alone! I'm the outlaw! But without saying anything, I finished my tapioca pudding, thanked Mom for dinner and beat it over to Taylor's to tell him about Wellesley.

Taylor and I decided to go to her house. The debate was whether to knock on the door or rap on her bedroom window. Neither one of us wanted to see her dad. I convinced Taylor that sneaking around made us look guilty—better to act boldly. Maybe I was learning something from Wellesley after all.

Mrs. Baker answered the door. Her face was colorless. She politely explained that Wellesley was "otherwise occupied" and wouldn't be able to come out. I hadn't seen Mrs. Baker up close since the night we spied on them. Stoop shouldered, with a quiet voice, she seemed deflated. Her eyes flitted nervously as if she thought someone might be listening. When Taylor and I reached the street, I turned and saw her draw the drape aside far enough to watch us through the living room window.

At the Rexall counter, we shared a cherry Coke. Taylor thought of putting a burning bag of shit on the front porch to distract them and rushing the back door. He loved to work with fire. I pointed out the obvious risks of his approach; besides neither one of us had to go.

Fifteen minutes later, we returned to the Bakers'.

No one answered the taps I made with a pebble on Wellesley's bedroom window. Her room was dark. As we circled the house, checking every room, we heard fingernails scratching glass near our feet. Wellesley was in the basement.

I got on my hands and knees and put my ear against the basement window. In a loud whisper, pausing between words, Wellesley said, "Push . . . the window . . . with your feet."

Planting my butt on the hardpan—these flower beds hadn't seen a spade since the house was built—I braced my back against Taylor's knee. The window must have been nailed shut.

"Kick it, Will," Taylor said.

"I don't want anyone to hear us."

Gradually, a crack appeared between the window and the frame. I moved closer for more leverage and, with a steady grunt, slowly pried the bottom of the window open. It swung free with a squeak from the hinges.

As I lowered myself feet first through the window, Wellesley wrapped her arms around my legs for support. She brushed the spider webs and beetles off the back of my pants. Then we helped Taylor down. We were in her coal bin. The scattered nuggets crunched as we moved. There were a few large chunks in the corners of the bin. It smelled smokey.

"What happened, Wellesley?" I asked.

She whispered, "My chain broke! The mechanic guy grabbed me before I could get to the road."

"What did he do to you?" Taylor asked.

"He put me in a hammer lock. Then he dragged me to the truck and dumped me in the back with a bunch of pipe fittings. We yelled at each other through the screen divider."

"Did he call the police?" I asked.

"No phone. He drove to the police station in his truck and marched me through the front door. You'd have thought he caught the Lindbergh kidnapper. 'Book this little witch,' he told the desk officer." Wellesley still had on the patched shorts, black tennis shoes, and frayed sweatshirt she wore at the dump. She hadn't bothered to wash her face. I could still see the dump grime in the sweat marks.

Taylor burst in, "Did you tell them about me and Bradford?"

"Hell, no! I'm no squealer. But the police kept asking me,"—she imitated the deep voice of the policeman— " 'Who were the two with you?' The Ferris wheel guy made a big point of it. I said I ran into you on the road and thought you were from out of state." Taylor sighed in relief. I felt worse. Wellesley had to lie to protect us. "Don't worry. The cops are too lazy to search for you in another state."

We sat on the floor under a dim bulb hanging from the ceiling. Taylor said no one at his house knew anything yet. I told Wellesley what Sergeant Payne had said. She took it all in. Until I asked her a second time, she wouldn't say what happened at her house.

"When the police called, Mom came down. I guess because I'm under sixteen and didn't kill someone, they let me go home." Her voice was sarcastic. "I asked if there was any way to keep it from my dad, but Mom said no. So she called him at the plant. He boiled over. Told her to put me down here till he gets off work tonight." Under her breath, she said, "He's probably at the Drift Inn."

Wellesley's whisper had grown thin when she started talking about her dad. Her shoulders drooped and she looked at the floor. "My dad gets spooked about police stuff," she said. "His younger brother, Elliott, got mixed up with a bad crowd and spent some time in the can." Sitting cross-legged, Wellesley formed a cross of coal particles with her fingers on the floor. "He blamed Elliott for his mom dying of depression. That left 'em with their dad. He hated his dad. Mom says, 'Your dad is only doing what's best for you and Tiffany. He doesn't want us to have the problems his family had.' Tiffany was smart. She moved out."

I wanted to get Wellesley out too. Watching her fingers fiddle in the dusk of the coal bin, I knew she'd rather face the carnival man or the police than her dad.

I remembered the time at the lake when I went into the girl's outhouse to see what it was like. Dad caught me and made me lie in the back of our station wagon on the dog blanket until it was time to leave. Just me and the spare tire. Waiting here had the same feeling of dog hair and dead rubber.

"Aren't you just scared shitless?" Taylor asked.

"It won't be the first time my dad's been mad."

"Why don't you just leave for a few days, come to my house?" As soon as I said it, I realized how impossible that would be.

"Thanks, Will, but I can't. If I'm not here when my dad gets home, he'll blame Mom."

Taylor scratched x's and o's on the floor with a piece of coal.

Wellesley took off her glasses and scrubbed both sides of each lens with her tongue, the same way I'd seen Grandpa Blane do it. He said there was nothing cleaner than your own water. She wiped them dry with the inside of her sweatshirt. "I wish Mom had some friends. She doesn't think she's good enough. She's embarrassed she only got to eighth grade. She thinks she's too plain. When she went to the Presbyterian sewing circle, people poked fun at her clothes. You know, being a Milltowner and all that." Wellesley bit her lip and sucked in some air. "Sometimes I dream of being rich and flying her to New York, just Mom and me. I'd buy her an expensive dress, get her hair fixed and parade through Clearwater from the back of a white convertible waving at the crowds on the curb. Everyone saying how stunning that woman is!"

The door opened suddenly, flooding the wooden stairs with light. "Wellesley!" Mr. Baker's slurred voice broke like a thunderclap.

I dropped my palms to the cement to get up, but where could I go? Taylor and I looked at Wellesley. We were in his house.

"Yeah, I'm coming," Wellesley answered dutifully. She motioned for us to stay put.

"Then get your butt up here! Now!"

"I said I'm coming."

Wellesley whispered for me and Taylor to wait until she was upstairs, and then go back out the window.

As Wellesley started up the stairs, he started down. I thought he was going to drag her back to the coal bin and find us. We were trapped. Instead, he grabbed her like a cat takes a kitten by the skin on the back of the neck and lifted her up and out of sight. He slammed the door so hard it bounced back open.

Mr. Baker's voice carried down the stairs. "So you finally got caught." Slap! "They should have just cooled your smart aleck ass in the jailhouse . . ." Slap! ". . . so you'd learn something . . ." Slap! ". . . but your mama feels so goddamned sorry she bails you out . . ." Slap! ". . . maybe that's the fucking trouble around here, too much fucking cover-up!" I heard table legs scrape, feet shuffle, and glass break. It sounded like Wellesley was bouncing against the kitchen furniture.

"Stop it, please! No . . ." It was Mrs. Baker's voice.

I didn't hear Wellesley say anything.

Something solid hit the floor with a thud. Then, Mr. Baker's boots left the kitchen.

"I'm sorry, Wellesley . . . oh God," Mrs. Baker sobbed.

Taylor and I just sat there on the concrete, waiting to make sure it was safe to leave. I sifted coal dust between my fingers.

When I got home, I leaned far enough into the living room to say, "Good night, Mom and Dad."

Mom was crocheting a sweater for someone, listening to classical music on the radio next to her chair. It was turned real low so it wouldn't bother Dad. Feeling sorry for all the radio people with good voices and homely faces who wouldn't make it on television, Mom had vowed not to give up the radio. Dad was reading the paper with his feet propped up on the footstool and a small plate of cheese, a can of Planter's Peanuts, and a box of Ritz crackers on the magazine table. The room was as bright as the school cafeteria.

"Good night, Will."

"Don't forget to do your sweeping tomorrow," Dad said, his mouth full of cracker. "The floors are starting to look like a dust bin."

"Okay, Dad." I would have agreed to anything. I wished he'd grounded me for something instead of letting me walk around as if everything was normal.

I flopped on my unmade bed, face down in the pillow, wanting darkness. How could anyone pound his kid like that? He should have been proud of her. I remembered her wading into the bedroom at the homestead to help Annie. My complaints about my dad seemed so petty compared to hers. If only Wellesley had what I took for granted, she'd soar. I didn't deserve what she couldn't have. The fact that I'd escaped at the fairgrounds made it worse. When things turned sour, I'd turned tail.

On the back of a magazine wrapper, I wrote a note to Wellesley explaining what a coward I was. Then I started an "Our Father" but dropped it during the part about trespasses, realizing I'd been hypocrite enough for one day.

I woke up kicking the next morning. The sheets were wet with sweat. Birds, feeding on our cherries, chirped outside the window. The sun streamed through the slits between the bath towels I'd draped over the flimsy gauze curtains. Wellesley's note, folded double, was still next to the alarm clock on the apple crate. I felt like I had a brick in my intestines.

11

Dad had come out of World War II with a wife, a kid, and no money. When Mr. Perry died, leaving Western Hardware to his widow, Dad stepped forward with ten thousand dollars he'd borrowed from Grandpa Blane to buy the business.

My dad was the family's unemployment office. When Aunt Violet lost her husband in the Korean War, she came to work at the hardware. Uncle Harold, who had six kids, convinced Dad he needed a second job. Joe Woodward, Dad's second cousin, dropped out of engineering in college and became the bike and lawnmower man and added television repair to his job when TV broadcasting started.

Without Dad even asking that morning, I swept the floors and filled beer bottles and wine jugs with paint thinner and linseed oil. Dad bought the stuff by the fifty gallon drum, screwed an ordinary hose faucet into the threaded hole on the end, and turned the drums sideways on a wooden rack in the back of the bike shop.

Joe patched tubes, replaced spokes, and greased axles while I corked bottles and taped hand-printed "Thinner" and "Linseed Oil" labels across Lucky Lager, Hamm's, and Marco Petri labels. Joe let me plug his radio into the socket next to the barrels. The radio had a plastic chassis fractured by the falls from his workbench but it played fine. I often wondered how many times my thinner would be mistaken for beer when the scotch tape broke. They looked the same in the tinted bottles.

Taylor came by to go swimming at the park after lunch. On the way, he bragged about a girl he'd met at the pool. He claimed a tall dame about sixteen couldn't take her eyes off him. Taylor had no sense of perspective. He acted as if last night at the Bakers' hadn't happened.

"No joke, swear to die, she swam up behind me underwater and gave my shorts a big jerk."

"Probably ugly as a crawfish too," I said, shouldering him off the curb.

"If I didn't have such a big hard-on, I'd have lost my pants," he said, laughing his way back next to me. Taylor liked to remind me he was maturing. What he used to call his wiener was now a bone or a rod. I suspected it was part wishful thinking, stuff he'd read in his magazines. "Some thug googled at her all afternoon but she wasn't interested in dog food. She wanted King Salmon!" Taylor puffed up his chest and strutted.

Thugs were just one of the reasons I preferred to swim at the river. Something about the smell of chlorine or the fact that it was fenced off like a zoo made people act crazy. Wellesley only swam at the river. Taylor preferred the pool because of the girls. I alternated depending who I went with.

I wore my suit under my pants so I wouldn't have to change in the locker room. Someone was always snapping towels at your butt or teasing you if you didn't have any hair on your crotch. Hair was beginning to sprout on me but it was still too thin to be obvious. Voices bounced off the cement walls like wet kickballs. Everyone was "dick head" or "butt face." I'd rather have peed in the pool than shower in there.

Once we were sitting inside the fence, I asked him about Wellesley.

"It's a bad break, Will, but what can we do?" He chewed and smacked his gum with his mouth open. "Us getting dutch for it isn't going to help her."

"That's only part of it," I said. "What about her dad?"

"I don't think he's any of our business."

"He's an animal."

Taylor had stopped listening. He leaned back against the cyclone fence watching the crowd. He was as far away as the train whistle at midnight.

The water was second day in and probably still freezing. Swimmers sunned on the coarse cement, trading goosebumps for indentations that made them look like they'd slept on a food grater. The pool churned with the energy of a hundred eggbeaters—skinny crewcut kids in goggles, Johnny Weissmullers swan diving from the high board. And Monica Amberly swimming laps.

"She's alone now," Taylor said, poking me in the ribs.

Monica climbed out of the pool where the rope separated the shallow from the deep water. With her heels resting on the splash trough, she tipped her head from side to side and tapped it to clear the water from her ears. She looked like a magazine model, even more curvy than I remembered her at Spirit Lake. My heart rapped lightly against the back of my chest bones as if to remind me.

"Maybe she'll come over here," Taylor said, "probably hasn't seen me yet."

One benefit of Taylor being stuck on himself was my ability to go nuts for Monica at the lake and have it go unnoticed by him. "You're nervous," I said. "The great Taylor Clark is shaking in his trunks."

"I'm still cold. Give me a minute." Taylor didn't take his eyes off her.

Before he could find the courage, Monica slipped back into the pool for another series of lengths. This time, she alternated backstroke one direction, crawl the other. On the backstroke, her breasts cut the surface of the pool like upside down teacups covered with leopard skin. Her long legs flashed with each kick. The shimmer of the water that trailed her shot beams of white light at me.

When she came out of the water, Taylor was there to greet her. They sat on the deck, both facing the pool, too far away for me to catch even a snip of their conversation. Taylor picked at his toenails. With her spine erect, Monica looked like a Muslim at prayer on his mat. Judging from the constant movement of his mouth, Taylor dominated their discussion.

Although they were the same age, Monica's full body made Taylor look like a sparrow. She raised her head and gently swished her black hair to dry it. When she stood, she was statuesque. Everything moved so fluidly as she separated from Taylor and walked to the girls' shower room.

Returning to me, Taylor clapped in slow motion, his teeth clamped together in a big grin. He forced himself to walk not run. "I told you so! I told you so!"

The seven-year-old girls next to me in matching ocean wave suits craned their necks to hear Taylor's news.

"What did you talk about so long?"

Taylor steered me by the arms backwards to an empty patch of cement in the corner, as if the swimmers there spoke another language. "She wants to go out with me!" Taylor paused, with his eyelids raised. "No shit!"

"I can't believe you actually did it!" He stuck his hand out and I congratulated him with a shake.

"I asked her what she's been doing this summer and she said nothing much since Spirit Lake. That was her signal! That meant no boyfriend! That meant, Mr. Clark, make my life exciting again! I picked up on it immediately and bragged a little about the crap we've been doing."

"You didn't tell her about Wellesley, did you?"

"No way!" Taylor rose triumphantly on his toes as he dropped the punch line. "Monica Amberly is my first date of the summer!"

"You mean of your life!" We laughed and headed for the turnstile.

It was a stretch to think of Taylor, my farting friend who hunted rats in the dump, picked his nose, and confused lettuce with cabbage, going out with the jewel of our class. I could see why a girl would choose Taylor though. His eyes were magnets. And you never knew what he'd do next. Taylor created fireworks.

Riding back from the pool, watching him weave his bike like a drunk driver, I felt defeated. If this worked, I lost Taylor and Monica. Why would he sit around cracking jokes with me when he could be with her? He had what he wanted. My crush on Monica had been exposed for what it was, pure fantasy. She was only nice to me so she could get my friend.

Taylor must have also done some thinking on the ride home. By the time he fell onto his bed, he was panicky. "What am I going to do with her, Will? There's no show at the Orpheum until the weekend. Besides she's probably seen it. I need a car."

"Take her golfing, you can borrow my clubs." I sat on the floor and probed the seam between Taylor's mattress and box springs with my hand. "Where are your magazines?"

"I don't know if she golfs." Taylor slugged his pillow.

"Play tennis."

"Girls are so uncoordinated, we'd both be embarrassed. And there's no way I'm going to show her off at the park in front of a bunch of goons rubbernecking at us through the fence. Wait till we get more established."

"You sound like you're planning marriage."

"You know what I mean. I don't want to run into Wizer or someone and have them ask how long we've been going out and me saying one hour!"

"Take her on a picnic. Mossyrock. You can walk. Nobody will see you."

Taylor smiled. The gears beneath those wavy locks were turning. "Not bad, Will. But what are we going to talk about for three hours? I just about shot my wad at the pool getting her to go out." Taylor propped himself on his elbows and looked at me. He furrowed his brow and filled his cheeks with air, waiting for my answer.

"Taylor, I've known you for fourteen years and you've never run out of gas. What makes you think you'll be struck dumb this time?"

"It's something about her. This afternoon, sitting next to her, I felt dizzy, like she was sucking up all the oxygen. Nothing I thought of sounded important enough." Taylor was talking to himself, each observation a question. Then, he planted his feet on the floor, leaned over and grabbed me. "I need you there, Will!"

"What? Are you crazy?"

"Really. You always have something intelligent to say. That's where I'm most nervous. I need to sound smarter than I am. She'll start talking about politics or literature or Beethoven or somebody. What will I do, show her my double belch?"

I started laughing. Taylor was sounding the way I'd always felt, unsure. "Taylor, she's not square. Tell her some jokes.

Make up stories." If it were only me, I'd make sure I had plenty to say. I'd go to the library this afternoon. I'd read *Crime and Punishment* tonight.

"Yeah, but if you were there, you could prime the pump." Taylor held my face, making me look him in the eye. "You have the right sense of humor, Will."

"She's going to think it's pretty stupid to have an interpreter on your first date. She'll think it was my idea!"

Suddenly, Taylor leaped with both feet together to the center of his bed. "You can bring your own date!"

"Who am I going to bring, my mother?"

"We'll figure that out." Taylor was jumping up and down on the bed like it was a trampoline. "Some dog in this town will go out with poor Willy."

Taylor phoned Monica after I left and she agreed to find someone for me. I was apprehensive. Playing altar boy to Taylor made me feel small and clumsy. Going out with someone else also seemed like a private act of disloyalty to Monica. I should have said no.

Taylor and I argued over what to eat at the picnic but ended up with the traditional—hot dogs, Nalley's potato chips, Coke, and Oreos. To save money, I brought catsup and mustard from home in folds of wax paper. The rest we bought at the IGA. It was probably obvious we were spending our own money the way we added up the total after picking each item off the shelves.

We stuffed everything into Taylor's Army duffel and headed for Monica's. Even in a crew-neck shirt and cut-off shorts, I was sweating and thirsty for the pop baking in the bag on Taylor's back.

Uncle Carl pulled over to the curb and poked his neck out of his Kaiser-Frazer like a chicken looking through the henhouse window. "Howdy, Will! What are you up to?"

"Hi, Carl! Yea, we're just heading up to Mossyrock. Probably do a little hiking." That's the same thing I told my Mom, leaving out any mention of females.

"You two be careful up there." Carl raced his engine. It backfired as he relaxed the accelerator. "How do you like my little bomb? Say, can I give you a lift?"

"No thanks!" Taylor and I yelped simultaneously.

Carl hesitated at the quickness of our refusal and looked again at the duffel bag for a clue. "Okay, boys, you have a good time at the falls. Don't do anything I wouldn't do!" He cackled and pulled his head inside.

Monica lived on Eden Circle, the newest development and only cul-de-sac in Clearwater. The houses gleamed in freshly painted pastels. Saplings stood at attention in cookie-cutter circles on the parking strip. Each yard was terraced with quartz, cactus, and nursery flowers. The people who lived here weren't customers at the hardware store. They could afford contractors to fix their toilets and move their light switches. They belonged to the country club, where Grandpa Blane said everyone used an electric cart.

Monica opened the screen door. She was wearing a blouse with broad red and white horizontal stripes and solid red shorts. She looked beautiful. We stepped onto the porch. "Will, you know Marilyn."

Behind Monica, looking unsure which side to pass, stood Marilyn Tubbs, Monica's protector. I should have guessed. Marilyn was the great granddaughter of Clearwater's first mayor. Her dad was a doctor and also a member of the city council. I had gone to him once at three A.M. with stomach cramps so bad I thought I was having a baby. He'd diagnosed it as appendicitis and cut me open before breakfast. I felt ready for the knife again.

"Hi, Marilyn, glad you could come," I said, still only able to see her head.

Monica ushered us into the living room. "Come on inside, my Mom wants to see you." The white mohair carpet was combed like a prize dog. I worried I had gum on my tennis shoes. The mirror covering the wall between the fireplace and the ceiling reflected the four of us, shuffling like strangers at the bus stop. On the mantel, gold-framed portraits flanked a candelabra with three unburnt rose candles—the pictures of Monica and her older sister on the left, Mr. and Mrs. Amberly on the right. Mr. Amberly, with suit jacket and tie, looked like Jimmy Stewart and, like his counterpart in *It's a Wonderful Life,* he was also the president of the local savings and loan.

Mrs. Amberly swept into the room like Loretta Young.
Her silk housedress billowed as she moved. "Hello, boys!
Monica, for heaven's sake, invite them to sit down. Can I
get you a cola or a juice?"

Monica prompted us with a pantomime.

"Sure . . . sure Mrs. Amberly," I stammered, when no
one else answered. "I'll have a Coca-Cola if you have it."

"You're Will Bradford, aren't you?"

"Yes, ma'am."

"I'll call you Will if you call me Beverly, okay?" Mrs.
Amberly drew me toward her as she spoke. Her hands slid
along my forearm until they formed an envelope around my
fingers.

I was starting to blush. Nobody else spoke. "Yes, Mrs.
. . . Beverly." Monica and Marilyn tee-heed. I pulled my
hand away to cover a fake cough.

We finally sat, Monica and Marilyn on the loveseat and
Taylor and I on matching high-backed throne chairs opposite them. *Fortune* and *National Geographic* magazines
fanned on the chrome and glass coffee table between us. On
a round silver platter, Mrs. Amberly brought four sizzling
Coca-Colas on ice in tall soda glasses that flared at the top.
Each glass had its own wooden coaster and red straw.

Maybe Mrs. Amberly asked questions out of genuine curiosity about our plans. I suspected she just wanted to remind us that Monica had a mother we would have to account to at the end of the day. Mrs. Amberly did most of the
talking. Monica did most of the answering—for the four of
us. Luckily, the question-and-answer period would end as
soon as we drained the Cokes.

Marilyn Tubbs sat pasty-faced through the entire conversation. Her green pedal pushers, a size too small for her
thick legs, choked her calves. The extralarge orange and
black sweatshirt camouflaged any shape between her hips
and neck. I studied her closed mouth, wondering if her lips
would puff out as much without her braces. She had a pretty
face, with no evidence of pimples. The blond ponytail tied
with a matching orange ribbon was the only sign of playfulness.

Once we left the Amberlys, Marilyn and I paired off. She

talked like a chain-smoker. As one story ended she lit another. It didn't seem to matter whether I commented or not. She said she was still grieving over Buddy Holly's death and promised to change her name to Peggy Sue the day she turned eighteen. Marilyn confessed getting in trouble with her mother for not telling where she went after school and generally not acting like a Tubbs. I did wonder where she went after school. Did Monica go with her? She called the Tubbs' tradition a bunch of crap, tarnishing any notion I had that being the descendant of Clearwater's most famous citizen was an honor.

I didn't want anyone to see us. We had one close call. Wizer and Beller coasted through the intersection ahead of us no hands, flying from the momentum of the downhill grade. If they had looked left, they would have seen a couple of tenderfoots on their first double date.

Twice, walking on the trail, I watched Taylor drape his arm on Monica's shoulder. Each time, she turned and said something to Taylor, making his arm drop harmlessly.

Mossyrock was named after the lichen which coated the boulders at the base of a waterfall in a stream that flowed into the Clearwater. On one side of the falls was a log shelter with a fireplace and iron pits with cooking grates. As planned, Taylor turned left at the fork to avoid the shelter and, of course, any people. We headed across a meadow with the kind of tall, sweet grass that I imagined deer liked to sleep in. Grasshoppers buzzed, snapped, and jumped to get out of our way.

We picked a spot on the far side of the meadow. The smell of pine from the woods drifted across us with the breeze. The grass leaned slightly.

Our fire died when the grocery bag and wrappers burned up without catching the branches. We tried grass for kindling but stopped when it sent a yellowish-green distress signal skyward. We didn't want to be rescued. Taylor convinced the girls that the wieners were precooked at the factory and safe to eat.

"Cooking them again over the fire," he said, "is just for color and atmosphere."

In the trek from the IGA, the wax paper envelopes I'd

made for the catsup and mustard had worked their way to the bottom of the load and burst. Taylor had forgotten the knives. So Monica and Marilyn smeared the condiments onto the flattened buns using the wax paper. Taylor and I scraped our fingers along the pack to recover what we could. The warm pop bottles spit and sprayed as we opened them against the edge of a rock. Only the Oreos were served as the manufacturer intended.

"Best meal I've ever eaten," Taylor sighed, as he disappeared into the grass next to Monica.

"Raw sirloin is a delicacy if it's ground up," Monica said, "why not raw hot dog?" Everyone laughed.

I saw the pieces of chocolate cookie trapped in Marilyn's braces when she spoke. "Wait till I tell Mom I had a cold wiener at Mossyrock," she said. Too late, she tried to muffle her words with her hand. Then she got the giggles.

Taylor opened a wooden matchbox and pulled out a single, slightly bent cigarette which he stuck in the corner of his mouth. "Nothing like a smoke after dinner," he said, letting the air out of his lungs.

The last time Taylor and I had tried cigarettes in my garage rafters, we'd both gotten sick. Taylor swore he'd never smoke again. Monica and Marilyn watched him inhale. He held it for a long time and smiled like someone having a bowel movement. Then he coughed so hard he had to stand up. When the fit subsided, he strained to speak. "Went down the wrong windpipe, I guess."

Monica patted him on the back like she was burping him. "How long did you say you've been smoking?"

"Will, how long would you say it's been?" Taylor asked, with half his voice.

This was why Taylor wanted me along, to pull him out of jams. "Let's see . . . I'd say about fifteen seconds!"

Monica and Marilyn tittered.

Taylor scowled. "Wise up, Bradford!"

I tried to redeliver what Taylor wanted in an earnest, no-fooling voice. "I was just kidding. You started smoking about a year ago."

Monica fixed momentarily on my eyes, confirming and

excusing my exaggeration in the same glance. We both knew Taylor was doing this for her.

When we lay back in the grass, Marilyn took off her shoes and worked her bare feet under my calves. I was afraid to move for fear I'd encourage her. She rambled on with more self-revealing stories to entertain us. Taylor snubbed out his cigarette and broke off a long weed to chew. Monica rested on her side across from me, her head propped up on one elbow. I studied her face, her length, her shape. She was still the perfect hourglass I remembered, but she was Taylor's.

Then Marilyn interrupted my daydreaming. "Have you ever kissed a girl, Will?"

I remembered the sixth grade production when I played George Washington and kissed Stephanie Bruce, playing Martha, on the cheek. "Sure, who hasn't?" I answered.

"How long without breaking?" Marilyn insisted on pushing this beyond the limits of my experience.

"God, Marilyn, who knows, we weren't using a stopwatch."

Taylor sat up, taking a new interest in this stocky blonde dressed like a pumpkin.

Marilyn beckoned with a crooked finger. "Come here, Willy, I've got something for you."

"Go for it, Will!" Taylor clapped his hands and grunted animal sounds through his puckered lips. The focus of the outing had somehow been turned. Marilyn and I were supposed to be background.

"Time this!" Marilyn said, suddenly pulling my head against her face and sucking my lips like a vacuum hose. I didn't know where to put my arms and just let them hang between us. Her grip was so tight there was no risk of losing balance. I kept my eyes open. She closed hers and made a soft humming noise in her throat. I could taste chocolate and mustard. Finally, she ran out of breath.

"Thirty-eight seconds!" Taylor announced. "Encore! Encore!"

I wanted to spit. Instead, I just wiped my lips with the front of my T-shirt and smiled.

"We can beat that," Taylor said, reaching for Monica.

"Not with me you can't!"

Taylor looked surprised.

Marilyn offered Taylor a try but before he could answer, Monica glared at her. "I think it's time to go."

On the walk home, Marilyn was quiet. So quiet she made me nervous. She left more space between us than before. I didn't know how to follow up on what she'd started. A kiss was supposed to make you feel all sugary. This one had backfired. Maybe it was just me.

12

I finished my chores at the hardware store and headed out the back door. Wellesley was pushing her red Schwinn down the alley, the chain draped over the handlebars. Rust had eaten away the edges of her fenders like termites.

"Wellesley! Where are you going?"

She turned, with a hangdog expression like she was trying to slink by without being noticed. "I got my bike back yesterday. I'm going to see if Joe can fix the chain."

"The police had your bike?"

"Yeah. They held it until after the arraignment."

"Arraignment?"

"You tell them whether you think you're guilty or not." Her hands were greasy. Probably she'd tried to fix the bike herself.

"What did you tell them?"

"Not guilty," she said, without hesitation. "Mom wanted me to just say guilty and get it over with." When she was on the hot seat, Wellesley fought back. That was one of the differences between us. I tried to look at both sides.

"Do you think there's a chance of winning?"

"I don't know. Mom said we can't afford a lawyer." She smiled her lopsided smile. "Breaking in at the fairgrounds is only a misdemeanor." Wellesley's arrest had forced her to become an expert on criminal procedures.

"What happens if you lose?"

"I go to juvenile prison."

"You mean Union Gap? That place is full of creeps."

"If I lose, that's what I'll be." Her eyes glistened through her glasses. She seemed tired, her spirit broken like the chain.

We walked around the building to the bike shop. A playing card flapped against her front spokes. I left her at the doorway, squeezing the handlebar as if it were her arm. "We'll think of something, Wellesley."

I started walking home, stepping on my own shadow, and realized I'd forgotten to ask if she got the note I put under her bike seat. The air was full of the sounds of summer, lawnmower blades turning, wheels clanking on sidewalks, sprinklers rotating. But something rang false.

I decided to turn myself in.

The Clearwater police station was downtown, in the basement of City Hall, a red brick building with two husky columns supporting a triangular recess. In the triangle was a fading mural with scenes of people at work, home, and play.

The interior of City Hall was as plain as the hallways of Adams Elementary. Maroon linoleum covered the floor and the first four feet of the walls. A black arrow painted on the green plaster wall turned the corner and pointed down the stairwell. Above the arrow, the sign said, "POLICE—GO DOWN."

The stairs creaked as I stepped on the rubber treads. On the landing, I stopped to inspect the gallery of Clearwater's former police chiefs. The man in the first picture had a full beard and looked like Grover Cleveland. Many had mustaches and long sideburns. Only the last picture resembled modern man—"Chief Vernon A. McGinnis, 1955– ." He must still be the chief. I recognized him as a customer at Western Hardware.

At the bottom of the stairs, there was a cage that looked like a cashier's window in a bank. A bald-headed policeman behind the grate was stamping the papers a tall policeman shoved through the opening. I studied the FBI "Wanted" posters pinned to the corkboard on the opposite wall. Most of them were men in their twenties with bad complexions. They reminded me of the carnival guy that had chased us out of the fairgrounds.

"Can I help you?" the husky voice in the cage asked.

I felt panic. "Uh, I was just looking."

"You know any of those fellows?" he asked, shaking his hand in the general direction of the posters.

"No, sir, uh no, sir."

"What do you want? I'm busy." His voice was gruff, like someone who hated kids.

The introduction I'd prepared seemed too weak in the face of this officer's attitude. I tried to call in the cavalry of resolve I'd had on the sidewalk. My blush was starting to rise the way it did at school when I had to hum a note in front of the class until it matched the pitch pipe. "Thank you," I said and beat it upstairs, two steps at a time.

I ducked out the main entrance and walked purposefully toward the end of the block. With the front of my T-shirt, I wiped the sweat from my face and held my arms away to let the pits dry.

I didn't have the guts to do it. There were plenty of excuses. They wouldn't believe me. They'd charge me for the worse crime of failing to report sooner. They probably still wouldn't free Wellesley.

At the door to the Rexall, I pulled my pockets inside out. A nickel, not enough for a cherry Coke. I leaned against the ceramic tile on the face of the drugstore and slid into a slouch on the cement, my knees higher than my head.

His bell was ringing before I saw him turn the corner. It was Laddie, pumping his bell with his thumb, rocking slowly as he glided by the front of the store. He came to a stop on the sidewalk a safe distance from me. One foot on the ground, the other on the pedal, he looked at me like he wanted to see if I was all right.

I shaded my eyes to get a better look at him, "Hello, Laddie, how are you doing?"

He started to smile and bit his lower lip nervously. Scooting forward, he showed me the seat; someone had taped the rip with adhesive tape. Laddie remembered. I started to get to my feet and give his bike a closer inspection when a man came out of the drugstore. Panic filled Laddie's eyes and he pushed away.

He'd stopped to help, I thought, the same way I'd helped him. Maybe his imaginary contacts in the police department had warned him. I didn't deserve his sympathy sitting here on my butt. Determined to be arrested, I returned to the police station.

"Back again?" the man in the cage asked.

I wasn't going to stop until I had said enough that they couldn't let me go. "I know something about a crime. I want to talk to whoever is in charge of the investigation. It's about the thing at the fairgrounds, the trespass. I did it." My pits were dripping again.

He studied me for a while to see if there was more. Then he pushed a button on the speaker box and barked into it, "Sergeant Carver, front desk! A kid here wants to make a report."

A buzzing "You bet, sir" came out of the box when the desk officer lifted his finger from the button.

I just stood there in front of the posters waiting to be taken prisoner. Wellesley wouldn't be the only one going to the detention center. My life was about to take a sharp turn south. Grandpa would have to find another golf partner. Someone else would take over the dirty job of bottling at the hardware. I felt relieved that Monica and I had never hit it off. She'd be spared the shame of it all.

A man I assumed to be Sergeant Carver appeared from the back of the cage. He looked familiar. His paunch stretched the buttons on his blue uniform shirt; only the gunbelt prevented him from bursting. Purple thread veins streaked his puffy cheeks. Sacks hung under his eyes and the wet part of his lower lip showed. The skin on his face looked several sizes too large for his skull, which was rimmed with a crown of hair.

He led me through a maze of cluttered desks and into a small room with nothing but a table and three steel chairs. An ashtray overflowed with cigarette butts. The air reeked of stale smoke. The walls were bare.

Sergeant Carver turned his chair backwards and sat down, his legs straddling the seat. "So, what's your name, son?"

"Will Bradford, sir." My voice was loud.

He looked up from his form. "Tom Bradford's boy?"

"Yes, sir, but I would appreciate you not telling my dad about this." My fingers shook but I was able to steady my voice.

"Why, I've known Tom all my life." He wiped the extra moisture away from the corners of his mouth as he spoke.

"Your dad and I bucked hay together when we were kids. He was a helluva good worker. I told him he should have stayed in farming." He laughed.

The way he talked about Dad I doubted he would keep this to himself. But I wasn't backing out again. "Sir, I want to turn myself in."

Sergeant Carver put his pencil on the table and looked at me very seriously as I explained the whole story, emphasizing my role and mentioning Wellesley as little as necessary. I was there when Taylor bought the matches. I agreed to go into the fairgrounds. I led the escape attempt. He asked me whether the man charged us before or after the matches were shot. It was hard to remember, because it seemed like he was going to come after us from about the first moment we started talking.

"Will, you've done your duty," he said, reaching across the table to pat me on the shoulder, "but I'm not going to arrest you. I like your old man too much." He nodded his head and twinkled his eyes like I should jump up and say thanks.

"Sergeant, you don't understand! I want to be charged. I want you to let Wellesley Baker go!" The possibility they'd turn me down never entered my mind. I couldn't even get myself arrested.

"Someone like you has no business getting mixed up in the law," he said, as he wadded up the page with his notes on it. He moved me to the door. "Now just get out of here and forget you ever seen our interrogation room."

13

The Fourth of July Junior Rodeo was the chance for kids in the county under eighteen to imitate the real thing, the guys who bucked broncos in Pendleton, Lewiston, and Ellensburg. Annie Curran told me I could ride Dolly in the barrel race as a reward for rescuing her at the homestead. I figured Wellesley had put in a good word for me. I hadn't seen Dolly or Bushner since that afternoon.

Wellesley was still on a short leash since her arrest. After some begging, her mom let her participate in the rodeo, mainly because her cousin Annie was one of the princesses. Wellesley kidded about the rodeo being at the fairgrounds, the same place she'd gotten into trouble.

The morning of the rodeo, I reached the grounds by sunrise and took Dolly on some practice runs in the arena. The weeds and oil stains had been thoroughly plowed under since the stock car races. Dolly handled like a bicycle, following my leans through an imaginary slalom course from one end of the field to the other. I took her at about three-quarters speed to save strength. When I steered her through the exit gate, she snorted and pawed at the ground like she wanted to do it again.

Wellesley and Annie showed up about ten A.M. and we strolled the grounds together. Annie wore a matching silk blouse and white tapered pants. There was fringe on the arms and sides of the legs and the chest was embroidered with red, gold, and green sequins shaped into two arching broncos with riders. Her silver spurs clanged as she walked.

Neither Wellesley nor I owned cowboy boots so we wore tennis shoes. I had jeans, a plaid shirt, one of my Dad's red hunting hats, and a bandanna tied around my neck. Wellesley wore a jean jacket and a banjo player's straw hat, with a string under her chin; it sat back on her head and made her look like she was walking in front of a small moon.

Wellesley and I were in the first event as partners, hog tying. We went to the stables under the stands to wait. The loudspeaker hummed and squealed, until someone lowered the volume. Sunny Crebbs' country voice crackled. "Ladies and gentlemen, welcome to a perfect Sylvanus County summertime day and to the twelfth annual . . . JUN . . . YER . . . ROW . . . DEE . . . O!" Sunny sat in the box draped with red, white, and blue taffeta at the top of the bleachers. "Let's give a great big grand entry hand for those pretty little ladies on horseback—ladies and gentlemen, QUEEN . . . JUDY . . . BRIGGS . . . and her lovely court!"

"Hey, Wellesley, how ya' doin?" It was Roland Bushner, sticking his head through the fence slats. His greasy hair was pressed in a rim where his hat had been.

Wellesley fired back. "I guess we know who's in charge of the horseshit down here!"

"Hey, calm down, let bygones be bygones," he said. Then he noticed me, "Is your buddy here going to catch a pig?"

"You bet," I said, trying to project the same confidence Wellesley did. Bushner studied my hunting hat. It was too big on me. I wished I'd left it home.

"Come here, I've got something that will help you." Bushner pulled a pint bottle of Old Crow from inside his leather jacket, twisted off the cap and pointed the top at me. "Don't be a candy-ass."

"Don't drink it, Will, you'll catch the same gonorrhea he carries!" Wellesley turned her back to watch the parade in the arena. Between the openings in the fence, I could see the flags carried by the queen's court.

Wellesley yelled, "Way to go, Annie!"

"No thanks," I said to Bushner, "you're the asshole." Wellesley turned, surprised, and smiled. It felt good to talk back.

"Piss off, Bradford!" He fumbled at his zipper. "Why don't you drink this then?" Standing on his tiptoes, Bushner aimed his stubby penis over the middle slat and directed a stream next to my shoes.

"You couldn't put out a candle with that dribble," Welles-ley said, pointing to the small puddle forming in the dirt.

When the whistle blew, about twenty-five hogs entered the arena from one gate and twice as many chasers from another. Everyone had to stick their hands into one of the five gallon cans of axle grease by the entry gate as they entered the arena. It had the texture of vaseline and was a purplish color. The hogs snorted, the kids yelled. From the stands, it must have looked like someone kicked the roof off an anthill. The smaller hogs looked easiest; the full grown ones were linseed barrels on legs. Next to the fence, I finally cornered a big one, wrapped myself around its neck and, temple to temple, twisted it to the dirt. Wellesley wrapped its two hind feet as fast as I could have tied my shoes and shot her hand in the air. We used the pig's bristly hide to wipe the gook off our hands.

We took second.

For the barrel race, I waited on board Dolly in a line of high-strung horses and riders. The course consisted of a be-ginning perimeter lap around the inside of the arena in a narrow lane between the flags and the fence. After the opening lap, you directed your horse through the slalom course in the middle of the arena and then finished with another lap next to the fence. Only one rider ran at a time. The fastest time won, including penalty time added for each barrel missed or knocked over.

The other riders patted horses they owned and rode every day. Their horses looked so handsome and strong— speckled Appaloosas, creamy palominos with blond manes, and shiny brown stallions. I wondered if stock car drivers had the same feeling that they were going to throw up be-fore a race. I hoped that Dolly's stomach wasn't as queasy as mine.

Then I was next to the entry gate. "Rider number nine today on . . . DOLLY! WIIILLL . . . BRAAD . . . FORD!" Sunny Crebbs's voice echoed.

"Good luck, Will!" It was Annie Curran, two riders be-hind me, on Apache.

Sunny's voice, rising in his familiar crescendo, said "Oh—pen—the—chute—boys!"

I slapped Dolly on her haunches and dug my heels into her midsection. She bolted into the arena and I reined her over to the lane next to the fence. Dad's hunting hat flew off in the first stretch. In the slalom, she wove gracefully between the red kegs. I didn't know if we'd been out there an hour or a minute when we finished the return run through the barrels and fixed our course for the final lap.

The fence rushed by so close I could have touched it. The colors in the stands were wet paint through my watered eyes. The applause was rain on a tin roof. I clamped my legs against Dolly and held my head parallel to her neck while she stretched forward trying to purchase ground with her chin.

Suddenly the earth seemed to open and Dolly dropped. I was catapulted over her head. My face slammed against the dirt.

Then there were voices, all talking at once.

I wanted to ask where Dolly was but when I moved my tongue, it pushed against a big bite of mud.

"Don't move him!"

"Get a stretcher!"

"His neck might be broken!"

The X rays at Mary of the Angels showed a fracture of my left arm. The emergency doctor set my arm in a cast and sent me home. He said I'd have a sore neck for a few days. The manure in the rodeo grounds had cushioned my fall.

Dolly wasn't as lucky. Alone in my bed that night, I cringed at the thought of her being destroyed with a pistol shot to the head in front of all those strangers.

Sunday morning, Mom insisted I stay in bed and served me corn flakes with strawberries, a glass of tomato juice, and two pieces of buttered white toast. She balanced the bread board across my legs. Breakfast in bed and staying home from Mass were some consolation.

While I was still propped up in bed, Grandpa Blane came by with a grocery bag which he set next to the door. My accident on Dolly was big family news. Mom told me that

Grandpa was always visiting old friends who were sick. It was like I was suddenly a sixty-five-year-old invalid.

"That should cure you of wanting to be a cowboy for a while," he said, puffing out the roof of his cap with his fist. "Darn lucky you didn't get tangled up in the horse. What do you think made her go down like that?"

"I don't know, Grandpa."

"You know, Will, I rode in one of the cavalry divisions in the war." For Grandpa, I knew that meant World War I. "A horse was a sacred thing then. In some states, they'd hang you for stealing one." Grandpa Blane shuffled his feet.

"Dolly might have won, Grandpa."

Suddenly he turned and handed me the sack. "Almost forgot," he said, placing it in my lap. Inside the sack was something about the size of a lunch pail wrapped in layers of newspapers. "You better open it, Will," he said, "it might be some barbells to rebuild your arms when you get that cast off." He chuckled with his teeth together like he was clenching a cigar.

It was heavy enough for a barbell. I peeled away the paper to find a brass horse in full gallop, with a jockey crouched in the stirrups.

"My parents gave it to me when I was a kid," he said. "I'm sure they'd be proud to know we have another horse lover in the family."

Later in the morning, I moved to the living room couch. Mom kept me quiet, sticking a thermometer in my mouth every hour and feeling my forehead. She fluffed my pillow, tucked in the blanket, and brushed my hair back every time she passed.

Taylor came by with the hunting hat I'd lost during the race; Wellesley had rescued it. She'd also given him the real scoop on what happened. "Will, you won't believe it!" He knelt next to the couch and pushed his face near mine so Mom wouldn't hear. "Guess who killed your horse?"

"Who?"

"Bushner! Roland Bushner!" Taylor must have wondered why Bushner would come after Dolly. For Annie's sake, I'd never told him the story. I knew my fall had something to do with catching Bushner in the act at the homestead. "No joke. He shoved a board through the fence."

I pictured Bushner crawling through the scaffolding under the stands, whiskey on his breath and urine on his hands. "Are you sure it was him?"

"They caught him. Wellesley's cousin chased him to the parking lot on her horse. Almost trampled him. I hope they lock him up and throw away the key." Partial repayment I thought for what Bushner had done to her. Good for Annie!

"They can do to him what they did to Dolly," I said, wiping my face with the couch blanket.

After Mass, Dad pulled a chair next to me and talked, just like when I was sick as a kid. "We'll have this ready by football tryouts, won't we?" I could remember Dad teaching me to spiral the football. He always talked about my playing high school football and said he was too small when he was my age. Playing football was one of Dad's dreams for me, as much as going to college or getting into heaven.

"Sure, Dad, I'll be ready. We Bradfords are tough." That was one of Dad's sayings, like "Work won't kill you" and "Men don't cry."

He stood up and smiled down at me, his hands planted on his hips, then joined Mom in the kitchen.

Dad was always softer in distress. When the family took a vacation in Canada one summer, the hail came down so hard it drove holes through the canvas roof of our old Plymouth station wagon. Dad just laughed it off. "They sure don't make 'em like they used to," he said. He wasn't so patient with things he thought were avoidable. When I was in first grade, he made me give away my puppy because I didn't help Mom clean up the dog poop in the yard. Mom felt terrible and later helped me pick out Plato from the pound, but he ran away while we were in Canada.

I lay on the couch, drifting in and out of sleep. Mom and Dad ate lunch at the kitchen table. I could hear Dad's spoon stirring the sugar into his coffee and his voice which, even at a whisper, easily carried to the living room. They must have thought I was asleep.

"I'm worried about Will," Mom said.

"It's a tiny crack in the arm bone," Dad said. "The doctor said it will mend in four weeks. Why don't you scoop me another cup of that tomato soup?"

"It's not just his arm. He's been acting moody. Something's bothering him."

"Audrey, he's a teenager."

Dad blew his nose. The talking stopped. A spoon tapped the side of the bowl followed by the slurping of the soup. I was wide awake.

"Tom, do you want another grilled cheese?"

"No thanks, I'm stuffed."

"Not much to brag about for a Sunday," Mom said, "but with Will down it didn't seem worth fixing a big roast."

"You better get used to eating more of these economy meals." The usual stiffener was missing in his voice. "Things still aren't so good at the store. Lot of people coming in the door but everyone wants to buy on credit. Our best customers have huge accounts overdue."

"Do you think it's getting worse?"

"I got a call from the warehouse yesterday. They've put everything on a cash basis until we get our bill paid. If our wholesaler cuts us off, we're dead."

"That's not fair! Did you tell him the trouble we're having collecting from our own customers? There's a recession in this town. You've been one of his best stores." I had never heard Mom raise her voice against anyone. She sounded mad enough to throw the dishes she was stacking in the sink.

"Audrey, this is business. They can't give the stuff away. We've just got to figure out a way to get them off our back."

"What will you do if we have to close the store?" I swallowed hard to make sure my ears were unplugged.

I could hear Dad picking and sucking with his toothpick. "There's not much else I know how to do," he said. "Maybe I could get on working at the garage. I've fixed a few car engines in my day. Maybe move back to the country and raise chickens and a big garden."

I felt sick. We were going to a farm.

"I think you should talk to Daddy, ask him for a loan."

"I can't do that! Barney doesn't have that kind of money."

"Tom, you're just too proud. What other choice is there? Daddy would be glad to help. You know how much he thinks of you and Will."

Mom had said it. This did involve me. I didn't want to move just when high school was starting. I couldn't imagine living anywhere but Clearwater. But I couldn't imagine staying if the Bradfords were broke.

14

I dialed Wellesley's number with my index finger on the button in case her dad answered. The phone cord was long enough so I could call from the laundry room. The door pinched against the cord. Wellesley answered.

"Hi," I said peeking out through the crack in the door to make sure Mom wasn't listening. "Have you heard anything more about Bushner?"

"More than I want to, that pinprick. Annie says her family is pressing charges."

"Good."

"You guys should have let me take another swing at bush-brains when we had him on the bed."

I released the receiver cord that I'd curled around my finger. "How's she doing?"

"She's sick about Dolly."

"I'll bet she's sorry she lent me her horse."

"No way, she's just glad you didn't break your neck. Hey, how's the arm?"

I lifted my left arm, as if Wellesley could see it. "The ache went away days ago, now it just itches. I'm tired of babying it. How are you doing?"

"I'm itching a little bit too. My hearing is August six-teenth." She talked as calmly as if she were ordering a Coke at the Rexall.

I thought of telling her about trying to turn myself in. But at a time when she was probably counting on the fairness of the system, it didn't seem right to tell her how whimsical it could really be. "I gotta do something for Grandpa. Maybe I'll see you later."

"Is he going to teach you to golf one handed?" She laughed.

"I wish!"

"He's a character."

I sensed admiration in her voice. Grandpa was one more thing I had that she didn't. "Wellesley . . . did you ever get my note?"

"What's it say?"

I laughed. "Hey, read the note! It's under your bike seat." She said good-bye.

I put the phone back on its cradle and held on a minute, marveling at the power of fate. A single grimy half-inch link in her bike chain split open and Wellesley ended up at the police station. My dad bucked hay with Sergeant Carver before I was even born and I can't beg my way into jail.

Mom had stopped treating me like an invalid. Instead, she'd promoted me to errand boy.

"This is a trade," she said, as she wrapped her new Mixmaster and two beaters in newspaper and stuck them in the bottom of a drawstring cloth bag. "Take the mixer to Grandpa and bring back the meat grinder. I'm going to grind that leftover stew meat into sandwich spread." Mom must have known the mention of the spread would be an enticement for me.

"What's Grandpa want with a mixer?"

"It's for Aunt Ruth. She wants to make angel food cakes for the bake sale." Another enticement, maybe we'd get the extras. Mom swatted me on the seat of my pants, like she used to do when I was a kid. "Shoosh, now get going. They're waiting for you."

As I crossed Willow Street, Taylor skidded his bike to a stop next to me, making a black mark on the pavement. "You look like the hunchback of Notre Dame! What's in the bag?"

"A Mixmaster. For my grandpa." I swung the bag off my shoulder and it clanked onto the sidewalk. "Why don't you come with me? It'll only take a minute."

We found Grandpa Blane hitting practice golf balls in the backyard. His two wood and a three iron leaned against the porch. The steps were pockmarked from his golf spikes. He worked with a pitching wedge, knocking hollow plastic balls into a formation surrounding an upside down hat in the center of the yard.

Taylor and I watched until he'd hit the last ball in the row next to him. "Hey, Grandpa, special delivery! I've got something for you."

He looked around, unsure where the noise came from. Then he spotted Taylor and me and laughed like we'd played a joke on him. "Where'd you boys come from? Say, you could use some practice shots yourself, Will." He looked at my arm, puzzled, like he'd already forgotten about the accident.

"Hello, Mr. Blane," Taylor said. Grandpa ignored him and started up the stairs to the house.

As we followed behind Grandpa, I reminded Taylor, "You have to talk louder." Taylor wasn't used to being around someone with bad hearing.

"I was almost in his ear!" Taylor leaned against me to demonstrate.

"He doesn't recognize your voice," I said. "Make sure he's looking at you. He needs to see your mouth move."

Grandpa let the storm door slam without turning to see if we were coming.

The antique dining room table was covered with an ivory linen. Stacks of old letters with red and blue diagonal borders and *Saturday Evening Post*s filled one side of the table. There was a small pile of foreign stamps that had been torn off the corners of envelopes. Grandpa's correspondence was worldwide, many of them pen pals he'd never even shaken hands with. He and an invalid buddy in Butte played chess by postcard, one move per stamp.

I set the bag in the space where the linen had been folded back to make room for Grandpa's writing pad. Grandpa unwrapped a caramel from the open box on the table and plunked it into his mouth. He bent over to peek at what I pulled out of the bag. His breath smelled more like tar than caramel. When I had the mixer out, he picked up the bag and stuck his arm in it, poofing out the bottom to see if there was something else. While I uncovered the mixer, he pulled the drawstrings, closing and opening the bag a few times. "That's pretty slick, isn't it." He stretched the bag between his hands and admired it, ignoring the mixer.

"Mom said you'd trade a mixer for a meat grinder, Grandpa."

"Oh . . ." he said, not finishing his thought. He had spied an article in the newspaper wrapping and flattened the paper on top of the stacks of letters.

I looked at Taylor and we both smiled. Grandpa had probably forgotten we were there. I thought that his hearing must be getting worse. He seemed more distracted than usual. Grandpa clicked his tongue as if he was disgusted.

I spoke into his hearing aid. "Grandpa, do you want me to just take this over to Aunt Ruth?" Grandpa's sister lived in the same house as Grandpa, in the two rooms that had been converted to her apartment. But we always referred to her as "over there" or "next door" to preserve Grandpa's illusion that he managed on his own.

"Isn't that something?" Grandpa asked, putting his finger on the newspaper. "The railroad claims they're hauling empty cars westbound. I guess the folks on the coast aren't buying our grain and potatoes."

"What's so bad about that, Mr. Blane?" Taylor looked straight at Grandpa's ear.

Grandpa turned to me. "Clearwater's in big trouble, Will."

I tried not to laugh at Taylor being ignored again.

Grandpa continued on as if someone had asked another question. "I had a chum once who'd rather hop a freight than ride a limousine. He and I covered the Northwest in those empty cars. Regular hobos." He seemed lost in reverie. "Riding the rails was something to be proud of in those days." Grandpa had no trouble remembering things that happened fifty years ago. It was the things that were happening now he forgot.

I held the Mixmaster, waiting for Grandpa to make the trade. Taylor played with the beaters, trying to see how many ways he could fit them together.

Grandpa studied the article again and shook his head. "The railroad just looked the other way, you know. There's a lot of folks couldn't get to jobs any other way."

Taylor shouted. "Sounds like fun, Mr. Blane!"

Grandpa turned to Taylor with a surprised look, then laughed. I could tell he wasn't sure what Taylor had said but knew from Taylor's grin that it must have been funny. Grandpa grabbed another one of Aunt Ruth's caramels and sat down to read the wrinkled newspaper again. I signaled Taylor to follow me to the kitchen.

Grandpa's kitchen smelled of wax paper and the oatmeal cookies Aunt Ruth always made for him. There was a row of cupboards on one side. The refrigerator, sink, and a two-burner stove were on the other. A wooden clothes-drying rack hung from the ceiling. A bar of black Lava sat in the soap dish between the faucets. A crooked stack of newspapers grew out of the floor and overflowed onto the top of the refrigerator. He bundled these and stored them in the basement for school paper drives. We found the meat grinder and discs with different sized holes behind the paper sacks on the bottom shelf.

Taylor had to go to the bathroom. When he came out, he carried Grandpa's razor blade machine. It looked like a rusty pencil sharpener with a flat stone that turned as you cranked the handle. The clamp holding the blade lowered, raised, turned over then lowered again to sharpen the other side of the blade against the revolving stone. Grandpa Blane never threw anything away. His house was a museum, full of inventions that were modern when he was a kid.

We said good-bye to Grandpa. He was still sitting on the edge of his chair bent over the old newspaper on the dining room table. With Taylor, I'd let on as if Grandpa was just a little peculiar, like some of his gadgets. But for the first time I was worried that Mom and Aunt Ruth might be right in arguing that he needed someone to help take care of him.

On the way home, I rode sidesaddle on the crossbar between the seat and the handlebars of Taylor's bike. It was the kind of day warm enough to take the chill out of the swimming hole, a day to take target practice throwing rocks at pieces of bark floating down the river. The cast was costing me the only fourteen-year-old summer I'd ever have.

The good part was the fact that Taylor had to give me a

ride without complaining. As he pedaled, he tried to convince me to hop a freight. "How 'bout it, Will?"

"It's not a good idea with my arm bunged up," I said. "Besides, we'd probably get in trouble."

Taylor answered between pumps, as we climbed the grade back to Willow. "Don't you . . . believe . . . your own . . . grandpa?"

"We'd end up in a car with some convict on the run."

"We'll reserve . . . our own . . . car," Taylor said. We laughed. The bike wobbled. "Let's ask . . . Wellesley."

"She's in enough hot water already," I said. "I talked to her this morning. She has a hearing date."

Taylor waited until we were on the flat to answer. "Okay, if Wellesley nixes it, we don't go."

"She'll think it's a bum idea."

"Ha, that's a ripe one!"

We found Wellesley at the park. She was playing touch football with a group of guys. Most everyone was barefoot with shorts. One guy had slacks he'd rolled up to his knees and a white shirt, like he'd just come from summer band practice. The defense tried to screw up the snap count with baseball chatter. "Hey, batter, batter. One down. Two's the play. Hey, batter, batter."

I wished I could have been in the game with her. I needed the practice for tryouts. When Wellesley shagged an incomplete pass near us, we said we had something important to tell her.

She panted, "Next play. It's fourth down."

Her team, the shirts, scored on a sweep right. Wellesley carried the ball behind a formation of blockers joined at the elbows.

We biked to the baseball diamond so we could be alone. Flattened cans marked the bases. The dilapidated scoreboard on the left field fence displayed, on removable boards, the score of the last American Legion game there, "Mustangs 6, Badgers 9." We parked in center field.

Wellesley thought the train idea was a winner. "I've always wanted to hop a freight, Will." Despite the sweat smudges on her glasses, the pull of her eyes felt as powerful as a pair of winches. "Come on, I'll go if you do."

"What about your hearing?" I really meant her dad.

Wellesley threw the grass in her hand toward home plate. "Forget it! I'm going to pay for that in August."

Taylor had turned his bike upside down and raced the pedals with his hands. "Here's the way I've got it figured," he said. "The chances of getting caught are a hair worse than zero. If we're caught, we'll say Mr. Blane said it was okay."

"Come on, Taylor, leave him out of it!"

"You heard him, Will. He as much as invited us to use those empty cars heading to the coast." Taylor grabbed the spinning rear tire. Pieces of grass from the tire came off on his hand and dropped to the ground like sparks from Uncle Joe's grinder. "Okay, forget Mr. Blane." Then Taylor spoke in a loud voice imitating Grandpa. "But I'd sure be proud to see my grandson in one of those boxcars."

Wellesley danced a dandelion under my chin. "Something to brag to your kids about, Will . . ."

They were ganging up on me. Taylor's willingness was predictable. But I couldn't believe Wellesley would even consider it, knowing what her dad would do if she got caught. "If I don't go, what will you guys do?" I asked.

"A diesel locomotive couldn't hold me back!" Taylor held up three fingers. "Scouts Honor!" Taylor had been kicked out of Boy Scouts when he was a Tenderfoot for missing too many meetings.

"What about you, Wellesley?"

She was still picking the grass in the space between her legs. "Sure, I think I'd go too." Then she looked me straight on, her lopsided smile building. "But I'd rather have you with us."

I had to choose between my doubts and my friends. I would never go on this trip if I thought I could keep Wellesley out of trouble by staying back. But if she was going anyway, I wanted to be there to share the blame. "Okay, I'll go," I said, "on one condition!"

"Anything," said Wellesley.

"It's a deal," said Taylor.

"I want to be the leader," I said.

Taylor's and Wellesley's chins dropped.

"I say when we go, where we go, when we come back. And no matches!"

Taylor wrapped his arms around me from behind and pulled me over on top of him. He kicked his feet like a kid throwing a tantrum. "I knew it! I knew it! I knew you wouldn't let your grandpa down!"

"Look out for his arm, Taylor!"

The arm felt fine. It was my head that throbbed, already worrying how to pull this off.

When I got home, I called the Great Northern freight forwarding office, with a dishtowel over the receiver. I said I was pricing a shipment from Clearwater to the West Coast.

The man said trains were made up twice a week, Tuesdays and Fridays. Freight had to be in the yard by five o'clock the previous night. Payment was "FOB, shipper," whatever that meant. All I cared about was his final statement, "The trains leave the yard by six A.M."

One more detail bothered me. Where did the train stop? I didn't want to get so far we couldn't get back the same day. If I called again, I was worried he'd recognize my voice and suspect something. Besides, why would a shipper care about stops along the route? It wasn't as if the freight had to stretch its legs.

I went to Grandpa Blane's and started talking about railroads. He unfolded a map he found in the stack of letters. It was yellowed and worn through on the creases. With his magnifying glass, he drew a circle around each town on the route he figured to be a stop—Olalla, Coles Corner, Spirit, Brush Prairie, Oakville, Castor, Finn, Relief, Midland, Jove. Finally, he drew a line through Union Gap, said the train should reach it by noon. He seemed pleased with so many train questions, never asking what I needed the information for.

To Grandpa Blane, the train was man's greatest invention. Rails were the arteries of the nation. The great railroad barons ranked with the presidents. Nobody built an overpass, bridge, or trestle in Sylvanus County without Grandpa

Blane's personal supervision. When the crews quit for lunch, Grandpa would climb into the ditches and check the forms and lay his nose against the new rails to make sure things lined up properly. He'd told more than one foreman how to do his job.

I wrote three lists which I folded and kept in my back pocket—supplies, instructions, and questions. It was like planning a military invasion. Supplies included bologna sandwiches, apples, canteens of water, pop, a list of the stops, and emergency money. Nobody balked at my instructions. I told Taylor and Wellesley to wear hobo clothes. No bright shirts or kids' insignias but old jackets in dark colors. Long pants. Old leather shoes. Hats with brims instead of bills. I thought we were less likely to be bothered if we looked older and poor.

Wellesley and Taylor had to clear their excuse—the story to tell the parents—with me. I told Mom and Dad I was getting up early to hunt for golf balls at the course and try and get a caddie job off the first tee. Wellesley said she was going to Annie Curran's to ride; her cousin had agreed to cover for her. Taylor's first story—he had a new job at the bakery—I rejected, explaining he would be discovered by his parents when he slept in the second day of work. So he borrowed my excuse. We'd both caddie.

I told Taylor and Wellesley to meet me behind my garage. We had to be in the yard at five to find an empty car before daylight.

15

I didn't sleep well that night. A train derailed at high speed and crushed us between two boxcars. Then a bridge collapsed and dropped us into the river. Wellesley's right leg was severed at the knee by the steel wheels of the car we were racing to board. When the alarm went off, I was so sweaty I felt like I'd run to Union Gap. The panic of the dreams made me think of something that wasn't on my list. I rummaged through the basement closet and found one of Dad's hunting knives. It fit the inside pocket of his leather pilot's jacket.

Taylor was late so Wellesley and I huddled against the back of my garage in the dark. She looked like a seasoned tramp in her baggy pants and derby hat. I shivered despite two shirts and the jacket.

"I found your note, Will. Thanks." Her voice was steady and reassuring. "I didn't want to say anything when Taylor was with us yesterday."

"If I had any guts, I'd have told you in person."

Wellesley elbowed me gently in response. "You don't have to apologize."

I guessed that meant she'd forgiven me for leaving her at the fairgrounds. Now I could tell her about my attempted confession. "Wellesley . . ."

"You know that night in my coal bin?"

Her mention of the place jolted me. "Yeah, I . . ."

"I feel so ashamed. My Dad . . . I don't know why he acted like that." She grabbed my pilot's jacket by the sleeve and twisted it. "I know you wouldn't say anything Will, but . . . I don't want everyone in town gossiping." The night was so still, like it must be listening to every word we said.

Wellesley didn't know I'd seen him in action before, when

he threw the drink at her mom. I'd already suspected this wasn't a freak thing. I wanted to get back at her dad, hurt him. Every time I thought of telling Mom and Dad, something turned me away. They wouldn't let me see her anymore. Dad would say mind your own business, you wouldn't want people telling us how to live. Most likely, nobody would believe me. "I haven't told anyone."

"Thanks."

Her mention of the coal bin renewed my doubts about the trip. "Wellesley, are you sure you want to hop the freight?"

"Lightning doesn't strike twice in the same spot, Bradford. Don't worry about it." The way she ground her shoes into the gravel, I wondered if the thought of it didn't bother her more than she let on. "Do you think Taylor said anything?"

As if waiting to hear his name, Taylor appeared. He clicked his dad's work shoes together and saluted. "Private First Class Clark, reporting, sir!"

Wellesley hissed at Taylor, "Where you been, asswipe?"

"Shh!" I warned. "Follow me, no talking."

The Clearwater freight yard was at the eastern edge of town, past A&M Wrecking. Grandpa Blane brought me here before I could remember my parents taking me to church. The dispatch office was a small barn-red building between the asphalt storage area and the tracks. There was a light on. Two men with bill caps were visible through the window. We used a stack of crates for cover and dashed across the asphalt away from the lights.

The yard behind the office wasn't lit. We let our eyes adjust to the dark. There were four tracks, with cars resting on each of them.

Taylor whispered, "Well, Captain, how are we supposed to know which one to get into?"

I hadn't asked Grandpa about this. I guessed. "See that locomotive? Watch where he goes. He's putting our train together."

The stubby locomotive played bumper cars, building up a small head of power, then ramming a row of boxcars. Metal clanged against metal. The ground shook. I thought I

smelled the same electricity in the air that my old Lionel
train set made. Then slowly, squeaking like a crank handle,
the locomotive drew a single car away from the rest of the
lot. When he was out of the yard, he screeched to a stop,
reversed direction and returned on the far track pushing his
captive. He released his car like the outside skater in crack
the whip and sent it hurtling toward the waiting line. When
the car hit, it set off a chain reaction of smaller collisions
through the row as the slack in each coupling compressed.

The train on the far track was ours.

We made a wide circle around the working part of the
yard to reach our train. Downwind, I inhaled the smell of
creosote and diesel smoke. The roughness in my throat
masked the softness in my belly. But there was no way I
could admit that to my friends. After all, I was in charge.

There were already about fifteen cars coupled. Starting
with the end car, we walked next to the train, looking for an
empty. The first car, rusty orange, said "Santa Fe, San Anto-
nio and Southwestern Railroad" on its side. The closed door
was secured by a steel cable. The "Southern Pacific and
Georgia" was also sealed. A flat car with logs smelled like
room deodorizer. We passed another closed boxcar with a
"Flammable" tag. Taylor mooed at the white-faced calves
packed into a cattle car. No response. They smelled like the
stables under the fairground stands. Where were all the
empty cars Grandpa said were going west?

We advanced along the broken granite bedding each time
the locomotive moved away from the train and ducked between cars whenever its headlight was coming toward us.

"Bull's-eye!" Wellesley slapped the floor of an empty.

I leaned back to read the inscription. "Looks like we'll be
riding courtesy of the Milwaukee Road."

"Always wanted to see Milwaukee," Taylor said, throwing
his pack through the open door.

Everything was bigger than I imagined, like the toys of a
giant. From the ground, the floor of the car came up to my
shoulders. The double wheels at each end of the car looked
more like the turbines in the generator at Clearwater Dam.

Wellesley and Taylor made stirrups out of their hands.

"Come on," Taylor said, "let's give our crippled leader a boost into the club car."

Once Taylor was in, we reached down and grabbed both of Wellesley's arms. "Ladies and gentlemen," Taylor said, "introducing the great Wellesley Baker." She felt so light she almost floated up to the lip of the car. When she landed, her derby hat fell off and rolled across the floor like this was part of a vaudeville act.

Inside, our voices echoed. The car seemed as big as a basketball court. The walls were covered with badly splintered plywood. Wellesley picked up two slivers as long as toothpicks. I'd forgotten to put gloves on my list.

When the sun came up, we realized the floor was covered with a fine gunpowder-looking dust that puffed with each step. I blew my nose and the dust came out soot black in my handkerchief. Taylor said he was bored and ate his first bologna sandwich while we sat in the yard. He pulled the lettuce out of the middle and stuck it to the wall like a wet dollar bill. Wellesley split a Hershey three ways.

We heard someone's feet grinding into the rocks and pressed ourselves flat against the wall on the open door side. None of us breathed. Still upside down in full view of the doorway was Wellesley's hat. It just lay there like we were hoping someone would toss in their change if they liked our act. The steps became louder. Then a man in striped overalls with a steel rod on his shoulder passed without stopping.

The assembly of our train took forever. Each time the locomotive hurled a car at us, we rocked, squeaked, and then settled again. Each collision was followed by a long silence.

Then the horizon framed by the door begin to move. Our car trembled. The wheels began to throb against the rails. I could feel the power of the engine pulse through the frame beneath us. The town rolled past us like a movie.

"This is great!" Wellesley said. "I can't believe we're really doing it."

The familiar backside of Clearwater looked cleaner and richer from the train. The A&M Wrecking yard looked like a playpen with pretend cars and trucks stacked on top of

each other. The grain elevators were castles. I. B. Henry
Lumber seemed like it had a fresh coat of paint. Cemetery
Road wound up the hill like the road to Oz. Once the train
passed out of the city limits, we dangled our legs out the
door. The motion of the train blurred the junk in the farm-
yards, making them into postcards.

Wellesley tousled my hair. "You did it, Will! And it didn't
cost us a dime."

"Damn smart for one arm," Taylor said, patting my thigh.
"Worked like a Swiss timepiece."

I felt like I'd shot a hole in one. Wellesley had never seen
me tell Taylor what to do. I let out the breath it seemed I'd
been holding since we arrived at the dispatch depot. "Wa-
Hoo!" My voice was lost in the rush of the wind sweeping
our faces.

We stopped in every town Grandpa circled plus others not
big enough to qualify for his Texaco map. Each time the
brakes squealed, we pulled our legs in and moved out of the
doorway in case there were railroad agents. In Coles Corner, our car stopped opposite a gully full of abandoned refrigerator crates made into lean-tos.

"There's some migrants," Taylor said, pointing at a group
of men squatted next to a small fire. Every summer, Mexi-
cans traveled to Sylvanus County to pick fruit and vegetables. Some of them bucked hay and worked the wheat harvest. We saw a man roasting a wiener and a piece of bread
on a stick.

Another man with a T-shirt over his plaid shirt crossed
the creek and climbed the bank to reach our car. His feet
slipped as the soil gave way. *"¡Buenos días, señores! ¿Cómo
están?"*

Taylor said, "He's all yours, Bradford."

His teeth were white and straight as piano keys. He had
laugh lines around his eyes and a knife in a leather sheath
on his belt. The strap for his cloth purse crossed his chest in
a diagonal. *"¿Hablan español?"*

"Don't look at me, Will," Wellesley said.

He'd scaled the bank and was panting when he reached
our car. While he studied each of our faces, he rested one

arm on the floor of the car to catch his breath. On his tiptoes, he stretched to see inside.

I mentally reviewed the steps I would take to reach my jacket on the floor and retrieve the hunting knife. "We just speak English," I said, enunciating each word. It was like talking to Grandpa Blane.

He laughed, like he was surprised. "Me speak English." His accent made hash of the last word.

"What is your name, sir?" I asked in a loud voice.

He furrowed his brow and cupped his ear.

"Name? Your name?"

His face lit up. "Pedro. Name Pedro." He extended his hand to me.

"Don't fall for it, Will," Taylor said through his clenched teeth, as if Pedro might read his lips if he moved them.

The men in the shade of the camp below us continued to mind their own business. A couple of them stood together like they were sharing a joke. The teller was gesturing dramatically. Both of them rocked back on their heels when they laughed. If this was a trick, Pedro was on his own. I braced my butt against the side of the car. "Cover me," I said to Wellesley and extended my good hand to Pedro.

He grasped my hand with both of his and made what sounded like a long toast. His voice rose several times as he pumped my hand up and down. Then, with his eyes closed, he spoke in hushed tones like a prayer. I was ready to jerk back if he made the slightest attempt to pull me out of the car. He ended with a *"muy bien"* that sounded like "amen," smiled warmly and bowed to each of us.

"¿Tienen hambre?" He chuckled and nodded his head. *"Sí, mis amigos, ¡tienen hambre!"*

His laugh was catching. I nodded my head with his and grinned even though I didn't know what he was saying. He hoisted the strap of his colored purse over his head, set the purse in the dirt, and reached inside. He pulled out three shiny Jonathan apples. I didn't know whether to take them. Then the train started to move. He stumbled to keep pace with our doorway, keeping the apples elevated with his outstretched arms. He pleaded in words I didn't understand.

Finally, I grabbed an apple. Taylor and Wellesley followed. He stopped running and broke into a big smile.

"Thank you, señor!" I called back as the distance between us grew.

He folded his hands together and shook them toward us, *"Adiós, amigos!"*

We waved and so did the two men watching from the edge of the camp.

Taylor and I argued until after our stop in Brush Prairie about whether I should have let the man grab my hand. Somehow my being more reckless had made Taylor more careful. "That was stupid, Will! Haven't you read about some of the crap those migrants do? He could have bounced you out of this car faster than you could say your name."

"Taylor, the man gave us apples."

"I'm not talking about just him. You were lucky. But don't think every bum between here and the West Coast is going to be Santa Claus!"

I didn't know whether Taylor was scared or jealous. "He wasn't a fighter," I said. "That man had a family. We probably reminded him of his kids. Besides, I had you two to cover me!" I tapped Wellesley and Taylor with my shoes.

"You did fine," Wellesley said. "I kind of liked the guy. He's just looking for work." I wondered if Wellesley's taking my side was partly a result of our talk behind the garage that morning. I wished I could have reassured her about Taylor. The truth was Taylor hadn't said much about the fight with her dad. But I was sure he'd have told me if he'd blabbed to anyone. Normally, he couldn't keep a secret from a stone.

Taylor pouted. He knew he was outnumbered.

Our car swayed and teetered as the train raced toward its next stop. *Pitapat, pitapat, pitapat.* The wheels thumping against the joints in the rails sounded like a printing press. The air was thick with the aroma of toasted summer wheat and green lentils from the fields we passed. Farmhouses and silos guarded the rolling hills. Power poles passed us like bicycle spokes. The sky was cloudless blue.

I finally broke the standoff with Taylor. "Okay, I'll admit it. I wished I'd had my knife closer to me."

Taylor's head spun. "What knife?"

I'd forgotten they didn't know. I leaned back, dragged my jacket out of the pack and found it.

"Jack the Ripper," Taylor said, as he pulled Dad's knife from the case, turned the blade in his hand, and tested the edge with his thumb. Then he plunged the knife viciously into the mustard stain from his lettuce on the plywood lining of the boxcar. "This baby stays next to me," he said. "Peace means being ready for war, my friends."

I was sorry I'd mentioned the knife.

Wellesley helped me out. "Let's rotate guard duty," she said. "Keep the knife where it is. We trade seats. What's our next stop, Will?"

I pulled the paper from my pants. "Oakville, then Castor and Finn."

"Good!" Wellesley said. "Will, you're Castor Oil and I'm Huck Finn!"

Even Taylor laughed. Custody of the knife was settled.

The train braked as our car passed the sign for Union Gap. Away from the shade of the mountains, the landscape looked parched. Tumbleweeds instead of live shrubs. A car traveling the opposite direction on the road next to us left a miniature tornado of dust in its wake. It was 12:35 P.M. We were later than Grandpa predicted, taking almost six hours to do what a car would have accomplished in less than half that time.

We wanted to get off before the rail yard. While the train was slowing, we dropped out of the car one at a time like paratroopers. I lost balance and slid down the ditch using my cast as a rudder. The rocks socked against my side like hundreds of angry fists. When I stopped moving and inspected the cast, it was gouged and scratched but intact. The only permanent damage was obliteration of the mermaid Taylor had drawn on the elbow.

Union Gap was the county seat of Thornton County, bigger than Clearwater by one high school and probably three movie theaters. It also had a J. C. Penney and a Sears. In our house, Sears was a bad name. It was one of Dad's competitors, the place people in Clearwater thought of when they needed big appliances like a deep freeze or a stove. I'd also seen one of their paint thinners in Taylor's garage. Instead of beer bottles, they used shiny, rectangular tin cans with a clean label that wouldn't come off when the scotch tape broke.

I thought of myself as a soldier coming home from the war as we ambled down Main Street with my arm in a cast. We gawked into store windows. The rabbits in Thornton Pets nibbled on the wood shavings. The smell of leather saddles on sawhorses was strong enough to seep through the glass at Texas Outfitting. Through the scratches in the green paint on the windows, we could see men perched on stools in the musky dampness of Archie's Tavern.

"Hey, look at that!" Taylor said, pointing to the yellow panel truck parked down the street. Plain as day, the black lettering on the side read, "Cirro's Road Shows."

"That's him," Wellesley said. "I rode to the police station in the back of that junker." The truck looked like it had been mistreated. It needed a wash. The only clean surfaces were the spaces on the front windshield where the wiper blades had rubbed.

"What are we waiting for?" Taylor said. "Let's go!"

"What are you going to do," I said, "shoot more matches at him?"

"Oh, come on, Will," Taylor said. "He can't do anything to us in the middle of Main Street. This is America!"

I looked at Wellesley for help. My command was in jeopardy. Wellesley was still staring at the truck as if it were a mirage. "I have to admit, Will, I'm a little curious to see what this guy looks like without a wrench in his hand. Let's at least get a closer look."

To avoid the mutiny, I took the lead in the direction they were headed. "Okay, follow me. Let's backtrack and cross the street down there so he won't see us. He's probably in that diner. I doubt he's fixing his hair in the beauty salon next door."

We crossed over and moved cautiously along the storefronts, peering in each window before passing. Sure enough, when we reached Maude's Diner, I saw someone sitting in a window booth with his back to us who looked big enough in the neck and shoulders to be the man that chased us out of the fairgrounds. There was a woman across from him. I was back in my military intelligence role, making sure I protected the troops. "Let's get something to eat."

Wellesley and Taylor smiled at each other and followed. I directed us to the booth by the window next to the suspect. The direct sunlight made the green vinyl upholstery hot to the touch. Two men drinking coffee at the counter swiveled their stools to take a look at us. We were newcomers. From a radio in the kitchen, the announcer was reciting barley, corn, wheat, and pork prices. The waitress dropped three laminated menus on our table and went to the next booth.

The carnival man ordered country chicken and pea soup, with a bottle of Lucky Lager. She just ordered a Lucky. Taylor pointed a finger against his chest. "That's him," he mimed without sound.

When I looked up, the woman faced me. She had fire engine lipstick that went outside the lines of her lips. When she put a cigarette in her mouth, the carnival man flicked his lighter for her. I could only see the tops of his muscular shoulders and the back of his tanned bow neck. His head was twelve inches from Taylor. I motioned with my hands flat to stay quiet.

The carnival man tapped his lighter on the table. "When's your old man getting back?" He made no attempt to lower his voice.

She took a drag as if the answer was in the tobacco. When she exhaled, her words chopped up the stream of smoke. "I told you not to worry. He's gone all week. On a load to Sacramento." She took another deep drag. "Then he picks up another move north before he comes home to his little ba-by." She fattened her lips and let the last word pop out slowly in two distinct syllables.

"Good! I'm going to keep his baby in practice. That bastard's probably got his stick in some pussy right now." Taylor raised his eyebrows and Wellesley covered her mouth to keep from laughing.

The woman didn't flinch. "You're no better than he is. I shouldn't even let you touch me. How'd you like that?"

"I'd fucking beat your moron brain in if you tried that shit."

Wellesley whispered. "I think we know who the moron is."

I tried to act normal. They were going to get suspicious if we didn't say anything. I spoke in a low but audible voice. "Do you guys want anything besides a milkshake?"

Taylor caught on. "Ah . . . no, a shake'll do it for me."

The waitress with her hair in a tight bun brought two brown stubbies of beer to the next booth. Then she stopped at our table. We had all our change on the table. Taylor had enough to line his up in the shape of a T. "You kids want anything?"

Taylor asked her what the soup of the day was and ordered a chocolate-banana shake. I ordered a root beer shake for Wellesley and me to split. Wellesley ignored the waitress and kept her attention on the conversation next to us.

The woman took a swig from the bottle. "At least Larry doesn't steal from his boss like some guys I could name."

The carnival man grabbed her wrist. "You keep your nose out of my business. You say anything about stealing and I'll break your arms off. Understand?" He let her go. "Fuck a little equipment. Cirro has insurance."

Wellesley whispered to me, "Crook."

"You gotta like this town," I said out loud, in reference to nothing, trying to avoid the attention of the couple in the next booth by being too quiet.

Taylor caught on again. "We sure could use a little rain though. The barleycorn's going to die of thirst." It didn't matter whether anyone around here raised barley.

We finished our shakes before he finished his country chicken, put our fifty cents on top of the bill, and slithered toward the door. The elderly woman in the kitchen waved at us with her spatula through the opening. Maybe it was Maude.

As we were walking to the end of town, a hailstorm broke, the kind hard enough to flatten the wheat. We ducked under the marquee of the Liberty Theater—*Spartacus* was playing —and watched the hailstones bounce off the street and sidewalk. They hammered the tin on the marquee and made the air smell like someone defrosting a freezer.

It was good weather for hitchhiking though. People must have felt sorry for us with hailstones melting in our hair because the fourth car we thumbed stopped.

Wellesley and Taylor took the backseat and I sat in front. It was a farmer from Rimrock with a steel hook instead of a right hand that I kept staring at. He said he'd come to Union Gap for an alternator for his wheel tractor.

"Lost it when I was your age," he finally said out of a dead silence. "Combine accident." He smiled as if to assure me it was okay.

He'd caught me. His missing hand had reminded me of what happened to Wellesley in my dream last night. "Oh," I said.

When he asked what brought us to the Gap, I said, "We were checking out the railroad, seeing if they had any work."

16

I caught the screen door with my hand to keep it from slamming. Mom, Dad, and a bald man in a shirt and tie were sitting at the dining room table arguing about something. They didn't notice me come in.

I whispered, "Mom, hi!"

She crossed a finger to her lips, left her chair, and came into the kitchen. "Did you caddie in that outfit? You look filthy."

Wellesley, Taylor, and I had taken turns slapping the box-car dust off each other before we separated but we hadn't gotten it all. "Taylor and I messed around afterwards." I wanted to change the subject. "Where's dinner?"

Mom glanced back to the dining room table, then spoke quietly. "Your Dad and I are meeting with Mr. Bartleson. I don't know when we'll finish. Why don't you fix something for yourself. Sorry." I'd snuck off to Union Gap and Mom apologized for not having dinner ready. It was just like her.

"What's the meeting about?"

"Business." Business meant it didn't involve me so don't ask questions. The last time I'd heard Mom and Dad talk about business it was bad.

I opened the oven to make sure Mom wasn't kidding. It was cold and empty. Holding the refrigerator door open, I stared at leftover macaroni and cheese, canned peaches, and ground stew meat with chopped pickles in a bowl. There were apples and oranges in one bin, wilted lettuce, rubbery carrots, and half a green pepper in the other. I pulled out the eggs, a jar of mayonnaise, catsup, and a bottle of milk.

I could see the three of them through the cutaway between the kitchen and the dining room. Dad balanced on the front of his chair, tilting up the back legs. Mom always had to remind us to keep the chairs flat so we wouldn't break the legs off. Dad leaned toward Mr. Bartleson and jabbed at the papers spread on the table. "Our sales are four times what they were when Audrey and I bought this place. Am I wrong, Ned? You show me if I'm wrong on that!"

Mr. Bartleson pulled a hanky out of his suit coat and wiped his forehead. He checked the hanky, wiped the top of his head and then checked the hanky again. "Tom, I don't want to argue with you. But you have to look at both sides of the ledger. You've also shown a corresponding increase in expenses. More employees, bigger mortgage payments, insurance . . ."

"That's a joke. The only time I made a claim on the insurance, they turned me down."

Mr. Bartleson's voice reminded me of our pastor, calm and detached. "I certainly understand your frustration, but there was no clause covering employee theft. It's one of those unfortunate things . . ."

I cracked two eggs into the spreading yellow pool of margarine in the frying pan. One had a double yoke, twin chickens. I pushed the knob down on the toaster until my Wonder Bread disappeared. The wires started to glow. What employee theft? They never told me the serious stuff.

Mom tried to soften the tension. "Would you like some more coffee, Ned?"

"No, thanks, Audrey." He gave Mom a forced smiled.

"Tom?"

"Sure, I'll have some." Dad shoved his cup toward Mom. "So what do we do about it, Mr. Accountant?"

Mr. Bartleson drew a deep breath. "First, we have to be patient. Second, we make some tough decisions."

Mom asked, "Like what, Ned?" She stepped between Dad and Mr. Bartleson with the percolator, aiming the dented spout at Dad's cup.

"Well, you could bring collection actions against some of your larger accounts receivable . . ."

". . . and lose our best customers in the process," Dad said. "What else?"

"You won't like this one but I have to say it." Ned looked at Mom for support, then Dad. "Reduce the payroll . . . release some of your help."

Dad winced, dropped his ballpoint pen across the papers, and sat back in his chair. His voice broke. "Ned, half the people working there are relatives. The rest are as good as family."

"Tom, if you don't start turning red ink to black, there won't be jobs for any of you."

The toast popped up. Dad spun his head toward the kitchen like I'd just flushed a quail from the bush.

"I'll tell you what I'm not going to do." Dad pushed his chin toward Mr. Bartleson daring him to take a swing. "I'm not going to fire anyone!"

I spread the mayonnaise and scrambled eggs on the toast, made a circle of catsup on top and closed the sandwich. They talked some more, Dad agitated, the accountant cool headed. Then Mr. Bartleson stood, assembled the papers into a neat stack, and slid them into one of the compartments of his zip briefcase. Dad just sat there watching him. Mom retrieved Mr. Bartleson's hat from the back of the large chair.

I finished my sandwich alone and wiped up the toast crumbs on the table.

The next morning, Mom said we were going to have a yard sale. She went into every room in the house with her clipboard, making a list of what to sell—my American Flyer sled, the Lionel train set, a Mickey Mantle glove, the set of wooden-handled golf clubs Grandpa Blane gave me, my bust of Lincoln bank, and sweaters, sweatshirts, and wool pants from my bottom drawer which Mom said I never wore. I stapled signs on telephone poles and taped them in windows at Western Hardware and the Rexall. Mom used our address but, at my request, left our name off the signs.

On the day of the sale, I helped Mom wait on people who came to the front yard. They sat in our chairs, tried on our clothes, and fingered Mom's ceramic figurines. People pointed to our things and whispered to each other. Some giggled. Kids from school came by, stood on their bikes at the curb, and just watched.

When Mr. Tracy bought our one-armed bandit, I lied and told him we'd outgrown it. There were still nickels visible in the glass vault on the front, which drained into the chute if you hit a row of three cherries. When we played, Dad always opened the back of the machine and let us reuse the coins we'd just spent.

Nobody paid the prices Mom had scotch-taped to each item. People turned things over and pointed out scratches, chips, and ink spots. I worried that each car stopping at the curb would be someone rich like Monica Amberly and her family. Sitting on top of crowded, tilted cardboard boxes, everything we had looked cheap. It was junk. I knew what the men in the gully at Coles Corner must have felt when we gawked at them from the train.

I kept track of my hours at the hardware in a book with purple carbon paper between each numbered invoice. At twenty cents per hour, I figured the hardware owed me thirty-seven dollars and seventy-five cents. When I asked Dad if I could draw down some of my pay to buy a new record player with Taylor, he said wait until the end of summer.

I didn't know if the trouble at the store meant we had less money or no money. There had to be enough to pay my bill. I was peeved the way Dad turned me down. It was as if I hadn't earned the money and wanted a handout.

Mr. Bartleson returned the next week with another man in a dark suit and narrow red tie. When I walked by the table real slow to go to the bathroom, I heard the new man say, "bankruptcy court." He was more edgy than Mr. Bartleson and constantly interrupted Dad when he tried to make a point. Dad looked like a steam boiler ready to explode as he listened to the new man rattle on.

The morning after the bankruptcy man visited, Dad stayed home in bed. He looked pale. Mom said he must have a touch of the flu. She took the keys and opened the store. I hadn't seen Dad stay home in bed in his pajamas since the time someone hit him in the eye at the stock car races. I remembered his eye socket turning the color of mimeograph ink. He hid it under sunglasses at work. When

I asked Mom who started it she was vague, which meant Dad did.

I couldn't remember ever being without the store. Every pair of cuff pants I owned probably had grains of that red sweeping compound in them. I used to pick the stuff out from under my fingernails in class, make a neat pile on the desk and then plow it over the edge with my ruler. I hated sweeping as much as bottling. Now, I was afraid to lose them.

The talks at the dining room table sounded of doom. I'd never seen Dad in a corner he couldn't get out of. He wanted to fight but there was nothing to attack except the stack of paper Mr. Bartleson carried in his leather case.

Dad went back to work next day. Everything seemed normal on the surface but I could feel the tension. We had chipped beef on toast for dinner. Dad announced we were selling the Buick. He wanted to get an older car, something more reliable. Mom and Dad got into an argument at dinner about him working too hard. She said he should have turned down the chairmanship of the Fair Committee.

After doing the dishes, I headed out the back door, letting the screen door slam. Mom called after me, asking where I was going, but I didn't answer. I didn't know. I wanted to be alone.

I took the same alley route Taylor, Wellesley, and I had taken to reach the rail yard. That had worked just the way I planned it. Nobody had even suspected we were out of town. Maybe this was my payback. God was getting even. By the time I started high school, I'd be another Bill Devine. His dad had injured a leg in a trucking accident and hadn't worked since fourth grade. Kids teased him, saying his dad was faking. Devine's neck was always grimy and his collar black from not bathing. He smelled like the insides of one of the used refrigerators for sale at the hardware.

At the end of our alley, I saw Laddie pumping his bike toward me. His head was down. I ducked behind two garbage cans. He pedaled by, mumbling to his feet, like they were horses pulling his carriage. He rang his bell three times, stuck his left arm out and turned at the corner. Laddie's universe seemed so reliable.

I went up to Cemetery Hill, feeling sorry for myself. Because of the cast, I couldn't swim, couldn't practice football and the summer was flying by. It felt like I was climbing a rope one handed. Dad's going broke was like smearing the rope with vaseline. When word leaked out, I was afraid that kids at high school would avoid me like the plague. A girl friend, always a long shot, was now totally out of reach.

The gate was open. The caretaker raked grass clippings. I told him I was just visiting and he went back to raking. I stopped at each tomb, counting the babies that had died before they were old enough to start school. Some of the family names I recognized, Mary Ann Tucker, Elizabeth Mae Crumbacher, Baby Tubbs.

I tried to think of somebody living I'd trade places with. Nothing quite fit. Taylor's parents were generous with allowance and independence but they didn't seem to pay much attention to him or his brother. Although I liked her mom, Wellesley's dad put her house permanently out of contention. The lucky ones seemed to be families I didn't know very well, like Monica Amberly's mom who served us Cokes without worrying whether we'd spill on her long-haired white carpet. Her dad's bank wouldn't fold like the hardware.

On the way home, I stopped at the Rexall to look at magazines. Martin didn't care as long as there wasn't a gang of us.

"Well, look who's here." It was Roland Bushner, triumphantly chewing a wad of gum. Because his family was a big supporter of the prosecuting attorney, they'd worked out a deal over his killing Dolly. Some people could get away with anything. His magazine was open to a picture of a woman in a low cut red gown. "What happened to your arm, partner?"

He'd caught me by surprise, same as he did at the fairgrounds. Suddenly, the Rexall was a steamroom. "I think you have a pretty good idea."

He had a smirk on his face, as he reached for his back pocket. "Hey, I've got something to show you." He glanced over the Band-Aid counter to see if anyone was looking. I thought he was going to offer me another drink of his whiskey. He had something worse. In the palm of his hand, he held a jackknife with an ivory handle and a silver insignia. "My uncle picked it up at a yard sale the other day. I guess some family in town's gone flat ass broke."

My adam's apple heaved as I swallowed. The knife had my Dad's initials, "TB," on the plate.

I didn't hear anything on the way home. It was as though I was swimming underwater. Some law of nature always put the information you most wanted to hide in the hands of the person you least wanted to have it. Bushner didn't have the brains to find the open end of a sack. Now, he had stumbled across a piece of bad family news and stuck it in my face.

Clearwater seemed the wrong size. It was too big to know everyone, but small enough that I couldn't hide our family's money problems. And people ganged up. Without ever meeting or taking a vote, they seemed to make decisions about who was good and who wasn't. We'd been okay because we owned a business. The Bakers were common because they worked for wages and lived in Milltown. Grandpa Blane played the public course, Mr. Amberly the country club. People like Laddie didn't count.

17

When I got home, everyone in the living room turned to look at me. Dad was in his chair. He still had his hardware smock on, probably just closed the store. Mom teeter-tottered nervously in her rocker. Aunt Ruth sat on the couch, her legs too short to put her heels on the floor. Nobody even said hello.

Something was wrong. I wished we still had my dog Plato. Whenever I came in the door, he'd run to greet me, licking the salt off my hands, rubbing figure eights inside and out between my legs. I smiled faintly. "Hi, Aunt Ruth, I didn't know you were coming over."

Before she could answer, Dad started. "Don't you have something to tell us, Will?"

Tombstones, jackknives, and Bushner's face rolled behind my eye sockets like the three wheels in our one-armed bandit. Did Dad already know what happened in the drugstore? My voice bleated like a lamb. "What are you talking about, Dad?"

"The week before last." His fingertips gripped the brass tacks on the front of the chair arms. He sat stiff like the chair was about to drop through a trap door.

I tried to make a connection. I imagined the bald accountant and the man in the red tie bearing down on me like they had on Dad at the dining room table. What had I done? I saw the girlie magazines I'd snuck out of Taylor's house. They were safe in my closet under the textbooks. Grandpa Blane held up the wrinkled article about the Great Northern. The train! My God, did he know about the train?

Nobody in the room helped me. Aunt Ruth held her face in her hands. Mom fidgeted, covering her mouth with the corner of her apron.

"Did you go to Union Gap?" Dad said Union Gap like it was a stick he was poking me with.

I rubbed my cast. "Yeah, we did, but . . ." I realized I'd said we.

"And you told your mother you were caddying?"

"Yeah, but . . ."

"How'd you get there? Look at me when I'm talking to you."

He hated lying. He'd rather I'd vandalized the tombstones in the cemetery. I closed my eyes until I heard my own words enter the room. "On the freight train."

Mom gasped.

Dad was still squinting when I looked up, his eyes wanting to drill a hole through me. "What in the hell did you think you could accomplish with a stunt like that?"

I felt like the mudflaps on a sixteen-wheel truck and trailer being driven by Dad. The gravel was spraying me so hard I couldn't think straight. "I just thought it was safe . . ." I wanted to tell him about Grandpa Blane saying how common it was in the old days, to ask him if he'd ever done something like this.

"I thought you might grow up this summer!" He shifted in the chair for the first time, letting loose of the arms. "I'm just glad your Aunt Ruth knows Maude McIntyre. She said you had lunch in her diner."

Aunt Ruth cleared her throat. "I didn't mean to get you in any trouble, Will. I thought they knew. Maude recognized the Blane face, and the cast."

I used Aunt Ruth's interruption to move past Dad's chair, to the other side of the room.

"We're not through yet!" He glared at me. The muscles tightened around his eyes. "What do you think we should do about this? You lied to your mom. You pirated private property. You broke the law."

Dad made me a candidate for the posters at the police station. "I don't know, Dad, I'm sorry. I guess I shouldn't have done it."

"Guess?" He gripped the chair again. "Who was with you?"

I didn't want to drag my friends into this. I felt like a

prisoner of war. But I knew Dad wouldn't quit until he'd dug this out of me. If there was a trap door under him, this was the time for someone to pull the latch. I took a long blink. He was still there. "Taylor Clark and . . . Wellesley."

Dad's eyes flared as though he just saw someone out front hit the hood of the Buick with a sledgehammer. "Didn't I tell you to stay away from her? What . . ." He left off and just shook his head.

Out the back window, behind Dad, I could see the corner of the garage and the lowest branch of the tree. On the next branch up, Wellesley and I had sat that night hiding from Taylor in kick the can. I needed a hideout right now.

"Audrey, bring me the phone," Dad said.

Mom picked up the phone, unraveled the extension cord from the chair leg, and cautiously placed it on the hassock like a piece of antique crystal.

Dad grabbed the phone and turned it so the dial faced me. In his hands, the phone was an anvil and he was going to reshape me over it. "Call the Clarks and the Bakers. Tell them we're having a meeting. Here. Right now. Tell them it's about you and their kids."

Dad had an instinct for picking the fitting consequence. Calling Taylor's and Wellesley's parents was the cruelest punishment I could have imagined. Mr. Baker would blow sky high when he found out. Dad wanted to use me as the fuse.

I dialed Taylor's house first. Mr. Clark answered in a chirpy voice. He asked how my summer was going. He must not have known about the train. I tried to be light, but with my Dad's face two feet from mine, I sounded more like a bill collector. He said he and Taylor would be right over.

Remembering Dad's warning to stay away from outlaws, I pretended I didn't know Wellesley's number and used the phone book. Wellesley answered. Dad whispered that I had to talk to her parents. She must have sensed I wasn't speaking of my own free will. When she put her hand over the phone, I heard Mr. Baker's voice in the background. Wellesley came back on and said her dad wanted to know what it was about. I explained it vaguely the way Dad instructed. I knew he wanted to spring the great discovery himself.

Dad became irritated that I couldn't get one of her parents and took the receiver away from me. He asked for her dad. We waited. Mr. Baker apparently came on and Dad explained there had been a trespass, something he'd want to hear firsthand. Dad planted the phone in its cradle and announced that Mr. Baker was coming too.

My heart dropped like an elevator. Dad's evasive reference to trespass had introduced a new problem. Mr. Baker probably thought this was about the fairgrounds arrest. Dad and Mom didn't know I was involved in that one. We were about to crash land.

Aunt Ruth scooted over to make room on the couch when Mr. Clark arrived. Like the gentleman he was, Mr. Clark shook Dad's hand and Mom's before sitting down. He wore a dark blue shirt and a string tie with a sliding clasp that read "Clark's." Taylor sheepishly followed his dad to the couch. I grimaced to warn him how serious this was.

I realized that I'd never seen Mr. Baker in our house. Maybe my parents had the same attitude toward Milltowners that everyone else did; leave them alone. Only something as serious as hopping the freight train would bring Dad and Mr. Baker together. From what Wellesley had told me about her dad's distrust of town people, I knew that an invitation under these circumstances would make him doubly angry. First, at Wellesley for getting in trouble and, second, at me and everyone else for publicly humiliating him.

Dad and Mr. Clark asked about each other's business and both said it was going fine. In Dad's case, I knew he was fibbing. Mr. Clark started into a long explanation of the problems he'd experienced doing repairs on the new Crosley television units. He was interrupted by a knock that rattled the screen door against its jamb. The room went silent and everyone stared at the massive man who clouded the screen.

"Come in," Dad called.

It was Mr. Baker, in a pair of soiled green work pants held up by black suspenders. His barrel chest expanded under his denim shirt as he eyed each of us like a dog smells a stranger. His whiskers darkened the lower half of his face. Instead of standing up to fuss about finding him a seat,

Mom seemed paralyzed by the giant that had just entered her house.

Wellesley was hidden behind him.

"Have a chair," Dad said, motioning toward the dining room without bothering to get up.

I felt the floor sag as Mr. Baker walked past the couch and picked up one of our dining room chairs by its back as easily as if it were his lunch bucket. His face had the look of a driver who'd just been rammed from the side and intended to get even. As he moved back into the living room with the chair over his shoulder, Taylor cringed like he thought Mr. Baker was going to break it over him. Mr. Baker stabbed the legs of the chair into the carpet directly across from Dad, turned the chair around and straddled it. He crossed his hairy forearms over the arch of the chair back.

Aunt Ruth looked like she might faint and started fanning herself with a *Cosmopolitan.* Dad sat stoically, like the priest waiting for everyone to stop rustling before he started his sermon.

Once her dad settled into position, Wellesley lowered herself to the floor and sat Indian-style next to him. Avoiding eye contact with me, she crossed her arms and stared straight ahead at the level of Dad's clenched hands. She looked more peeved than scared.

Dad cleared his throat. "Let's get this over with. We've got a problem. Bear with me and I think you'll understand why I called you away from your dinner tables. Aunt Ruth," —he nodded to Aunt Ruth fanning herself on the couch— "happened to mention that her friend Maude saw Will in Union Gap a couple weeks ago. She and Maude go back to high school. Anyway, I didn't think much about it until Will's mother figured out that was the same day he'd caddied at the golf course." His eyes pointed to me and I felt everyone's stares. "Any fool knows you can't caddie eighteen holes here and eat lunch at Maude's Diner the same day." When Dad looked down, I purposely looked away and focused on the side of Mr. Baker's head. "You're probably wondering how he got there?" Mr. Clark had moved to the edge of the couch so as not to miss a word of the speech. He nodded his head up and down in response to Dad's question. "Fifteen minutes ago, Will solved that mystery. He told us he hopped a freight train." Dad shook his head in disgust. "He hopped a freight train. And he wasn't happy just getting himself in trouble, he had to take your two down with him!" Taylor collapsed his head into his hands, facing the floor like he was ready to vomit. Wellesley looked straight ahead, not flinching, a replica of her dad. "Am I telling you something you already know?"

"First I've heard of it, Tom," Mr. Clark said, glancing quickly at the back of Taylor's head.

Mr. Baker didn't say a word. His glare was trained on Dad. He was so tense I thought the back of our dining room chair would break if he so much as swallowed.

"That's what I thought," Dad said, nodding. "So there's no confusion, I didn't drag you over here to blame your kids. You'll handle them as you see fit. As far as I'm concerned, it was Will's fault. He knows better than to pull a stunt like this."

From the circular motion of Mr. Baker's jaw muscles, it looked as if he was grinding his teeth, probably insulted Dad would imply that Wellesley didn't know any better. By his silence, Mr. Baker had attracted everyone's attention. Even a curse word from him would have helped. I imagined him slapping the chair into toothpicks against the hearth. Was he angry at me for leading this thing, Dad for telling, or the rest of us for listening? No matter who he was mad at, I knew exactly who he was going to take it out on.

Wellesley's spine was straight as a plank. I could see the frustration in her face. She had survived the savage beatings from her father and never peeped my name or Taylor's. Within two weeks of the train mission, my Dad had gone public with it because I couldn't keep my mouth shut. She deserved to be bitter.

Dad licked his lips. "I don't care what you two do about this mess but I'm going to make Will set up an account with the railroad and pay them back for the use of that boxcar. From here to Union Gap. And I don't care if he's still paying when he's twenty-five." I'd have to fill and label enough beer bottles to stuff a boxcar. Dad's punishment wasn't surprising. For him, customers not paying for services rendered was a serious offense. That's why the store was failing.

When Dad was done, Mr. Clark thanked him for the way he'd handled things and volunteered Taylor to pay half of the freight bill. Taylor gave a "guess so" with his eyebrows.

Mr. Baker pulled out a handkerchief, doubled it and wiped some spit off his tongue. When Dad stood up, Mr. Baker crooked his finger at Wellesley and turned for the door.

Our front porch was a favorite place to sit on hot evenings. I used to swing in the bench that hung by the chains while Dad and Mom reclined in their swayback chairs listening to the radio and drinking iced tea. That's where they listened to the '56 Democratic and Republican conventions. The radio on the porch railing was connected by an extension cord that snaked through the crack in the door to the outlet behind the couch. After the meeting with the Clarks and Bakers, the porch was like a church vestibule. Dad shook hands again with Mr. Clark. He patted Taylor on the shoulder. Everyone hesitated to leave, like people who only saw each other at Sunday Mass.

When Wellesley stepped onto the porch, her dad gripped her by the back of the neck and hissed at her, "You ain't getting off so easy!"

Wellesley ducked and shook her head like a horse resisting the bit.

Mr. Baker grabbed her arm and jerked her toward the steps. "Wise up, you little bitch!"

Everyone backed away, except Dad. "Hold on a minute, sir. You don't use language like that on my property!"

Mr. Baker turned, dragging Wellesley through a pirouette. "This is my property," he said, offering Wellesley's elbow to my Dad's chin.

Dad shot back, "That's no way to handle it, Mr. Baker! Let go of her!"

Mr. Baker's eyes bulged. The pressure of figuring out what to say was going to push them right out of his skull. I noticed his lower lip quivering. He stammered in his heavy voice. "Shit . . . the shit it ain't!"

Wellesley squirmed to straighten her arm. She kept

watching Dad to see what he'd do next. Dad scowled at Mr. Baker, daring him to move. Next to Mr. Baker's bull body, Dad was a calf.

Mr. Baker spit in Dad's face.

Dad moved in slow motion between Wellesley and her dad, ignoring the gob of saliva on his cheek, and grabbed Mr. Baker's arm and hers to separate them.

Mr. Baker let go of Wellesley and hammered Dad's chest with the palms of both hands.

Mom screamed.

Dad gathered his balance, crouched, then charged Mr. Baker. His right shoulder landed hard between Mr. Baker's suspenders, driving him into the column that supported the overhang of the house. The porch shook. Pieces of dirt and paint chips fell from the ceiling.

Mr. Baker stooped, like he'd temporarily lost his wind. Wellesley ran to his side and tried to move him down the steps. He pulled his arm loose and bristled at Dad.

Nobody moved.

Mr. Baker finally sucked some air into his lungs. "You won't get away with this." He eyed each one of us, stopping on me. "Next time, I'll pound you through that porch and drop your skinny ass kid in on top of you." Everyone on the porch moved into a "V" behind Dad. "You fancy ass people think you're too good for us. Well, sorry ladies, but fuck you all!"

Dad stepped back and reached his arm around Mom. As she sobbed against his shoulder, Aunt Ruth stroked her with a hand twisted from arthritis, every knuckle swollen like a Boy Scout knot. Mr. Baker put his hand on Wellesley's neck and steered her toward the street.

I was scared. Something horrible had been unleashed by Dad. The setting sun, like an orange squeezed against the juicer, had discolored the sky. The same anesthesia which had numbed me in Wellesley's coal bin slowly spread from a dark spot in the center of my stomach. I took charge of the trip to Union Gap to make sure there'd be no trouble. Now it felt like the stick I'd launched so gleefully into the wild blue yonder had circled, returned, and was about to clobber Wellesley.

Mr. Clark stepped forward and slapped Dad on the back. "I got to hand it to you, Tom, you did the right thing."

Dad finally wiped the spit from his face, looked at his hand, then reached for his back pocket. "Thanks, Ted."

"Mr. Bradford, you really belted him!" Taylor said, his face taut with admiration.

"I don't make it a habit, hitting another man, Taylor," Dad said, "but I wasn't going to turn the other cheek." Dad gave me a knowing look, probably wondering if I'd remembered Father Dominic's sermon.

I wanted to be enthusiastic, but could only be trite. "Nice going, Dad . . . you really showed him who's boss."

Mom invited everyone in for a lemonade. Mr. Clark declined. Taylor shrugged, disappointed. I knew he wanted to talk more about the fight. Dad headed for the bathroom and Mom to the kitchen. From the living room, I could hear Dad cupping water against his face in the sink, blowing to keep it out of his mouth. He returned, fingering the moisture in his ears with his hanky.

No one could keep a conversation going. Dad seemed anxious to change the subject. "Say, I've got some work to do in the basement. Maybe Audrey can run you home, Ruth. I'm rebuilding the furnace ducts."

I was relieved. It was a chance to go to my room and sort things out.

"That doesn't excuse you, Will!" Dad said as I started backing out of the living room. "I need your help in the basement. You can start earning your way back to respectability."

We started next to the furnace. It was encased in asbestos, like a mummy. Galvanized metal ducts grew like arms out of the topside, disappearing behind the sheet rock on the ceiling. With a crowbar, Dad found the seam in the sheet rock and started prying. A chunk of plaster dropped to the floor. Then another. Dad seemed oblivious to the pieces landing on the overstuffed furniture and boxes of Christmas ornaments that hadn't sold in the yard sale. My job was to follow along and sweep up the pieces. He worked quickly, ripping and tearing. White dust coated his face. He blew to clear pieces from his mouth like they were gnats.

"What's eating at you, Will?" Dad aimed his words at the vein of duct work he was exposing over his head.

I knew it was coming. He wanted to go over the whole train episode again. I decided to keep it short and cut to the ending. "I'm sorry about lying to you and Mom."

He let the black crowbar hang loose at his side from the crook in the J-end and looked at me. "You sure that's it?"

When I didn't answer, he turned to attack the ceiling cover again. "Hey, I shouldn't tell you this," he said, "but I hopped a freight once. Don't tell your mom I told you." The plasterboard bounced off his head. When stubborn pieces clung to the ceiling, suspended by the paper sheathing, Dad swatted them down with his hand.

He kept ripping and talking to the ceiling. "But you want to know something?" He paused again and let the bar hang limp. "It's not the freight train that made me mad, it's the lying . . . I know, I did it too. Fibs, white lies, it's no excuse."

My hands were chalky from the pieces I'd crammed into a cardboard box. I was tempted to confront him with his own white lie, the hardware store. When I looked at him, I had to blink to clear the dust in my eyes. "Dad, I didn't like the lying part either. But nobody got hurt."

I guessed we'd reached the heat vent for the dining room because the duct turned, and Dad's path of destruction with it, toward the register next to the couch. A multicolored bundle of threads and cloth scraps dropped at my feet. It looked like a dirty hat. Dad said it was a nest, a place for a pack rat or squirrel to keep warm in the winter.

"So what's eating at you?" he asked again. The sticky fiber of a spiderweb marked his face like the tracings of a fine point pen. "Are you mad because we caught you? Or just mad about paying back the railroad?"

I felt a burn in my throat at the junction where words are supposed to form. I cracked a triangular piece of sheetrock in two and dropped it into the box. "It's the fight!"

Dad paused, but kept the bar poised over his head. "You mean with that"—he ripped the bar violently between the duct and the joist, cutting the plasterboard like it was butcher paper—"Baker!" Then he put his hands on his hips and looked at me. "So what about the fight?"

"Mr. Baker isn't going to come after you," I said. "He'll take it out on Wellesley."

"Well, that's a hell of a note!" Dad seized a hanging chunk of the ceiling and smashed it against the floor. "I step in to protect your friend and now you're upset! What did you want me to do?"

"Dad, don't get so mad!" I was surprised my voice had some muscle in it. "I'm not blaming you for what happened. I was glad you stopped him." The skin around Dad's eyes softened, like he'd been waiting for my okay. "But don't you see what I mean? He's not going to let up once they're home!" I kicked the box of scraps.

"Slow down, slow down, Will! You're jumping to conclusions. Mr. Baker was mad. So was I. But he's not going to beat up on her!"

Some obligation to Wellesley kept me from saying what I really knew. When Mr. Baker slammed into the column, Wellesley could have hung back. She ran to him because she wanted to protect something. Maybe she wanted us to believe that her dad was as good as anyone else's. I couldn't casually add her secret to the wreckage on the floor of our basement. And I wanted Dad to be right.

About ten o'clock, Mom came down. She tiptoed around the edge of the room to avoid the mess. I knew she wanted to say something about the filth covering the furniture. "Tom, don't you think it's time you two quit for the night?"

Dad straddled an end table with wobbly legs that still had the $7.95 yard price taped to it. He looked like a snowman. "Your mom's right, Will. Let's hit the sack. We've created enough damage for one day."

I twisted in bed like a corkscrew, drenching the sheets with sweat. When I heard Dad snap off the TV after the national anthem, I pulled on my jeans. I had to go to Milltown.

At midnight, Clearwater was deserted. No cars. No pedestrians. The glow from corner streetlights punctuated each intersection. Hammocks were abandoned. Empty porch chairs faced the street, grouped for tomorrow's conversation. Bed lamps went out as I passed. A scraggly orange cat appeared from under a car and followed me, meowing for a stroke.

I hesitated at the edge of Milltown. Without street lamps, it was darker. Porch dogs, backyard dogs, and the muffled barks of hallway dogs sounded off. Each mutt seemed to have the precision of a surveyor, barking as I crossed the boundary line onto its lot and stopping precisely as I left it.

Wellesley's house was pitch dark and as still as an abandoned homestead. I just stood there, with my free hand in a pocket, staring, wondering what had happened behind those blank windows earlier. In the middle of the night, it was possible to confuse peacefulness with emptiness.

There was no sign of life in the backyard either. I sat on the running board of the Pink Lady and watched the house, waiting for Wellesley to come out the side door with her knapsack and a smile on her face. I imagined inviting her to come with me. "We're leaving tonight, Wellesley! You, me, and your mom. Tell her to get her things ready."

She'd be hypnotized by the determination in my voice. "Where are we going, Will?"

She put her hand on mine as I spoke. "We're going to a farmhouse at the foothills of the Rocky Mountains. We'll have a hundred wild horses. You and I will tame them. We'll come back to the ranch dog tired at night to your mom's home cooking. Then sit on the porch and watch the sunset together. Just telling stories until we hear coyotes howling at the moon."

I shivered against the cold metal of the Pink Lady, wondering how its driver had settled the score from last night's fight. The whistle of the train sounded in the distance, warning everyone to clear out of the way. A sliver of moon hovered over Wellesley's roof like a boomerang.

18

When I riffled my hair in front of the mirror over the sink, it snowed gypsum dust. One eye at a time, I fingered away the grit that had collected in the corners from last night's work.

On the kitchen table, the salt and pepper shakers held down the edges of a note that wanted to curl. Dad's oversize block printing filled a page torn from one of the "Western Hardware" pads that could be found in our house in silverware drawers, on nightstands, and propping up short table legs.

> "WILL—
> WE NEED A GOOD MAN
> TO BOTTLE UP SOME
> PAINT THINNER THIS
> MORNING!!
> ME AND THE RAILROAD
> APPRECIATE IT!
> DAD

Mom had lightly penciled on a corner of the note—"I'm at the food locker, see you after your work." I used to love Polar Storage. We'd go there to retrieve venison steaks or bear meat from one of Dad's hunting trips. Walking through the aisles was like eating ice cream too fast.

I had Wheaties with bananas while sorting through the mail on the table. There was an opened letter from Commissioner Hanson to the "Labor Day Committee" thanking them for the program they'd organized. The schedule was stapled to the letter. My eyes caught on: "Saturday, 8 p.m.– Midnight, Youth Dance (modern band)." The fair had never had anything but square dancing. I rinsed my bowl and stacked it with the other dishes on the counter. Then I called Wellesley.

The phone rang and rang. I imagined she'd run away. Or she was hurt and couldn't come to the phone. I should have burst into the house last night and found her.

Finally, she answered.

"Are you okay?"

"I'm fine." Her voice was a dishrag.

Something had happened but it was like we had a pact where she wouldn't tell me about it and I wasn't supposed to ask. The only currency we could trade in was safe stuff. "Why don't you meet me after I do my bottling at the hardware? I'll challenge you to Ping-Pong."

"I can't today, Will . . . I've got some things to do at home." Usually, she'd have teased me about creaming me the last time we played.

"Tomorrow then," I said. "Doctor says this cast comes off next week. It's your last chance to get me one handed!"

"Yeah, maybe we can."

We hung up and I headed for the store to get my work over with.

While I sat on an upside-down mop bucket in the back of the lawnmower shop, watching the thinner rise in each beer bottle, I kept thinking about Wellesley. It was spooky hearing her talk like someone had yanked the claws out of her paws. I liked it better when she was threatening to beat Bushner's balls to mush. Or staring down the three guys who'd stolen the raffle money at school until they coughed it up. But I guessed her dad was another matter.

Joe let me switch the radio from country to rock and roll. "Hey, you cool dudes,"—the disc jockey spoke in a voice that could smooth wrinkles out of a shirt—"this next piece has climbed to number fourteen on our nifty fifty. How about 'A Big Hunk of Love'?" His voice dropped to a whisper. The next beat was the record. By the time the barrel glugged, then sputtered and ran out of paint thinner, I'd decided to go over to Taylor's.

*   *   *

He was in the garage hooking an insignia to the back fender of his bike.

"What's the skull and crossbones for?" I said.

Taylor straightened the metal plate and leaned back to check the alignment. "Pretty cool, huh?"

"It's kid's stuff."

"It's what they put on rat poison! Anybody messes with me, they're dead. It's perfect!" He stood and thumped me on the cast with his screwdriver. "You want to read magazines?"

"Naw, not today."

"It's too hot, let's get something to drink."

I nodded toward the house. "Anyone home?"

"No. Dan's working at the lumber yard." Taylor flipped the screwdriver into the air and caught it by the handle.

In the kitchen, he turned on the radio and opened the refrigerator in one swoop. "Rock Around the Clock" was playing.

"Guess what? There's going to be rock and roll at the fair."

Taylor spun in his stocking feet with a quart of root beer in his hand. He kicked the refrigerator door shut with the bottom of his foot. "No lie?"

"I've seen the schedule. Dad gets all that stuff."

Taylor turned the radio full blast and planted his feet, legs spread. With each phrase by Bill Haley, he moved one foot forward and snapped his fingers, legs more or less parallel, leading with his pelvis. He looked down and sneered, like he was on a stage surrounded by screaming fans. He shouted over the din, "Watch me!" His knee convulsed suddenly and then snapped erect again. He laughed and I helped myself to the root beer.

I danced like someone who had just emerged from an iron lung. My body parts either didn't move at all or, when they did, they looked like they were acting under orders. Each move was stiff, separate, like a series of still photos. Taylor was part snake. Shakes rippled through his body. He had no internal dividers. Things like a dad beating up on his daughter seemed to flow in one end of him and out the other. Nothing stuck.

When the deejay came on again, I turned the volume down. We finished the bottle with about two swigs each. Taylor let loose a huge belch and we moved to the living room. Stretching out on the sofa, he braced his head with two Persian-looking pillows. "I'm beat."

I took off my socks and lay down on the floor, propping my legs on the sofa next to Taylor's feet. The room was cool and, with the drapes drawn, it was dusk. The Clarks were one of the first families to buy a TV in our neighborhood. They still had the biggest, a 21″ Motorola in a mahogany cabinet with doors. The same cabinet held a radio and the Clarks' collection of *Reader's Digest*s neatly faced on the shelf.

"Some night last night," I said.

"Your dad's tough," Taylor said. "I wish my dad had the guts to slug somebody like that. He's afraid to shake hands too hard."

"What about the rest of it?"

"What do you mean?" he asked.

"Your punishment? Wellesley?" I couldn't see his face.

"My dad didn't say another word. He'll forget about it in a few days. He only said something to go along with your dad."

"What about Wellesley?"

"Let's not talk about stuff we can't do anything about, huh?"

"It feels like we're ditching her again."

"You worry too much, Bradford." I stared at the ceiling. Maybe he was right, I was all worry and no action. "Do you think Monica will go to the dance with me?" he asked.

I sighed. He didn't want to talk about it. "She went to Mossyrock with you, why not?"

"That's what's got me nervous," Taylor said. "The first time you ask a girl out, they go because they don't know you. They're curious. They just hope for the best. Now she knows."

"Knows what?" I asked.

"Knows. Just knows what I'm like." Taylor sat up and put his feet on my legs. "In a way, I'd hoped she'd acted a little more like Marilyn did."

"Taylor!" I grabbed his foot and stomped it up and down on the carpet. "You mean kissy face?"

"You know what I mean. Monica seemed a little afraid of me."

I lay back and closed my eyes trying to visualize bopping with Marilyn. "I'm not sure I'll go."

He kicked me. "You can erase that brainstorm. You're going."

"I'd feel stupid dancing. Besides, I don't want to abandon Wellesley."

"Damn it!" Taylor slapped his hands on the couch. "We're in high school now! She's got to take care of herself."

I felt a stab of pain. "Piss on you! That's not fair. Look at all the crap she's gone through. You've seen it, same as me!" He looked surprised. "I can't just waltz off to the dance if she's in jail. Or the hospital!"

Taylor spoke calmly. "Okay, okay, I wasn't talking about that. I just mean, if she wants to go to the dance, she'll find her own date."

"The three of us have always gone together."

"If you're so worried about Wellesley," Taylor said, "why don't you take her to the dance?"

I shook my head. "She's not somebody you date."

Taylor didn't push it.

I found my shoes on one of the kitchen chairs and got ready to go. At the door, Taylor made a bridge to my shoulders with his arms and shook me gently. We parted without saying good-bye.

I'd never gotten mad at Taylor before. It felt like Taylor and Wellesley and I were standing on a big slab of ice in the middle of the ocean. Something had fractured the slab and now we were drifting in different directions. We could still see each other, but I had to cup my ear to hear them. Things I could have just whispered before I had to yell now. So, instead, I didn't bother to say anything.

For two days, I didn't see Wellesley. I was afraid to go to her front door in case her dad was there. So I resorted to our most primitive method of communication—the underside of the bike seat.

After dinner, I walked to her house. Their dusty red station wagon was parked in front. That meant he was home.

I backtracked and walked down the alley with a straw hat pulled over my eyes. Her bike lay on its side in the backyard. The first try I chickened out and kept walking, imagining that Mr. Baker was watching. Behind the next door neighbor's garage, I took the hat off and wiped the sweat on my forehead. I decided I wasn't going to let my imagination stop me. If he wanted me to leave, he'd have to chase me.

I plotted a path that would get me within about five feet of the bike behind cover of the Pink Lady. Leaning against the garage was a garden rake, the handle wrapped with black electrician's tape that covered most of a bad split. Gripping the rake under my arm, I hunched down and slunk to a spot behind the front tire. I closed my eyes to focus all concentration in my ears, straining to hear a hinge swinging or a knob turning. My hands gripped the rake handle like a baseball bat in case I had to fight him off. Silence.

Slowly, I stretched the rake toward the bike, hooked the teeth into the rear spokes and dragged the bike to me. Then I leaned over and looked under the car to make sure he wasn't coming. The mud caked against the bottom of the car had the same arena dirt smell I remembered from the time I was knocked off Dolly. Pulling the note from my pocket, I read it one more time:

Wellesley—where are you? I'm worried. Things aren't the same out here without you. Give me a signal. If you want to see me, leave a note on my bike. Are you still mad?

Your friend, W. B.

Then I folded it and slipped it under the seat springs.

I returned the broken rake to its place and beat it toward home. Instead of the shortcut up Sawyer Street, I decided to walk the river.

* * *

The Clearwater River drained the snowmelt from the Clearwater Mountains. Grandpa Blane brought me fishing here the first time when I was in kindergarten. He said the river used to be the chute for logs heading for saw blades in the Clearwater mill. The logs were so thick in those days you could walk across the river with your eyes closed and never wet your boots. When the mountains were logged off, the mill closed. But the river was still home to the best steelhead in the Northwest.

I walked along the edge of the riverbed, hopscotching from dry stone to dry stone. The spring runoff was muddy, carrying topsoil scoured from the banks as the Clearwater ricocheted its way through each bend. In late summer, the water was low and clear.

The Route 16 bridge was a giant version of my erector set —green steel beams riveted together in a series of triangles. Next to the bridge, I found cardboard boxes with empty paint cans spewing onto the gravel shore. From the faintness of the "Fullers" labels on the cartons, I guessed the boxes had been sitting in the sun for a while. They bowed and separated at the seams. Some people in Clearwater treated the river like another dump. They figured the river would eventually flush everything through.

A hundred yards past the bridge, the river made a dogleg. I hopped to a perch on a boulder that was flat as a park bench. In a still pool, a school of minnows wiggled in formation, each facing the same direction. I dropped a pebble the size of a BB. The fish disappeared like bread crumbs shaken from a napkin. Then a single minnow returned. And another. Gradually, the whole school was back in session, all eyes to the front. They didn't have human memory. They'd already forgotten the bomb I'd dropped on them forty seconds ago. Maybe they thought the next pebble would be an egg they could feast on. When I leaned over, they darted out from under my shadow.

I couldn't get out of the shadow of the freight train fiasco. If Taylor were more concerned, we could've figured a way out. He'd scattered like a minnow when I even mentioned Wellesley's name. I was alone in this one.

I picked my way downstream on a path of smooth stones

spilled like jelly beans in the riverbed. When I returned to shore, I spotted someone squatting on the bank in a patch of trash. His arms were wrapped around his knees and he stretched a book wide open between his fists. The handlebars of a bike poked out of the bushes like a pair of chrome antlers. I recognized the bell. It was Laddie. Like me, he had come to the river to get away from things. I sat ten yards away and watched.

The rush of the water masked whatever noise I had made. Laddie seesawed on his feet as he looked at the book. He had trouble separating the page he wanted to turn. When he caught the page, he put his whole hand behind it, folded it over and pressed it into the other side of the book until he secured it with the opposite hand. With both fists firm, he rocked again, lifting his behind up and down off the skinny white calves showing between his socks and pants cuffs. I couldn't hear him, but when he bared his buck teeth like a neighing horse I thought he must be laughing. This place was part of Laddie's world. What the citizens of Clearwater threw off the bridge in the dark of the night, Laddie rescued.

Then he carefully put the book down, still open, in the trash pile and watched to make sure it wouldn't move. He picked something out of the pile and, with one hand holding the pages flat, started writing on them.

A squirrel scampered down the dirt bank and stopped next to him. When Laddie looked up at the squirrel, he saw me and let go of the book. I didn't want him to leave. He was here first, I was the intruder. If I stood up, he might bolt like a deer. He raised his hand as if he was going to wave but it froze in midair. When he got up, his pants stuck half way up his calves, like he was ready to go wading. His eyes kept flitting from me to his book.

I moved slowly, hands at my sides with palms facing him, the way you approached a frightened animal. "It's okay, Laddie." He rubbed his hands nervously on his stomach. "I like it here too," I said, trying to draw the river closer to us with my hand.

He smiled shyly, showing his teeth. The gray hair on his head was shorn almost as short as the stubble on his face.

One side of his shirt was tucked and the other flapped outside his pants. He pushed the bike up the bank on a course marked by his own tracks. A branch of a blackberry bush had snagged in his seat springs and stuck out like a radio antenna. He mounted the bike and pedaled out of sight, never looking back to see my wave.

I walked into the middle of the debris where Laddie had sat and picked up the book he'd left. A broken green crayon lay in the seam between the pages. Except for the watermarks on the edges, it looked like the same *Bambi* I used to pull out of Grandpa Blane's glass-doored bookcase by the piano. On the open page, Laddie had crudely traced the outline of the deer in crayon.

There were more children's books in the pile, tennis shoes, a rusted pair of roller skates, and dozens of empty Campbell soup and tuna fish cans. I picked up a wooden letter opener and scraped the mud off it with the cover of the book. Someone must have used it to stir a pot of beans. On its side, the opener read, "Reno, Nevada, the Biggest Little City in the World!"

I checked my bike seat that night and the next morning for a note from Wellesley. Nothing. I called. When nobody answered, I hung up and decided to check things out.

Mr. Baker must still have been working the swing shift at the plant because the station wagon was out front again. I detoured and went down the alley. The bike was leaning against the garage. She'd moved it.

I slipped into the open door of the garage. It smelled of motor oil. A beam of light shone from the paned window to the dirt floor. As my eyes adjusted to the dark, I could see engine parts caked with black grit on the bench next to the wall. The pieces were scattered carelessly as if someone had tossed them. Through the spider-webbed window, I could see the back of the house.

A person walked by the kitchen window. Then the back door opened: it was Wellesley. She was carrying the garbage pail. I waited until she was next to the garage door. "Psst! Wellesley!"

Her head jerked up. "Will!" She stopped and looked over

her shoulder toward the house. Her right eye was ringed with a sickly yellow color I recognized as the leftovers of a black eye. The upper lip was slightly swollen.

"He got you, didn't he?"

She shrugged. "I'm okay, Will. You shouldn't be here. My dad's home."

"That bastard!" I wanted to get back at him somehow, pound those engine parts against his skull. But anything I did to him he'd double and use it against Wellesley. "I had to see you. Did you get my note?"

She smiled and shifted the pail nervously to her other hand. "Sure, thanks, Will. You're turning into a regular spy, you know." The fat lip made her flub her words.

I wanted to pull her into the garage and hug her. "It's kind of slow out here without you. I was at the river yesterday with Laddie."

She tried to laugh but looked back at the house.

"When are you going to come out?" I asked.

She blinked and gulped, a little choked up. "I don't know . . . the hearing is day after tomorrow. . . ." Suddenly, she turned, tapped her pail against the side of the garbage can to empty her load and headed for the house.

Through the dirty window, I watched her set the bucket on the back steps. She wiped her face against the sleeves of her sweatshirt and disappeared through the door.

19

On the morning of the hearing, I woke up shaky. My insides were screwed tight as a hose nozzle. I'd decided what to do after seeing Wellesley's black eye. Dad had already left to open the store. When I came upstairs, I could hear Mom's sewing machine thumping in the bedroom. "Good morning, Mom."

She jumped and the machine stopped. "You scared me, Will! Good morning. I didn't expect you up so early. Your dad didn't tell me you were working today."

I sat on the bed, so perfectly made that the ribbon border of the spread defined the edges. The vapor from one of Mom's spray bottles on the dresser made an invisible violet bouquet. "I'm not."

She waited for an explanation. None offered, she returned to feeding the big yellow and orange pansied material to the needle. The sign she'd posted at church for sewing and tailoring had brought her a lot of work. Every other time the doorbell rang, it was someone with a bolt of cloth for curtains or a sack of socks to be darned.

"Mom, I have to go to Sylvanus."

She stopped sewing again and looked at me. "What's the matter, Will?"

"There's nothing the matter. I mean, there is something . . . but it's nothing I can tell you right now."

"Are you in some kind of trouble?" She covered her mouth with her hand. "Is this something to do with . . ."

"No, Mom, it's got nothing to do with the train. It's a favor." She studied my eyes for clues. "I didn't want to lie, so I'm telling you where I'm going. But please don't ask me details."

I think she wanted to believe me. Mom was a forgiver. "How are you getting there?"

"My bike."

She studied me some more. "What time are you getting home?"

"I'm not sure . . . before Dad gets home." I'd never been to court before, but assumed it closed before the hardware.

She put her hands on my knees and looked at me. "Will, promise to be careful. Remember, you can't go as fast with that arm."

"I'll stay under the speed limit."

She finally laughed. "I mean it, Will. I worry about you."

I put my hands on top of hers. "Mom, you don't have to tell Dad about this, do you?"

She straightened up like she was disgusted I would bother to ask. "I don't see why he has to make all the decisions around here."

I wolfed down a bowl of corn flakes and banana slices, changed into school clothes and headed for the back door.

Mom intercepted me. "My, you look like you're going to church."

"You're getting warm."

She gave me a hug like I was going off to battle. "Good luck!"

The town of Clearwater sat at the foot of the mountains, far enough away that you could imagine a long time ago it just floated downriver and coasted until the terrain was flat enough that things jammed up and stuck. And around that logjam people started building roads and schools and having babies. Farther west, the land became flatter yet and drier, carpeted with acres and acres of dry-farmed crops. The road north to Sylvanus ran parallel to the mountains on four miles of road that was routine in a car. On my bike, with only one good arm, it felt like the climb to Pikes Peak.

I arrived in Sylvanus, winded, about 9:20.

The county courthouse was the only three-story building in town with a steeple, bell tower, and American flag on top. It was designed like something built during the American

Revolution, even though the plaque over the entry read "1911 A.D." Men with wrinkled brows and briefcases strode up the cathedral steps leading into the courthouse. People gathered in twos and threes next to the railing like they were waiting for someone. They looked at their watches and then up at the clock tower. They were all adults.

Just beyond the revolving door there was a directory with black letters slid into the grooves of a white plastic reader board. It was the same kind the IGA used to show the price of fresh produce. I expected things to be more permanent here. Most entries concealed the true nature of the enterprise: Assessor, Auditor, and Equalization Board. Under Licenses, they grouped "Business, Dog, and Marriage" in the same office. Courtrooms were second floor.

As I ascended the stairs, I felt my corn flakes floating upstream and catching against the trap in the back of my throat. The metal guards on the edge of each step were loose and made a tinny sound. The banister railing had been worn thin between supports like a piece of stretched brown licorice.

Scotch-taped to the oversize varnished door to Courtroom No. 2 was an official-looking piece of paper that said "State vs. Baker, 9:30 A.M." As soon as I cracked the door, I could hear voices. It had already started. The door squeaked up the scale as it opened and down the scale as it closed. The judge glanced up. I prayed that he wouldn't stop the proceedings. I tiptoed to the last row of the pews and sat stiff as a statue.

The judge looked just like I had imagined—white hair, thick horn rim glasses, draped in black. He was kind of short and had to lean forward to see what I guessed was a lawyer talking to him from in front of the podium. I thought the courtroom would be packed. There were only three people in the front row, Wellesley's mom in a birds' nest hat sat alone on one side. The pair on the other side, a police officer and the man from the fairgrounds, sat so close together I thought they must be handcuffed together.

Wellesley was next to an older woman at a table between the communion railing and the judge's bench. They faced the judge. The lawyer must have been using the table with all the papers scattered across it. The choir box with twelve chairs was empty.

The lawyer looked young, with a scrubbed face and tie. Except for his gold wire glasses, he reminded me of the high school graduation picture of Uncle Scott that Grandpa Blane kept on his buffet next to Mom's picture. But he fired his words fast and with the confidence of someone quite practiced, never looking at the yellow tablet he carried.

When the lawyer finished, the judge nodded to the woman next to Wellesley.

She rustled her papers and then stood, tugging on her jacket to cover the sleeves of her blouse. "Your Honor, Mrs. Thistle from Juvenile Services. Miss Baker and I have discussed the pros and cons of contesting the charges against her and she insists on going forward. She is ready to proceed."

The judge leaned forward to get a good look at Wellesley. He spoke to Mrs. Thistle as if Wellesley didn't know how to talk. "Does she have any witnesses?"

I flinched.

Mrs. Thistle and Wellesley whispered to each other. "No, Your Honor. But the defendant wishes to testify."

The lawyer called the first witness. "Sergeant Robert Payne!" The sergeant must have done this before, because he walked up and set his hat on the witness chair like it was home, turned to face the judge and raised his right hand. He was handsome and athletic. The sergeant explained that he was the arresting officer. The suspect was brought to the police station by the victim, Mr. Rodney Sparkman, the employee of Cirro's. He interviewed Mr. Sparkman and Miss Baker and completed the police report, which the lawyer handed to the pale woman sitting at her own small table at the base of the podium. She stamped it and wrote something. The lawyer thanked him for his testimony. Sergeant Payne pressed his hat under his arm and stepped down from the witness chair with a triumphant look.

The next witness was the carnival man. He walked tall, glancing down at Wellesley as he passed, in a crushed corduroy sport jacket and yellow tie. His neck was stiff like the tie might be cinched too tight. I thought it wasn't fair that he could change clothes. He should have testified shirtless and greasy the way he was when it happened. The shirt and tie were a lie.

Each time he answered, the carnival man wrung his hands together. He spoke so politely it made me mad. Then the lawyer asked him to describe exactly what happened. The carnival man sucked in his breath through his teeth. "Well, sir, I was minding my own business fixing the Ferris wheel, like I said. I had my hands around the innards of the machine when three kids snuck up behind me."

"What did you do, Mr. Sparkman?"

"I said hello and started making what you'd call polite conversation. I get along pretty well with kids, you know. My brother has a pack of 'em." He looked at the judge and smiled; the judge was stone. "Anyway, I was afraid they might get hurt around the machinery, so I encouraged them to run along once I was done answering their questions." Mr. Sparkman alternated glances between the lawyer and the judge, like he wasn't sure who he had to convince. He tried to sound friendly, the kind of guy who put little kids on his leg and played galloping horsey.

"What happened then, Mr. Sparkman?"

"Well, sir, that's when all heck broke loose. I turned my back for a second and next thing I knew, the girl was shooting matches at me like a flamethrower. I got pretty scared. You see, I had solvents all over the place from working on those machine parts. Any flame reaches the gasoline tank and poor Mr. Cirro could say good-bye to his truck! I'd 'a felt pretty rotten. I been working for Cirro's for more 'n five years." Mr. Sparkman bowed his head like it was painful to contemplate.

I felt cheated. Somehow, the carnival man had repainted the picture of what happened. Using all the same objects and people, he had added shadows and colors that weren't there.

"Mr. Sparkman, you said there were three kids, what happened to the others?"

I stiffened again.

"Sir, they beat it out of there and left the girl behind."

"Did you ever find out who they were?"

"No, sir, but I wished I could've caught all three of 'em."
He raised his chin and voice in a way that made him sound
like some kind of citizen hero.

When Mr. Sparkman stepped down, the judge banged his
gavel. "Recessed until ten forty-five!"

Everyone stood. The judge swooshed out the door in the
corner of the courtroom. I was caught by surprise. Sergeant
Payne and Mr. Sparkman started toward me down the center aisle. I decided I had to go to the bathroom and beat
them out the door.

The "Gentlemen" sign in the hallway was lit green like an
exit in a movie theater. I went in, ran cold water in the sink
and hoisted it to my face. Then I heard them outside the
door, ripped a towel from the dispenser, and ducked into
one of the stalls. Sergeant Payne was talking. "You almost
had me feeling sorry for you."

Mr. Sparkman chuckled. "You think I overplayed my
hand? Sounded pretty good, huh?" I heard his stream pour
into the pool in the urinal.

"I didn't remember you explaining it with such a flair
before," the Sergeant said.

"I guess I dressed it up a little bit." Quietly, I pulled down
my pants and sat on the toilet seat in case one of them
looked under the door. "She gonna serve any time for this
one, Sergeant?" Then he flushed the urinal and the water
roared.

"Afraid so," Sergeant Payne answered when the water
settled.

I felt someone slap the stall next to mine, "Goddamn!"

When they left, I flushed, waited a half minute to let them
get ahead of me and came out of my stall. Just then, the
lawyer walked in and I made myself busy washing my hands.
In the mirror, I noticed he must have had some acne when
he was younger. His eyes were dark brown and piercing,
someone determined to get wherever he was going.

"What brings you to the courthouse?" he said.

Since I was the only one in the bathroom, he must have
been talking to me. "Uh, I'm just observing," I said, and
then thought of something intelligent I'd heard Grandpa
Blane say. "Seeing how our taxes are being spent."

The lawyer looked at me sidewise from the urinal and laughed. "You're a cautious man. 'Never test the depth of a river with both feet.' "

"What?"

"It's a proverb. It means look before you leap."

I toweled off my hands for the third time and wondered if I should go ahead with my plan.

When I returned to my spot in the back of the courtroom, Wellesley was standing at her table. I'd never seen her in a dress. It was a satiny dark purple with white sailor flaps in front and back of the neck. She seemed nervous, like Beller's wire terrier the time we dressed her in human clothes. When Wellesley sat, she turned and looked straight at me. I thought she winked. She knew she wasn't alone.

We rose to attention when Judge Lally slammed the door to announce his reentry.

The lawyer reached his table just as the judge settled into his chair. "The county rests its case, Your Honor."

Judge Lally peered down at Wellesley's table. "Your turn, Mrs. Thistle."

Mrs. Baker dabbed at her eyes as Wellesley walked straight for the witness chair and sat down. The judge asked her to stand and be sworn. I was five times more anxious about what Wellesley was going to say than I was about the county witnesses. I didn't know whether she was going to be sorry or mad.

The judge swiveled in his high-backed chair to face her. "If you had counsel, Miss Baker, I would let him ask you the questions. Instead, I'll be doing it. When I'm finished, the county's attorney, Mr. Feinberg, may have a few. Understand, the purpose of my questions is not to trick you but to give you the opportunity to tell your side of the story." He gave her a practiced smile. Wellesley's lip had shrunk to normal size and, from the back of the courtroom, I couldn't see the ring around her eye.

"I've read your file," the judge said, "but I'd like to ask you to tell me about your family." Without knowing it, he had clawed an open sore.

She hesitated. "I don't see how this affects my case, sir." Wellesley wasn't taking the sorry path.

The judge dug in. "Young lady, I'm here to help you. Please."

Wellesley straightened up. "My mother is here with me. She's a housewife. My dad works at the rendering plant. I have an older sister, Tiffany. She just finished high school but she's not living at home anymore." Wellesley rushed to get her answers out, volunteering nothing but the bare facts.

"Do you have any trouble at home?" I wondered how much the judge knew from the report he'd mentioned. Wellesley didn't want this. I guessed she'd rather have pled guilty than talk about what happened in that house. She squirmed in the oversized witness chair, rubbing her shoe against the cross brace and looking down. "Miss Baker, did you understand my question?"

"Yes, Your Honor." With one finger, she pushed her glasses straight. "We have some arguments. My dad is pretty strict. Is that what you mean?"

The judge waited to see if she would elaborate. Wellesley wasn't going to let him in. "How do you do in school?"

Wellesley shook her head, like she was frustrated with all these preliminaries. "I guess I do pretty well, mostly A's and B's. I'm not the teacher's pet, if that's what you're wondering."

The judge smiled. Finally, he got to the meat and potatoes. "Now tell me, in as much detail as you can recall, exactly what happened when you arrived at the Ferris wheel."

Wellesley sat up in the chair and looked at Mr. Sparkman. "That man was stooped over fixing something. I didn't sneak up on him. We just had a conversation. He started acting like a . . . like he owned the place." Mr. Sparkman whispered to the sergeant as Wellesley spoke. "He started swearing at us and told us to get out of there. Then I shot a match at him."

"Excuse me," the judge said, "how did you shoot a match at him?"

"You mean, what kind of gun did I have? Well, it's made out of a wooden clothespin. You turn it inside out so you can cock it. When you pull the trigger, it scrapes the tip of the match and lights it, they're wooden matches, and flicks it toward the target." For the first time, Wellesley seemed to relax. Her description of the rat gun seemed encyclopedic in comparison to what she was willing to say about her dad.

The judge seemed fascinated with her explanation. Taylor would have been proud of the attention his contraption was getting. "Why did you shoot at him?"

Wellesley rested her hands on the enormous flat arms of the witness chair. The arms were so high they made her shoulders hunch up. "It didn't hit him, sir. I don't think it even came close. I guess I was just mad. I felt like throwing something. All I had was the match gun." She looked at the judge to see his reaction. He chewed the inside of his cheek and studied her. I wanted her to say more—what the guy felt like, how he dragged her into the truck, that it wasn't her idea, something to draw the judge to her side.

"Who were the two kids with you?"

My heart bounced off my insides! The courtroom started to float. Wellesley's eyes moved from the suspended light globes to her lap. I expected her to look at me. "Sir, I don't think it's fair to get them involved," she said.

Feeling like I'd just turned upright from balancing on my head, I stood. Like a ventriloquist, I threw my voice into the light-headed dummy standing in my shoes. "Your Honor, I was one of those kids."

Everyone turned to look. There was no getting out of it now. The judge seemed perturbed at my interruption. "You! Come to the front!"

I used the back of the bench for support. The center aisle stretched like a blurry highway from me to the judge. When I reached the front railing, I held on to steady myself. An airplane propeller was spinning in my stomach. The county's attorney seemed amused. I was testing the depth of his river with both feet.

"What's your name, young man?"

"Will Bradford, Your Honor. I was there." I heard the voices of the sergeant and the carnival man whispering behind me.

"Do you want to testify?"

Sitting in the back row, I'd thought of all my points. The closer I came to the judge, the more everything scrambled in my brain. "Yes, Your Honor, I do."

The judge asked Wellesley to return to her seat and waved me through the gate. I stood in front of the judge's throne with my hand raised. It was like I'd been watching the show at the Orpheum and suddenly I was in it. My heart beat like a tom-tom. He skipped any questions about my family or school. "Mr. Bradford, tell the court what you think happened."

I tried to spear the ideas in my head. Wellesley looked distant, like I was seeing her backwards through a telescope. "First, Your Honor, I was there as sure as she was and if she did something wrong, so did I." Just saying it out loud relaxed me. The spinning slowed. "There are some things everyone else left out. I've replayed what happened at the fairgrounds that day a thousand times. One thing I'm certain of. Mr. Sparkman was waving a big wrench in his hand and, before anyone flipped any matches at him, he was charging like he was going to smash us."

"That's a lie!" The carnival man thrust his fist at me.

The judge hammered his gavel. "Order! Please." He scowled Mr. Sparkman back into his seat. "Continue, Mr. Bradford."

"About the trespassing. It's true we came through the gate and it was chained. But Your Honor, anyone who lives in this county knows the caretaker doesn't care if kids come in there. I've squeezed through the gate before to help Mr. Brisco. He's even paid me to do it. Some days, it's wide open and some days it's closed but we all know it's okay to come in as long as you don't wreck anything." Everybody was in focus now. Mr. Feinberg tapped his pen on his tablet. Wellesley smiled. The juvenile lady's face started to defrost.

"Do you have anything more to say, Mr. Bradford?"

"One more thing, Your Honor. Mr. Sparkman made it sound like he was real worried about his boss's truck. The matches were miles away from the truck . . . well, twenty yards anyway. Those clothespin things won't shoot as far as that railing."

"Thank you, Mr. Bradford. Mr. Feinberg, any questions?"

I'd forgotten about him. He'd be mad that I'd evaded his question in the bathroom. Now he had me under oath.

"Yes, Your Honor, I do." He stood slowly and walked over in front of me. "Mr. Bradford, is Wellesley Baker a friend of yours?"

"Sure."

"And Mr. Sparkman is the enemy?"

"Well, not exactly . . ."

"And you think Mr. Sparkman intended to hurt you that day. Isn't it likely he was just trying to protect his company's equipment?"

Mr. Feinberg's question took me straight back to Maude's. I looked at the judge, needing someone to tell me if this was fair to bring up. "There's something I'm not sure how to explain, sir, because it didn't happen at the fairgrounds. But I don't think he was trying to protect the equipment because"—I looked over at Mr. Sparkman— "because I think he's been stealing from Cirro's Road Shows."

Mr. Sparkman leaped to the railing. "He's lying!"

The judge pounded his gavel. "Mr. Sparkman, sit down or I'll hold you in contempt. Do you understand?"

Sergeant Payne tugged on the bottom of Mr. Sparkman's sport coat. He'd end up in handcuffs yet. I was starting to feel a lot safer next to the judge. He let about fifteen seconds pass before asking Mr. Feinberg to proceed.

"Mr. Bradford, that's a very serious accusation," Mr. Feinberg said. "Can you please explain."

"Well, sir, it was just a coincidence. But about a month ago, I was in Maude's Diner in Union Gap. Wellesley was there too. We were sitting in a booth having milkshakes . . . next to Mr. Sparkman and a lady friend of his. They were talking real loud and drinking beer. The woman said her husband didn't steal from his employer the way Mr. Sparkman does. Mr. Sparkman got real mad and grabbed her arm. He told her to 'keep her pretty little nose out of his business.'" I purposely cleaned up his language out of respect for the fact that we were in a courtroom.

Mr. Feinberg gave a dirty look to Mr. Sparkman who was leaning forward like a bulldog on Sergeant Payne's leash.

Wellesley grinned and covered herself to hide it from the judge.

"No more questions, Your Honor."

The judge excused me and I walked back to my seat. I felt the same excitement rising in me as the morning the freight train pulled out of Clearwater and we turned our faces to the wind. Maybe the Union Gap trip had been worth it after all.

Judge Lally asked for closing comments. Mr. Feinberg spoke carefully, summarizing the story in a way that sounded bad for Wellesley. He reminded the judge that it was Wellesley not Mr. Sparkman who was on trial.

Mrs. Thistle's remarks were sincere but lacking the hammer quality of Mr. Feinberg's. When she finished, the judge asked Wellesley to stand.

"Miss Baker, although you are only fourteen, this county and the state hold you responsible for your actions. I take juvenile offenses very seriously." The judge spoke in a solemn tone, letting each sentence sink in. Wellesley's worst fears on the floor of the coal bin were coming true. "I've listened very carefully to everything that was said this morning. I'm impressed with your willingness to take full blame for this incident. On the charge of trespass, I'm going to find you innocent. Mr. Bradford's testimony regarding the practices at the fairgrounds exonerates you. However, your decision to fire a lighted match at Mr. Sparkman is another matter. I believe your conduct carried the threat of harm and I find you guilty on the assault charge." The bottom of my stomach fell open. She was going to get it. "But since it's your first offense, I'm going to suspend the sentence and put you on probation for six months. If you stay out of trouble, the charge will be expunged from your record." Judge Lally slapped his gavel down, turned, and glided out of the courtroom.

It was like the movie had ended and the theater lights came on. Everyone started talking. Mrs. Thistle shook Wellesley's hand. The lawyer stuffed papers into his briefcase. Mr. Sparkman's head bobbed up and down as he talked at Sergeant Payne. Wellesley looked at me across the courtroom and clasped her hands over her head like a prize fighter. She looked prettier than I'd ever seen her. Mrs. Baker pushed through the swinging gate and hugged Wellesley so hard her hat fell off.

Sergeant Payne escorted Mr. Sparkman down the aisle. The carnival man and I locked on each other's eyes until he went out the door. I resisted the urge to shudder.

When Wellesley and her mom started to leave, I did too and waited in the hallway. It seemed homier than before the hearing. The ceiling wasn't as high. The wood paneling on the walls wasn't so polished. The seats along each side of the hall looked like park benches where people could read the newspaper.

Wellesley came out surrounded by Mrs. Thistle, her mom, and Mr. Feinberg. She walked toward me, with her lopsided smile fully cocked. I moved my cast away from my stomach, to make room for a hug. As a reflex, my eyes closed, expecting to feel her sailor dress against me. Instead, she just shook me by the arms. "You creamed 'em, Will!"

I blushed. The stares of the three adults discouraged me from crushing her into my chest.

Mrs. Baker nodded politely. "Thank you, Will."

"Wellesley," Mr. Feinberg said, "I want to apologize for something. As you know, I work for the prosecuting attorney and it's my job to try whatever's on the calendar. I'd never met Mr. Sparkman until this morning. All I knew about him was what it said in the police report. We should have done our homework. If I'd known what your friend explained on the stand, we'd have probably dropped the case. He wasn't a witness you'd like to stake your career on." Everyone laughed politely. "I'm glad the judge split the charges and gave you probation. I owe you one." He put out his hand, Wellesley slowly drew hers up, and they shook.

"Put this whole thing behind you," he said. "I'd just as soon never see you down here again." He winked at me. "Nor you. And don't report this one to the taxpayers."

"Are you going to bring any charges against Mr. Sparkman for snitching the tools?" Wellesley asked.

Mr. Feinberg switched his briefcase to the other hand. "You don't let up, do you? I doubt we can get him on the basis of one cafe conversation, but maybe we'll have a word with Mr. Cirro." He'd seen the same thing everyone else had. When I said steal, Mr. Sparkman had jumped like a drill hit a nerve in his tooth. "Unfortunately, I won't have the pleasure of prosecuting him even if we have a case. I finish three years with the prosecutor at the end of this month, then I'm giving a try to private practice."

At the top of the stairs, Mr. Feinberg said good-bye. I wished we'd talked more. In person, he'd shown a kindness I wouldn't have expected in someone who just tried to put Wellesley in the detention center. Mrs. Thistle took Wellesley's mom into an office on the first floor to sign papers.

Wellesley guided me to the other side of the corridor. "Will, last night I was so scared I'd go to jail that I actually prayed. Somebody must have heard me and sent you."

"Yeah, but you didn't get off entirely."

"Mrs. Thistle told me probation just means I have to report once a month to somebody in Juvenile Services, maybe her. After thinking of jail bars for the last two months, that sounds fine."

"Then it's fine for me too."

"You singed 'em, Bradford! But I never expected to see you here this morning."

"Wellesley, I had to. If I'd sat this one out . . ."

"I owe you something."

"No! You don't owe me anything."

"I know you'll never need a rescue from this kind of jam. But, promise, I won't foul up again." Her eyes opened wide, inviting me in.

I shook my head. "Wellesley, you're going to be something grand."

She laughed. "You mean grand larceny!"

Mrs. Thistle stepped out of the office. "Wellesley, can you come here for a minute?"

"Okay," I said, "I've got to get home."

She grabbed me and hugged. I wasn't ready for it. My cast caught between us like a fence rail. My free hand pressed between her shoulder blades. She felt firm. Mrs. Thistle backed into her office. It was over in a second.

"Good-bye, Will!"

"See you back in town."

"Summer starts over today, okay?"

"Okay!"

Wellesley winked, twirled and disappeared into the room that said "Court Administration" over the door. I imagined waltzing down the hall with her. The lightness I'd felt when I first stood up in the courtroom had returned, but this time it made me giddy instead of faint. I couldn't wait to tell Taylor. He should have been there to see it. And Dad. Maybe I had inherited some of Dad's ability to wade in and start swinging. He would have been proud. No lies.

But the most important person never showed. Wellesley's dad. Working swing shift, he had no excuse. I wondered whose side he would have been on anyway.

On the sidewalk in front of the courthouse, a kid with a cowlick was selling cherry Kool Aid out of his wagon. I remembered when I did this and Mom and her friends bought from me. Six different-sized glasses rested on the dish towel in the wagon bed. The pitcher was full. The wobbly letters on the sign taped to the empty MJB coffee can said: "5 Cents Glass."

The kid wiggled like a puppy when I ordered a glass. There was no ice. The only thing I had in my pocket was a quarter; it was hardly going to make a dent in my bill with the railroad. I told him to keep the change.

I felt like Robin Hood.

20

Mom was napping on the couch when I got home. I crept closer to see if she was sleeping.

"You're back." She shaded her eyes with her hand.

"Yeah, hi Mom. Hey, what gives? You never take naps."

Mom crinkled her face, fighting against the puddles in her eyes. "Grandpa . . ." She sat up and sponged her cheeks with a wad of Kleenex. "Your Grandpa Blane . . . fell." I sat down, knowing she was going to tell me he was dead. "He broke his hip . . . we think he fell off the back porch." Mom concentrated on the rug, like she would cry again if she looked at me. "Thank goodness, someone found him and called the ambulance." She pressed her hand against her throat. "We don't know how long he lay there."

"How is he now?"

"He's at Mary of the Angels. We think he's doing fine." She patted my leg like she used to do after washing dirt from a cut or pulling a sliver. "Your dad and I just got back from the hospital. Daddy's still pretty woozy. They put him under sedation."

"He's going to be all right, isn't he?"

She watered up again. "Oh, Will . . . this kind of injury is serious for someone your grandpa's age." Mom's voice strained as if her words were forming in the roof of her mouth. I'd seen her cry after a show or at birthday parties, but never like this.

I put my arm around her and she leaned her head against me. "He's a pretty tough guy, Mom. He won't let this thing whip him."

The win at the courthouse seemed pretty small now. Bad news always seemed to push aside good news. Mom had enough to worry about without me telling her about the fairgrounds thing. The prospect of losing Grandpa Blane scared me. His playfulness had always given me hope that grown-up life didn't have to be so dull.

Dad came home at five o'clock to take Mom to the hospital. I begged to go along. Dad didn't think Grandpa was ready for visitors yet. I raised my voice. "Dad, I'm not just a visitor! I'm family."

Dad looked surprised. He licked his lips. "We don't want to wear him out. Let's wait till he gets some strength back."

"If I were in the hospital, I'd want Grandpa to see me. No matter how tired I was."

"Let him come, dear," Mom said, "it might do Daddy some good."

Dad shrugged, he knew he couldn't beat Mom. It was her dad who was in the hospital. "Okay," he said, "but don't get him excited."

I sat in the back of the car with my chin perched on the front seat, asking questions on the way to the hospital. Mom was in a mood to talk about Grandpa and I wanted to find out everything I could. Getting by Dad felt like I was in on something. He didn't say much. I recognized it as a Bradford pout.

"Your grandpa's been acting funny lately," Mom said. "Maybe it had something to do with causing the fall. Two weeks ago, Melba Scruggs called to say she'd seen Daddy urinating on a tree in front of her house." Mom shook her head like she didn't believe it. "Then, last Friday, we got a call from Captain Alexander at the Fire Department. He said they responded to a call in Milltown. When they got there, a little old man in a fishing hat was warming himself on a small bonfire at the curb. It was Daddy."

"What was he doing?" I asked.

Mom chuckled. "He said he was burning litter, must have thought he was in his own front yard." Dad hiccuped and braced his arms against the steering wheel. Mom checked him with a glance and went on. "Last winter, Aunt Ruth smelled smoke coming from the basement. When she peeked downstairs, your grandpa was feeding newspapers into a fire in the garbage can. Aunt Ruth had the sense to smother it with the garbage can lid." She shook her head. "He said he was just tidying things up."

I draped my arms over the front seat and fiddled with the clasp to Mom's purse, two gold prongs with a knob on each end. My knees had worked to the floorboards, with my toes hooked on the backseat. The slouch position felt familiar; I'd practiced it plenty between the pews in church. "I've never heard any of these stories."

"These aren't things we want to advertise, Will," Mom said. I knew what she meant. People would treat him like Laddie.

Dad tapped his thumbs against the steering wheel, waiting for the car with its left signal blinking to turn into the Phillips 66 station. He'd transferred his impatience with me to the driver in front of us. That load lifted, he finally spoke. "We took his matches away. If he wants a cigar, he has to ask Aunt Ruth for a light. One match at a time."

I thought how humiliated Grandpa Blane must be to have to ask his younger sister for a match. Cigars were a badge of his independence. It's what he did to feel rich. Knowing Grandpa, he'd already figured out a place to squirrel away his own supply. It was odd. Both of us had gotten in trouble for playing with matches this summer.

We parked in the visitors' lot behind the hospital and crossed the yellow striped horseshoe drive labeled AMBU-LANCE. The hospital was three stories of sandy brick. The windows on the first floor had bars on them. Somewhere in there, I knew they had a ward for crazy people. It's where they brought Bill Devine's uncle when he showed his dong to the people coming out of Mass. The following Sunday, Father Dominic excused it by saying he'd been possessed by the anti-Christ. I knew better than that; Taylor had done the same thing at the swimming hole once to clear people off the rock.

Conversations in the hospital lobby seemed to slide across the freshly waxed linoleum. From the center of the room, I could plainly hear the high-pitched complaint of an elderly woman on a cane arguing with a nurse by the newspaper stand on one side of the room and, from the other side, a young couple goo-gooing into the blanket their baby was wrapped in.

The counter at the information desk was decked in marigolds planted in green, gold, and red foiled pots with price stickers. The cardboard sign printed in biblical letters said the proceeds went to St. Paul's Altar Society.

I'd never been at the desk on official business. Taylor and I often stopped here when he needed to borrow money from his mom. Her shift at the desk must have been over because a nurse with thick arms and a gruff voice handed Dad the sign-in book. He asked why he had to sign. While they stared each other down, I thought we'd be left standing there. It was just as well that Taylor's mom wasn't on duty.

The elevator stopped on the second floor and we stepped back to make room for a bed on wheels. A tube ran from a hanging bottle into the nose of a patient that I thought was an Indian. The sheets were pulled up to the chin and glossy, straight black hair spilled across one side of the pillow. I couldn't tell whether it was a man or woman.

Dad nudged me off at the third floor. It smelled like they had mopped the floors with Merthiolate. I stole a peek into every open door we passed. People lay on their backs in tilt-up beds. Some rooms had visitors huddled around the bed; others just had radios playing.

There was a shriveled man asleep in the first bed in Grandpa's room. A shower curtain separated the two of them.

Taylor's mom was sitting at Grandpa's bedside. "Hello," she said. "Mr. Blane's been asking about you. He's looking pretty chipper, don't you think?" She held Grandpa's hand, like she was family. "My shift's over so I just stopped by to say hello."

Grandpa looked terrible. He lay motionless against the pillow. His face was pale, with beads of sweat on his forehead, his hair thin and disorderly. Without glasses, his eyes wandered.

Mom took Grandpa's hand from Mrs. Clark as if it was detached. "Daddy, let me put your glasses on so you can see us. Can you hear me okay?"

"Where's Olive?" he asked. His voice was sad, like he was lost.

Mom bit her lip. "She's not here, Daddy." I'd never heard Grandpa say Grandma's name out loud.

"Olive will take me home," he mumbled. "We have to go to the store." Mom just petted his hand. "Somebody's got to mow the lawn. The grass is too wet." As he spoke, he brushed the sheet with his free hand like he was looking for the car keys. His face skin sagged like melting wax.

"He's still feeling the effects of his painkillers," Mrs. Clark said.

"Don't leave me here," he said. "I want to go home."

"Daddy," Mom said loudly, "Will's here to see you!"

His eyes flitted around the room.

Mom motioned me next to her. I was nervous. I didn't want to make him more confused. "Hi, Grandpa," I said, trying to sound cheerful like Mrs. Clark had. "When are we going golfing?"

He smiled faintly. "That's quite a game. I've never been much good at it myself."

"Maybe you'll get a hole in one next time out!" I spoke loud enough to wake the man behind the curtain.

Grandpa laughed gently, keeping the back of his head pressed against the pillow and looking toward the ceiling. "Say, do you remember that time on number eight? Pretty darn lucky." He was getting his bearings. The deepest grooves in Grandpa's head were the ones made with his golf swing.

"You better get well pretty quick, Grandpa," I said, "before they move the pins to the temporaries." He hated the temporary greens. You might as well just add a stroke a hole to your score before you stepped on the course he said. The ball jumped like a bedbug when you putted it on that crabgrass.

I rotated back to the end of the bed, trading places with Dad. Mrs. Clark whispered to me, "He understood you."

Dad was the only person Grandpa was really afraid of. Dad sometimes bawled him out in front of us. Mom always made Dad talk to Grandpa about business matters and getting along with his sister, Ruth. I imagined they'd had a few man-to-man talks about some of the things Mom told me in the car.

I turned over the clipboard hanging on the footboard so I could read it. Patient: "Harrison B. Blane." Mom told me he detested Harry. His nickname Barney was more friendly. The chart showed his age—69, weight—140, and height—5'5". In the space after employment, it said "Social Security." Grandpa always complained because he made more money on Social Security than he did when he sorted mail on the train to Butte. That was one of the things wrong with this country he said. Near the bottom of the form, it said: "Patient found on cement patio by passerby. Apparently injured in porch fall—4 steps. County ambulance delivered." In large cursive, black ink instead of blue, it said: "X rays—positive, hip fracture."

Dad pulled back the sheet to look at Grandpa's hip. I thought he would have a monstrous cast. Instead, his spindly legs, white as the inside of a coconut, stuck out from under the hospital gown.

The bells chimed and a soft voice came over the intercom. "May I have your attention, please. Visiting hours are now over. Our visiting hours are now over. Thank you!" We all looked at Mom knowing how hard it would be for her to leave. She kissed Grandpa on the forehead and stroked his hair back. Then she tucked him in, straightening the sheet across his chest and under his arms. I shook his hand. Dad patted him on the shoulder in 'atta boy fashion.

From the doorway, I took a last look at Grandpa. His complexion was almost as pale as the white sheets and walls. The whole scene looked bleached. I still controlled my breath, taking in as little as possible to avoid the germs I imagined floating in the air.

In the hallway, we had to dodge the food cart rattling with dirty glasses, cups, and unfinished plates of mashed potatoes, brown gravy, mixed vegetables, and jello. Mom stopped to talk to a woman whose green badge said "LEONA—Registered Nurse." While they talked, I read the announcements in the Staff Bulletin on the corkboard. Blood donations needed. Chief of medical staff speaks on wisdom of wonder drugs. Sylvanus County Labor Day Festival. Dad's Committee was doing its job. Nurse Leona told Mom that Grandpa was still running a fever. They were giving him something to kill the pain; she called it a wonder drug.

Mom asked whether the bone would heal straight. The nurse said he would have a limp no matter what. "He's a tough old buzzard, but his dancing days are over."

As we started out the double doors, Dr. Robinson came in. "Well, well, I'll bet you're here to see Barney." He slapped Dad on the back and laughed. "He's doing all right for a seventy year old who swan dived to his patio, huh?" The rest of us were silent. I wondered if medical and nursing schools had courses in sick humor.

Dr. Robinson ran his fleshy hand through my hair. "Will, don't we have an appointment tomorrow to get that plaster off your arm?" He looked at his watch. "If you folks have ten minutes, I can break it off right now." He herded me across the lobby. That was another thing I didn't like about doctors; they didn't treat kids with any respect.

In the emergency room, he pulled the curtain around a narrow bed and told me to hop up. With a pair of scissors as heavy as cable cutters, he cut a slice from one end of the cast to the other and pried it open like the jaws of a great white shark. I was afraid to move my arm. It felt cool. The skin was pruny the way it gets when you leave a bandage on your finger too long.

Dr. Robinson manipulated my new arm—over the head, behind the back, across the chest, straight out, straight down. "Does it hurt? How's that? What about this? Huh?"

The only thing that hurt was thinking of Grandpa, three floors up. I visualized him staring at the ceiling wondering when his wife would come by to take him shopping.

On the way home, Mom and Dad spoke in collapsed tones. Their faces were drained of the false cheer I'd seen at Grandpa's bedside. Dr. Robinson had told them something they weren't telling me. Grandpa's condition was another family secret.

21

For the first time since the Junior Rodeo, I slept on my left side. When I woke up, I flopped on my back, stuck my arm in the air and squeezed every inch of it to test for feeling. My bicep was as soft as a soaker hose. When I held the two arms next to each other, they were chocolate and vanilla.

I slid to the floor to do push-ups, still favoring the right arm. Maybe Dr. Robinson had taken the cast off too soon. He seemed so casual about it. I should have waited until the appointment. After ten push-ups, I checked again. The muscles were still flabby.

Dad wasted no time in putting me to the test. His note on the kitchen table listed work needed at the hardware:

UNLOAD PAINT AND FERTILIZER IN VAN
STOCK SHELVES
REMOVE TILE IN LAWNMOWER SHOP

Taylor would have to wait to hear about Wellesley's trial.

By 8:30, I had finished my cereal and toast, biked to the hardware, and swung open the back doors of the van. Dad's suppliers hadn't cut him off yet. J. P. Lilly fertilizer bags were piled against the wire mesh divider behind the driver's seat. Boxes of Fuller paint, four high, filled the rest of the floor. The load made the truck look raked, like a hot rod.

With my right arm, I pulled one box at a time to the end of the van, braced it against my stomach, carried it down the alley, through the back door of the store, and stacked it in the paint aisle. I separated exterior from interior, quarts from gallons, to avoid moving them a second time when I shelved.

Working solo, I had lots of time to think. Scenes alternated in my head. Judge Lally pounded his gavel. The carnival man poked his fist at me. Wellesley opened her arms. Mom covered her tears. Grandpa's lips trembled. It was like I was allowed a fixed number of wins. If Wellesley was saved, then someone else was lost. I was sure it would be Grandpa Blane.

Uncle Carl stopped to watch me balance a box against the doorframe while I turned the knob and pushed the door open with my hip. "This'll fix that arm of yours!" His cigarette waggled from the corner of his mouth as he spoke. "Why don't you carry two at a time?" His laugh made him cough and he pounded his palm against his chest.

I stood in the doorway, waiting for Carl to stop hacking. "I forgot to tell you, Carl. I'm doing the paint. Dad wants you to unload the fertilizer." He smiled then started coughing again.

I stacked the fifty-pound bags of ammonium sulfate on two pallets in front of the store. Dad said he would move the van closer but by the time he broke free, I only had two bags to go.

Stocking the shelves was easy. I had to make sure the new paint was stamped with a price on the lid and put it behind the old cans. Dad must have thought everyone was going to paint their houses Frost White because I unpacked six boxes of it. I had to move the Emerald Green and Canary Yellow to another shelf to make room. I chuckled out loud when I opened the Pink Flamingo, trying to imagine anyone in Clearwater ever using it.

While I faced each can, making the shelves look full, I overheard Dad and Uncle Harold talking by the paint shaker. Dad said the paychecks would be delayed a week. Harold mumbled something and Dad gave him money from his wallet.

With a hammer and putty knife, I pried the tile off the floor. Each piece was a surprise. Some of them came off in two or three chunks. The glue was so strong on others I had to chip them off like dandruff flakes. Cousin Joe kidded me about making so much noise. He said he couldn't hear the grinder against the lawnmower blades. Neither one of us knew why Dad suddenly wanted the old tile removed. The cement underneath didn't look any better. I figured Dad was thinking up ways to help me with the railroad bill. But how was he going to pay me if he couldn't give Uncle Harold a paycheck?

My arm throbbed by the time I biked home. I showered and fixed a bologna and Velveeta sandwich. When the phone rang, I was chewing on a giant bite. "Hello," I said through the sandwich, wiping the mayonnaise and mustard from the edges of my mouth.

There was giggling at the other end of the line. "Is this Will?"

I swallowed the sandwich in my mouth whole and it rolled down my throat like a golf ball. "Yes, it is," I said, when I could breathe again.

"Do you know who this is?" More giggling.

"Uh, I think so." I could never forget the voice that went with those lips. "Is this Marilyn Tubbs?"

"Good for you . . . don't!" Someone was trying to cut us off. "Shh, get away . . . *click* . . . *click* . . . are you still there Will?"

"Yeah, what's going on?" I blushed.

"I'm calling on someone else's behalf," Marilyn said. "It was a dare . . . no!" There was more scuffling. "You don't know why I'm calling, do you?"

"Huh, no. . . ." My laugh rattled like a grapefruit seed in a pencil box. "Something about . . . uh . . . school?"

"I have to ask you something, Will."

"Sure."

"Are you going to the Labor Day Festival?"

I knew this wasn't the question. Everyone went. "Yeah . . . sure, my Dad's chairman of the committee." Why did I say that? It sounded like I was going because he made me.

"I meant are you going to the dance?"

I didn't know. "Sure . . . uh, are you?" I did my nervous laugh again.

"Are you going with someone?"

I was starting to figure this out. Marilyn wanted a return bout. "Maybe . . . uh, I'm not sure yet."

"How would you like to go with someone really special?" A voice in the background said, "Stop it, Marilyn!"

I visualized Marilyn's pudgy smile parting to show her steel braces. "Do I know this person . . . ?"

She cut me off, like she had to talk quickly or lose the phone. "Will you go with Monica Amberly?"

"Monica?" I was afraid my voice would break. What happened to Taylor? Was this a joke? "Really?"

"Cross my heart. She was afraid to ask you. Well, yes or no?" Her voice was sincere. The giggling had stopped.

I stuttered, trying to settle the golf ball bouncing in my stomach. "Oh, I see . . . I'm . . . sure, I'll go!"

Marilyn said something else but all I heard was, "It's a date!"

When we hung up, I jumped and touched the ceiling with the fingertips of both hands. I finished my sandwich and headed for Taylor's still trying to sort it out. What made Monica call me? When I saw her at the Rexall two days ago, I thought she ducked into the soap section to avoid me. Taylor would flip his lid.

No one answered when I knocked on Taylor's door. I went around back and found him in a rare position—bent over a shovel in the garden.

He saw me immediately. "Hey, Will, no cast!" He stabbed the shovel into the ground with both hands. "All right."

"Came off yesterday," I said. "Looks sick, doesn't it?"

"Like you been soaking it in Purex!" Taylor grabbed my arm and shook it, wagging my hand. "Are you sure everything's still connected?"

"Hey, don't break it!" I pulled free. "Taylor, I've got some news."

"Hey, so do I!" His face went electric. "Guess who called me?" He stooped to a half crouch and slapped his thighs to keep from laughing. "Big Lips Tubbs!"

Maybe I had been fooled after all. "When did she call?"

"About five minutes ago."

"What did she want?"

"She wanted me to go to the dance with her!" He could barely keep the lid on his laughter.

"Really? What did you say?" Maybe this would work out better than I thought.

"Are you kidding? I said no! I didn't have the heart to tell her I'm asking Monica."

I'd rarely beaten Taylor at anything, never when it came to girls. I wasn't trained at disappointing him. "Taylor, that's one of the things I wanted to tell you." He was still smiling, but I had his attention. "Marilyn called me too!" I might as well fire my shot. "She asked me to go to the dance with Monica."

Taylor looked sick. "What?"

I took one more look at the ditch Taylor was digging between the tomato vines. "I told her yes!"

Taylor stomped his foot. *"Crap! Crap,* Bradford!" His face was between crying and slugging. "She's mine. How could you stab me in the back like that?"

"Taylor! She called me! Don't you see? They made a deal. You got Marilyn and I got Monica!"

Taylor folded like a clothes drying rack onto the grass. "But you could have said no! I said no to your girl. Where's your loyalty?"

Taylor's question hit me like the back of his hand. "Taylor, that's not fair!" He was flat on his stomach and I screamed at his backside. "I didn't see you at Wellesley's trial!" Except for his toes working back and forth in the grass, he didn't move. "I'm sorry about Monica. I thought about you, but I couldn't say no." He didn't react. "Taylor. Taylor, say something."

He rolled over and squinted into the sun. "I feel like all of a sudden, everyone's pissing on me."

I sat down next to him. "Look, I've got it figured this way. Monica is nuts for you. She's just trying to make you jealous!" This came from my head out of a deep-seated belief that I wasn't meant to ever have a girlfriend. But my heart desperately hoped I was lying.

Taylor burped a small laugh. "You're crazy too, Bradford. What do you think I did wrong?"

I slapped his shoulder. "This is my second date. You think I know?"

Then Taylor asked me about the trial. I told him the

whole story, how Sparkman said we attacked him, how fascinated Judge Lally was with the match guns, how pissed Sparkman was when I told what he had said at Maude's. We had a common enemy again, the carnival man. The old Taylor loved it.

When I finished, he shook my hand. "Nice job, Willy!" His blue eyes blinked back some wetness. I couldn't tell if it was leftovers from the laughing or regret at not being there with us. I felt almost like telling him I wouldn't go with Monica.

"Hey, I gotta go home," I said.

When I turned, he caught my arm. "Sorry about your grandpa. Mom told me about his hip."

I cuffed him lightly. "Thanks, Taylor." Anybody that cared about Grandpa was instantly forgiven.

At home, I found Mom's note to call Dad at Beller's. He was at a Fair Committee meeting. Dad told me Mom was with Grandpa. There was something inevitable in his voice. He volunteered none of the usual Pablum about everything being fine. I hoped it was just worry over the hardware. We were on our own for dinner.

Dad swung by to pick me up on the way to the hospital. He'd sold the Buick, so we drove the orange and blue delivery van with "Western Hardware" in large block print on each side. I sat on the metal engine hood next to the driver's seat and leaned against the inside of the windshield. Like a rearview mirror, I could only watch the places we'd passed —Superior Tire and Wheel, Padgett's Body Shop, Lincoln Savings, Peckenpaugh Portraits. These were Grandpa's places.

I remembered when Mom organized a family portrait at Peckenpaugh's. The photographer kept turning Grandpa's head so his hearing aid wouldn't show. He finally gave up. In the photo on Mom's dresser with three generations of Blanes, almost everyone stood taller than Grandpa and you could clearly see the wire leading from under his collar into the plastic plug in his right ear.

We stopped at the Arctic Cafe. I had a grilled cheese sandwich with potato chips and a chocolate milkshake. It was less than Dad's buck fifty limit. His cheeseburger, fries, green salad, and coffee ran forty cents over.

Dad bent a fry with a fork and dragged it through a puddle of catsup on his plate. "He's getting worse, Will."

I relaxed my mouth grip on the straw. "He isn't going to make it, is he?"

"I don't know, Will." Dad trapped two fries and swished them in a quick circle on his plate.

In the car, Dad talked about work he needed at the store. I just listened and said, "Sure."

When we arrived at the hospital, Grandpa was sleeping with a mask over his mouth. The elastic strap pushed the top of his ears away from his head. I stood next to him and watched his chest rise and fall under the gown. I'd never seen a grown man so helpless.

Mom sat in a hard-back chair facing the bed, her hands folded on her lap. A pile of used Kleenex covered the tray on the nightstand.

Dad and I left when the chimes sounded to end visiting hour. Mom stayed in her chair, staring at Grandpa's mask.

22

Dad's shaking woke me in the morning. He was in his bathrobe. "Will, Grandpa Blane died."

I bolted up.

"Your mom called about half an hour ago." He smelled of after-shave lotion. His hand rubbed my knee through the blanket. "I'm going down to the hospital to help out."

"Grandpa's dead?"

Dad nodded with his mouth closed like he was sucking on something.

When he left, I felt so alone. What if Dad didn't come back? If Grandpa could fall down and die, why couldn't Dad? Last time we golfed, Grandpa beat him by a stroke. I wanted to tell Dad I wasn't mad anymore about him not paying the money I wanted. I wondered if Western Hardware going broke could kill Dad the way that fall had knocked out Grandpa.

Mom must be turning inside out. She'd lost her mother, now her dad. She always called him "Daddy." I liked that. So did Grandpa. I remembered once when Grandpa dropped in by surprise and Mom was smoking a cigarette with her coffee. When the doorbell rang, she ran water on the cigarette, threw it in the garbage sack and swished the back door to make the smoke go out before she let him in. She told me later that Grandpa didn't know she smoked. Poor Mom. Grandpa was a regular smokestack. If she'd only asked, he would have said okay. Now it was too late.

I wanted to bawl out loud. There was a lump near my tonsils but no tears. I tried to picture things I'd done with Grandpa, his teeth clamped on a cigar while he showed me how to back the hook out of the throat of a steelhead, the time he taught me to grip a horseshoe on the arch to make it open at the peg. On the golf course once, he'd introduced me to a friend as the next Sam Snead. In the mirror, I checked my eyes. I couldn't squeeze out a single drop.

When Mom came home, she gave me a big hug. I held her as tight as I could. She felt softer and fuller than Wellesley. I thought she'd just go to the bedroom and cry. Instead, she made phone calls to her brother, her sisters, and friends. I sat at the kitchen table listening. She answered everyone's questions. It happened about four-thirty in the morning. Pneumonia had filled his lungs with fluid. His heart wasn't strong enough to fight back. It was lucky, she said, he went peacefully.

Within a few hours, people started ringing the doorbell, people I didn't think even knew Grandpa. Parents of kids at school, customers I'd seen at the store. They brought bouquets of flowers, then casseroles, potato salads, fried chicken, sweet rolls. Martin came by in his Rexall uniform with a pink canister of Almond Roca for Mom and comic books for me. Mrs. Tucker, who'd squealed on Taylor and me when the gas caught fire in his garage, brought a flat chocolate cake with a yellow frosting cross in the middle. The pan was still warm.

Aunt Ruth arranged the flowers wherever she could find a flat space. Then she cleaned out the leftovers in the refrigerator to make room for the new food, vacuumed the rug, and mopped and waxed the kitchen and bathroom floors. She showed her grief at the loss of her older brother in square inches of scrubbed space.

Mom took charge of the funeral arrangements. Grandpa's services would be at the First Presbyterian. Going to church was one thing I'd never seen Grandpa do. Mom said he'd stopped going regularly when Grandma Blane died. Grandma would have insisted on a church funeral she said. It was set for 9 o'clock Tuesday morning. We had two nights and a day to get ready.

After dinner, Dad left to close the hardware store. Mom cornered me in the hallway when I came out of the bathroom. "Will, I'd like you to help out at the funeral."

"Sure, Mom, whatever you want." I figured she needed

someone to set up tables and chairs, haul boxes or sweep. These were talents the family recognized.

"I want you to give part of the eulogy," she said.

"What's that?"

"It's a chance to thank Daddy for what he meant to all of us." Mom's face weakened. "It's something traditional at funerals."

"What exactly would I do?"

She smiled. "You stand up in front of the church, by Daddy's casket, and say what you feel."

"Out loud?"

"It's like a short speech," Mom said, as if the shortness made it tolerable.

"Does anyone else have to do it?"

"You're the oldest grandchild, so you'll be speaking for your generation."

The more she explained, the worse it sounded. "Mom, I'm afraid I'll goof up."

She laid her hand on my clenched fists. "You'll do fine. Just be natural, like you're talking to Grandpa."

Aunt Eleanor and her family arrived from Fargo the next morning. Mom's brother, Scott, and her other sister came in the afternoon. I had to share my bedroom with the eight-year-old twins, Darrell and Daniel. They acted like we were the same age. I had to play catch with the kickball in the backyard. They wanted to learn how to climb into the tree from the garage. They found my old rubber-band glider and took turns seeing who could make it go the farthest. Mom gave me money to take them to Martin's for a cherry Coke. When Taylor came by, I made him help. We put them on our backs and played cowboys and Indians. But all I could think of was the eulogy.

The dinner that night was a family reunion, Dad's side and Mom's. I counted thirty-one people. Nobody sat at the table; it was too crammed with food. Instead, people balanced plates on their laps and used the couch, folding chairs, stools, a foot locker, and the porch steps. The screen door slammed as people came in and out for more casserole, green salad, soft rolls, beans, punch, cake, coffee. Aunt

Ruth inspected the table regularly, rearranging the dishes, scraping the remains of one dish into another, putting out still more food. It was a regular Fourth of July party.

I helped put the twins to bed on army surplus cots in my room. They begged me to read a story. I didn't have any children's books so I read from the *Archie* comic book that Martin gave me. They asked a lot of questions to delay turning out the lights.

Mom, her sisters, and Aunt Ruth set up an assembly line for stacking, washing, and drying the dishes. They made it look fun. Dad sat on the front porch talking with my uncles about work. No one noticed me sneak out the back door. I walked around the block, then sat in the garage tree trying to think of something to say about Grandpa Blane. The stars were easy to see. I imagined him up there chuckling at me.

The morning of Grandpa's funeral was a perfect day for golf, solid blue sky with a gentle breeze.

I sat in the first pew next to Mom. I'd never been to a Presbyterian service. Despite Mom's Protestant upbringing, she and Dad had raised us in the Bradfords' religion, Catholicism. Compared to Saint Paul's, the church looked bare. There were no altars, no statue of the Blessed Virgin, no saints. Instead of a pulpit that you had to reach by stairs from the back, there was a simple brown wooden stand facing the congregation. No one was nailed to the large flat crucifix mounted on the front wall. The windows were stained in pastel greens and yellows instead of purples and blood reds.

Mrs. Crumbacher played something on the organ that sounded like bagpipes as Dad, my uncles, Captain Alexander from the Fire Department, Mr. Scruggs, and Dr. Robinson carried the casket down the aisle. They walked with slow, halting steps. The music ended as they set the metallic gray casket on the carriage at the front of the church. The funeral director stepped over and propped the lid open.

The minister walked to the foot of the casket, bowed, and opened the Bible to the page marked by a green ribbon. Over his suit, he wore a thin white gown that looked like the linen curtains in Grandpa's kitchen. He read something from the Gospel according to St. John. It sounded Catholic. Then he repeated, "This is my commandment, that ye love one another, as I have loved you." He used those words to start his sermon. I hadn't thought of using scripture.

I could just barely see Grandpa's face over the edge of the casket; it was chalky and serious. He would have laughed if he knew that Mom had put his #1 wood into the casket. He would have preferred the whole bag. You never knew which club you needed until you stood behind your ball and studied the pin.

The minister kept preaching, putting Grandpa in places that would have surprised him. He had him working as God's main go-between here in Clearwater. Everyone who knew Grandpa liked him, but I'd never heard Grandpa spend much time talking about faith, hope, and charity. More often, he was pretty impatient with anyone who didn't get out of his way.

Then the minister signaled for another piece of music. Pumping the organ like she was pedaling to heaven, spindly Mrs. Crumbacher made the windows vibrate. The echo of the closing note was still ringing when the minister resumed. "Now I'd like you to hear from some of Mr. Blane's family. Let's start with his grandson, Will Bradford."

I wanted Grandpa to climb out of that box and say he was okay. Cancel the eulogy. The crowd hushed like the minister had covered it with a blanket. I walked past the front of the casket, glancing at Grandpa. He was dressed in a suit and vest with a maroon tie knotted tight under his chin. It was the same thing he wore for the family portrait at Peckenpaugh's. When I turned around, a garden of hats and faces stared at me. Everyone looked gloomy except Mom, who was trying to smile.

"Good morning," I said. My voice was sponged up by the huge space. I had to speak louder. "I tried to think what Grandpa Blane would have said this morning if he were in my shoes." Saying his name in front of the casket, like he wasn't there, choked me up. "No offense to the Bible or anything, but Grandpa wasn't very easy around big words and great literature. He liked the outdoors and kids. I think sometimes he would have rather been a kid than a grandpa." The spit in my mouth felt pasty. When I licked my lips, they were sandpaper. "Grandpa," I said, turned toward him but not letting myself actually look at his face, "I want you to know that where you're going you can be a kid again. There's a big river running through the clouds up there, wider than the Clearwater. It's so thick with fish that you can catch them with a gunnysack if you want. And next to it, there's a golf course as big as all of Sylvanus County." I felt like I was going to cry. "You'll never have to play the same hole twice. You don't have to wait for anyone to get off the green. At every tee, there's a rack with free balls and fresh cigars. And when you reach the clubhouse, you won't need a car to go home. There'll be a mail train and a red caboose with your name on it." The faces were getting blurry. I had to finish before something broke inside me. "And Grandpa . . . someday . . . all of us grandkids are going to join you . . . to carry your bag . . . and help clean the fish."

I didn't remember walking back to my seat. The next thing I knew, Mom was sobbing into my right ear, running her hand through my hair with her black glove. The lump in my throat never broke; I couldn't cry.

Everyone turned their lights on and joined the procession to Cemetery Hill. Our family rode just behind the hearse in Uncle Carl's Kaiser-Frazer. There were so many cars I couldn't see the end of the line. We passed through the middle of town. People with grocery bags in their arms stopped to watch. We drove by Western Hardware. I didn't know if it had ever been closed on a weekday before. At the intersection of Willow and Sawyer, I saw Laddie. He stood half off his bike watching us, with his blue messenger hat over his heart.

We wound up the same road that Wellesley came down in the Dragon Lady in June. The skid marks where I'd spun into the ditch were gone. I wished she'd been at the funeral but this was mainly a family affair. It didn't seem right to ask someone to come help bury your grandpa.

At the cemetery, we gathered under a green canopy

pitched near the back fence. They set the casket on wide black straps stretched over the rectangular pit. I stood in front next to Mom and Dad. There was a mound by the hole, covered with a canvas tarp hiding the dirt that would go on top of Grandpa.

The minister read a couple more prayers from his prayer book. Mom handed him an American flag which he draped over one end of the casket. The flag was frayed at the edges, probably the one Grandpa hung from his front porch on holidays. Everyone with flowers stepped forward and dropped them on top of the casket. Aunt Eleanor tossed hers too hard and it slid off into the hole. Then the minister asked us to pray silently.

Everyone bowed their heads. I could hear the flap-flap of the rotating sprinkler on the other side of the cemetery and the sobbing. I wanted to look at anything except the hole. For the first time, I realized I didn't have Grandpa anymore to ask questions. I should have told him what was happening to Wellesley. I knew he'd be on Wellesley's side; he was partial to the underdog.

Mom was crying pretty hard, with Dad bracing her up, as we walked back to our car. Dad was dry eyed. I realized I'd never seen him cry. He was always the one saying to toughen up, it wasn't the end of the world. Maybe it was his Catholic upbringing. Suffering was a necessity. Compared to hell, all other pain was supposed to be acceptable. I wished I could just weep with Mom.

Nobody talked on the way home. Dad drove with one hand on the wheel and the other around Mom.

23

Once we were home, Mom brought out rolls, made coffee and tried to act cheerful. It was like when you can't stop shivering at the pool. Then something clicks and suddenly you're calm.

Darrell and Daniel tackled me, one on each leg, when I came out of the bathroom. "Will, take us to the park!" Daniel said.

"Yeah, Will, we're getting bored," Darrell chimed in. "Ask your mom if it's okay." They figured the same parental rules applied to me as them.

"Why don't you do something with your cousin Ginger?"

"She's a girl," Darrell said, still wrapped around my knee.

Daniel joined. "She's not as much fun as you!"

I couldn't disagree but I wanted to get away. "I'll check with my mom."

"Yeah!" They released their grip and followed me, stepping on the back of my heels.

"Hey, you guys, it's better if we don't gang up on Mom," I whispered. "Just wait here." I winked and they nodded eagerly. Darrell and Daniel stood at attention, so close together they could have fit into one pair of shoes.

I found Mom alone in the kitchen transferring another batch of warm rolls from the cookie sheet to the plate. "Mom, is it okay for me to leave now?"

Mom looked surprised. "Well, this is a nice turn, asking your mom if you can go."

"This isn't a regular day," I said, "with the . . . you know." I didn't want to say funeral and break her mood.

"Sure, I think it would be fine if you disappeared for a while," she said, borrowing a phrase I might have used.

"Mom, one more favor?"

She stopped in midair with a cinnamon roll.

"Can you tell Daniel and Darrell that I can't take them to the park?" I saw the twins peeking through the hallway, one head above the other.

"Oh, Will, you conniver you . . ." She sounded almost happy that I'd ditch them. "Okay, but check back in a couple of hours. Your aunts and uncles will be leaving this afternoon. They'll want to visit with you some more."

"Thanks, Mom!" I started an about-face.

Mom pinched my shirt and set her spatula down. "Just a minute, young man, not so fast!" She wiped her hands on the apron. "I haven't told you thanks. Your eulogy was perfect!" She kissed me on the cheek.

I bounded downstairs to my room. There was no time to hang up the white shirt and tie. I had to get out of there before Mom gave the news to the twins. My dirty jeans and tennis shoes felt so comfortable.

As I reached the fence, the twins reached the back porch. I hummed the words to "Don't be Cruel" so I wouldn't hear what they were yelling as I cruised off on my bike. Without a cast, I could pull up full force on the handlebars and bear down harder on the pedals. I made it to Taylor's in record time. He was sunning himself on the roof of the garage.

"Come on down, you look like a tomato!"

He threw his towel, crept to the edge of the roof and sprang into the air, beating his chest like Tarzan. We called Wellesley and agreed to meet at the bridge.

Wellesley was already there, throwing rocks into the river, when Taylor and I arrived. She wore a pair of tan shorts and a sleeveless T-shirt. Her black high-top tennis shoes were laced every other eyelet.

"Hey, jailbird!" Taylor said, kicking the stand down on his bike. "Will told me what a job you guys did at the hearing!" Taylor stood with his hands on his hips. "Doesn't sound like you needed the first string."

Wellesley threw a rock at Taylor's feet, making him dance. "You clown! You wouldn't have come if they'd sent you a subpoena." She smiled; it was easier to joke now that it was over.

"Where do you guys want to go?" I asked.

"Hey," Taylor said, crouching to give his idea dramatic effect, "let's go to the fairgrounds!"

Wellesley bellowed between her hands, "Boo!"

"How about the swimming hole?" I asked. I'd been dying to go since my cast came off. "Follow me, I'll take you a new way."

I dug out, kicking up gravel and puffs of dust with each downward stroke of the pedal. The trail I wanted was on the north side of the river. It came out next to the sign that read, Bridge Clearance—12′6″. When Taylor and Wellesley started to gain on me, I swerved left down the shoulder and drove into the brush. Except for deer and an occasional fisherman, probably nobody used this trail. Weeds flapped against my jeans. The spokes beheaded wildflowers that leaned over too far. I ducked under live branches and bounced over dead ones. We were heading upstream.

By the time I reached Devil's Elbow, the sweat on my arms had collected petals like a roll of flypaper. I squatted on the bank and cupped handfuls of water to rinse off while I waited for Taylor and Wellesley. The swimming hole was my favorite spot on the river. The Clearwater made a sharp turn there. A rock wall prevented it from going straight. The Elbow could be reached more directly in a car, using an old logging road. At night, you could spy on teenagers necking in their cars or watch stars from the rocks. Today, no one else was there.

When Wellesley and Taylor showed up, we decided to rock jump, hopscotching in the shallow edge of the riverbed. We played follow the leader. If you slipped into the water, you went to the end of the line. Wellesley was the hardest to knock out of the lead. She was agile as a cat, leaping the length of her body, then braking on stones as slippery as bowling balls. Taylor and I changed second and third places frequently as we overshot or undershot our targets. Sometimes it was slow death, as one of us teetered, waving arms wildly to catch a solid pocket of air for balance. Other times, it was a spread-eagled explosion into the water.

Once we'd worked our way upstream as far as the base of the dam, we raced back on the tops of the rocks. Taylor and

I ganged up on Wellesley, giving her friendly nudges whenever we could. We spent as much time in the water as out,
scrambling like escaped convicts dodging bullets. By the
time we returned to the Elbow, all three of us were laughing
so hard we couldn't keep our balance.

My jeans, soaked from the belt to the cuffs, felt as heavy
as a suit of armor. Taylor stripped his off, laid them across a
rock to bake and dove into the pool in his underpants. I
looked at Wellesley to see her reaction.

She grinned. "It's okay, Will, go ahead!"

I pulled off my shoes, socks, and shirt, turned away from
Wellesley, and undid my jeans. I jumped before she could
get a good look at me in my shorts. The water was as cold as
first day in at the pool. "Come on, Wellesley! It's great!"

She climbed to the top of the rock and waved us away.
"Look out below!"

"Don't miss the deep water," I yelled, unable for as long
as I lived to forget about the friend of Grandpa's who broke
his neck here.

She jumped, tucked her knees, and smashed into the river
in a cannonball. A mushroom-shaped bush of water rose
behind her. When she surfaced, she looked different. Her
curly hair was plastered against her head.

"Wellesley, your glasses!" I said.

"Shit! I forgot all about them!" She slapped the water
with the flat of her hand.

"Hold on!" Taylor yelled. He drew a breath and turned
over like a duck, his white shorts flashing momentarily
above the surface.

The hole was probably twelve feet deep. I put my head
under and watched him circling near the bottom. A stream
of bubbles came out of his mouth and rose to the surface.
The sunlight projected Wellesley's and my shadows to the
bottom of the pool next to Taylor. He patted his hands
against the rocks and weeds. Suddenly, he flipped over,
reached for something by his shoulder and shot back to the
top.

Brushing the hair out of his eyes and blowing, he extended his hand to Wellesley. "Madam, did you misplace
your spectacles? I beat 'em to the bottom!"

Later, the three of us climbed to the top of the wall and stretched out to dry. The rocks were warm. The river rolled by below us. We hadn't been to the swimming hole together since the second day of summer. Most years, we would have been here twenty times by now. I watched the waterdrops evaporate on Wellesley's lenses. Her T-shirt clung to her flat chest.

Taylor's mouth against the rocks added a huskiness to his voice. "Are you going to the fair, Wellesley?"

She hesitated. "Sure, don't we always?"

"What about you, Will?" he asked.

Damn Taylor! Why did he have to get into this in front of Wellesley? "Yeah, probably." I tried to sound mildly interested.

Taylor didn't let up. "What about the dance?"

Wellesley spoke. "Is there a dance this year?"

"You bet, ask the big bopper there who he's taking."

Wellesley turned to me and shielded her eyes. "You've got a date?" I couldn't tell if she was disappointed or just surprised.

"A miracle, huh?"

"Who is it?" she asked.

I hesitated and Taylor answered for me. "Monica Amberly."

Wellesley grinned. "That's great, Will! She's really smart!"

"If she were smart," Taylor said, "she'd go with me!"

"That proves my point," Wellesley said.

Taylor rolled over and grabbed Wellesley's wrists.

"Glasses! Glasses! You can't throw in someone with glasses."

They both laughed. Wellesley broke loose and handed me her glasses. They faced each other in wrestlers' crouches, hands ready to fend off a charge. Slowly circling, each of them trying to look more hard-boiled than the other, their quick slaps found only air.

Suddenly Taylor lunged at her. Wellesley sidestepped and gave him a congratulatory pat on the back as he rushed by and fell into the hole screaming, "I'll get you! I'll get you!"

Wellesley was right, summer had started over. Without

making a blood oath, or even mentioning it, the three of us had agreed to not look back. The matches, the probation, and the problems with Mr. Baker had all washed downstream.

24

Dad recruited me to hang signs and banners at the fair-grounds. The theme of the fair was "Harvest of Plenty." We strung orange, white, and green taffeta on the archway over the entrance. The weathered banner read, "Welcome to Sylvanus, Home of the World Famous Timber Carnival."

Outside the gate we stood up a huge replica of Paul Bunyan and Babe the Blue Ox. The wire-framed sculptures had been dented over the years from hauling them in and out of the storage rafters of the John Deere dealership. These models, the creation of an earlier Fair Committee, were used every year regardless of the theme.

As the opening drew closer, I became more anxious. The idea of walking around the fair with Monica petrified me. I couldn't imagine her and me in the same picture. I kept seeing her with Taylor.

Dad's chairmanship of the Committee turned out to be a curse. Saturday morning, he told me I'd have to be one of the greeters. Two of the people signed up had called in sick.

"That's kids' stuff," I said.

"You're wrong," he said. "Most of my volunteers are over thirty."

When the gates opened at nine o'clock, I was peering out the eye holes of a corncob, shaking hands with people as they entered. Uncle Harold was a green apple. Grant Beller was an Idaho spud; his dad was on the Committee too.

My cardboard cob was covered with burlap stiffened by light green paint. The burlap peeled away near the face to show the yellow oilcloth that was stitched in rows over wads of mattress stuffings. When people stroked me and made corn jokes, I ignored them. My shift ended at noon and I headed for the office to change as fast as I could. With my feet so close together I walked like a pair of tweezers.

Then I wandered around looking for the best place to buy lunch. The Kiwanis booth was still serving its pancake breakfast. A huge grill sizzled with little pig sausages. A man in a floppy chef's hat waved a cookie sheet, sending the flavored smoke over the counter. "Step right up, folks, best breakfast in the county! Proceeds for charity!" Cooking the grease out of pigs is how they paid for the Kiwanis picnic shelter that kids carved swear words into.

Nurses from Mary of the Angels ran a booth covered with white butcher paper. They lined their instruments along a towel so neatly it looked like an operating room. I watched a woman in a nurse's hat split a triangular biscuit and ladle melted butter and then a big gob of raspberry jam on each half. It smelled warm like Aunt Ruth's bread.

I ended up where my stomach warned me we would—at the last booth. A large woman wrapped in a red and white plaid tablecloth stuck pointed sticks into the ends of wieners. She handed them to her twin who twisted them in a tub of cornmeal batter and dropped them into a vat of boiling oil. As the batter became crispy brown, she fished them out with tongs and laid them on a newspaper transparent with grease. They didn't look as good as last year's but I bought two anyway, on the theory that you should eat at the fair what you never get at home.

But everything lacked the mystery of past years. I'd heard all the jokes. New clown posters were pasted over layers of old ones. And, I couldn't get the dance out of my mind.

Taylor arrived in time for the Lumberjack Show. People who wouldn't set foot in Milltown oozed with admiration for the pretend loggers in the annual competition. This town hadn't had a real logger since the mill burned down.

The log-rolling contest was held in a watering trough in the middle of the arena. A burly guy in a full beard, suspendered pants, and heavy boots stood at one end of the trough. A clown with a red-ball nose and rag-mop hair stood at the other. The clown warmed up with exaggerated stretches. Each time he bent over to touch the toes of his tennis shoes, his billowing pink and black pants legs hiked up to show the frilly garters around his ankles. He was the same clown as in last year's show.

I already knew the result.

The clown nonchalantly trotted to keep up with the rotating log, checking his fingernails, then his watch, as if he was waiting for eggs to poach. They teeter-tottered as the log continued to spin. The crowd clapped. Up, down, up. The logger struggled to stay upright.

Ker-whoosh! The logger landed flat on his back in the pool, sending a wave of water over the edge of the trough. The crowd roared. As the logger pulled himself back onto the platform, the clown lit a cigarette, walked to the end of the log and offered it to the angry lumberjack. Last year, the clown lit a cigar.

"Who was the Miller that fell?" Taylor asked.

"I don't know but the clown's Randy Zander."

"What a talent!"

"Hey, look who's in the sawing contest!" I said.

"Bushner and one of his asswipe friends! There's a team," Taylor said.

Their opponents were a couple of older men in white dress shirts who looked ready to pass the collection basket.

"Bam!" The starter fired a blank into the air.

The two men drew their first stroke slowly across the top of the log, letting the teeth of the crosscut saw find its groove. As the teeth disappeared into the wood, they increased the tempo, alternating the workload. One man eased off while the other dragged the saw viciously in the other direction.

I beat my knuckles into my palm. "Come on whiteshirts! Pull it!"

Bushner slipped and lost his grip. Then his saw bowed as he tried to force it through the log. Daylight appeared between halves of the whiteshirts' log, then it dropped to the ground. The men raised their saw over their heads like a banner. Taylor and I jumped up and yelled while Bushner and his partner collapsed next to their log. Their saw, still stuck in the log, wagged harmlessly.

Of course the winner didn't exactly get rich. Grand prize

was dinner for two at Popeye's Galley. Last year was better
—a 21″ Hoffman television.

Mom gave me a ride home around dinnertime so I could
shower and change clothes for the dance. Dad had to stay
on the grounds to make sure no one ran out of paper cups,
refrigeration, or patience. Being chairman of the committee
had turned out to be a grunt job. Whether it was the
thought of Monica or the heartburn from the corndogs, I
turned down Mom's offer to grill me a cheese and pickle
sandwich.

I inspected my face in the mirror for pimples and dabbed
Clearasil on two red ones not ready to squeeze. They
blended into a spray of freckles when I stepped back from
the mirror. From my left side, maybe she wouldn't notice.

On the way out the door, Mom stopped me. "You look
nice, Will." She studied the short-sleeve shirt with alternating red, white, and black triangles she'd given me for my
birthday. "You check with Monica's parents to see how late
she can stay. I think eleven-thirty is a nice hour. And you
call if you need a ride."

"Sure, Mom, thanks." I had no intention of asking her or
Dad for a ride. It would be hard enough to keep the conversation interesting without my parents in the front seat.

I walked to Monica's using side streets. All I could think
of were things that would go wrong. What if I got a boner
that showed like the day Mr. Dennehy called me to the front
of class for spelling and I had to keep one hand in my
pocket? I moved my jaw up and down to loosen the skin. I
practiced smiling. Out loud, I tested different ways of greet-
ing her when she came to the door. "Hi, Monica, you look
great!" Too much Sunny Jim. "Hello, Monica, it's a perfect
evening for the dance!" Too stiff. "Hey, you didn't change
your mind, did you?" Too honest.

Mrs. Amberly answered the door. "Don't you look handsome, Mr. Bradford?" She swept me into the house.

My clean jeans, brown oxfords, and triangle shirt quickly
lost value in the Amberlys' sumptuous front room. Mr.
Amberly smoked his pipe in one of their throne chairs, his

feet stretched across the hassock. He lowered the newspaper. "Hello, Will! So tonight's the big night."

I didn't know exactly what he meant. "Yes, sir, it should be pretty good." Where was Monica? I didn't have anything else to add.

Mrs. Amberly still held my arm in hers. "We'll probably skip the dance," she said, "but Monica told us you needed a ride." She squeezed me. I had the feeling she was counting the blemishes on my face.

"Oh, that's all right, Mrs. Amberly, we can walk."

"I wouldn't hear of it!" she said. "Besides, you'll need your strength for the dance." My weak knees must have showed.

Mr. Amberly released several cherry-smelling smoke clouds that hung in the air between us. "How's your dad doing these days, Will?"

I answered in reflex, "He's doing great." Maybe Mr. Amberly had turned Dad down for a loan at the bank. His question sounded like he knew about the store. I cringed thinking of Dad sitting in front of Mr. Amberly's desk at the bank in his hardware smock, hands greasy from threading a length of galvanized pipe. Mr. Amberly had probably never cut a pane of window glass or wrestled a new freezer down a set of cellar stairs or gashed his hand against the razor edge of a roof flashing. His friends at the country club were accountants, stockbrokers, and dentists. Why would Monica want to go out with someone from a hardware store that was going broke? Mrs. Amberly finally let go of me and sat on the chair arm next to her husband. He just puffed on his pipe and waited for me to go on. "He's been pretty busy running between the hardware and the fair," I said, trying to think of something safe.

"Sorry, Will!" Monica appeared on the staircase, in a white skirt with ruffles and a peach top. "I hope my parents aren't being too nosey." With her lipstick, she looked nineteen years old.

"Will was just telling us how proud he is of his father for chairing the Fair Committee this year," said Mrs. Amberly, rising to meet Monica. "You look glorious, dear!" Mrs.

Amberly had a way of stealing, then elevating the conversation.

All I could think of was dittoing her. "Yeah, Monica!"

Monica shrugged her shoulders and clasped her hands back to back so her elbows turned out. "I'm so excited!"

She descended the stairs, stopped in the middle of the living room, and twirled slowly. In the mirror over the mantel, I could see myself standing lopsided in my triangle shirt next to her. I looked like her little brother.

Mr. Amberly drove right to the gate, forcing people on foot to make way for his big Mercury. When I jumped out and slammed the door, Monica stayed inside. Mrs. Amberly rolled her window down and whispered loud enough for Monica to hear, "A gentleman would cross over and open the door."

I did. Monica used my hand getting out of the backseat, just like I figured her mother would. Fortunately, she let go in time so we could walk through the gate uncoupled. I forgot to keep her on the opposite side of my new pimples.

The sun was low enough on the horizon to flame the sky. Merry-go-round music from the midway and a fresh Juicy Fruit smell washed the grounds. Kids chased each other with squirt guns. Balloons popped. The crowd had grown since the afternoon.

Walking next to Monica was like being on stilts; I felt light-headed and everyone else looked small. Beller went past us, then turned around and walked backwards to make sure he'd seen it right. A few minutes later, he showed up tugging Woody by the sleeve. Woody had to see it to believe it.

Monica asking me out had certainly hoisted my status. People in town admired the Amberlys, I guess, because they had what everyone else wanted—money and respectability. I just wanted their daughter.

We wandered into the midway area. The merry-go-round, zeppo plane, octopus, tea cups, jack-dragon, mixer, bronco buster, and Ferris wheel spun, bumped, and twirled with lights. When I squinted, the colors moved like a kaleidoscope.

"Will!" It was Wellesley by the Ferris wheel with her mom.

"Hey, look who's here," I said to Monica. "Come on!" We weaved through the crowd to reach her.

Wellesley wore the satiny sailor dress from the trial. Her mom had a bright red bow in her hair and a full skirt like the kind people square danced in. I'd never seen Mrs. Baker without a gray face. She looked younger.

"Hey, Wellesley, you made it," I said. "Hello, Mrs. Baker." I turned to Monica. "Mrs. Baker, this is Monica Amberly."

"Hello, Monica," Mrs. Baker said, extending her hand.

Wellesley beamed. "This is the first fair Mom's gone to since high school."

Mrs. Baker examined her cotton candy. "Wellesley, you don't need to . . ."

"Every boy in town chased her in those days," Wellesley said, leaning back and hooking her elbows around the top rail and resting the heel of her shoe on the bottom one.

"What was it like back then, Mrs. Baker?"

"You talk like it was another century, Will," Mrs. Baker said. "I'd say it was the same kind of feeling as tonight. The fair was the biggest event of the year. We didn't have a movie theater in those days, never even heard of television. People came to the fair to laugh, try their luck at one of the games, maybe fall in love with someone." She smiled at Monica.

"Did that happen to you, Mrs. Baker?" Monica asked.

"Well, kind of . . . but then he married someone else." She looked up, realizing what she'd said.

Wellesley saved her. "Don't you think Mom looks like a million dollars?"

Monica and I chimed in chorus, "You look great, Mrs. Baker!"

"I love your dress," Monica added.

"She made it herself."

"Wellesley . . ." Mrs. Baker picked at the cotton on her stick again.

"Mom's a professional seamstress," Wellesley said, raising her voice over the screech of the Ferris wheel dragging to a stop. The car behind Wellesley rocked on its axle as two kids pumped it like a swing. "I'm trying to get Mom to go for a ride with me. She says she's scared of heights."

"I'm a little scared of Ferris wheels myself, Mrs. Baker," —I looked at Wellesley—"especially this one." I didn't trust anything Mr. Sparkman had fixed.

Wellesley winked back.

The Ferris wheel rotated an eighth of a turn, creaked to a stop, ejected the kids and let in a new twosome. "You guys have fun at the dance," Wellesley said. "We'll come by and watch you!"

The fewer people that saw me dancing the better. "It's going to be pretty crowded," I said.

"We'll be looking for you," Monica said, grabbing my hand to leave.

I turned sideways so they wouldn't notice Monica's hand on mine, but Wellesley glanced down. "Have fun, you guys," she said, smiling.

When I looked back, they were still standing there, tugging cotton puffs off their sticks and watching us. I had never seen Wellesley and her mom at anything so public. Maybe they were celebrating Wellesley's probation.

As the sky darkened, Monica grew more stunning and I grew more worried. The matchbook covers I'd folded into the heels of my shoes to look taller had slid under the arches. When I put my hand in front of my nose to check Dad's Old Spice, I could only smell the steel from rubbing the Ferris wheel railing. The lotion was evaporating along with my confidence.

We circled the barn so many times Monica said she was getting dizzy. The big doors on each end were wide open. So were the flaps along the side of the barn that used to be horse stables. People lined the openings and gawked inside waiting for the music to start. I paid for each of us and went inside. Monica treated it so automatic. I'd never paid someone else's way to anything.

The band members plucked their electric guitars on the makeshift stage to test the sound system. Four guys wore identical black sport coats and fluorescent lime ties. The drum face read, "Rock Hounds."

Although the county long ago had converted the barn into a meeting hall, with floorboards, electrical outlets, and rest rooms, everything higher than your head was still just barn. The paint left off where a tall man with a brush couldn't reach. Loops of rope and cable still hung from pegs in the lofts at each end. If you sniffed real fast, you could still smell dry hay.

When the band opened the show with "Long Tall Sally," the floor cleared like someone had yelled fire. Everyone huddled along the perimeter and stared at the empty dance floor. The Rock Hounds had overestimated the willingness of local people to make fools of themselves.

The leader had greasy hair parted down both sides and a spit curl in the center of his forehead. He stepped to the mike, "Maybe Sally better duck back in the alley till you folks get warmed up a little bit." The amplifier system squealed like a signal from outer space. People tittered nervously. "How about a little slow dancing to get acquainted with each other?" He turned to his group. They nodded no, then yes, like baseball pitchers communicating with the catcher. The lights dimmed and they played "Love Me Tender," with the spit curl guy singing.

A brave couple on the other side of the barn strolled hand in hand to the middle of the floor. "My God, that's Taylor!" I said. "With Marilyn!"

Monica grabbed my arm. "Didn't you know?"

"Taylor told me he turned her down!"

"Well, two days later he changed his mind!" She made an "isn't it amazing" grin and we both laughed.

Taylor had almost made me sorry for him when he complained to Wellesley about me going with Monica. He already knew he was going with Marilyn! She nestled her head against Taylor's chin like they were going steady. Taylor held her close, leaving no air between them. Other couples joined them on the floor.

A voice inside me said it wasn't going to get any slower than this, ask her! My legs felt like they'd gone to sleep. I'd concentrated on holding my arms away from my sides so my armpits wouldn't get the shirt wet. I glanced down to see how I looked. My shirt puffed out above the belt. My toes pointed like ducks' feet. I reviewed the steps I'd practiced in my room then leaped. "Monica . . . you don't feel like dancing to this, do you?"

"Oh, sure, I love this song."

I put my arm around her and placed the flat of my hand against the back of her blouse as we started moving. Silently, I counted the steps, two to the left, two to the right. We were wearing a path. Monica kept us a safe distance apart, as if she had fresh paint on her front. When the song ended, we followed Taylor and Marilyn back to their side of the barn.

"Hey," I said when we were in earshot, "who is that cool dude in the black?"

Taylor spun around. He had black shoes, black pegged pants, a black short-sleeve shirt with the collar turned up and a thin white belt holding his low-slung pants. He dropped Marilyn's hand like we'd caught him playing with himself. "Hey, you guys, where you been?"

Marilyn giggled. "Hi, Mon', isn't the band great?"

Monica stepped back to admire Marilyn's creamy gown with sequins that blinked as she moved. "Your dress is fantastic!" Marilyn's neckline had worked its way to one side from dancing so that the lace in her brassiere showed.

Taylor looked Monica up and down. I suspected he was still jealous. Then he whispered in my ear, "You didn't expect me to stay home and mope, did you?"

The Rock Hounds started playing "Wake Up Little Susie." Taylor wasted no time pulling Marilyn back onto the floor. Monica tested the rhythm by bouncing her head with the music, then reached for me. This was it, my first fast one.

By letting her direct my hands, I could do anything I wanted with my feet. My body behaved like a stage horse, with one character playing the head and another one the hind end. I moved us as close to the center of the floor as possible, out of range of the spectators leaning through the horse windows.

The dance was better and worse than I expected. Monica seemed happy. She threw her head back when she danced, hummed to the music and went out of her way to bump into friends. I wondered though whether she enjoyed me or just the dance. She was so pretty I knew everyone was asking themselves how she ended up with me. And there would be a line of guys outside her door tomorrow who thought they were better dancers.

I couldn't help comparing this to past years when I would have been leaning through the horse windows laughing at Taylor's jokes or watching Wellesley make monkeys out of the braggarts in the amusement alley. Now, Taylor was putting the make on a girl that he'd turned down for the dance and Wellesley was walking the grounds with her mother.

When the Hounds took their first intermission, I convinced Monica we had to go outside for fresh air. The hangers-on by the door made wisecracks as the dancers filed out.

"Hey, muscles!"

"Hey, skinny!"

"Hey, beautiful, trade him in!"

Away from the barn lights, we found the Big Dipper, North Star, and, according to Monica, some constellations called Andromeda and Pisces. She told me the story of each. It was the first time all night I'd relaxed.

Then some yelling started over by the stables. We ran over to see what was happening. Under the pole light, there was a large man against the fence. It was Mr. Baker, shouting at Wellesley and her mom!

"What goddamn business do you have here anyway?" His speech was slurred. He held onto the fence to steady himself. "Fucking empty house . . . HUH? . . . DO YOU HEAR ME? . . . sonofabitches." He muttered, yelled, and then muttered some more.

Wellesley stepped toward him. "You're making a fool of yourself doing this. We're going home."

"You're goddamn right you're going home!" He pushed himself away from the fence, boots still planted, upper body swaying. He swore at the ground, "Bitches."

A man stepped forward and tried to steady Mr. Baker. "Let me help you."

Mr. Baker jerked his hand away. "Hands off, you bastard!"

At the edge of the circle of light, the horses in the pen

huddled together, their heads poking over each other's
necks to watch. Another couple from the dance and a tall
man in cowboy boots smoking a cigarette stared at Mr.
Baker. Then I saw Laddie by the fence, gripping both han-
dles of his bike, ready to escape. He looked as skittish as the
horses.

Mr. Baker started to walk. He combed his hands through
his hair. His stride was determined and heavy.

"Wellesley, what happened?" I asked.

She supported her mom by the arm. "Shit, he's pissed off
because he had to heat up the dinner Mom left for him!"

Mrs. Baker sobbed. Her youth had vanished, her face
sagged again.

"He's just torqued off," Wellesley said, "because Mom
and I are having some fun for a change. Goddammit! Why
does he have to embarrass us like this? He can yell his lungs
out at home!" Wellesley took her glasses off and wiped her
eyes on her sleeve. She looked around to see if anyone was
watching.

"Don't kick yourself about this!" I said. "It doesn't sound
like it was your fault."

Wellesley gritted her teeth. "I don't care what he does to
me, it's Mom! Goddammit, she fixed him a casserole and he
hauls over here and screams 'cause she wasn't there to set it
under his nose!"

"What are you going to do?" I said.

Wellesley kicked the ground. "Go home like good little
dogs, I guess."

"Do you want me to come with you?" I glanced at
Monica, hoping she'd understand. She stood reverently,
hands folded across her ruffled dress.

"No, Will, thanks," she said, looking at Monica and me.
"Don't let this ruin your night. We'll be fine, won't we,
Mom?"

Wellesley and her mom walked away, arms around each
other's waist. Laddie followed them at a distance. The
horses sidled back to the railing, looking for sugar cubes.

We returned to the barn without talking. I couldn't get rid
of Mr. Baker's staggering, whiskied frame. Every time
Wellesley started to enjoy something, he snapped her back

as if he had a leash hooked to her. He'd created the prison Wellesley thought she'd escaped.

The dance floor was jammed and the air sticky with cigarette smoke, sweat, and the twang of guitar music when we returned. Ticket takers had abandoned the gates, letting people too cheap to pay admission join the dance. When the leader asked the crowd what they wanted, they yelled "FASTER! FASTER!" I felt like I'd missed something. The dance had skipped from tentative to reckless while Monica and I were at the stables.

Monica sensed something was wrong and didn't make me dance or bubble and joke when people came up to us. When the band played "Red Sails in the Sunset" though, I asked her to dance.

"You and Wellesley must be close," she whispered in my ear.

"We're pretty good friends, I guess." That sounded incomplete but I didn't know what else to call her.

She pressed gently against me as we danced. The paint had dried. And somehow she'd learned to follow my wooden soldier cadence, changing directions without resistance. I was tempted to tell her some of the things I'd seen and heard at Wellesley's. But Monica had already seen more than Wellesley wanted anyone to know.

"Why don't we call my mom and tell her we're walking home?"

I could have hugged her. "That suits me great!"

Taylor saw us leaving and cornered me. "You mover, you," he whispered behind his hand, "I can see makeout written all over your face! Where you taking her?"

To feed Taylor's fantasy and maybe mine, I lied. Tomorrow, I could tell him the truth. "She wants to go to the meadow at Mossyrock!"

Taylor's eyes were dollar pancakes, "No shit?" Monica and Marilyn were busy in their own conversation. "Marilyn's all over me," he said. "I've never danced so close. I can feel the pattern in her bra through my shirt!"

We laughed. Monica trading with Marilyn had worked. I thought of telling him what happened at the stables, but he was in no mood for someone else's problem.

* * *

The walk to Monica's was about a mile and a half by way of the highway. We decided to take the longer route, using the dirt road that goes by the dump, to avoid having every car leaving the fair offer us a ride. The light from a banana-shaped moon paved the road like cement. Crickets chirped. The bushes rustled whenever our footsteps flushed a squirrel or bird into the woods. Out of view of the crowd, I found Monica's hand.

She squeezed to let me know it was okay. "This reminds me of Sleepy Hollow," she said. "Remember the spindly little school teacher who left the dance alone. What was his name . . . Ichabod! I remember him walking through the forest to go home. Without a moon." She looked up to find ours. Her face shone.

"And the guy who stole the pretty girl from him at the dance, the headless horseman?"

"Brom Bones!" She shivered as if to shake loose of the image.

"So, which one am I?" I surprised myself. We hadn't even finished our date and I'd asked for the results.

She pressed my hand again. "Let's see. You have some of Ichabod's shyness . . ."

"I'll get over it."

"I like shy people! They feel safer to me. But you've also got some of the Brom Bones. It's hidden, but I can see it. Like the way you offered to help Wellesley. If someone took something you wanted, I think you'd fight for it. So I guess you're both of those guys."

I'd ridden this road a hundred times on my bike in the daytime. Never again would I be able to think of it as the road to the dump. Monica's voice, the pressure against my fingers, our conversation had transformed it.

She told me how frustrating it was to be the banker's daughter. There was so much she missed out on. She had to get perfect grades, use perfect manners, wear the right thing. People were afraid she'd freak if they talked to her about anything reckless. She wanted to be someone regular.

Neither one of us mentioned what we'd seen at the stables.

When we got to her house, she held the screen open but made no attempt to turn the doorknob. "Thanks for taking me. I hope you've forgiven me for having Marilyn call you up like that."

"I'd forgotten all about it . . . I mean, of course I remembered, but it wasn't a problem or anything." My conversation was turning awkward again in the flood of the porch light. I didn't know how to end it.

Monica acted as if I'd forgotten something. My hands moved in and out of my pockets like I was sorting mail. I thought she wanted me to kiss her, but what if I misjudged? She'd refused Taylor at Mossyrock. Maybe that's why she asked me to the dance instead of him. I was safer. She rested one foot on the bottom of the screen and rode it back and forth, making it groan.

"I guess I'd better go," I said.

"Me too. I don't think you want Mom to join us for twenty questions." Her smile broke slowly, then she looked deep into me.

My head wafted toward her.

She closed her eyes.

I pressed my lips against hers, like stamp to ink pad and held until she retreated.

Then she spun, opened the door, and disappeared.

I stared at the brass crest on the closed door, with "Amberly" engraved on it. I would have swallowed that fixture to have Monica's name inside me. We had danced on each other's feet, laughed at the same stupid jokes, held hands . . . and kissed.

Leaping from the top step, I cleared the holly bush and landed spread-legged in the front lawn. Throwing both arms into the air, I trapped a shout in my clenched teeth so that only a muffled small animal sound escaped.

From the sidewalk, I looked back to be sure this was really the house of the girl I'd secretly watched since first grade. Any moment, I expected a buzzer to sound and a voice to announce, "The game is over, everyone please return to their own desk!" Only in daydreams did I get the prettiest girl. But Monica was more than just pretty.

In the center of the bay window, I saw her head peeking

out, the drapes a cape drawn snug under her chin. The soft light from the living room darkened her silhouette. She'd seen me lunge like a madman into her yard. Who cared? I blew her a kiss.

Once out of sight, I exploded into a combination twirl and broken field run, dancing off the trunks of trees and telephone poles. A black Scottie dog with white eye patches chased me to the end of his block, stopped at the curb and barked at me. By the time I reached Willow, I was winded and slowed to a dreamy stroll. A breeze soft as a ceiling fan blew against my face.

Monica's asking me out wasn't a mistake. Her words echoed in my head, ". . . I like shy people." Summer could end and high school start. I imagined how different it would be sitting across the aisle from her now, studying her mouth.

At the streetlight, I sat on the curb and untied my shoes. The makeshift supports had made my arches itch. I tipped the sweaty match covers out of each shoe and one at a time flicked them into the center of the intersection.

25

Mom and Dad were standing next to my bed when I woke up. Mom's face was ashen. Dad, in his hardware smock, looked mad. He'd probably heard me come in late last night. I tried to see the clock on my nightstand.

Dad spoke. "Mr. Baker's dead."

"What?"

"He's dead. They're holding Wellesley."

I tried to raise myself on my elbows, to get upright. "It can't be, Dad."

"Mrs. Baker called the police about twelve-thirty last night. They couldn't save him. It was a direct hit at close range." He towered over me. Each statement he dropped seemed to pin me harder to the bed.

I was trapped. Why was he doing this to me? I felt feverish and needed to move but I couldn't. "How could it be Wellesley?"

"Sergeant Payne said she confessed. Happened in their own kitchen. Wellesley's in the county jail."

"Oh, Will, I feel terrible," Mom said.

"Will,"—Dad's voice was grim—"do you know anything about this?"

"I don't think so."

"What do you mean, you don't think so?"

"I . . . the only thing . . ."

"The only thing what?"

"There was an argument . . . last night at the fairgrounds."

"What happened?"

"Mr. Baker came by . . . he was yelling at Wellesley and her mom. Dad, she didn't do anything! Mr. Baker had been drinking. You've seen him. He was mad because Mrs. Baker didn't fix his dinner or something."

"Then what?"

"Wellesley said they'd go home. And they did. Dad, that's all I know."

Mom's face was blotchy and swollen like at Grandpa Blane's funeral. She shook her head.

"You're going to have to tell what you know to the police," Dad said.

"Yeah, Dad, I know."

He said he had to get back to work and left the room.

I pushed my palms against my head like a vise and stared at the ceiling. "Mom, you don't think she did it, do you?"

Mom sat on the edge of the bed. "I know how you like that girl." She rubbed a small circle onto my forehead.

I'd thought of Mr. Baker as the destroyer, bludgeoning whatever got in his way. But now Wellesley was the one in jail. "Mom, can you give me a ride?"

She looked at me with merciful eyes. "Sure, Will, but I have to change first. Are you sure they'll let anyone see her?"

"I don't know, but I can't just stay here."

The Sylvanus County Courthouse was closed on Sunday. A sign in the glass panel next to the revolving door instructed "Night and Weekend Visitors" to push the white buzzer.

A blue-uniformed man with receding hair answered on the second ring. We were too late for morning hours and too early for evening. I begged him, explaining that we'd just found out she was there. He studied his watch and asked what relation we were to the prisoner. Mom had to show her driver's license.

"It'll have to be quick," he said, then led us to the basement.

Our steps echoed as we descended the steel stairwell. The floodlights made it brighter than natural daylight. When we reached the bottom, he pulled on a chain in his pocket until he reached a ring of keys and unlocked a steel door held together with rivets. "Damn Sundays," he muttered, "I'm desk sergeant and maid. Lucky the count's down this time of year."

Mom and I waited on a wooden bench in an area about the size of my bedroom. A fluorescent light fixture in the ceiling buzzed like a housefly. The two metal ashtrays crammed with bent cigarette butts made my nostrils itch. "Mom, can you wait here? I'd like to see her alone."

She looked around the room as if to make sure the walls wouldn't close in on her when I left. "Sure, I'll be fine."

When a heavy metal door clamped shut somewhere, Mom and I looked at each other. Then I heard voices. Another door slammed. Then a clap sounded like one of those movie director's boards. The jailer's head emerged from the crack in the door.

"You can come in now," he said.

Mom put her hand on my knee and I stood. He led me down a hallway that dead-ended at a set of bars. The cramped space reeked of disinfectant. Before opening the gate, he searched me with his eyes, "Have you been here before?"

"No . . . ah, no sir."

"The rules are simple," he said. "You're on one side and she's on the other. Don't touch the bars. Not with your face, your hand, nothing. And don't give her anything. Not a pencil, not gum, nothing. Understand? You've got ten minutes." He turned his key and activated a series of sliding movements inside the lock. The door swung open silently and he pointed to the left.

Wellesley looked at me through the bars. All my images of her on the way to the jail had not prepared me for the real thing. I took another breath. Her curly hair was matted and stringy. The long-sleeved green gown fit her like a sack. Stoop shouldered and slouched on the stool, she looked defeated. I straightened the chair in front of her and sat. The room was old, with unpainted concrete that was cracked like the walls in Grandpa Blane's cellar. Steel bars partitioned the room in half, floor to ceiling. There were three other stalls behind the bars. A bare light bulb hung over each empty stool.

Wellesley tried to smile but her face contorted into a cry

when we looked at each other. She fought against it. "Thanks for coming, Will." Through her glasses, her blood-shot eyes were enlarged.

I wanted to be hopeful but it felt that just by being there I'd touched a finger against the tent canvas and let rainwater drip in. "Wellesley, I only have ten minutes." I started to put my hands on the bars and remembered. "What happened?"

She fiddled with her fingers and looked down. "You don't really want to know."

She was right. I was scared of what she might say. "I do, Wellesley."

Her face was raw and streaked. "I shot him, Will!" Her eyes watered again and she let her tears drip off her cheeks to the counter. I gulped, empty of anything to say. "I wanted him dead. Every day of my life, I'd prayed he'd die. I'd even dreamed of killing him. Now I have." She convulsed with sobs.

There had to be an explanation. "Did he do something to you? I mean . . . your dad . . ."

She raked her hair and shook my question away. "I shouldn't have shot him." Her voice caved. "He's dead, Will!"

Her abject misery trivialized whatever lame consolations occurred to me. "What did your mom say?"

"She thinks it's her fault! She says if she hadn't gone to the fair, it wouldn't have happened."

"That's crazy," I said.

There was another long silence. "I pulled the trigger," she said. "Mom didn't even see it."

I avoided looking directly into her eyes. Her pain scared me. "It's okay, Wellesley."

"Time's up, mister!" The jailer's voice startled me as he yelled from his swivel chair behind the desk in the next room.

"Wellesley, I know you didn't mean it," I said as I stood, even though she'd given me little reason to believe that was true.

She locked her eyes onto mine and I wished I could pull her out through the bars.

* * *

"These things have a way of working themselves out," Mom said on the drive home.

I had learned a long time ago that it was Dad's job to prepare me for the clouds and Mom's to paint the silver linings. The truth was, I favored Mom's way. I wanted to believe that Wellesley would be rescued. But it was almost as if she wanted to be punished for what had happened.

Mom had to raise her chin to see the road over the steering wheel of Grandpa's Chevy. He'd left it to Mom in his will and so she was determined to drive it. She kept her back as straight as an ironing board. "Tell me more about your time with Monica," she said. That was the start of it. I should have gone with Wellesley and Taylor. Mr. Baker could have had his stupid casserole. There wouldn't have been the fight at the stables. But there wouldn't have been Monica. Mom poked my arm. "Will, are you listening?"

"Yeah . . . Monica. She was great, Mom. I was thinking of something else."

"They're a very nice family, you know." It felt like this was a comparison to the Bakers. She was coaxing me toward a substitute for Wellesley.

"I feel so shabby when I'm in their house, everything's so tidy. The pillows match the couch fabric. The couch matches the rug."

"That's nice."

"I'd be more comfortable if they wore overalls and tracked mud into the house."

Mom was distracted by the car passing us. She tightened her grip on the wheel. I looked at the speedometer; the red needle wavered just below thirty. "There's nothing wrong with cleanliness, Will. They were probably just trying to make an impression on you."

"Huh! Monica could have anyone she wants. She doesn't need her parents' help."

Mom eased the car into its parking place in front of our house until the tires wedged against the curb. Then we went inside. The house was still cool. I flopped onto the couch and stared at the ceiling. Flecks sparkled in the plaster like distant stars. I studied the formations. Triangles made cat ears. I found a wagon, then a mule pulling the wagon. And a pistol. When Mom turned on the kitchen light, the galaxy disappeared.

Then it hit me. Mr. Feinberg. I'd call the only attorney I knew, the man I'd met in the rest room at Wellesley's hearing. He'd know what to do.

The phone book on the end table was dog-eared at the edges. It covered Clearwater, Olalla, Coles Corner, Divinity, Alfalfa, Nestor and, of course, the county seat, Sylvanus. There was only one Feinberg, Aaron L., at a residence in Sylvanus. Too soon for his new office to be listed. The phone rang and rang. No answer.

I walked over to Taylor's. To my disappointment, Marilyn Tubbs was sitting on the front porch next to him in her pink pedal pushers and white sweatshirt, looking very chummy. Whatever Taylor produced, it was honey to Marilyn. They didn't notice me until my shadow touched them. "Hey, Bradford!" Taylor said. "You must have dropped out of the sky!"

"Hi, Will," Marilyn said, "did you and Monica have a good time?"

They must not have heard what happened at Wellesley's yet. I wasn't in the mood to rehash the dance but I suspected that everything I told Marilyn would be reported in detail to Monica. "Yeah, it was great. I hope Monica had as much fun as I did."

Marilyn didn't really want to know about me and Monica. "We had a scream," she said. "Taylor is so funny. And sooo . . . romantic!" She tugged on his arm like it was an inside joke. "Wasn't the band great? I just loved the singer. Didn't he remind you of Sal Mineo? His voice imitations were sooo . . . perfect. I could have danced all night. Especially the slow ones." She fluttered her lashes and nudged Taylor.

He leaned back against the steps, relaxed, soaking in her flattery. Taylor had a convert. I wanted to snap my fingers and turn her to smoke. I had to tell Taylor, without Marilyn cheapening it with her chatty ooh's and ah's. "Excuse me, Marilyn, I have to ask Taylor something."

"Sure, shoot!" she said.

"In private." I pointed to the yard with my head.

"Ooh . . . men talk, I'll bet!" Marilyn raised her eyebrows.

Taylor followed me hesitantly. Marilyn turned her ear to pick up whatever she could. I pulled Taylor all the way to the sidewalk. His mouth hung open as I told him what happened.

Then he stomped the heel of his tennis shoe into the concrete. "Damnit, Will! She's cooked! Her old man's going to get her again."

I could have hugged him. "I'm glad you're mad." I'd feared he'd find a way to pass this off or, worse, blame Wellesley.

Marilyn was about wetting her pants wanting to know what was going on. She'd moved to the bottom step and craned her neck. Taylor waved to her and Marilyn put her thumbs in her ears and made a face back. "Is it all right to tell her?"

I gently cuffed Taylor's gut. "She'd beat you up if you didn't! Sure. By tonight, everyone in town will know."

"Thanks, Will." Taylor rubbed the side of his tennis shoe back and forth in the crack in the sidewalk. "God, I can't believe this happened. Tell her we'll get up a collection. I hope she beats this thing."

Mr. Feinberg remembered me from the trial. I told him what little I knew from talking to Wellesley. "What's going to happen to her, Mr. Feinberg?"

He let go a breath of air into the phone. "I'd like to tell you everything is going to turn out fine, Will. But I can't. It sounds like murder all right. The only question is whether it's first or second degree. Not enough information. A good defense attorney would try to negotiate the charge to manslaughter. At least this time she better have an attorney." The words he used, murder and slaughter, sounded so vicious. They described Mr. Baker, not Wellesley. "Even though she's a juvenile, the prosecutor will go all out for a murder charge."

"What happens if she loses?"

"Prison terms for juveniles are indeterminate. She could serve as much time as an adult, maybe longer."

"Mr. Feinberg, she'd die in prison. Is there any chance she'll get off?"

"From what you tell me, not much. Even self-defense is hard to establish without a witness. The law comes down hard on people who pull the trigger, especially in small towns. People get nervous when a kid kills her dad. It could happen to them."

"You make it sound bleak, Mr. Feinberg. Talk to her. You've got to help."

"Are you trying to hire me?"

"No, I didn't mean it that way, I just . . . I just didn't know who else to call." I wanted to tell him something that would convince him of Wellesley's innocence, to explain how she'd always had the raw end of every deal. But he was right. The town would believe in Mr. Baker. My own dad doubted he'd do anything to hurt her even after their fight on the porch.

"Don't get down, Will. I like Wellesley. Let me think about it." His voice had that same quizzical sound as the day he quoted the proverb to me in the bathroom. I hoped he knew something he wasn't explaining. "You're Catholic?"

"How did you know?"

"Pray for a miracle."

26

Ever since the day Dad took me to Hunter Memorial Field in the fourth grade to watch the Clearwater Loggers play the Sylvanus Roughriders, I'd yearned to go to high school.

We sat in the front row that day, on the ten yard line. I remembered that the numbers on the Loggers' gray and crimson uniforms, pale from being laundered too many times, were impossible to read in the sunlight. Some of the second stringers wore gold instead of gray pants. They were practice pants, Dad said. The third string was more of a thread; we counted only two extra players.

The opponents fielded an army in fresh blue and white uniforms that warmed up in the end zone closest to us. Their coach, in a matching windbreaker and cap, blew his whistle like a drum major to announce drills. Two long whistles and the players quickly formed rows. Three short bursts and they broke into jumping jacks.

Clearwater High served the farms in the western half of the county. The kids who played guard and tackle in the fall baled hay in the summer. The backs and ends were mostly town kids.

The Clearwater cheerleader on our end, with a long pony tail, sparkled as she called instructions to us through her crimson megaphone. I yelled so hard I had laryngitis the next day. She bounced and did cartwheels in front of the stands, not caring if her underpants showed. I'd never seen such enthusiasm.

I idolized those players in the faded jerseys, with helmets as varied as a stamp collection. They were outnumbered and outclassed that day but they weren't outscored. Clearwater won 21 to 20 when the Sylvanus try-for-extra point bounced harmlessly off the butt of their center with two minutes to go.

Since that game in fourth grade, I'd counted the days until I could be a Logger. I imagined walking the halls with classmates saying, "Nice catch, Bradford!" and the cheerleaders wanting to be seen with me.

Approximately one thousand nine hundred and seventy-five days after that game on Hunter Field, I woke with a bad case of heartburn. My throat felt thick and raw. Until I'd swallowed some water from the bathroom faucet, I thought I had laryngitis again. High school was here and I didn't want to go. Wellesley's absence had changed things.

First day was a series of fire drills. We met each teacher, introduced ourselves, talked about homework, and how many points for each test. Then the bell rang and we ran for the exit to find the next room.

The hallways boomed, with lockers slamming and people yelling to catch up with friends. It seemed so fake. Kids I'd seen pick their noses and wipe it on the inside seam of their pants in grade school acted so mature, repeating words like "algebra" and "grade point" in their conversation. Everyone pretended this was the happiest day of their lives. I tried. But inside, I knew I was faking too.

Lunchtime in the cafeteria, I sat next to three farm kids from Olalla. Mom encouraged me to meet new people. "It's easiest on the first day when kids don't know each other," she said. The Olalla kids were big enough to use me as a pencil. I listened to them talk about football.

"How much you weigh now?"

"Hey, I been runnin' twice a day this last month, how about you?"

"We're gonna' be number one in the state as soon they let me play!"

They laughed when I told them I was turning out. "You're too small!" they said. That's how I felt.

Predictably, Taylor had risen to the occasion. He sat at the end of one table, balancing a banana on his finger while a cluster of girls laughed at whatever he said. Marilyn was nowhere in sight.

On the way to fifth period English, Monica caught up with me. "I'm real sorry about Wellesley," she said. Her face was scrinched up like she really meant it. We walked together until the stairs. She had to go to social studies, with Mr. Fitter. I wanted to tell her thanks again for the dance and all that, but I couldn't bring myself to even talk about it. The memory of that night had been smeared with a chalky eraser.

All afternoon I thought about freshman football tryouts. For the first time since my beginner swimming lessons at the park pool, I decided not to show up for something I was supposed to. I walked home alone, with a stack of used textbooks so heavy I had to switch arms every block.

The maple trees on Chinook Street were mottled with yellow and orange leaves. Someone was burning trash in their backyard; I could hear the crackle of dry boards. Fragments of smoldering paper rose like small ashen carpets over the roofs of houses. Things were starting to die in Clearwater.

The feeling of being in the wrong place excited me. I was tired of varnishing over mistakes and misimpressions. Because I enunciated the Latin so clearly, I was Sister Gabriela's favorite altar boy at St. Paul's; she didn't care that I had no clue what the words meant. At the hardware, Dad's clerks said I worked harder than any kid my age, but I felt like a martyr because Taylor carried more money in his pocket from allowance. Now that I had a chance with Monica, I was worried she'd find out Mom took in sewing to make ends meet.

I heard Laddie's bell in front of the Durgans' house. He stopped his bike in the street, lifted it over the curb and blocked my path. Usually Laddie kept a safe distance from people. His eyes begged me with their eagerness as he grunted a sound, two syllables and nasal.

I had no idea what he was saying. "What's wrong, Laddie?"

He looked at me hopefully.

"I'm listening. Tell me again." I didn't know how I expected him to explain it. Nobody had heard Laddie say even his own name.

He yanked on my arm, almost making me lose hold of the books. A line of drool had worked its way out the edge of his mouth.

"You want me to come?" I raised my voice. "Come?"

He nodded repeatedly and I nodded back until we moved in unison. He smiled.

I had followed Laddie before when he fell from his bike and twisted his handlebars. This time, instead of soup cans and potatoes, I carried textbooks. He moved with determination, turning frequently to make sure that I was still there. We walked together for blocks. At each intersection, he stopped, looked both ways and listened, just like his mother must have taught him. He took us to Milltown and then to Wellesley's house. He hesitated at the edge of her yard, waiting for permission to go farther.

"Go ahead, Laddie, what is it?" He stared at the house, frozen. "Show me, Laddie."

With baby steps, he crossed into the backyard, clutching his bike. The grass hadn't been mowed in weeks. The dandelions had turned to seed. He brought me next to the same kitchen window where Taylor and I had eavesdropped. One hand on the handlebars, Laddie faced the house and leaned toward the glass. The sun reflected off the window. On the sill I could see a black plaster of Paris cat with yellow gems for eyes. Laddie squinted trying to see inside. His whole body trembled. He'd seen it! He must have sensed that Wellesley was in danger at the fair and followed her and Mrs. Baker home.

"Yes, Laddie!"

He slowly raised his left hand and pointed with a bent wrist into the window. I put my books on the ground and held my hands against the glass to shade the sunlight. Inside, it looked about the same as I remembered—a table with chrome trim and three empty chairs in the middle of the kitchen. There was yellow tape on the floor, probably where they'd found Mr. Baker.

"Did you see it, Laddie?" I wanted to shake words out of him. Pointing to the window, I repeated each word, "Did . . . you . . . see?"

Reluctantly, he nodded up and down, like he was in trouble for it.

"What? Laddie, what did you see?" I tried to use my calmest voice.

He leaned the bike against his hip and drew his hand away slowly. When he was sure the bike was secure, he made a fist with his right hand. With his other hand, he pried the index finger loose and pointed it inside the window. The gun! I could have leapfrogged the house. Laddie was Wellesley's witness. But how was Laddie going to convince someone he'd seen it if he couldn't even talk? And would what he saw help or hurt?

I patted Laddie on the shoulder and motioned him to follow me. As we walked, I imagined he must be bursting with things he'd seen in this town. People in Clearwater considered him a fool. Nobody had spent ten seconds trying to make contact with him. Maybe that explained the trapped animal look in his eyes. His unspoken memories just festered.

27

The smell of laundry bleach stung my nostrils. The wicker basket on the folding table overflowed with a load of dark clothes. Mom had pulled the pockets of Dad's pants inside out to make sure he didn't leave any gum or keys in them. I messed up twice dialing Mr. Feinberg's number. A woman with a slight accent answered. I guessed it was his wife. She gave me the number for his office. Dad was going to ask about all these long distance calls to Sylvanus.

"Law offices, good afternoon."

"Is Mr. Feinberg there?" I sounded panicky.

"May I tell him what this is regarding?"

"Tell him it's Will Bradford and I have what he wanted."

"Just a minute, please."

The first tumbler in the lock was moving. I could hear faint voices coming from somewhere deep in the phone line, like I was intercepting conversations from another continent. Silently, I prayed "Hail Marys" that the discovery of Laddie would help.

"Hello, Will?"

"Mr. Feinberg, I found him!"

He chuckled. "Slow down. Found who?"

"A witness for Wellesley! Laddie Tilford. He saw it." He didn't say anything. "Remember, you said Wellesley needed a witness to prove it was self-defense. That's how she'd get off." My finger had made a circle in the soap crystals spilled on top of the washer.

"I said it was a possibility, Will." His voice was calm; I wanted excitement. "Have you also found her an attorney?"

"No, uh, I was hoping you'd do it!" My request was totally unplanned, but Mr. Feinberg seemed like the right man. He was different, someone who wouldn't start out with the usual presumption that a kid from Milltown was a loser. I'd found out from Martin at the Rexall that Mr. Feinberg had grown up in the East and met his wife when she was a student at Brandeis. They moved West to take care of her mother who was in a nursing home in Sylvanus.

"Hold on! She's indigent and I'm trying to make a living."

"What do you mean?"

"No money. Her mother's unemployed."

"Mr. Feinberg, remember what you said?"

"What?"

"You owed her one. This is it. She needs someone fresh like you."

"Fresh also means less experienced. I've never defended anyone. A week ago, I was still a prosecutor."

I closed my eyes and shamelessly did what Dad had taught me never to do; I begged. "Please, Mr. Feinberg."

"You don't play fair, Bradford." His calling me by my last name was encouraging. Maybe he was considering it. "You remember promises. Who'll feed my pregnant wife? We can't penalize her for my rashness."

"We can't leave Wellesley in jail. You've got to help. We'll figure out a way to pay you. Promise."

He was laughing. "I'll think about it. People aren't exactly breaking the door down to hire me yet. How good's your witness?"

When we hung up, my circle in the soap had spokes sticking out of it, like a brilliant sun, or a tarantula. Mr. Feinberg said Laddie might not be allowed to testify. The prosecutor would argue he was incompetent. Besides, we still weren't sure what he'd seen. Mr. Feinberg said there'd have to be another dimension to the case. Something telling. He didn't elaborate. Neither did he say he wouldn't represent her. He wanted to talk to his wife.

I sat in the laundry room trying to figure out what to do next. When I was little, I used to watch Mom load the washer and dryer. They were new then. She let me put clothes into the rising pool of soapy water. The rubber hub churned the clothes back and forth. The room was so full of mysteries then. It seemed so ordinary and recognizable now.

Mom's iron stood on its heels on the ironing board. Parts from the vacuum cleaner head and a broken belt were spread out on the folding table, waiting for Dad to put it back together. A stack of boxes marked "Hardware Invoices" with dates on them blocked the cupboards. Everyone used the room to dump what didn't fit anywhere else. I heard Dad's voice in the kitchen. He was the last person I wanted to see. I tucked in my shirt, opened the door and tried to walk like everything was as usual as the smell of the dirty clothes basket.

"There he is!" Dad's voice boomed. He had a proud look on his face. "How was practice?"

I'd forgotten all about tryouts! "I couldn't go. . . ." I wanted to be more truthful. "I didn't go."

Dad fed himself peanuts from the opening in the end of his fist and stared directly at me. His jaw muscles bulged under the temples as he chewed. "How do you expect to make the team if you skip practice? You think the coach is going to beg you to play? He doesn't even know your name!" Dad's sneer reminded me of Bushner. Mom watched from the other end of the kitchen. "Why didn't you go?" he asked.

At least he'd given me a chance to explain. I could tell him I had a stomachache, the truth, and ignore the reasons for it. Dad wanted an answer. He chewed harder. But something inside made me firm. Dad's stare wasn't melting me into the usual babble. "I had something more important to do," I said. He dumped the rest of his peanuts into the dish and brushed his hands together like the conversation was finished. "Don't you want to know what?"

He raised his eyebrows as if to make sure who he was talking to. "Okay. You've got an excuse? Let's hear it." Mom moved into the kitchen and sat, worry lines breaking out on her face. She probably recognized the same familiar tone I did, the way Dad laid out the bait before pouncing.

I took a breath. "I'm worried about Wellesley . . ."

"Damn! I told you . . ."

"Dad, I know what you told me. Listen. She's a friend whether you like her or not . . ."

Mom reached her hand to smooth things out. "Will, that's not the point your Dad's trying to make . . ."

"Audrey, stay out of this!" He didn't even look at her.

"Don't worry, I'm not involved in Mr. Baker's death. But that doesn't mean I'm going to pretend it didn't happen. If I'd gone to football today, I would have been doing exactly that."

"Are you going tomorrow?"

"I don't know." My voice was softer again. "That's not the main thing on my mind." No interruption. For the first time in my life, he seemed to be listening. "I have to tell you something else." I checked Mom's face. We were skidding out of control and she was bracing for the impact. "Remember the trouble Wellesley got into at the fairgrounds with the man from the carnival company?"

They nodded.

"I was with her," I said. "She got caught and I didn't . . ." Dad raised his hand. "I know what you're going to say. I already tried to turn myself in. The police ignored me. So I went to Wellesley's trial and told the judge what I'd done. I should have told you, I'm sorry . . . but I was afraid to say anything." I stopped, to let Dad unload.

He moved slowly, like he'd been awakened from a deep sleep. He licked his lips, dried out from listening, furrowed his forehead and looked around the room to get his bearings. Mom held her breath. "Is that all?" he asked quietly.

"I carried that fairground thing around all summer. It was like a tumor growing in my head. I was afraid I'd get caught. Then I wanted to be caught." It was so quiet I thought I could hear Dad's wristwatch ticking. "What happened with Wellesley and her dad makes it seem so small now." There was a sense of relief in letting them know that I wasn't their little angel anymore.

Dad sat down, braced his elbows against his knees and rubbed his face in his hands. I was still looking at him when he raised his head. "I should chew you up for this," he said, squinting slightly. "You know how much I detest disrespect for the law. And lying. I must be getting old. The only point of punishing you is so you'll understand what you did." His eyes seemed to water a little bit as he spoke. "It sounds like you already know what the score is."

"Will," Mom said, "you're not responsible for what happened between Wellesley and her dad . . ."

"If I'd told someone what was going on in that house, Mom, maybe it wouldn't have ended in a shootout."

"Oh, Will," Mom said, "don't even think that way . . ."

"Mom, I know you're trying to protect me." For the first time since I'd entered the kitchen, I moved off my spot between the refrigerator door and the counter. From her chair, Mom tackled me around the waist and burrowed her head into me. Awkwardly, I put my hand behind her neck and patted her hair.

"Listen, Will," Dad said, in a firm voice, "there's a lotta problems out there. No ten of you or me are going to solve them. You're not some garbage collector that has to pick up everyone's trouble."

"I know, Dad, but when it's one of your friends, you can't just stand there and watch them suffocate in it." I paused. "That's why I didn't go to football." Dad's eyelids looked heavy, like they carried the weight of all that garbage. "Sorry, Dad."

The three of us sat around the kitchen table while I told them what I knew about Mr. Baker's death. Mom kept shaking her head and crying. When Dad started filling his fist with peanuts from the bowl again, I asked him. "You'll think this is crazy but can you and Mom help pay for Wellesley's attorney? It can be a loan, Dad."

Dad's chewing slowed as his eyes met Mom's. In that glance, they carried on a whole conversation, both apparently agreeing that it was okay to tell me because Dad did. "Will, you've been keeping something from us this summer that you shouldn't have. But we've been keeping something from you too." He looked at Mom again and his eyes welled. "We're selling the hardware."

My stomach knotted. "Really?" When the accountant's visits to the house had stopped, I'd assumed Dad had taken care of things the way he 'always did. In my preoccupation with Wellesley's hearing and the dance, I'd forgotten about the hardware store.

"I could tell you we wanted to sell it, but the truth is we have to. That or go bankrupt. I feel sick about it. Your mom, of course, says it's for the better."

"Maybe we'll see more of your dad," she said, "when he gets a normal job."

"Maybe you can get on as the bottler with the new owner," Dad said, smiling through his wet eyes.

"Do we have to move?" I still carried around the picture of that chicken farm Dad had mentioned when he didn't know I was listening.

Dad laughed. "Why would we do that? We're losing the business, not the house! Don't worry, I've already got an angle on a job. You think the only thing I know how to do is run a hardware?"

"I just thought . . ."

"We're staying! Hardware or not, we're staying right here!" He spread his arms and gripped the edges of the tabletop.

"Everything will be fine with us," Mom said. "I'm more worried about Wellesley and her poor mother. What a horrid thing!"

"Mom, when I asked about the money for Wellesley's attorney, I didn't . . ."

"I didn't drag all this out as an excuse to tell you no," Dad said, "but if want to talk money, then let's talk. You're too old for the tooth fairy." He grabbed some more peanuts and talked with his mouth full. "Just 'cause we're selling doesn't mean I'm going to lose my shirt. Your old man wasn't born yesterday. Our biggest creditor is Jensen-George. So that's who we're selling to. They're taking over all the debts plus . . ."—he stabbed his salty index finger next to the Planter's can—"plus, keeping the employees."

"Uncle Carl?"

"Yep."

"Joe?"

"Joe, Harold, and Vi!" Dad said, counting them on his fingers. "The family stays on, except for the boss. They want new management."

"They'll live to regret that," Mom said. "It'll take three people to do what your father did."

Dad dismissed Mom's comment with a wave of his hand, "You asked about money for Wellesley. Let me tell you something else you don't know. Your Grandpa Blane had a couple of War Bonds. One for ten thousand dollars with your name on it. We were figuring on keeping it a secret till it was time for college."

"Ten thousand dollars?"

"You want to spend it on legal fees?"

Dad had a way of attaching responsibility even to a pure windfall. Although Grandpa Blane didn't make it through high school, he always said there wasn't a better investment than college. But I also knew Grandpa would get his friend out of jail first. "Won't you need the money . . . because of . . . well, until you get a job, Dad?"

"Your grandpa meant this money for you," Mom said. "We're not going to starve."

"This hardware store business has taught me something, Will." Dad set his jaw and spoke in his most serious voice. "For the past twelve years, if I had an extra minute, I asked myself what could I do at the hardware. When we had a good month, I found a way to spend it on something at the hardware. Bigger display windows, a pipe threader, a new delivery van. Bunk!" He rested his hand over Mom's. "I've let your mom darn people's socks and sell her antiques off our front yard just to keep the hardware going. Someone should have kicked me. The damn hardware was a thing! Life's for people!"

"You sound happy about it, Dad."

"You know? I am," he said. "I can start paying your mom back for all those times she's waited up for me to close the store. Maybe I owe you something too."

I'd never thought I'd hear Dad question the hardware. It was his religion, not just the Sunday Mass kind, but seven days a week. He drew his energy from the confusion of gadgets and fix-its that filled the bins. In the failure of the hardware, he'd suffered a conversion in Wellesley's favor.

After creamed tuna fish on toast dinner, I called Mr. Feinberg again. When I explained about Grandpa's War Bond, he knew I was serious. He said he'd do it if Wellesley wanted him.

Then I called Taylor.

"That's pretty weird," he said, when I told him Laddie had been there when it happened. "I wonder what else that old coot's seen he's not telling."

"Taylor, I also told Mom and Dad I was with Wellesley at the fairgrounds."

"Damn, Bradford, what's gotten into you? I'll kill you if you said anything about me."

"What are you afraid of?"

"I'm that close to getting a raise in my allowance," he said. I imagined him holding his thumb and index finger next to his eye like a microscope. "That kind of news would pretty well poison it."

I laughed out of habit, but I didn't care how big his allowance was. Dad had stopped mine three years ago when he realized I could push a broom. "Have you seen Wellesley yet?"

"Did you see that girl I was sitting next to in the cafeteria? She's in my algebra. God, what a looker!" He paused for my answer, while I clamped my eyes shut in disbelief. "Will? Do you read me? Hello, Willy . . . wake up."

I was tired of being Taylor's chorus. Taylor's dominant instinct was still personal survival. The Clearwater Dam had burst, washing away the bike paths and back alleys that joined our lives. Wellesley's raft was losing air and he was paddling in the other direction. I felt alone. But I also felt a rising strength like Dad must have felt when he stood up to Mr. Baker on the porch that night. "Taylor, I don't give a crap who you flirted with at school today. Tell me about it when you've done something for Wellesley."

The line was hushed. "You're right. I haven't done shit. I guess I just wanted everything to be the way it was."

"So do I, Taylor. But we're kidding ourselves to think that way."

"Can't we just nurse a little fib between us?" he asked.

"Something to dream about, you mean . . ."

"Yeah, something harmless."

* * *

School next day was a clock on the wall. I watched the red second hand sweep the face. Each bell at ten minutes to meant I was one hour closer to seeing Wellesley. When I was called on in ancient history, the class laughed when I said, "The Greeks?" It turned out he'd just asked if I'd read the first chapter. My face must have looked like a new brick.

Mom drove me to Sylvanus again. From looking ahead in the history book, I recognized the courthouse entry as Doric architecture. I'd been inside so often the place felt more familiar than the high school. Mom volunteered to wait in the pew outside of Licensing instead of going to the jail lobby in the basement. I wished now I'd made Taylor come with me. More than anything else, Wellesley probably wanted to see her friends. But Taylor was going to Yell King tryouts in the gym.

There was a new officer at the desk. He put a mystery novel facedown next to his sandwich on the wax paper when I stepped to the window—*The Case of the Blue Petticoats.* On the cover, a woman with perfectly combed auburn hair lay on her back, a glass with ice cubes spilled on the carpet next to her. The left knee hooked awkwardly over her right leg, exposing layers of ruffled, powder blue petticoats.

I signed the log and put "Wellesley Baker" in the prisoner column. Glancing up the page, I saw that Mrs. Baker had been Wellesley's only other visitor that day. The officer chewed on his sandwich while he spoke, sending a sardine odor through the talking hole in the window.

The metal clanged and bolts disengaged from invisible clasps as I waited. It was as if Wellesley was being brought to me in an iron gondola. Finally, the steel door in front of me moved and I entered the visitors' bay.

Wellesley was on the same stool as before, in the same oversized green gown. "Hello, Will," she called, as if we'd just met in front of the Rexall, "I was hoping it was you."

I squared a chair in front of her and sat down. Raccoon rings still showed around her eyes from lack of sleep. "You look great," I said, stupidly.

"Don't get so used to this," she said, pinching her shirt front and letting go with a snap of her fingers. "I thought you wanted to get me out of here."

"I do. Listen." I scanned the room again to make sure we were alone. "I found a witness."

She lowered her chin in a disbelieving frown. "You mean Mom?"

"No, Laddie Tilford!"

She tilted her head sideways.

"He was standing outside your kitchen window the whole time." I raced to get it out. "Laddie saw it." Now I was the Yell King, trying to whip Wellesley into a frenzy.

A worried look came over her face. "What did he see?"

"Mr. Feinberg's working with him to find out. I forgot. He said he'd take your case."

She looked away, as if she was upset. The air in the room felt used and sticky.

"What's wrong, Wellesley? You act like you want me to butt out." My voice was raised. I wanted to shake her. "Stop trying to be a martyr."

"I'm sorry. It's just that I'm not sure I want anyone to know what happened." She was firm and looked straight at me as she spoke. "The idea of someone looking in my window . . ."

"It's just Laddie. He doesn't have a harmful bone in his body."

She shook her head and seemed to shift gears. "You're crazy, Bradford." She straightened her shoulders and pushed the glasses back up her nose. "Do you really think Laddie can help . . . I mean, people think he's loony." Her laugh was almost a shiver. "Pretty fitting. They probably think I'm loony too."

"He's what we've got."

"But he doesn't talk," she said.

I didn't want to run out of time. "What do you think of Mr. Feinberg?"

"He came by. All he wanted to talk about was my childhood. God, he even asked me if I sucked my thumb! Who's going to pay for him?"

"I think the court appoints him or something." I'd already decided not to tell her about Grandpa Blane's money, in case she refused to cooperate. "But how do you think he'll do?"

"Beggars can't be choosy. I like him or lump it, I guess."
Authority figures always rankled Wellesley. Why did I expect her to change just because it was someone on her side?

"He's smart. Dad said he's from one of those high-pow-
ered Eastern law schools."

"I just . . ." Wellesley stopped and let her jaw soften.
"I'm sorry, Will, you're turning the town upside down and
I'm being a jackass." We laughed. Both of us knew she was
right. She crammed her eyes shut, like she was making a
wish. "I'm not mad about the lawyer, he'll be great." She
looked at me again. "It's just that sitting in here, I get so
angry at myself I could piss through my eye sockets. Mom's
miserable. She can't sleep. She thinks she's a failure. One
kid a runaway, the other in jail. I wanted so hard to make up
to her for Tiffany. Maybe for Dad too. The more I tried, the
worse it got."

"Wellesley, you're too hard on yourself. You didn't
choose your dad, I didn't choose mine. You could have been
Grace Kelly and married the prince."

She laughed softly. "Or maybe the toad."

"Maybe then I could have beaten you arm wrestling."

The guard knocked on the open door. "Time's up, son!"

I quickly rattled off the news from the outside. "You're
not missing a thing in school." That was true. "Everyone's
worried about you." From the stories I'd heard in the hallways at school, it was probably more curiosity. "Taylor
thinks we're going to spring you out of here like a slingshot." We both laughed. Taylor's cartoon version of the
world tickled Wellesley's funny bone the same as mine.

"You mean in flames, like one of his matchstick guns."
She grinned her famous crooked smile.

28

The weekly edition of the *Clearwater Chronicle* carried the story of Mr. Tug Baker's death on the front page, complete with a picture of him resting one foot on the running board of the Pink Lady. It was probably one of many Baker stock car pictures in the *Chronicle* files. The headline read: "Stock Car Veteran Slain." Wellesley's name appeared in the story only as one of those who Mr. Baker was "survived by." Even though the explanation given for his death was vague, "a bullet wound inflicted by a member of the family," everyone knew who did it. Dad said the paper never printed the names of juveniles until they were convicted.

People asked me two questions. What did I think really happened and why hadn't I turned out for football? I'd never realized until then how much I'd been connected to Wellesley in people's minds. Part of the answer I knew rested with Taylor who, even though he'd still not visited Wellesley, had become her chief press agent. As he nodded in hallway conversations, kids would turn to gawk at me while I opened my locker or tied my shoe. It was as if everyone wanted to believe Wellesley killed her dad in cold blood. When I protested, they said it was because I was soft on her. You'd believe anything she told you, Bradford. I could have been more convincing if I really knew what happened.

Mostly it was the football players who asked why I'd chickened out of tryouts. For them, I guessed there wasn't anything more important to talk about. Coach MacDonough was cracking ass, they said. No place for someone who's daydreaming about a dame in jail.

It was almost a relief when the *Chronicle* ran the story about the hardware. I needed a change of subject, even if it

was more bad news. The same issue which featured a picture of Khrushchev visiting an American farm in Iowa carried the story of Jensen-George's takeover of Western
Hardware. The story didn't actually use the word failure but
"business reversals" amounted to the same thing. The survi-
vors in this story weren't listed by name. Nor was any mention made of the real cause of death, but I knew what it was:
the customers who bought Toro power mowers, Black and
Decker quarter-inch drills, and furnace filters on credit
without paying their bills.

I doubted most freshmen read the business page and con-
cluded they heard about this one at the dinner table. The
conversations were easy to imagine. Don't you go to school
with the Bradford boy? They always seemed so prosperous.
It was like Mom had sponsored a giant yard sale on the
practice field behind school, laying out our remaining tat-
tered possessions for nickels and dimes. Kids started teasing
me about my old man being flat ass broke. Beller said the
business went tits up. They used body parts for emphasis. I
told them Dad wanted out; he had a choice of new jobs. The
truth was he was still circling and calling phone numbers in
the *Chronicle.*

What they whispered behind my back, Taylor reported.
"They say it's no wonder you and Wellesley like each
other."

"What is that supposed to mean?"

"Milltown," Taylor said. "You're in the same boat with
'em."

"They can shove it! What's wrong with Milltown? Maybe
we'll decide to live in Milltown, so what?"

"Don't tell them that," Taylor said.

"My dad's given away more money than most of them will
ever make. What about you, Taylor?"

"What do you mean?"

"Have you joined them?"

"Jesus, no! I'm just telling you what I hear. Don't get so
worked up about it! It's connected to Wellesley's thing, you
know. People are trying to figure it out. They'll forget about
the hardware as soon as her mess blows over."

"I wish it were that easy. Have you been to see her yet?"

"I've been busy . . ."

Taylor finally went. He said it scared the bejesus out of him, partly because he'd always assumed he'd end up there one time or another himself. It also gave him claustrophobia. "The place echoes like a morgue," he said. "I get the creepy feeling . . . don't get mad at me for saying this . . . I get the feeling she's going to lose."

"You didn't tell her that, did you?"

"Do you think I've got soup for brains?"

"Did you act depressed?"

"Come on, Will, get serious."

"Why do you think she'll lose?"

"It's just a hunch. I guess I don't trust adults that much. There's a side of Wellesley that scares them."

If Grandpa Blane were watching, he'd say we were getting our money's worth out of his War Bond. Mr. Feinberg's name came up as often as next week's high school football opponent. He was pestering everyone in town who knew the Bakers. I found his old Ford with the gray primer on the fender parked in front of Mr. Baker's old haunts—Larry's Barbershop, Western Auto, the Drift Inn.

People asked what the point of his search was; everyone knew who did it. If Mr. Feinberg didn't believe them, why didn't he ask his client? Larry, the barber, said that Feinberg was just using the case as an opportunity to build his clientele. Win or lose, he'd know everyone in Clearwater. Pretty shrewd, Larry said.

He interviewed Dad, Mom, and me separately. When I asked him how the case looked, he was poker-faced. "I think Mr. Baker has more friends dead than he ever had alive. But I'm working on an angle."

Mr. Feinberg tried to get Wellesley out on bail, while waiting for the trial, but he said state law didn't expressly provide bail for juveniles. His former boss, Mr. Dutcher, who was the prosecutor, had refused to even consider it given the gravity of the offense. Mr. Feinberg explained to me that pretrial detention was normal in this state for incorrigible delinquents and that's how the system classified Wellesley because of her two offenses. The court's refusal to let her out just made Feinberg more determined. He called it punitive.

Whenever I got close to Monica Amberly, she seemed to be late for class or in a hurry to meet someone. At the game under the lights against the Sylvanus Roughriders, I saw her walk in with a junior who looked like Roland Bushner, with his pants riding so low on his buttocks I could have put a quarter in the crack in his ass. I should have warned her but instead I just moved to the higher bleachers so I wouldn't have to watch them. High school had reshuffled the deck. The hand I held at the Labor Day Fair had been dealt to someone else.

Out of refusal to believe that life could change so quickly, I went to the Rexall for a cherry Coke. Martin still pumped the same two squirts into the Coke, pushed a white straw into the glass, and set it gently in front of me. He was my best source.

"What's the news, Martin?" I was the only one at the counter, ahead of the after-school rush.

"People are skeptical of your Mr. Feinberg, Will."

"So? He's not on trial."

"He's an outsider." Martin said the word like it was the name of a foreign country.

"So is most everyone. This is a small town."

"And he's Jewish."

"I'm Catholic, so what?"

"It's been mentioned, that's all I'm saying, Will." Martin polished dry a Coke glass with the dish towel as he spoke. "You know how people are. Like your friend, Laddie. He's the sweetest guy in town, but ladies grip their purse a little tighter when he rides by." Martin pushed his bushy eyebrows closer together. "They just don't know how to figure him, I guess."

"I'm worried about Laddie too. This thing's done something to him."

"How so?"

"He seems scared to show his face," I said. "The other day he turned around and hightailed it when he saw me coming, like I was going to put a net over him or something."

Martin started chuckling. "He's never been very sociable, Will. That's his way."

From watching him pedal these streets since I was a kid, I knew there was something else. We'd started to make a connection; now he was acting like he wanted nothing to do with my world. I couldn't blame him. It had to be the trial. Mr. Feinberg had been working to get him ready. "Do people talk much about the trial, Martin?"

He laughed. "Not as much as you, my friend. But sure, I hear 'em talking at the counter. They just assume I'm not listening."

"What are they saying?"

"Mostly saying what a tragedy it was. Poor Mr. Baker and all that. It's funny, but I always thought most people were kind of scared of that guy. But he's remembered fondly. One of the few of us anybody outside Clearwater had ever heard of. The ladies mention Mrs. Baker, saying what a shame to lose a husband with two kids to raise. Mostly they're curious how she'll support herself. You know, practical considerations."

"Doesn't anyone worry about Wellesley?"

"Sure, the kids do. They make their jokes but I detect a serious tone to it. She was a bit of a loner, but kids respected her, don't you think, Will?"

"Sure, Martin, some did. Did? You've got me talking like it's over."

Martin turned the glass in his hand upside down and put it under my chin. "Hey, keep it up there, pardner! Somebody's got to make up for all those pessimists."

I couldn't get to the jail every day because of school and having to beg Mom for rides. But the bike still worked and my legs were staying in good enough shape to play football. Next year maybe.

When I was with Wellesley, I took Martin's charge seriously. But it was hard to think of anything that wasn't depressing to someone sitting out first semester of their freshman year in a jail cell. Anything good that happened she was missing out on; anything adverse seemed a bad omen. Through the school office, I made arrangements to get textbooks for her and then she started asking me English comp.

and history questions. As a tutor, I was a complete failure; her questions always hit on the feature I knew least. Martin came to visit her once, she was ecstatic, and Tiffany twice. She was surprised. I always spoke hopefully of the future, reminding her of the things we'd do when she got out. She said she'd be happy to just pedal down to the river and go swimming.

On the day after Halloween, I decided to visit Mrs. Baker. Except for meeting her in the corridor at the jail once, I hadn't seen her since the fair.

She seemed delighted to see me. "I'll get you some cookies, Will," she said. "Would you like milk with them? Wellesley always wants milk with her cookies."

"Sure, Mrs. Baker, that would be great." I'd just eaten the Twinkies I'd saved from my lunch sack.

The living room was dark, with the curtains drawn, and held the itchy smell of snubbed-out cigarettes. She led me into the kitchen and pulled out a wooden chair with a split in the leg. The back gave when I leaned so I didn't put all my weight against it. There were nicks and gouges in the wall plaster and, next to the light switch, a hole the size of a fist. The scuff marks on the linoleum took me back to the night in the coal bin. The cupboard doors sagged so that the crack between the doors widened from top to bottom. The ceramic cat, with one eye missing and a stubbed tail, was still perched on the windowsill. In the center of the table, a bowl with bananas and green apples rested on a lace doily.

Mrs. Baker served me store-bought Lorna Doones on a saucer next to a glass of milk. She pulled her chair to the table and watched me eat. It was so quiet that the crunch of the cookies in my mouth sounded like a storm. I tried not to look around and make it so obvious that I was looking for signs of him. I half expected to hear the front door slam and see him barge into the kitchen and dump me out of the chair.

"He's not here anymore, Will."

"No . . . I, of course, I know. How did you know what I was thinking?"

"It's written all over your face," she said, her hands resting softly on the apron in her lap.

"I couldn't help but think of him, he's so . . ."

"Unforgettable."

"Yeah, he sure was." The topic was wrong, one that would just upset her, but at the same time I couldn't leave it. "I didn't really know him that well though. I'm sorry, Mrs. Baker, about what happened."

"I have mixed feelings about it, Will." Her voice was so quiet I had to stop chewing to hear. "I'm heartsick about Wellesley. That poor dear. Some mornings I check her room to see if I haven't just been dreaming. Her father was such a bully. Always had to have things his own way. I know he loved the girls . . . he just didn't know how to show it. He expected so much of them. You should have known him when he was your age, Will."

"What was he like, Mrs. Baker?"

"He was a drifter who showed up one summer day and started doing odd jobs in our neighborhood, washing windows, painting houses, changing sparkplugs. I thought he was the most handsome man I'd ever seen. For some reason, he took a shine to me." Mrs. Baker looked down at her lap like she was still embarrassed about it. Her hair was coiled in a tight bun, every hair in place. "Next thing I knew, we were married."

"In Clearwater?"

"Only place we've ever lived. It was great for a while . . . until the girls came along. Somehow he resented having to share. Then he started drinking again, just like his dad. When I reminded him of that, he said it was different. But it wasn't." Mrs. Baker looked as if she was willing her tears to stay inside, but they disobeyed. When she dabbed with her finger, I took a drink of milk to take the attention off her. "I think he did it to forget things, things his dad had done. His dad was so vicious. When he found out Tug hadn't passed third grade, he took the gun and shot right through the screen killing his dog. Can you imagine, Will? His dad said the dog was wrecking the door with his scratching."

Wellesley had never told me the whole story. I squirmed in my chair, wishing there was another Lorna Doone to chew on. It made me uncomfortable, hearing Mrs. Baker tell things that were obviously so secret. I rubbed my fingers along the dented chrome strip, pushing it back against the table edge so that the nail heads poked out.

"Does it feel like I've trapped you? I'm sorry, Will. I don't get many visitors."

"No, Mrs. Baker, I'm fine, I wanted to see you . . ."

"With Wellesley gone, there's no one to talk to, you know, just these walls," she said, holding up her hands and looking around. She smiled and tried to make a joke of it. "I've not been very active in the social circles. Always too busy here at the house, I guess." She paused again. I thought she might say something about how the church sewing club humiliated her over her Depression clothing or explain why Mr. Baker never took her anywhere, but she was too polite. "I'm so glad you came by, Will. It's meant so much to Wellesley the way you've kept in touch with her."

"She's going to be back in school in no time, Mrs. Baker," I said, pushing two of the loose nails back into their holes with my thumbs.

"I admire your spirit, Will. I'm praying for the same thing."

She led me back through the living room and opened the door, staying close enough for a hug. But neither one of us was able to make the first move.

When she'd closed the door, I walked around to the back of the house, past the basement window I'd pried open once and into her backyard. The front end of the Pink Lady was propped up by concrete blocks. I walked over to Wellesley's Schwinn, tilted on its kickstand next to a stack of old tires by the house. Without a note to leave her, I just gripped the seat, closed my eyes and made a wish.

Walking home, I got madder and madder. It wasn't fair. When Grandpa Blane died, people wouldn't leave us alone. Besides food and gifts, they offered to do our yard, take Mom shopping, go on picnics. We'd never had so many friends. But Mrs. Baker found her husband dead on the kitchen floor and the same people ignored her. The death of a Milltowner was a disease that nobody wanted to catch.

29

The day of Wellesley's trial it poured rain, not surprising for the week before Thanksgiving. Some years, we'd already had snow by this time. As people entered the courthouse, they shook their umbrellas and turned them upside down in the foyer.

Judge Lally's courtroom was about half full and smelled like coats and galoshes in a school cloakroom. When I sat down with Mom and Dad, Mr. Feinberg was already at his table, looking over a stack of notes. Mrs. Baker sat in the front row wearing one of those hats with black netting that goes over the face. Annie Curran sat next to her; she'd probably gotten permission to miss school the same as me. She must have thought the law was blind in one eye. Bushner killed her horse and would have raped her if it hadn't been for Wellesley but here we were at Wellesley's trial.

Each time the door creaked, I turned to see who it was. Mrs. Thistle carried a folder in her hand and sat in the back. I wondered if she was going to be testifying for or against. I recognized Mr. Coughlin, the reporter for the *Chronicle*. He had his sleeves rolled up and a pencil over his ear ready to report what they said was the first murder trial in the county since before Russia launched Sputnik. Some people connected the two events, saying how both showed the moral decline of the country.

Tiffany came in with a sneer on her face in a red oilskin coat; her boyfriend followed, his hair slicked down from the rain. Instead of sitting with Mrs. Baker, they slouched down in the first empty space next to the aisle. Although I didn't really know her, I held a grudge against Tiffany. It felt as if she'd deserted her mom and sister.

I almost clapped when Taylor walked in with Mrs. Clark. He didn't tell me he was coming; I'm sure he didn't mind the idea of missing classes but that also meant he'd sacrificed lunch period with what's-her-name.

Escorted by a stern-faced matron with a ring of keys hanging from her belt, Wellesley finally appeared. Her face looked as petrified as her hair, which hung stiffly over her ears where it had been combed out. The matron whisked her through the gate in the railing and into the seat next to Mr. Feinberg, who patted her on the shoulder and eked a slight smile out of her.

"All rise, please!" The clerk in front of the podium projected his voice to the back wall. "Court is now in session, the Honorable Judge Randolph P. Lally presiding!"

And there he was again, entering on cue, the same judge who'd already convicted Wellesley of assault. His tan slacks showed beneath his robe as he ascended the two steps to his high-backed leather chair. My stomach tensed and I looked over at Wellesley to see how she was doing. "Please be seated," he said. "Bailiff, please call the next case."

The bailiff yelled, *State* versus *Baker,* Case No. Ten Seventy-five," as people lowered themselves to their seats.

Then Judge Lally called for the jury panel and another door opened. The courtroom had more doors than a train station. A single file of ordinary-looking people entered, filling the twelve chairs in the jury box as well as a row of folding chairs on the floor in front. The men were red-faced and bald, the women heavily powdered in bright patterned dresses and carrying purses of every size and shape. The jurors were so serious, like they'd been plotting something in the side room.

The presence of a jury represented a victory for Mr. Feinberg. Unlike adults, he'd explained, juveniles were not guaranteed the right to a jury trial. But Feinberg had insisted. He told me it was part of his plan. Judge Lally said he could see no problem in too much justice, despite the prosecutor's opposition. Besides, the judge had pointed out, the prosecutor had gotten his way on the bail.

Working from a notepad in his hand, the judge asked the panel a series of questions—whether they were related to or personal friends of the defendant or members of her family, whether they or anyone in their family had ever worked for the police department or the prosecutor's office. The jurors shifted nervously in their seats, looked around at each other and shook their heads no to each of the judge's questions. It was as if they'd agreed to consult.

Then the judge opened it up for questions from Mr. Dutcher, the prosecuting attorney, a tall skinny man in a tweed sport jacket with brown patches on the elbows that matched his slacks. With each question, he hitched up his belt buckle and made a check mark with his pencil on the tablet. I whispered to Dad, asking if he knew anyone on the panel. He held up four fingers and whispered, "Customers." I checked their faces again to see if I could pick them out. Everyone survived the prosecutor's questions. Mr. Feinberg's turn.

He stood, fastened the middle button of his jacket, and walked over in front of the box. "Good morning, I'm Aaron Feinberg, counsel for the accused, Wellesley Baker. My questions will be a little more personal, I'm afraid. Please understand the spirit in which I approach this. It's my job to insure that my client has the fairest possible trial." Although I guessed he was much younger than the prosecutor, Mr. Feinberg's wire glasses and his bald spot made him look older than he was and smarter. "Sometimes, there are things in our background that prevent us from being fair. For example, my grandfather was beaten and nearly paralyzed by a group of Nazi hoodlums in Frankfurt before his family fled Germany. Therefore, it would be difficult for me to sit on a jury for a neo-Nazi accused of mugging an old man." This was another reason for liking Mr. Feinberg. He had a special feeling for his grandpa.

Wellesley sat straight up on the front of her chair. I wondered if she knew where Mr. Feinberg was going with this. It seemed totally unrelated to her problem. The jurors fidgeted while Mr. Feinberg strolled slowly in front of them, seeming totally relaxed. "Have any of you . . . please answer this honestly, there will be no repercussions for being honest . . . how many of you have ever slapped one of your kids in anger?"

The prosecutor jumped to his feet. "Objection, Your Honor! Mr. Feinberg's question is totally out of line. The jury panel is not on trial here. He's prying into matters of domestic privacy."

"Your Honor, my client is being prosecuted for something that took place under the canopy of the prosecutor's so-called domestic privacy. I am entitled to *voir dire* the prospective jurors on their attitudes regarding this subject."

"Mr. Feinberg knows better, Your Honor." The prosecutor seemed agitated and hiked up his belt buckle repeatedly. "His question is demeaning and without relevance."

I didn't have to understand all the words to know that Mr. Feinberg was the right lawyer for Wellesley. He was determined to do this his own way even if it meant remaking the rules. "Feinberg's a fighter," I whispered to Dad.

"The question is unusual," Judge Lally said, "but I'll allow it. This is *voir dire*. But be careful, Mr. Feinberg."

The prosecuting attorney shook his head in disbelief, but folded his lanky frame into the chair. Mr. Feinberg repeated his question and, hesitantly, checking with each other first, almost half of the panel raised a hand.

"How many of you have ever used a closed fist?"

Mr. Dutcher objected again and the judge overruled him. A couple of hands raised about halfway. Mr. Feinberg looked the jurors in the eye, waiting to make sure there weren't more.

"What about a belt?"

Mr. Dutcher shook his head but stayed in his seat. Wellesley scooted back in her chair, but without taking her eyes off the action. Nobody in the jury box made a move and Mr. Feinberg repeated the question as kindly as if he were complimenting the ladies on their loud dresses. The jurors looked at their laps, the ceiling, the judge, everywhere but at Mr. Feinberg. "Okay," he said when no one put their hand up, "how many of you have ever repeatedly struck your child or a spouse with your hand or with any object?" The slow twirl of the ceiling fans wasn't enough to offset the heat Mr. Feinberg was putting into the room. Mom put her hand reassuringly on my leg. "Does anyone have to answer 'yes' to that question?" Mr. Feinberg asked.

A few women shook their heads no, then others followed. A man in the back row stood up. "Your Honor, rather than answer the question one way or the other, I'd just like to be excused if that's all right with the court."

"Juror number nine is excused," the judge said. "Thank you. Is there anyone else who wants to be excused?"

Juror number nine worked his way between the knees of his neighbors to the end of the box. "Is he a customer, Dad?" I whispered. He shook his head negative. Maybe his son was one of those football players from Olalla. I wondered how many others were just too scared to do what number nine had done.

Mr. Feinberg asked more questions about disciplining children; the prosecutor objected and Judge Lally refereed. But nobody else stepped down. Finally, the judge invited a lady from one of the folding chairs with a hump in her back to step into seat number nine, excused the other prospective jurors and swore in the jury.

While the bailiff folded the extra chairs and stacked them against the wall, I kept thinking of Wellesley's first hearing in this room when she only had a judge to convince. Now she had a group of ordinary citizens, the ones who drank Cokes at the Rexall counter, the ones Martin said were more concerned about Mr. Baker. These were the people from Mrs. Baker's sewing club who'd laughed at her clothes. This was supposed to be a jury of Wellesley's peers, Mr. Feinberg said, but nobody up there remotely resembled Wellesley. I hoped that Mr. Feinberg's getting his jury didn't turn into what my history book called a Pyrrhic victory.

Mr. Dutcher called the county coroner as the state's first witness, a man with a string bean physique that made him look like a Dutcher relative. The coroner explained that the thirty-eight caliber bullet that pierced Mr. Baker's heart was fired from the pistol with Wellesley's fingerprints. The prosecutor handed him the gun to hold. He fiddled with it nervously while he answered the prosecutor's questions. One bullet passed through the abdomen and lodged against the lumbar vertebrae. A second one passed through the bladder. The fatal bullet entered laterally about elbow distance down from the armpit and severed the pulmonary artery.

"All were fired at very close range," the coroner said, "judging from the powder burns on the victim's clothing. There is no way to know the order of the shots or the elapsed time between shots. It could have been a few moments, it could have been minutes."

Mr. Feinberg cross-examined, asking if the coroner had any idea which way Mr. Baker was moving when each bullet entered.

"There's no way to know but either the victim was moving, or the shooter," the coroner said, "because the trajectories of the bullets are different." For a man who made a living examining dead bodies, he seemed very friendly.

"Could there have been a struggle?"

"Yes, that could account for it."

The second witness was the policeman who answered Mrs. Baker's call that night. He showed pictures of the body which the judge let the prosecutor pass to the jurors. From their grimaces, I imagined the pictures were pretty gruesome. He described finding blood on the kitchen table, one of the chairs and, of course, the floor, leading him to conclude that the victim was still walking after the first shot. In addition to the three bullets found in the deceased, he said there was a fourth hole in the kitchen floor and they found the fourth bullet in the basement coal bin. He also said Wellesley admitted she'd fired the gun.

Then, Mr. Feinberg stepped up. "Where were Wellesley and her mother when you arrived?"

"They were huddled together in a corner just staring at the victim's body."

"How did they seem to you?"

"How do you mean, sir?"

"What was their mood as far as you could observe?"

"I'd say they were scared. The mother was still bawling and the daughter was trying to comfort her."

"Did Wellesley make any attempt to get away?"

"No, sir, she didn't."

"Did she cooperate in answering questions?"

"Well"—he hesitated—"she seemed to be in a kind of fog at first. Her words came out in spurts. I thought she wasn't going to be able to tell me anything. But finally, she got it out."

"She cooperated?" Mr. Feinberg asked.

"She answered my questions, yes, sir, she answered my questions."

Mr. Feinberg moved closer. "Did you examine Miss Baker that evening for injuries?"

The policeman almost cracked a smile, acting as if that was a dumb question. "Sir, it was the father who'd been shot."

"Then how do you know whether or not there'd been a struggle? Isn't it possible she was trying to defend herself?"

"Objection, Your Honor, pure speculation! No foundation." Mr. Dutcher rose up on his toes, leaning into his table, as he spoke. He wasn't letting this one through.

"Sustained," the judge said.

Mr. Feinberg had the scent but the judge had just blocked the trail. He backed off and returned to his table. "No more questions."

After the morning recess, Mr. Dutcher called Sergeant Payne. From the first hearing, I'd expected him to be a Wellesley convert. Mr. Feinberg raised an immediate objection, and the judge excused the jury to the back room while the two attorneys argued whether Sergeant Payne could testify about Wellesley's conviction for assault. The judge said he normally heard evidence of prior convictions when juveniles were involved and overruled Mr. Feinberg's objection. *"Parens patriae,"* the judge said. "The state is her parent here." Wellesley was getting the worst of both the juvenile and the adult worlds.

"Yes, sir, I would have to describe the match gun as a dangerous weapon," Sergeant Payne said when the jury returned. "At least at close range." He started to add something else but the prosecutor cut him off.

"And were there any flammable materials within range of her gun?"

The sergeant didn't seem to be enjoying this and kept looking at Wellesley as he answered. "Well, yes, there was the generator which powers the Ferris wheel and a gas tank close by." Wellesley had to just sit there, grind her teeth, and let Mr. Feinberg do the fighting.

Mr. Feinberg seemed upset when he finally got his turn. "How big a man was Mr. Sparkman, the man working on the Ferris wheel that day?"

"Oh, probably about six feet two, two hundred pounds . . ."

"And my client is less than half that size?"

Sergeant Payne looked at Wellesley again. "In weight, that might be right . . ."

"And Mr. Sparkman chased her down with a pipe wrench in his hand?"

"Yes, sir, he did."

"It doesn't sound like Mr. Sparkman was in much danger, does it, Sergeant?"

"As it turned out, no, sir, but . . ."

Mr. Feinberg rushed in with his next question. "And isn't it true that Mr. Sparkman was smoking when this happened?"

The sergeant hesitated. "I'm not sure . . ."

"Didn't Mr. Sparkman smoke?"

The sergeant seemed flustered. "I believe he did, but . . . the point is the girl attacked the man, sir."

"No more questions. Thank you, Sergeant."

As Sergeant Payne returned to his seat, Dad whispered to me, "That one is a customer."

Mr. Feinberg was doing the best he could to diminish the impact of the prosecutor's witnesses, but I had the feeling the jury was still wondering why a trial was even necessary. Wellesley had admitted shooting her dad. According to Sergeant Payne, this was a kid with a criminal record, someone who had already been convicted once for assault with a dangerous weapon. This was the kind of delinquent whom people expected from Milltown.

I almost snapped my neck when the prosecutor called "Mr. Roland Bushner." What did he have to do with this? Just the mention of his name made my tongue search the roof of my mouth for phlegm. Bushner came down the aisle with a snicker on his face in a white shirt and a tie that hung down his front like two flags. If only I could spit. Wellesley must have been cussing to herself. She considered Bushner a step down from a night crawler.

Mr. Dutcher introduced him with questions that let him explain how his dad was county auditor. It finally clicked. No wonder the charges for destroying Dolly had never been pressed. Bushner's dad and the prosecutor were probably buddies. They worked in the same building.

I wondered what Annie was thinking. The only thing I could see was the back of her head. Then it clicked again. The prosecutor wanted to ask him what Wellesley did at the homestead. Mr. Dutcher had done some digging of his own.

"My girlfriend and I had ridden her horse to this old house not far from her place." Bushner spoke very calmly. He sounded half intelligent when he talked about something besides pissing in the dirt. "Well, we started necking, one thing led to another, pretty soon she had her clothes off." Poor Annie, she'd held off telling anyone about this to save her pride and this worm was using it to get Wellesley. "That's not usually the way things went with us but, I guess the romance of riding out there on the same horse and all, we were feeling pretty strong."

"Mr. Bushner, I have to ask you. Did you engage in sexual intercourse that day?"

"Oh, no sir. There was nothing like that." Bushner shook his head, insulted at the suggestion.

"Did Wellesley Baker follow you?"

"Yes, sir. She and her friend Bradford snuck up on us."

"What did she do?"

"Well, she came at me with a two-by-four and hit me across the ribs with it. I don't think I've ever seen anyone so mad. She was practically foaming at the mouth. She would have hit me again, but her cousin, that was my girlfriend, called her off." Bushner tapped the ends of his fingers together in a way that made a cage out of his hands. That's where he belonged.

"Did you sustain any injuries?"

"They took the horse and left me there alone. I could hardly walk. Every time I took a breath, it felt like she'd hit me again." He creased his brow in mock pain as he spoke.

"My dad made me get some X rays." He held up his fingers. "Two cracked ribs."

"Mr. Bushner, what damage do you believe she would have inflicted if nobody was there to stop her?"

"Objection!" Mr. Feinberg said, not bothering to stand. "The question calls for speculation."

The judge sustained the objection and Mr. Dutcher sat down with a snicker of his own.

Mr. Feinberg had a whispering session with Wellesley and then walked over in front of the witness stand. "Mr. Bushner, your girlfriend asked you to stop before Wellesley entered that room, right?"

Bushner played with his tie. "That's not the way I understood it. She said something about not doing it there and it wasn't a good time, but girls always say that."

"You ignored her, didn't you?"

"We had a discussion about it, but it wasn't as if she was trying to run out of there or anything. Besides, I wasn't planning on going all the way with her if that's what you're suggesting."

Mr. Feinberg stayed calm, despite the snivel in Bushner's voice. "And if Wellesley Baker hadn't stopped you, exactly how far were you planning to go against that girl's wishes, Mr. Bushner?"

This time Mr. Dutcher objected for speculation and the judge sustained him. I thought there was a big difference. Bushner didn't know what Wellesley would have done next but it was crystal clear to him where he was heading.

I didn't think the jury liked Bushner too well. He had an oily quality to him. But his testimony hurt. There was no denying the fact that Wellesley had a temper. And she wasn't afraid to hurt someone to protect a cousin or a mother. The truth was she'd probably have taken another swing at Bushner right there in the courtroom if someone had handed her that board.

I was learning that a trial was war. Nobody was allowed to excuse themselves from participation if they carried something one of the warring parties needed. That's why I felt sorry for Johnny Wizer. He was one of the few kids who'd not jumped on Wellesley's case since her dad's death. I'd

even seen him sticking up for her in an argument with Beller
in the can. But he had something the prosecutor wanted, so
they called him as their witness.

"I saw Wellesley and her dad in the parking lot at the
Drift Inn," he said, shaking openly. I thought his teeth were
going to chatter. "I was walking home from my friend's.
We'd been listening to records. It was definitely an argument."

"How close were you?"

"I was on the sidewalk, probably about as close as I am to
Wellesley right now."

"Could you hear anything they said?"

Wizer squirmed in the chair. He still looked grade-school-
ish in his crewcut and oxfords. "I'm afraid I could, sir."

"Can you tell the jury exactly what you heard?" Mr.
Dutcher fanned his hand toward the jury box and stepped
back.

"I heard Mr. Baker tell her to 'go home.' He said she had
'no damn business there.'" Wizer's gaze probably took in no
more than the lowest board on the quarter-high partition
that separated the jury from the rest of the courtroom.
"Then she said . . ."

"Speak up, Mr. Wizer."

"She said, 'I hope someone catches you and blows your
ass off.'" Wizer lowered his head again. He'd done his duty
and I could tell he felt pretty low about it. Of all nights, why
did he pick that one to walk by the Drift Inn?

Mr. Feinberg rose slowly from his seat like he was searching for the right question to undo Wizer's damage. Unlike
Bushner, Wizer was clean-cut, almost angelic in appearance.
His nervousness made him totally believable. "Was there
anyone else in the parking lot, Mr. Wizer?"

"Well, not exactly in the lot, sir. But there was a woman
sitting in the car with the door open. I could hear the radio
playing."

"Do you know who it was?"

"I'm afraid I didn't get that good a look. It was almost
dark."

"Did you recognize the car?"

"Oh, yes sir, it was the Bakers' station wagon."

With a five minute slice of the morning left on the pendulum clock, the prosecutor rested his case and Judge Lally instructed the jury not to talk to anyone, even each other, about the case. He dismissed us for lunch recess.

Everyone stood, turned and stretched as the courtroom became a Babel. I heard the woman behind us tell her husband Wellesley was guilty. It was hard to argue with her. The jurors had almost gagged when the prosecutor passed around the photos of the body. And what Wizer had heard of their argument, Wellesley sounded like someone who wanted her father dead.

Taylor and his mom joined us for lunch in the Golden Gavel across the street. "Looking kinda' bleak for our side," Taylor said, as he squeezed into the booth next to me.

Now that he was here, I resented it. Taylor had a way of getting in front of a parade. "How do you figure? We haven't even had our turn. Feinberg'll run circles around Dutcher."

"What's he going to do?" Taylor asked.

My dad spoke up. "I know he's going to call me."

"Is he, Dad? When did he decide?"

"He caught me in the hallway this morning. So you won't be the only Bradford testifying."

Taylor swung around, knocked his glass over, and sent a waterfall over the edge of the table into my lap.

"Geez, Taylor!" A stripe of water across my zipper soaked through my pants as the flow slowed to a drip. Everyone threw their paper napkins to wipe up what little was left on the table. I spread my legs and brushed the water off the vinyl seat cushion to the floor.

"I'm sorry, Will, are you really testifying?"

"Only if my pants dry." I knew Taylor would find a way to foul things up.

"Will," Mrs. Clark said, "you can borrow Taylor's pants."

"No way, Mom! I'm not going to wear his."

I thought of protesting; my pants would probably dry by the time court resumed if I scrubbed them with paper towels. But Taylor's suntans looked newer than mine and still had a crease showing. Why save Taylor? He pushed the glass over. "Thanks, Mrs. Clark, I think I will. Let's go, Taylor."

On the way to the rest room, I turned my front away from the booths with people in them as Taylor pleaded with me. "This is sick, Bradford! People are going to think I pissed my pants." He walked sideways so he could face me. "What are you going to say on the stand? Who do you think that guy was who copped out on the jury? Please, Will, let me keep my pants, just name your price."

Dad told us to order whatever we wanted. I did, but it was wasted. After half my BLT, I thought I'd have to trade for Taylor's shorts too. The thought of testifying gave me the runs. I excused myself and hurried to the bathroom again. Sitting on the toilet, I went over in my head the things Mr. Feinberg said he'd ask me.

People were still shuffling into their seats and kicking the pews when Mr. Feinberg called Mrs. Baker as his first witness. She unpinned her hat, handed it to Annie and walked hesitantly up to the witness stand. She looked so frail, filling only part of the chair. Mr. Feinberg, on the other hand, seemed larger and his voice flowed more smoothly now that it was his show. He took her through the whole history with Mr. Baker. Obediently, Mrs. Baker described each incident. The prosecutor objected continuously, saying these anecdotes had nothing to do with the shooting. Mr. Feinberg said it was foundation and the judge let him go on.

"I'd brought Wellesley to bed with us in the middle of the night because she had the croup," Mrs. Baker said. Her voice was soft as a fresh diaper. "She couldn't have been eighteen months yet. Her wheezing woke my husband. He reached over and grabbed the bottle of apple juice I was feeding her and threw it against the wall. His yelling made Wellesley cry again and he kicked us onto the floor."

While Mrs. Baker spoke, Wellesley covered and uncovered her face. No matter what verdict the jury delivered now, Wellesley had already tasted the punishment—her mother was telling everyone what she never wanted anyone to know went on in that little imitation brick house in Milltown. I felt sorry for Mrs. Baker too. The good-looking drifter who took such a shine to her had turned into a monster.

"Mrs. Baker, what happened between Mr. Baker and his daughter, Tiffany, shortly after she turned sixteen?"

Mrs. Baker started to weep for the first time. Her tears came with an aching voice that moaned uncontrollably.

The judge leaned over to assess the situation.

Mr. Feinberg looked distressed. Receiving the judge's nod, he walked over to her, bent down on one knee, and whispered something. She shook her head sideways and whispered something to Mr. Feinberg. He stepped away.

Then Mrs. Baker looked over at the jury, her face ready to shatter. "He raped her . . . my husband raped her." Her voice trailed off and she squeezed her eyes closed. "Please, don't make me say anything more about that night."

"I won't, Mrs. Baker, except to ask if Wellesley was there?"

"She didn't see it, but she came home just after it happened. She knew. It's why Tiffany ran away."

I wanted to turn around and see if Tiffany was still in the courtroom. I wanted to apologize for all the times I'd looked down on her for not sticking it out.

Mr. Feinberg had steered his ship through treacherous waters. But it was clear he knew where he was going. If Judge Lally had polled the jury at that moment, I didn't see how anyone could have voted for Mr. Baker.

The trouble was, as the prosecutor soon showed, Mr. Baker was not on trial. His daughter was. Mr. Dutcher used the same events and turned them against her, asking why if these fights were so common there was suddenly a need to shoot him. "Wasn't he just a man with a temper when he drank like a lot of other people you know in Clearwater?"

"Sir, there's a difference between a bad temper and being knocked unconscious with the butt of a gun," she said.

"But that wasn't the first time he'd ever struck you, was it?"

"No, sir, it wasn't," she said, controlling the tremble in her chin. "And I'd like to know what you would have done." Her voice weakened. "We're only human, sir."

Mr. Dutcher seemed befuddled by her response. "I'm

sorry, Mrs. Baker, for what happened. I have no more questions."

She walked back to her seat kind of wobbly in the knees. Whispers rose from the audience like the crackle of grasshoppers in a dry field. The same pride showed in Wellesley's face that I saw the night she boasted about her mom to Monica and me at the Ferris wheel. Mrs. Baker had shown her grit.

When Dad took the stand, Mom gripped my hand like we were waiting for the zeppo plane at the fair to take off. Mr. Feinberg asked him to describe what happened on our porch that night. My eyes were on Mr. Dutcher's elbow patches even before he stood up to object to the relevance of this line of inquiry. More foundation, Mr. Feinberg answered, and the judge let him keep on building.

As Dad told his story about the fight with Mr. Baker, I felt the same pain in my intestines I had that night. Instead of her dad, I feared the jury this time. The way they just sat there, you didn't know if anything registered.

Mr. Feinberg then asked the same question I'd tried to ask Dad that night. "Didn't you think Mr. Baker would hurt Wellesley when he got her home?"

"In the back of my mind, it occurred to me."

"Why didn't you say something to the authorities?"

I'd never seen Dad so nervous. He rubbed his thumbs together like he was trying to scrape off some glue that'd hardened. "I thought it was none of my business. She was somebody else's kid." When he paused, Mr. Feinberg started to ask another question and Dad cut him off. "But I was mistaken, I should have done something to get this thing out in the open. There are too many secrets in this town. We all gossip behind each other's backs and then act surprised when someone loses his store . . . or someone is shot. Always blaming someone else." Dad turned and looked straight into the jury box the way I'd seen him scowl at me for leaving tools out in the rain. "If you don't pay your bills, I can't keep my store and if you ignore what's going on in your neighbor's house, it's going to be something worse."

Mom let go of me and fingered the chain links on her purse like rosary beads. We knew Mr. Feinberg's question had touched Dad's nerve center, where the Catholic, father, and storekeeper fibers joined.

When Mr. Feinberg called my name, I expected to collapse the way I used to on First Fridays after I'd fasted. It should have been harder than the first hearing because of what was at stake. But instead it felt like the chance to get rid of what felt like a sack of cement I'd been carrying around since summer.

As I described my spying through the Bakers' kitchen window that first time with Taylor, I realized I'd never told Wellesley. She must have wondered what else I knew. Then I told about the slamming and slapping I heard from the basement as I sat paralyzed in the Bakers' coal bin. The prosecutor moved to strike my answer when I said that Mr. Baker had hit Wellesley. He asked how I could see anything. Judge Lally instructed me not to speculate, but I don't think anyone in the room doubted what caused those noises.

"Why didn't you tell someone about it?"

"I guess I always had an excuse. I thought my parents wouldn't let me see Wellesley anymore. Then I decided nobody would believe me. The truth is I was just scared."

Mr. Feinberg stood close enough that I could see the five-pointed silver star on his tie clasp. "Scared of what?" he asked.

"Scared I'd hurt Wellesley." I could see her just past Mr. Feinberg's suit coat. "If her dad knew we'd seen him, he'd have just hit her harder. Besides, I had the strong feeling Wellesley didn't want anyone to know. I think she was trying to protect her dad's reputation."

"Anything else?"

"Maybe I was scared something would happen to me too." Because Judge Lally asked me not to speculate, I left out mention of dreams where Mr. Baker chased me on my bike in the Pink Lady or cornered me in his garage with a pitchfork. "I was scared of Mr. Baker."

Mr. Feinberg also gave me a chance to say what really happened at the homestead. Maybe the jury was still nervous about the way Wellesley slammed Bushner's ribs with the lumber, but at least I wanted them to know why she did it. And I set the record straight for Annie, in case someone had the mistaken notion that she wanted it with that guy.

When I finally stepped to the hardwood floor, my shirt and the waist of Taylor's pants were damp with sweat. I hardly felt like a hero. It was clear Mr. Feinberg had only one loyalty in that courtroom and it was to the girl at the defense table who nodded to me ever so slightly as I walked by. The rest of us were just his tools.

Mom patted me on the seat as I stepped by her to sit down. I glanced behind me and Taylor winked, grateful I was sure that we had traded pants instead of places.

Judge Lally studied the antique clock behind him for a few moments before announcing that we were adjourned until morning. Everyone stood while the judge and jury filed out. Then the buzzing started. More than anything, I wanted to talk to Wellesley. But the matron with the key ring appeared out of nowhere and, all business, escorted Wellesley over to the railing where she leaned across and hugged her mother. Then Wellesley, Mr. Feinberg, and the matron hurried out of the courtroom.

Mom, Dad, and I mingled with Mrs. Baker and Annie in the aisle for a while. It felt more like a funeral than anything else I could think of. Through Mrs. Baker's black netting, I saw a face that was as tenderized as a piece of cube steak. She'd had the heaviest lift of the day, dredging up memories that condemned her husband in order to help her daughter.

30

Taylor insisted on riding home with Dad and me and Mom went with Mrs. Clark to keep her company. He tried to be serious. "Mr. Bradford, what do you make of all the prosecutor's objections to relevancy?"

"I think you've got that backwards, Taylor," Dad said, "he's objecting to irrelevance."

"That's what I meant."

"He's trying to shape the case his own way, that's his job," Dad said, talking over his right shoulder to Taylor in the backseat.

"Every time the prosecutor objects," I said, "Feinberg is getting something he needs."

"The prosecutor looks like a jack-in-the-box jumping up like that," Taylor said. "Or a jackass."

"Mr. Feinberg had his share of objections too," Dad said. "When all the shouting's done, the jury's got to ignore what the attorneys have done and focus on the evidence."

"How do you think it's going for Wellesley, Mr. Bradford?"

"I'm no expert, Taylor, but I'd have to say it's fifty-fifty."

For dinner, Mom fixed "something easy," coney sauce we could ladle over a hot dog in a bun, topped with chopped onions. With my potato chips, I scooped up the sauce that dripped to the plate. We talked about who was at the trial and how people looked rather than the case itself. I couldn't have been more tired if I'd played two football games. As soon as *You Asked For It* was over, I went to bed. Stretched flat on my back, I realized how tightly I must have been holding myself all day because my muscles sang hallelujah.

Dad's knuckles on the door woke me. "Will, Feinberg's

on the phone." The sound of his name jolted me back to the nightmare that was daytime. The light was still on but my alarm clock showed only 9:30 P.M. This didn't make sense.

"I'm coming."

Dad turned the TV down when I reached the phone.

"I went by to get Laddie ready for tomorrow and he's gone." It was Mr. Feinberg all right. "His mother is worried. She hasn't seen him since lunchtime and he never stays away this long. I need him, Will."

I was groggy and slow to put the pieces together. But Laddie's going AWOL the night before his testimony confirmed my suspicion that he wanted out of this. We organized a search party. Mr. Feinberg recruited a squad car from the police station; I got Dad and Taylor. We agreed to meet at the Arctic Cafe. It was the only public place open past nine o'clock. Besides the police were used to meeting there.

Lill Bonner waited on us. She had a mole on the corner of her lower lip that made her imitation smile look like a frown. While holding a coffeepot in one hand and a fistful of mugs in the other, she shoved a table next to the booth with her hip. Dad tried to help her but she ignored him and had the table squared before he could touch it. "Coffees all the way around?" She looked at me and Taylor as if we were the ones in doubt.

"Sure," Taylor said.

The two patrolmen gave hand signals Lill seemed to understand.

Dad said, "No thanks."

"Me neither," I said.

Mr. Feinberg ordered a milk. "It's hard enough to sleep during a trial," he said.

Taylor looked at Feinberg, then switched. "I'll have a milk too."

Everyone knew Laddie and everyone had their theory where he'd be. The officer with "Reynolds" on his nameplate spoke first. I figured this was Timmy Reynolds, the halfback who broke all the records when he played for Clearwater. He told about the time he'd gotten a call from a hysterical woman who said someone was stalking her. "The creeper turned out to be Laddie," he said. "Found him in her toolshed. He had a cat in his lap who was purring like a power mower." He took a loud slurp of his coffee. "I say we start with the garages."

"We have to look where there's no people," I said.

Everyone turned.

"Brilliant," Taylor said. "That covers most of the county."

"I mean deserted places. He's not very sociable."

"Can you be a little more exact," the other officer said, dipping a spoon with three fast-melting sugar cubes in and out of his coffee. "I'm off shift at midnight."

Taylor laughed out loud.

"Mike, people are creatures of habit," Mr. Feinberg said, pointing at the officer. "I think Will's on the right track." Taylor's chuckling stopped. "More likely than not, he's someplace obvious. We just have to use our heads."

"The Rexall's closed," Taylor said, gripping the chrome flashlight his dad had made him take. Taylor's milk mustache undercut the seriousness he obviously intended. "Next best bet is probably the park. I've seen him stare for hours at the Lincoln statue."

Resting her free hand on officer Mike, Lill poured two more coffees. The sound of the liquid reminded me how badly I had to go to the bathroom and I excused myself. I knew we weren't going anywhere until the police finished their coffees.

The wall between the Men's and Women's was so thin I could hear two ladies talking as I peed. With my stream, I tried to melt the remains of the pink deodorant cake the way Officer Mike had melted the sugar cubes on his spoon. Someone had drawn a curvaceous female body on the wall over the urinal using a long sentence in small print that started in the crotch and ended there with an exclamation point that looked like a penis. Something a Bushner with talent might have done.

When the flushing stopped, I heard one of the women say "Baker" and put my ear against the wall, inches away from the naked lady.

"I don't blame him," the voice said. "His wife was such a cold fish." They both laughed.

"With his appetite, I doubt even warm fish'd be enough."
Laughter. The wall felt cold on my ear. I turned to use the
other ear so I could see the door in case someone opened it.

"I'd love to be at the trial. But there's no way Moran is
going to let me off. Someone's got to answer her phone.
Speaking of cold fish." They laughed again. Alvera Moran
ran the Hometown Insurance Center.

"You think they'll let the girl off?" It was the nasal voice
again.

"I think it's her mother's fault anyway. She neglected
those kids. One's practically a streetwalker. Shacking up
with the Mueller kid. The other turns out to be a killer. My
God, wonder what she'll get for Mother's Day." More tit-
tering. Their voices seemed inches away from my ear.

"Mother, may I shoot Dad?" the nasal one said.

"Oh God, Marna, you're terrible." Laughter. They must
have spent the evening at the Drift Inn and came here to
sober up and fix their makeup. Their teasing sickened me. I
figured what people would say to each other in the privacy
of a bathroom betrayed how they'd vote in the jury room. If
those two gabbers represented the conscience of Clearwater, Wellesley was had.

When I got back to the table, the others had already
drawn toothpicks for teams. Dad had Officer Mike; Taylor
would ride with the football star in the squad car. That left
me and Feinberg.

Taylor was puffed up, probably figuring he'd gotten even
for me taking his pants. The teams were fine with me.
Maybe Mr. Feinberg would tell me why I didn't need to
worry about what people were saying in rest rooms about
Wellesley.

As soon as the engine turned over, Mr. Feinberg pushed
the choke knob into the dashboard and looked at me. "You
know him better than I do, scout, where do we start?" The
faint scent of gasoline seeped through the floorboards. It
made the defense attorney seem human. Grandpa Blane
used to flood his Chevy the same way.

"I'm thinking." I remembered the time I'd met Laddie at
the river. "Let's start at the bridge."

"You thinking of jumping," he said.

"Could you tell?"

"You just look like this whole thing is getting you down," he said. "When you came out of the bathroom, your chin was dragging."

"Am I that obvious?"

He reversed into the middle of the street. There was no traffic. I squinted to see who the two women were at the table in the Arctic but the shade was pulled down just far enough to block their heads.

"You did fine in court today," he said. "I hope you don't resent me putting you on the spot like that."

"I'm Catholic, remember. Suffering is good for the soul."

He shifted into second. "Catholics don't realize where they got it. My people suffered through the Old Testament before you even came along. We invented anxiety."

"Will it be over tomorrow?"

"I'm trying to distract you but you won't let me."

"Will it?"

"It might be over tonight if we don't find your friend." He shifted as smoothly into third gear as he argued in court. "Cases like this run on a thin margin. All the sympathy I generate for Wellesley evaporates unless I can prove she had to do it. Laddie's the only one that can corroborate her story."

I winced. "You don't think it's going very well, do you?"

"Let's just say that's another lesson I've learned from my ancestors. Always work as if you're twenty points behind."

I stopped asking. He wasn't going to sugarcoat anything for me. We passed Dad's store. One of the e's was burned out in the red neon sign so that it read "Western Hardwar."

We parked on the shoulder about fifty yards short of the bridge and found the footpath through the brush. Neither one of us had a light. The moon was a dim flashlight trying to shine through a rain cloud. But I knew where the trails were. Once my eyes adjusted, I was able to lead Mr. Feinberg to the bank. He looked out of place here, in a raincoat buckled snugly at the waist.

As we got closer to the river, the dull background noise became louder and more detailed. I could hear the water breaking over rocks and washing against the gravel on shore. The surface of the river reflected what little light there was.

"You think this is really where a man would come who was scared?" Mr. Feinberg asked. He scrunched his neck into his collar and looked around.

"If you grew up on the river, you'd feel differently."

"I grew up in a Brooklyn apartment. The river was for rats and longshoremen."

We walked about a half mile, far enough to lose sight of the bridge girders. The ground was dewy from the day's rain and the mist of the river. It smelled of frogs and moss and reedy plants. Mr. Feinberg's feet were used to walking on floors and he slipped frequently, cursing something each time. But there was no sign of Laddie.

Next we tried the cemetery, which was spookier for me than the river. Mr. Feinberg felt at home. In Brooklyn, he told me the cemetery served as a park at night for the kids in his gang. I felt legal squeezing between the bars in the gate with an ex-prosecutor leading the way. We squatted down on our haunches in the lowest corner and watched for movement against the horizon. There weren't many places to hide in there, although if a person sat still enough he'd be mistaken for a tombstone. I called for Laddie and listened. The breeze rustled the dry leaves in a wreath someone had placed on the concrete cross next to us. A pigeon cooed.

"You're right, Will," he whispered, "this isn't as good as my old cemetery. Everyone here is dead."

On the way out the gate, Mr. Feinberg popped a button off his coat. He reached back through the grates and felt along the ground until he found it. "Bought this in Boston. There's no way I'd ever match it here."

On the way back down Cemetery Road, Mr. Feinberg put his car in low gear, letting the engine moan. It was 11:25 and still no hint of Laddie. Part of me didn't blame Laddie for fleeing. But I couldn't believe he'd leave Wellesley in the lurch. Maybe Laddie had also seen and was sickened by what Mrs. Baker begged not to talk about. The thought of it got me worked up again. Laddie had to come back.

I watched Mr. Feinberg's steady hand on the wheel. He was lost in thought too, probably reviewing in his head what he had to do tomorrow—with or without Laddie. I wondered how Mr. Baker's story compared to other cases he'd tried. The thought of more than one Tug Baker in this town made me shiver and I gripped the window knob.

"Let's call in," Mr. Feinberg said. "Maybe someone else has had some luck."

I'd forgotten there was anyone else on the search. "Sure, how do we do that?"

"Where's a phone booth?"

"Outside the Rexall. Just stay on this street."

Neither one of us had a dime. Then Mr. Feinberg thought of running his hand along the seam between the cushions in the front seat. He found a fountain pen, an Adlai Stevenson campaign button, bread-crumb dustballs, a nickel, some pennies, and, finally, a shiny dime. Mr. Feinberg was starting to seem like a regular guy.

He knew the man on night desk, who left him hanging while he called Reynolds' car. Reynolds had talked to Mike. Between them, they'd gone as far as the dam in one direction and the fairgrounds in the other.

"Who's on graveyard tonight?" Mr. Feinberg waited for an answer. "Ask Leonard to keep looking. I've got to find him. Tell him the man may be hurt."

When we were back in the car, Mr. Feinberg slumped in the seat. "I'm sorry, Will, but I've got to call it a night. Trial tomorrow." He glanced at his watch. "It's almost midnight."

"What if you don't have him tomorrow?"

"We're thirty points behind. The court's not going to stop the trial and let us go on a manhunt. I don't have a choice."

The thought of Laddie lying out there hurt seemed likely. Mr. Feinberg said so himself. He could have had another bike wreck, slid off the road, this time broken an ankle or a neck. He might even have tried to hurt himself. "I'm not tired," I said.

We headed for my house. I didn't complain. It was important that Mr. Feinberg be at his best tomorrow. As we got closer, I suggested we take the alleys. We might as well search while we drove. The car jostled us as the tires went in and out of the potholes. People dumped grass clippings and stones sifted from their gardens into the holes but the rain always seemed to form new ones.

When the headlights hit my garage, I saw it.

"That's his bike!" It was leaning against the door. I knew it was Laddie's from the high seat and the tape he'd used on the rips.

"Didn't someone say we should start with the obvious?"

"Douse the lights," I said.

Mr. Feinberg shut off the lights and the ignition. It was pitch dark again. The door squeaked when I opened it and I closed it with the button held in. Officer Reynolds had found him in a garage so that's where I headed. Mr. Feinberg followed and waited in the doorway.

"Laddie, it's me," I said. The branches from the tree rubbed against the roof. I could smell fresh soil from Mom's garden and the cut grass stuck to the mower blades. "It's okay." I waved my hand overhead trying to find the string for the light. It was in the middle of the garage but Dad had his sawhorses with some boards set up right where the pull string was.

"There." I found it. The light instantly popped the room open, showing the screens Dad had taken down when he put the storm windows on, our hand mower, shovels, rakes, the wheelbarrow standing on its nose, and the peat moss I'd smelled. But no Laddie. "He's got to be close. He'd never abandon his bike."

We walked into the backyard. The faint light from Mom's reading lamp in the bedroom only made it harder to see under the bushes. With me calling, we made a wide circle in the yard. It was too dark. I looked up, trying to get help from the moon. The clouds had thickened. But the sky seemed lighter between the tree branches.

"Mr. Feinberg, he's in the tree." Perched next to the trunk like an owl, with his knees in front of his chest, was a man. He'd done the same thing I'd done before Grandpa's eulogy, retreated to the worry tree.

"Is it him?"

"It has to be. Laddie?"

When he didn't answer, I ran to the fence, climbed the garage roof, and walked into the tree. He was shaking. The

back of his hand was as cold as sheet metal. "He's freezing,"
I called down to Mr. Feinberg, who stood under the tree
with his hands in his overcoat pockets. Laddie clung to the
tree trunk like an animal who'd escaped from a ground pur-
suer. His eyes were glassy as marbles. I thought we'd have to
call the Fire Department to pry him loose.

He'd retreated into some kind of cocoon. When I spoke,
he stared straight ahead like he was watching the horizon
for some hint of sunrise. "Laddie, everything's going to be
all right. No one's going to hurt you." I put my hand over
his. "Wellesley needs you, buddy. You have something nobody else in the world has. You saw it." No reaction. I
turned to search his target on the horizon. A street lamp
haloed in vapor seemed to float in the distance. "You're not
alone, Laddie. Mr. Feinberg down there, me, you, Wellesley,
we're on the same side. When it's over, we'll all leave you
alone, let you go back to your regular deliveries for your
mom."

At the mention of his mom, he looked at me, like he'd
forgotten something. Then his grip on the trunk loosened
and he tested the air with his foot looking for a place to
plant his foot. I scooted down and took hold of his shoe,
which felt loose, and directed it to a limb. Slowly, he twisted
around so that his back was to me. As he lowered himself, I
supported him with my hand, forcing his shirt to work out of
his pants. Standing on the same branch, he was a head taller
than me.

"Down we go, Laddie," I said, and took the big step to
the roof, going to all fours to keep from sliding on the shingles which seemed more slippery than usual. He landed stiff
legged on the roof but kept his balance by grabbing my back
pocket.

Mr. Feinberg met us at the fence. "He looks like he's seen
a ghost," Mr. Feinberg said.

"I have a pretty good idea I know whose," I said.

We put Laddie's bike in the trunk and tied the lid down
with a piece of twine from Mom's trowel bucket. Laddie sat
in the middle, holding his knees tightly together so he
wouldn't bump Mr. Feinberg's shifting hand.

The light from the street lamps moved across Laddie's

face as we passed each intersection. Mr. Feinberg's floor heater turned full blast was unable to thaw Laddie's frozen stare. His usual curiosity had retreated deep inside, to some warmer region of his body. I decided that, fortunately for us, he'd wanted to be caught. Why else would he have hidden in my tree? Laddie probably knew a hundred caves and cubbyholes in this county where nobody would have ever found him.

For the second time in my life, I saw the insides of the Tilford house.

We stayed by the door out of respect for their privacy. Laddie padded to his mom's side like a puppy waiting to be petted or scolded. It didn't matter which; the attention was what counted. Mrs. Tilford sat in a wooden wheelchair with a blanket draped over her legs and a stringy, soiled shawl around her shoulders. A table lamp that looked like it had canned peaches in the base cast an orange glow into the room. Three sleeping cats nested into each other on the caved-in seat of a rocking chair, the kind with a brake handle on the side to keep it from moving. The upholstery was frayed where the cats had sharpened their claws against it. Tinted bottles and jars of various shapes lined the windowsills and filled a buffet. A bowl with prune pits and a spoon sat on the stool next to the wheelchair. There were only two small windows in the room and they were closed. The air in the room was so stale I wanted to prop the front door open and turn a fan on.

"He knows he's not supposed to be out this late without telling me," she said. Her voice was raspy like she didn't use it much. But she spoke with great forcefulness. She was how I imagined my dad sounding when he was seventy.

"Don't be too hard on him," Mr. Feinberg said. "I think he feels bad enough on his own."

She smiled at her son. "Thanks for finding him."

That's the same thing Mr. Feinberg said when he stopped to let me off in front of my house. "He'd still be in that tree if it hadn't been for you," he said. Then Mr. Feinberg shut off the engine. "I'm worried about him, Will. In focusing on how to win this thing for Wellesley, I think I've ridden roughshod over Laddie." It was too dark to see his eyes behind the wire frames that moved as he spoke. "The man's beside himself for some reason. I'm not sure he knows Mr. Baker is really gone. His wife cremated him without services. Laddie's old fashioned like me. When you die, they bury you. He hasn't seen any funeral."

"I think you're right."

"All you have to do is look at those eyes."

"That means Laddie thinks Mr. Baker might be sitting there in the front row watching him when he testifies?"

"That's my theory."

"No wonder he was hiding."

The windows of the car were starting to fog over, making my conversation with Mr. Feinberg seem even more secret. As the air cooled, I could smell the vinyl slipcover on the front seat again and ran my fingernail along the ridge seam. Mr. Feinberg rubbed his palms against the steering wheel. "Can you do a favor, Will?"

"Sure."

"I want you to check on him in the morning. If you don't think he's able to do it, I want you to leave him home."

"Yeah, but . . ."

"I mean it. There's a nurse coming by to pick him up. Can you get there first?"

"Sure, Mr. Feinberg."

"Now that we're working together, it's Aaron."

I'd never heard of anyone named Aaron except in the Old Testament. It sounded more like a last name. "Aaron, sure," I said, smiling in the dark.

In the privacy of my bedroom, Mr. Feinberg's assignment haunted me. He'd made me a judge, pitting Laddie's pain against Wellesley's salvation. I must have finally fallen asleep because the rain woke me in the middle of the night. The gutters were spilling onto the bed of gravel Dad had built at the end of the downspout. The wind whistled through the lips of the crack between the casement and the basement window. I said another prayer that it would be Wellesley's last one in her basement cell. Finally her house was safe and she'd still never spent a night in it without her dad.

31

In daylight the decision seemed obvious. By the time breakfast was over, I'd turned single-minded. If Aaron Feinberg thought I'd be fair, he'd turned the job over to the wrong person. This was a campaign. I had to get Laddie there.

My bribe, which I carried safely under my belt as I pedaled over there, was a *Bambi* book just like the one Laddie had abandoned at the river. It was one of the books from Grandpa Blane's bookshelf for grandkids that Mom had boxed up and given to me. It was the only thing I had that I knew Laddie wanted. Maybe it would return the glow to his face I'd seen when he colored in it that day.

When he sat down on his porch steps with me, I gave it to him. His eyes lit up as he studied the picture of the wobbly little deer on the cover, smoothing it with his hand.

Mom said he had the mind of a child. What kid wouldn't want a book read to him? So that's what I did, start to finish. It was a shameless attempt to gain his confidence. As the forest fire raged through the pages, Laddie chewed his lip and wrung his hands. He knew exactly what was happening as Bambi's private world disappeared around her. The fight in the Bakers' kitchen was the fire forcing him unprotected into the open, where he'd have to testify in front of the whole town. He probably thought the fire was his fault. Somebody wanted to punish him for what he'd seen.

When I was done, I closed the book and handed it to him. His eyes were soft and compassionate again. The nervous biting had stopped. He took his book inside and I waited on the porch. The nurse pulled up in an old Ford with a mangled front fender. The socket where the headlight used to be tilted toward me like someone trying to look out of the corner of his eye.

The door opened and Laddie stepped out in a stiff white shirt and tie. No sweater. No messenger cap. No bicycle. He turned to wave at his mother watching him from the wheel-chair parked just inside the doorway. The three of us walked to the nurse's car and she drove us to Sylvanus for the second day of the trial.

The sun baked wispy steam clouds off the wide sidewalk as we marched into the courthouse. I thought people stared at us. We were an unlikely combination, a nurse in full uni-form, a kid playing hooky and a thirty-five-year-old boy. Laddie wanted to return everyone's stare and I had to mo-tion him to watch where he was going.

The crowd in the courtroom was bigger today. That was no surprise. Yesterday's testimony by Mrs. Baker was as scary as any movie that ever played the Orpheum. And, for the gossipers, there was enough material for a banquet.

The nurse ushered Laddie into a seat near the back. "He'll be fine. You can go sit with your folks."

As I walked to the front, I made sure Laddie watched me so he'd know I was still there. After all, I'd promised him we were a team. He followed me with his unflinching gaze to my seat where I gave him a thumb's up and sat next to Mom and Dad.

I checked everyone who came into the courtroom, Taylor, Mr. and Mrs. Clark, Johnny Wizer and his mom, Dr. Robin-son, Sergeant Payne, Uncle Carl. After yesterday, I wouldn't have been surprised if Tiffany sat the rest of this out but she was there again with her friend. They'd moved a few rows closer to the front. Martin came with a woman I presumed to be his wife. Instead of an apron, he had on a dark brown sport coat but the red bow tie was the same one he wore at the Rexall. Mrs. Baker and Annie Curran entered together and I wondered why Annie's mom, who was Mrs. Baker's sister, hadn't come.

The jail matron brought Wellesley in. Instead of the green Christmas tree-colored dress she had yesterday, Wellesley wore my favorite, the one with the sailor bibs front and back. She seemed tighter than a telephone wire and her eyes darted from one person to the next as she moved down the aisle. Everyone turned to stare, probably trying on in their imaginations the stories they'd heard about her yesterday.

Mr. Dutcher, in a solid brown jacket, again with reinforced elbows, carried a briefcase that ballooned out at the bottom like a pear. When he reached the railing, he pivoted and pushed the swinging gate open with the backs of his knees. The knees must have been as sharp as his elbows.

Finally, Mr. Feinberg showed. He walked slowly down the aisle, surveying the audience. When he spotted the nurse's headpiece, he seemed relieved and leaned across a couple of people to say something to Laddie. The rest of the team was here but Laddie still looked stiff as a paintbrush somebody had forgotten to clean. Mr. Feinberg hurried to the front, faced the gate head-on, and walked through it knees first.

The jury looked sleepy as they filled the two rows in the exact order in which they'd been sworn. They looked around and waited for the judge the same as the rest of us. One grandmotherly lady in the front row seemed to be studying Wellesley and I studied her to see if I could read anything from her face. She seemed sympathetic but I couldn't tell if it was concern for what had already happened or regret for what she knew was Wellesley's fate.

It sounded like the waiting room at the doctor's, everyone sniffling and coughing, clearing their throats, rustling old magazines and newspapers. The feet hitting the seat supports sounded like rubber clubs.

"I wonder if Feinberg told Wellesley about our wild goose chase last night," I whispered to Dad.

"She's going to question the competence of her defense team when she finds out where we found him." Dad's team was the last to get back and the farthest off the scent. They'd gone to the freight yard and Dad had made officer Mike walk the tracks with him halfway to Olalla. Mike overshot the end of his shift by an hour and a half, which Dad said was doubly irritating to Mike because the man we were searching for was a witness for the defense.

We stood for Judge Lally's entrance as if this was High

Mass. The judge seemed grumpy, wasted no time in trying to make the jury feel comfortable the way he did yesterday, and asked Mr. Feinberg if he was ready to call his next witness.

I didn't recognize the man who took the stand until he identified himself as the driver of the Little Brown Jug. He was the man Mr. Baker drank with over the hood of the Pink Lady in the infield that night after the races. His real job was as a carpenter and he looked strong enough to hold a ceiling up with one hand and nail with the other. Mr. Feinberg asked him how long he'd known Mr. Baker (he said about seven years) and how they got along.

"About like everyone else," he said, in a cowboy twang.

"What does that mean?" Mr. Feinberg asked.

The carpenter rubbed the inside of his riding boots together. "I stayed out of Tug's way, you might say, especially if he was mad . . . and that was pretty often."

"Did Mr. Baker ever hit you, Mr. Freeman?"

He stroked his chin and looked around at the jury. "He shore did."

"More than once?"

"Yes, sir."

"Who started these fights?"

"Let me put it this way. He's the last man I'd ever pick a fight with."

"Why's that, Mr. Freeman?"

He looked down and spread his legs momentarily as if he wanted to check the shine on his boots. "Well, sir, let's just say I was afraid he'd beat the living crap out of me."

"You were scared he'd inflict serious bodily harm on you?"

"That's a fancy way of saying it, sir. Most of the people I know would just say he scared the sh . . ."—he held the word with his tongue and glanced at the judge—"scared the shinola out of 'em."

Mr. Freeman described the time Baker had held court in the Drift Inn. Somebody called the barmaid, Faye, an uncomplimentary name. Tug rubbed the guy's nose so hard on the felt of the pool table that it bled. Three of the guy's friends attacked Baker with their cue sticks. "Tug chopped 'em down one by one. His hands were lethal weapons. As they tried to get up, he let 'em have it with those size twelve . . . with his kickers. In the head, the groin. It didn't much matter to Baker. Nobody dared to break it up." Mr. Freeman shrugged his shoulders and looked over at the jury. "Wasn't my fight."

"Did Mr. Baker ever tell you he'd hit one of his kids?"

"Objection, Your Honor, hearsay," the prosecutor yelled.

"Sustained. Mr. Feinberg . . ." Judge Lally's voice had a scolding tone.

"Do you think Mr. Baker was the type of person who was capable of inflicting harm on his kids?"

The skinny prosecutor shot out of his chair like a stubborn weed that wouldn't stay down. "Objection, calls for speculation, Your Honor, Mr. Feinberg—"

The judge used his gavel. "Sustained. Mr. Feinberg, stick to what this witness knows."

The prosecutor took his turn with Mr. Freeman, who admitted that he'd had his own fights with other stock car drivers. And Mr. Baker had never threatened him with a gun. "But sir, that man didn't need a gun," the witness said. Mr. Dutcher seemed exasperated, started to ask something else, and finally told the judge he had no more questions.

Mr. Feinberg asked for a few minutes to consult with his client, which the judge granted. Everyone else used it as an opportunity to do their own whispering. Mom tapped her finger on my leg. "You see now why I didn't want you hanging around that tavern."

Dad leaned over. "Will's going to get the idea you know more than you should, dear."

"Yeah, Mom, how do you know what goes on in there?"

"Some things you know by instinct," she said.

I looked around at Taylor. Freeman's testimony must have stirred him because he was explaining something to his mom with his fists doubled. Taylor loved to talk about fights but I couldn't remember him ever risking his face in one. He knew that a medium-fast tongue was still better than a quick left jab.

Laddie sat stone silent.

Judge Lally gaveled the courtroom to attention and Mr. Feinberg called his next witness. "Wellesley Baker."

The room hushed again. I thought Wellesley's heart must be spinning faster than the ceiling fan that rotated overhead. She nodded her head slightly to the jury as she passed, as if they'd just been introduced and she was anxious to get along to something else. She wasn't much good at small talk.

As Mr. Feinberg asked questions, Wellesley added details her mom had left out of the stories. How she'd worn long shirts on hot days to cover up bruises on her arms, how she'd skipped PE to hide the belt marks across her back. The marks changed shapes. Sometimes they were a spatula, then the handle of a pair of scissors, or the prongs of a fork. I felt so foolish to have missed these signs when I'd seen Wellesley almost every day since kindergarten.

Returning from the evidence table, Mr. Feinberg unrolled a thick black belt that looked like it had rawhide shoestrings woven into it. "Have you ever seen this, Wellesley?"

"Yes, sir. That's my dad's."

"Did your dad ever wear this belt?"

She hesitated. "I don't think so. That's the one he kept in our broom closet."

Mr. Feinberg walked over in front of the jury box, flexing the belt tight from one hand to the next. "What did your dad use this belt for, Wellesley?"

She spoke in a low voice. "For beatings."

"I want to make sure everyone heard you, Wellesley."

"For beatings."

"Who did he beat, Wellesley?"

"Mom once in a while. Usually Tiffany . . . and me."

"When was the last time he used this belt on you?"

She looked out at the crowd. I thought maybe she was trying to find me. "In July, after the fight on the porch Mr. Bradford talked about. When we got home, he pulled my shirt off and hit me with it."

Mr. Feinberg's voice was respectful and almost as quiet as Wellesley's. "How many times did he hit you that night?"

"Three times, I think."

Mr. Feinberg walked over to his table, picked up Wellesley's chair, and set it in the middle of the courtroom. With his grip on the belt buckle, he wrapped the belt around his hand once. "How hard did he hit you, Wellesley? This hard?" Mr. Feinberg slapped the chair with the belt, making a loud crack. There was a collective gasp. My pulse surged.

"No, sir, it felt harder."

With a roundhouse swing, he beat the chair again. Whap! The sound echoed in the room like a gunshot. The jury recoiled and I felt my own back bend away from the whip of the belt.

Wellesley spoke. "Yes, sir, more like that."

"Three times?"

"Yes."

Mercifully, Judge Lally took the morning break. I didn't even stand for his exit. All I could focus on was that sound, still rippling in waves back to the night Mr. Baker finished with his belt the fight he'd started on the porch with Dad. I'd feebly protested to Dad that something was wrong and let the subject be ash canned like the plasterboard Dad pried loose from the basement ceiling afterward.

"Let's get a drink of water," Dad said, moving toward the aisle.

"Yeah, just a minute," I said, half paying attention. Dad went on by me and he and Mom headed for the hallway. I didn't need water as much as a reassuring word. I turned. Even Laddie was being escorted out by the nurse. The courtroom was emptying. I stumbled toward the railing where Mr. Feinberg and Wellesley were talking with Mrs. Baker and Annie. Wellesley saw me approaching and met me at the gate.

"Pretty ugly stuff, huh?"

"I didn't expect it to be pretty," I said.

"I feel like a robot. He asks me the questions and something inside me answers. Anybody could do it."

"If they had the robot inside?"

"That's the hard part, huh?" Wellesley made a continuous figure eight on the top of the railing with her index finger.

"Maybe, if you let the robot spill its guts, you can get rid of it."

"When I think of you and Taylor listening to all this, I feel ashamed."

"Ah, come on, Wellesley. You haven't done anything wrong. As far as your dad . . ."

"I feel ashamed of him too."

"I didn't mean it that way."

"Whatever I say about him is still going to land on Mom . . . and Tiffany."

"Wellesley, this may sound funny, me telling you, but don't hold back." She laughed half-heartedly. "I mean, it's too late to protect him."

She shook her head. "I know. But you don't know everything that happened."

Once everyone had settled again, Wellesley took her seat in the witness chair. The belt was back on the table. Mr. Feinberg moved to the night of the Labor Day Fair. Wellesley described walking the‧ grounds with her mom, eating treats, mostly watching the people. Joy showed in her voice. I realized from what I'd learned these last two days how special that kind of time was. Out of the house, they were away from the belt.

When Mr. Feinberg asked about meeting Mr. Baker at the stables, Wellesley took a deep breath. The joyfulness fled as she faithfully repeated her dad's cussing just as I'd remembered it. "I thought there was something else bothering him. It wasn't just Mom not being there to serve his dinner."

"Do you know where he'd been?"

"At the Drift Inn."

"What happened when he got home?"

"He was shouting, knocking over furniture, throwing things at the walls. Then he went to the bedroom. I thought he was going to just pass out and leave us alone. But he came back with his pistol." She shuddered when she exhaled. "He stuck it against Mom's temple . . . said he was going to blow her brains out . . . for screwing around on him." She directed her answers to Mr. Feinberg, ignoring the jury. I suspected his language was worse than Wellesley was letting on. She sniffed and wiped her eyes. "Mom begged him to stop talking that way in front of me. He laughed and hit her in the side of the head with the gun. It knocked her down." She pressed her hands together and paused. "Then he fired a shot into the floor next to her. I was petrified. He said he'd teach her a lesson for dreaming about . . . screwing around with her old boyfriend at the fair." Her voice trailed off, she was shaking. I remembered the coal bin—skin slapping against skin, chairs scraping on the linoleum over my head, and Mr. Baker hollering.

Mr. Feinberg spoke softly. He was easy to hear because nobody else dared move. "Wellesley, you mean that first bullet, the one they found in the coal bin, was fired by your dad, not you?"

"Yes."

"What happened next, Wellesley?"

"He kicked her and kept cussing. I hollered at him to stop. Mom wasn't even trying to protect herself. I thought she was dead." Wellesley stopped and twisted her hands together. "Then I said, 'You're the one that's been screwing around. With that slut at the tavern.' That stopped him. His lip was quivering the way he gets when he's about to explode." Wellesley was also trembling and looked like she was trying to retain her composure.

"Then what, Wellesley?"

"He said, 'That's none of your god-damned business. Maybe if there was someone worth screwing at home, I wouldn't need Faye.'" Wellesley glanced up to check her mother. Mrs. Baker held her head high. Then Wellesley added, as an afterthought, "He said Faye was a piece of shit anyway. She'd turned him down."

"He said what?" Mr. Feinberg perked up like it was something he'd not heard before.

"She'd turned him down that night. That's what was bothering him."

Mr. Feinberg looked pleased at the discovery. "What happened next?"

"He seemed like he was going berserk. He kept yelling at Mom, 'Hey, Ethel, I'm going to hump your daughter. Wake up and watch me hump your daughter.'" Wellesley covered her face with her hands and Mr. Feinberg walked over and patted her on the back. The judge took his glasses off and looked down at the two of them.

"Are you okay?" Mr. Feinberg asked.

She mumbled something into her hands, then rolled her shoulders back and sat up.

"What happened after your dad yelled this?"

Wellesley scooted against the back of the seat. "He pulled me by the arm over to the sink and took a bottle of his Scotch out of the cupboard." She took a visible breath. "When he set the gun down to get some ice, I grabbed it and backed away. He turned and started yelling worse than before."

"Did you say anything to him?"

"I told him to get out of the house or I'd shoot! I just said it . . . I didn't want to . . ." She shoved her hands under her glasses to cover her eyes. The jerking pulse of her sobbing moved like a wave from her face to her waist.

"What did he do, Wellesley?"

"He just kept coming." She raised her voice and gripped the front edge of the flat armrests. "I said, 'No, Dad! Please, don't come any closer!' " It was like she was imagining him there in the courtroom. She collapsed her head and convulsed with sobs. I'd never seen Wellesley cry in public. Nobody I knew could bend her arm or squeeze her head hard enough to make her cry. Mr. Feinberg pulled a handkerchief out of his back pocket and approached Wellesley. Her voice cracked when she looked up at him. "I'm sorry . . ." She looked out at the crowd. "I'm sorry, Mom." Then she took off her glasses and wiped her eyes with the sleeves of her dress. I don't think she'd even noticed Mr. Feinberg's hanky. Mrs. Baker leaned forward. I thought she might go to Wellesley's side.

"We're almost done," Mr. Feinberg said as he pushed the handkerchief into her hand. Wellesley used it to wipe her glasses. Even the gnarled old jury man in the corner seat closest to the front had pushed his glasses to the top of his head and daubed at his eye sockets with one of those red and white patterned hankies bums tied their belongings in. "Wellesley, we can ask the court for a short recess if you want."

Judge Lally nodded his head in support of Mr. Feinberg's suggestion.

Wellesley said, "No."

"Was your dad holding anything when he came at you that night?"

"A bottle," she said, struggling to talk normal. "He had his bottle."

"How was he holding it?"

"By the neck. His fist was around the neck and he held it next to his head. Whiskey was gurgling out of it, it must have been open." Her voice sounded nasal from the crying.

"What were you thinking at that moment, Wellesley?"

"It was a blur . . . but I kept thinking of Mom . . . I thought she was dead." Wellesley pushed the handkerchief hard against the bottom of her nose, as if to stop a nosebleed. "I thought he was going to get me next. I had his gun."

"Did you think he was going to hit you with his bottle?"

"Yes."

"Did you think he was going to rape you like he did your sister?"

She looked up at Mr. Feinberg, her face on the verge of cracking again. "Maybe. I didn't know."

"Why did you shoot, Wellesley?"

"To stop him, just to stop him."

Mr. Feinberg paused and looked kindly at her. "Wellesley, I'm sorry I had to take you through all this again. Thank you. No more questions, Your Honor." He returned to his seat with his eyes downcast, leaving Wellesley alone on the stand. That seemed to be her fate, always the last one standing.

Wellesley was right. I'd underestimated again. It was more awful than I'd imagined. But she hadn't held back. Mom was doing everything she could to contain her crying. I could smell the tears. They were funeral tears. When I patted her on the skirt the way she always used to do for me, she set her hand on mine. The Kleenex in her hand was damp and warm. Dad just cleared his throat and watched the prosecutor as he pushed his chair under the table and slowly moved over to Wellesley.

Mr. Dutcher tried to make his voice friendly, as if he didn't want to get Wellesley riled up again. "Miss Baker, you said you and your dad had a lot of fights?"

"Yes, we did."

"Many of them violent?"

She hesitated. "Yes, sir."

"So, why this time did you think you had to shoot him to stop him?"

Wellesley studied Mr. Dutcher carefully. "Sir, that's the same thing I've been asking myself since it happened. Some days I've answered it one way and some days another. If you're suggesting I made a big mistake, probably I did. I know that. But there wasn't a lot of time to analyze things." Wellesley had calmed, maybe because she knew Mr. Dutcher was someone she had to be on guard for. "My dad hit us with his belt, his boots, chairs, extension cords, anything he could reach, but that night was the first time he brought out a gun. The way he'd kicked Mom, I thought this time he wasn't going to stop. Once I picked up his gun, he went nuts. I felt like an insect. If I didn't do something, I knew he'd just crush me."

I could visualize Mr. Baker in his stock car overalls, twisting a cigarette butt into the fairgrounds dirt.

"Wellesley, one of your friends testified about the argument with your dad in the Drift Inn parking lot. Is that the way it happened?"

She licked her lips. "Pretty much, yes, sir."

"Why were you so angry at your dad that day?"

Wellesley looked over at her mom in the first row, then back at Mr. Dutcher. "Because he was cheating on Mom."

Mr. Dutcher looked skeptical. "With whom?"

"With Faye Doherty." Wellesley snorted the woman's name.

"Miss Doherty worked at the Drift Inn?"

"Yes."

"Wellesley, were you mad enough about your dad and Miss Doherty to want him dead?"

"Yes!"

"Objection, Your Honor." Mr. Feinberg's objection came too late to stop Wellesley. "I move to strike the question and the answer. The question is argumentative and irrelevant." Mr. Feinberg was upset. "My client's state of mind during that argument in the parking lot is not relevant to the charges before the court."

"Approach the bench," Judge Lally said.

The three of them argued just quietly enough that we couldn't hear what they were saying. Finally, the judge waved them away with his gavel.

"The question and the answer stand," the judge said.

"No more questions," Mr. Dutcher said. Then he hooked his thumbs behind the lapels of his jacket and strode back to his seat. He'd won a big one. Wellesley had admitted she wanted her dad dead.

Mr. Feinberg set his glasses on the table and rubbed his eyes. He'd stayed out too late last night. He was wearing down.

"Any redirect, Mr. Feinberg?" the judge asked.

He calmly exhaled and put his glasses back on, making sure the wires were snug behind his ears. "No, Your Honor."

I was surprised he'd leave it at that, but what could he do? If he'd asked her how many other times she'd wished her father was dead, she'd probably have said plenty.

Aiming my curse at the back of Mr. Dutcher's giraffe neck, I wanted him to choke on his smugness. Mrs. Baker was right. We were only human. What would you have felt, Mr. Dutcher, if the woman in the parking lot had been your wife? Besides, wasn't it obvious her wish had nothing to do with what happened? If it were just a matter of wishes, he'd have been dead a long time ago.

Judge Lally excused Wellesley. She looked wrung out and worried.

Mr. Feinberg saved Laddie Tilford for last, as if he wanted to clear away the main fighting first to create a less threatening atmosphere. As I watched the nurse urge Laddie up the aisle, half a step at a time, I wondered if he was going to just turn and run out the door when she let go. Laddie always had trees to hide behind. Now we'd flushed him out.

At the swinging gate, Mr. Feinberg met Laddie and led him to the podium. Judge Lally asked him to raise his right hand; when Mr. Feinberg and the judge raised theirs, so did

Laddie. Judge Lally recited the oath and, at Mr. Feinberg's urging, Laddie nodded. Then Mr. Feinberg brought him to a card table the bailiff had set up in front of the jury box. The jurors straightened up in their seats to look at the big sheets of paper on the table.

Judge Lally explained to the jury that Mr. Tilford apparently couldn't speak in an intelligible fashion but he seemed to understand questions so the judge had given the defense permission to let him illustrate his answers. Although this was an unusual situation, the jury was instructed to give the same scrutiny to Mr. Tilford's testimony as it would to any other witness. While the judge spoke, Laddie just stared openly at those twelve faces as if he were protected by one-way glass.

Mr. Feinberg pulled his own chair next to Laddie's and drew something on the paper. It was so quiet you could hear his crayon unstick itself from the paper each time he lifted it. Then Mr. Feinberg asked if this was the window of the Bakers' house. Laddie seemed confused. Mr. Feinberg repeated himself. Laddie bit his lip. He tried to speak, but it was gibberish. Sounding frustrated, Mr. Feinberg handed Laddie a crayon and asked him to draw what he saw through the window. Laddie stiffened. Mr. Feinberg encouraged. The jury fidgeted.

"Your Honor, may I have a conference with you and Mr. Dutcher?"

"Approach the bench," Judge Lally said, motioning with his hand.

The prosecutor's head was high enough that he could have rested his chin on the judge's podium; Mr. Feinberg had to look up as the three of them carried on a private conversation. It looked like another argument the way their heads shook in different directions. Then the two attorneys backed away and Judge Lally spoke. "Will Bradford, can you step forward?"

My heart jumped. The seats creaked as people turned to look at me. Mom pulled her knees to the side to make it easier for me to get out. "Go ahead, Will," she whispered, "you have to do what the judge says."

I joined the huddle under the podium. The judge explained that Mr. Feinberg thought Laddie might be more comfortable with a familiar face. So, he wanted me to ask Laddie the questions.

"Here," I said, "in court?"

"That's what we're asking, Will," Mr. Feinberg said. It would have never occurred to me that this Eastern law school graduate needed help at his trade. Maybe he was too educated to communicate with someone as simple as Laddie. I looked over at Laddie. He was shaking like a dog that had just been given a bath on the lawn in the middle of winter. "Sure, I'll try, but no promises."

Mr. Dutcher spoke. "My objection is still noted for the record, Your Honor."

It was poetic justice, as Mom was fond of saying. After all, I was the one who got Laddie hooked into this. Whether he knew what was going to happen or not, Laddie seemed pleased that I was joining him at the card table. He hadn't taken his eyes off me since I passed through the gate. Laddie had a good sensor for fear and he must have known I was as scared as he was. It was hard enough to communicate at Wellesley's house when we had the real window. But I knew the only thing the jury would ever believe Laddie saw was what I could get him to draw right here under the globe lights.

I held out both hands and he responded by extending his, still holding the green crayon Mr. Feinberg had given him. His hands were cold. His blood must have flowed to his legs, where it was usually needed to pedal away from trouble.

The purple window frame Mr. Feinberg had drawn on the white butcher paper was approximately the same size as Wellesley's kitchen window, with the sill that divided the window in half, but something was missing. The cat! Using a black crayon, I drew the plaster of paris cat with no tail that was still perched on the sill when I visited Mrs. Baker. In the tiny eye holes, I colored yellow to match the beads in the real one. Laddie remembered animals better than people. With the cat staring at us, he seemed to know where we were because a captive smile escaped through his face.

Then I had another idea. "Your Honor, can I put the

paper on the floor?" The first day I'd seen Laddie coloring in the book at the river, he worked without table and chairs.

"I guess that's as permissible as anything else we're doing here."

So I spread the paper out on the hardwood and helped Laddie from his chair. Mr. Dutcher and Mr. Feinberg scooted the table away so the jurors could see us. Then Mr. Feinberg asked the judge's permission so that Wellesley could join us. I situated Laddie with his back to the jury, thinking this would work best if Laddie forgot they were even there. He still clenched the green crayon in his right hand. Our knees rested on opposite sides of the paper. Wellesley, Mr. Feinberg, and Mr. Dutcher stood in a semi-circle next to us. The jurors in the back row peeked between heads and those at the ends scrunched in closer to get a good look at the window. They reminded me of a family picture, everyone squeezing together to fit into the camera lens.

"Laddie, is this Wellesley's window?" I traced the purple frame with my finger. "Wellesley's window?"

Biting his lower lip, he moved his head up and down slowly.

"Good boy, Laddie." I must have sounded like a Dick and Jane reader to the jury, but I had to keep it simple. "Show me. Did you see Wellesley?" I emphasized her name.

He found Wellesley's feet and his gaze followed up her legs and skirt to her face.

"That's right. Wellesley. Show me Wellesley." I pointed to the large space in the bottom pane and tapped on the paper, "Wellesley!"

Laddie touched down at a point in the center of the window. Without lifting his crayon from the paper, he drew the outline of a small person in a skirt that flared broadly just above the two stubs I understood to be feet. Her sailor dress. Laddie's upper teeth bit against his lip so hard I thought he'd draw blood. I encouraged him with my hand to continue. He moved slowly as if tracing a faint outline visible only to him. On the head of this dough-girl figure, he scribbled tiny circles for her hair. Then, without encourage-

ment, he drew a stick jutting from the arm that had to be
the gun.

"Good, Laddie, good job!" He smirked shyly. It was
working. "Was Mr. Baker there? Where is Mr. Baker?"
Laddie studied the picture as if he was trying to find him.
His grimace returned. He let me pull the green crayon from
his grip when he realized that he got a brown one in ex-
change. "Mr. Baker! The dad! Where is the dad?"

I held down the edges of the paper again as Laddie
leaned over and lowered his crayon like a surgeon to the
exact spot he wanted in the space between the left casement
and the green girl in the green dress. He started at the head,
making it larger than that of the other figure, then to the
first arm, fat and raised up like the boom of a crane. When
he completed the outline of the figure, it dwarfed the girl.
The brown lines ran onto the edges of the window frame.
Laddie glanced at me and returned to his work. He moved
with certainty. On top of the misshapen, upraised hand, he
drew a rectangle with bulging sides and a long neck—the
whiskey bottle. Then he straightened slowly and opened his
palm to give me the crayon.

My heart was galloping. "The dad?" I asked, pointing to
the new figure.

He nodded vigorously.

"Wellesley?" I said, putting my finger on the skirt.

Again, he nodded.

We both looked at the paper. "What did Mr. Baker do,
Laddie? What did he do?"

Laddie made a ball with his fist, grunted and pounded
downward, stopping about three inches above the green girl.
Then he clamped his teeth tightly and uttered guttural,
abrupt gunshot sounds. "Cuh! Cuh! Cuh!" My eyes watered.
Laddie had done it! His crude wax crayon drawing was as
telling as a photograph and he'd even added the sound effects. Wellesley had her witness, someone who could testify
she was under attack.

Mr. Feinberg broke the silence. "Are you finished, Mr.
Bradford?"

"Yes, sir, I think he's finished."

Mr. Feinberg stooped over and lifted the butcher paper

from the floor, holding it carefully by the edges as if the crayon figures were still wet. "With your permission, Your Honor, I move to admit this as Laddie Tilford's testimony."

As Mr. Feinberg dragged the easel next to the jury box and mounted the drawing, Laddie still rested on his haunches, ready for my next command. Mom's word was right, he was an innocent. Watching him gazing at Wellesley, I had the feeling that Laddie's head, uncluttered with all the words we'd heard in the courtroom, carried the purest verdict. He'd watched from Wellesley's shoulder. He had to size up the same fear she did.

I led Laddie out the gate. People stared at us the same way they did the day I walked him home after his bike wreck. Instead of taking him to the back, though, I turned in next to Mom and Laddie sat between us. I couldn't let go of him after what he'd done. Mom reached over and squeezed his hand as if to say good job. She seemed as natural as butter.

Mr. Feinberg rested his case. The judge asked Mr. Dutcher if he had any rebuttal; he said no.

"It's almost time for the lunch break," the judge said, "but I'd prefer to keep going if that's all right with the parties."

Both attorneys consented.

He turned toward the jury. "I guess I should ask you too. Does anyone object to moving straight ahead with closing arguments?"

Everyone shook their heads no. It was one of those questions that was really a statement. The judge wanted to finish.

"Good. Thank you. Mr. Dutcher, please proceed."

Mr. Dutcher hitched up his belt and strode over in front of the jury box. The arms and legs of the law were long. The jurors in the front row had to bend their necks to look up at him. He worked off a sheet of tablet paper folded to about the size of an envelope that he buried under the opposite armpit each time he crossed his arms.

"There was no question what happened in the kitchen," he said. He walked over to the evidence table and picked up one of the bullets with a tag dangling from it. "The Bakers had another fight. This time Wellesley took her dad's gun and sent this piece of lead through his heart." He showed it coming to rest against his breast pocket. "Miss Baker herself admitted it. Three shots. She wanted to make sure."

Mr. Dutcher thrust his chin out in a way that lifted his Adam's apple away from his collar. "You'll hear the argument made that it was self-defense. The law is clear, and you'll be so instructed by the judge, that a person can only take the means necessary to avoid the immediate threat of harm. You can't use an elephant gun if the assailant has a bean shooter. If you have the means of escape, you must do so rather than use any weapon at all." He recited these rules as if he'd memorized them from some law book.

Then he snuck a look at his paper which he was holding about waist level. "So what about Miss Baker? She told you herself she'd faced off against her dad plenty of times. She was used to his yelling, his drinking, his threats, even his hitting. Better than anyone else, I think Wellesley knew that his threats were just the ravings of a man who'd had too much to drink." Mr. Dutcher walked over next to the jury box as if he was stepping out of his role of prosecutor and wanted to make a personal comment. In a loud whisper, he asked them, "Couldn't she have just left the kitchen until her dad cooled off?" He paused and let his question hang over them. "If she had, the night would have probably ended like other nights in the Baker house, with everyone pretty agitated . . . but still alive."

The jurors gave Mr. Dutcher their total attention. The mouth of the old man in the corner seat hung open, unhinged from his jaw. Next to me, I could feel Laddie's gaze wandering, checking out the tiles in the ceiling, the plaques on the walls, the people. He'd seen the real thing; he didn't need Mr. Dutcher's version of how it might have been.

Mr. Dutcher returned to his pacing, covering the width of the jury box in three strides of his long legs. "You've heard the testimony. Wellesley Baker is a kid with a history of violence. She wasn't afraid to go after just about anybody who got in her way. Last summer, she was arrested for shooting matches," he emphasized shooting, "at a maintenance worker at the fairgrounds. Mr. Bushner, a friend of her cousin's, told you how she attacked him with a club, cracking two of his ribs. And most telling of all, a friend of hers, a school chum, overheard Wellesley Baker make a threat against the victim in a downtown parking lot. She . . . wanted . . . him . . . dead."

I slid the soles of my good shoes back and forth in the depression in the floor tiles between the seats. The judge took his glasses off and gazed into space, then put them back on, and returned to his note taking. "Did Miss Baker have to pick up the gun? Was this an act of self-defense or did she become the aggressor at that moment? Miss Baker's an intelligent woman. Her head's not clouded over like Laddie Tilford's. She's accountable for her actions the same as you and me."

The prosecutor was beginning to grate on me. I'd gotten in my first fight, with Wizer, when he'd called Laddie a spastic. Mr. Dutcher was making my adrenaline run the same way it did on crosswalk patrol that morning. When I looked over at Laddie, he caught my eye and smiled. He'd missed Dutcher's slur.

"She had the motive. The defense went into great detail about how Wellesley resented her father's firm hand. Wellesley also imagined that her father was seeing another woman. There's no real proof of that, of course. The defense didn't even produce the alleged paramour. But it doesn't matter if it was real. Wellesley thought it was and she wanted to protect her mother's honor. So she threatened her dad. And when Mr. Baker carelessly left a loaded pistol on the counter, Wellesley had the means to make good on her threat. Motive . . . means . . . murder." The prosecutor slowly counted off the last three words on the fingers of his right hand, letting each word stab the jury.

His neat little package made me angry. He'd ignored the fact that Wellesley had spent a lifetime protecting her dad, that she was devastated by his death, that even today in front of the jury she questioned whether she should have pulled the trigger. Mr. Baker was despicable long before Mr. Dutcher knew it. Of course she'd dreamed of him dead. Who wouldn't? But he was her mom's husband and she loved her mom. And he was the only father she'd ever have and she ached to have a family she could be proud of.

Dutcher had also conveniently ignored the danger Wellesley was in. Maybe it was impossible for a strapping man over six feet tall like the prosecutor to understand the panic that a fourteen-year-old girl must have felt when her dad says in front of her own mother that he'll rape you.

He glanced at his notes again, then folded the paper and stuck it into the pocket of his jacket. "The state believes that Miss Baker wasn't merely trying to defend herself that night. Rather, she used this opportunity to get rid of someone whom she badly wanted to get rid of. As sympathetic as we all might feel for this girl's upbringing, we have to enforce the law. The law of life, 'Thou shalt not kill.' It applies on the broadest public street in Clearwater. It applies with equal force in the privacy of our own homes. Thank you."

The courtroom benches groaned as people stretched and whispered. I had to admit Mr. Dutcher's argument was effective. He was right, Wellesley had committed the ultimate offense. Maybe she could have run. But it just didn't seem fair. I wanted to pull Dad aside and ask him. What good were all his lectures to obey the law and tell the truth if Mr. Baker could cheat on his wife, beat his kids, and then Wellesley goes to prison for doing the only thing she could to stop him? Dad stared unflinchingly ahead, arms folded firmly on his chest, as if challenging Mr. Feinberg to earn his War Bond.

Mr. Feinberg buttoned his jacket and moved to the front of the jury box. I prayed, hoping that my Catholic God would see fit to help the only Jewish lawyer in Sylvanus County. The courtroom hushed again. Whatever Mr. Feinberg intended to say, he'd memorized it because he carried no cheat notes.

"Ladies and gentlemen of the jury, the prosecuting attorney has made a fine speech. He did his job, which is to argue for the conviction of my client." Mr. Feinberg's voice polished where Mr. Dutcher's only scrubbed. "But people can view the same water and see different things. One calls it a creek, the other a river. At normal flows, it's drink for his crops; at flood stage, it's a threat to his barn. The difference comes from something inside each of us. Our view of the world is shaped by our own value systems. I will show you another view of what happened in the Bakers' kitchen that night and let you decide whether that comports better with the values inside each of you."

The jury had no trouble seeing all of Mr. Feinberg without bending their necks. He didn't pace like Mr. Dutcher; instead, he stood firmly rooted in the hardwood floor like a spreading maple tree, gesturing gracefully, never taking his gaze off the jurors. They'd have to climb him to get by. I felt better already. Mr. Feinberg had a way of attaching everyday things to some broader scheme for the universe. But he did it using elements that a retired dirt farmer from Clearwater could understand. I nudged Dad and gave him an okay sign. He nodded approvingly.

"There are two myths inherent in what the prosecutor just told you. First, he is treating you as spectators. Second, he says the law works the same regardless of location. I am fond of proverbs. I guess it's because they pack so much wisdom in a small bundle. There's a Cameroon proverb which says that 'Rain does not fall on one roof alone.' That's also true of domestic violence. I think many of us heard the rain falling. Mr. Bradford heard it coming down when Mr. Baker called his daughter a 'bitch' and twisted her arm on his porch that night. When Mr. Baker spit at him, he even felt it. But Mr. Bradford thought he was a spectator, that the quarrel was between Wellesley and her dad." Dad unfolded his arms and wiped the palms of his hands on his pants. He was squirming the way he had on the stand.

"Will Bradford heard the rain; he stood in it outside her window. But he didn't tell anyone because he thought the rain would only get worse if he tried to help." I couldn't move a muscle. Mr. Feinberg's words paralyzed me the same way seeing Wellesley through the window had. I wished for that night back, right now. I should have gone to Grandpa Blane with it. We could have gone to the police together. He once told me they'd imprison a man in the infantry for mistreating his horse. He wouldn't have let Mr. Baker get away with it. I missed Grandpa Blane more than ever right now.

"Many of you," Mr. Feinberg said, "even if you didn't feel the rain, you saw the clouds. At the stock car races, you cheered for Mr. Baker as he hammered and clawed his way through the pack. We put him on a pedestal for his violence, never following up on our suspicion that maybe he treated his wife and daughters no better. After all, we were just spectators." I didn't know how Dad felt to be criticized but I had no complaints. Feinberg had accurately put me just where I'd been too long, on the sidelines. If it was any consolation, I had plenty of company.

"Mr. Dutcher also said the same laws apply in our kitchens as in our public streets. That's a myth, isn't it? Even Mr. Dutcher doesn't believe it. You saw him. When I started to inquire into the miserable list of brutalities that Mr. Baker had inflicted on his family, the prosecutor said it wasn't relevant. He wanted to draw his curtain of 'domestic privacy' over it." From behind, it looked like Mr. Dutcher was tugging at his collar, trying to pull his neck farther out of his shirt. Several members of the jury turned to stare at the prosecutor.

"If you or I had broken a chair over our neighbor's head in front of the Rexall or used our belt to put welts on someone's back in the church parking lot because we didn't like their answer to a question, we'd be arrested. There's no doubt about that, is there?" Mr. Feinberg's voice raised, challenging the jury. The woman who sat in seat number nine nodded her head vigorously in agreement. "I asked you all before the trial started whether you'd ever struck one of your children." He was personal and subdued again. "You probably wondered at the time if I wasn't going too far. Nobody likes that kind of question. Ladies and gentlemen, the law is the same way. It gets real cowardly at the welcome mat. Instead of knocking on the door and checking things out, it usually turns away and worries instead about the kid who slips through the gates without paying at the fairgrounds." Mr. Feinberg wasn't letting anyone off the hook, even himself. He was the one that had prosecuted Wellesley for trespassing. "Home sweet home!" he mused. "It wasn't so sweet in the Baker home for the past fourteen years, was it?"

My gaze kept drifting to Wellesley. She sat on the edge of her chair wound tight as a spring, fully preoccupied with Mr.

Feinberg's speech. Now I knew why she'd never invited Taylor or me into her home. I always thought it was because Milltown wasn't on the way to anyplace or because her dad was sleeping off the night shift. A lot of things she'd done and said made sense now. The night we hid in my tree during kick the can she'd asked what it would be like to be someone else. I thought it was a kid's fantasy. Now I knew it was as real as the rust holes in the fenders of her Schwinn. Wellesley hadn't been a kid for a long time. The girl I'd grown up with, same grade, same town, had aged with these experiences.

"If Wellesley or Tiffany or their mom had complained, I wonder what would have happened." Mr. Feinberg couldn't have been more intense if he were pleading for his own daughter. His voice filled the courtroom. "When's the last time a father went to jail for beating his kid in this county?" He paused and looked up and down each row. Some jurors shrugged their shoulders, others stared blankly. "I checked it out. It's been eighteen years as far as I can tell and that one only happened because the boy was hospitalized in a coma and died. The father was out again before Wellesley Baker was even born."

I could almost feel Mom shudder. Grandpa Blane's death was fresh enough that I was sure her imagination easily recreated the horror of someone slowly dying in a hospital bed. Mr. Feinberg's words must have hurt in another way too. Growing up, whenever I complained because Clearwater was a small town with nothing to do, she said it was a good place to raise a family. Less things to get you into trouble she said. And, although I groused, I believed her. Mr. Feinberg was challenging Mom's dream. Her little paradise was hiding something ugly.

"Unfortunately, ladies and gentlemen, the first myth prevailed in this case and it shouldn't have. We were all spectators to what happened in Milltown. Maybe we believed that the law would magically intervene as a shield between Wellesley and her dad the way it does on those broad Clearwater streets the prosecutor mentioned. That's the second myth." I pictured Wellesley, Taylor, and me making big S's on our bikes, riding no-hands down Willow on our way to the Rexall, unafraid of anything. The breeze washed past our ears as we tested how close we could come to the curbs and parked cars.

"Santayana says 'habit is stronger than reason.' Our habit in Clearwater, in the whole county for that matter, has been to stand back and let things be, sometimes even when we knew it was wrong." Mr. Feinberg had just said the same thing Dad said when he scolded the jury about not paying their bills. But Mr. Feinberg had a way of drawing on some great thinker who didn't live in Clearwater to make his hard points. It was a good strategy. People here were smart enough to respect what got printed in a book.

"For fourteen years, we left Wellesley alone to defend herself against her dad's belt. And she was alone again the night of the Labor Day Fair when a man weighing two hundred and forty pounds charged her with a whiskey bottle, coming back for his gun. Was that a loving father? Or was it a rapist and a killer? Look at Laddie's picture, what do you see?" Mr. Feinberg had left Laddie's drawing on the portable easel about ten feet from the jury box. Even from where I was, I could see violence in the bold lines Laddie had used to outline Mr. Baker. He was a monster in brown crayon. I knew there was no doubt in Wellesley's mind who was charging her that night. She'd studied that meaty face a thousand times and watched that lower lip go off like a fire alarm. She'd confronted him with his affair. He wasn't going to stop with the belt this time.

"Should she let him crush her skull with his bottle and hope she survives another blow?" Mr. Feinberg raised an imaginary bottle over his head and leaned toward the jury. The jurors unconsciously drew back. "Should she let him have the gun back?"

Mr. Feinberg cast his eyes to the floor as if Wellesley's open grave were there. Slowly, he raised them and reengaged the jury. "The prosecutor showed you a picture of the victim on the floor of the Bakers' kitchen. As horrible as that scene is, I believe it would pale next to the picture of what Mr. Baker did day in and day out to Wellesley and her family. The defense doesn't have any photos. You'll just have to imagine what it looked like when it was Wellesley's turn on the floor or Tiffany's or their mom's. And you'll just have to imagine what malice Wellesley must have seen in her father's eyes the night she had to shoot." The man who played games in the Brooklyn cemetery as a kid must have seen more than he'd let on. From the passion in his eyes, it was clear that the vision was real to him. Maybe it was something else he'd learned from his ancestors. "Wellesley Baker was in danger of losing her virtue and her life and she acted in self-defense! The war that started on the morning Mr. Baker kicked his wife out from under the bedsheets and sent her and the new baby sprawling to the floor culminated in a final deadly charge last Labor Day weekend. Wellesley had to do what she did. It was her father's prick, or the pistol . . . or both."

Wellesley's hands were folded against her lips. She'd had to bare so many shameful secrets. At least she had a Feinberg to shout her innocence. She'd always kidded me about being Catholic. We could do anything we wanted and rinse it off in the confessional. And what passed through that flimsy green curtain in the dark was only for the ears of a dottering parish priest numbed to the litany of commonplace venial and mortal sins. The Catholic way had another advantage over the jury system. The priest had to acquit.

"Members of the jury, it comes down to values. None of us wanted to see Mr. Baker or his wife or his daughter killed that night. But things had escalated to the point where death was inevitable. Do you want to live in a community where a child cannot defend herself against an abusive father?" The only audible response was the tick of the pendulum through the clock casement. "When something as tragic as the shooting death of·another human being happens, there is something in all of us that wants to find and punish the guilty party. If there's a guilty party in this case, it's us. By our indifference to the conditions that existed in the Baker house, we let it reach the point of no return. Wellesley Baker is the innocent. Show her what kind of values you have and set her free. God knows she has suffered plenty already and God knows that, despite your acquittal, the pain will punish her forever."

When he was finished, Mr. Feinberg simply nodded to the

jury and returned to his seat. Wellesley reached over and clasped his hand. He'd just done what I'd been wanting to do, thundered against Clearwater for its blindness. He'd drenched Dutcher and the rest of us with his Cameroon rain. He'd empaneled a jury so that Wellesley could not only be vindicated in the courtroom but in her town. I only wished that every doubting simpleton who sipped Cokes at the Rexall counter could have heard him.

Most of the crowd milled around in the hallway when the judge sent the jury into deliberations and dismissed us. Wellesley was returned to the basement of the courthouse. There was an easiness in the air. Most people seemed subdued by Mr. Feinberg's closing. Taylor was pepped up by it and repeated his condemnations, as if he'd been preaching the same thing all along.

Laddie, Mom, Dad, Mrs. Baker, and I went to the Golden Gavel to wait for the verdict. Mr. Feinberg said he'd send word as soon as the jury returned. I figured it might have been the first time Laddie had ever been served a Coca-Cola on a coaster. He knew what to do with the straw, however, and drained his glass without taking a breath. He still had to learn the difference between drinking to quench your thirst and sipping to be sociable. Maybe he was just making sure he'd drowned that forest fire in his belly. When Dad noticed his empty glass, he ordered a second one.

Sitting through two days of trial together had made us closer to Mrs. Baker. I didn't think my parents were anti-Milltown but I'd never heard them say anything good about the place either. As with a lot of things that mattered to them, they just kept quiet. The description of life with Mr. Baker was worse than anyone's worst fears about Milltown. Ironically, it felt as if the more we knew about each other's shortcomings, the more comfortable we were.

Mrs. Baker and Mom ordered chef's salads. The rest of us had burgers and fries. Laddie also had two slices of chocolate cream pie. Somehow, because he didn't say much, I'd imagined he didn't eat much. It was the reverse. No wonder he had so much energy for pedaling.

I could tell Mrs. Baker was particularly anxious. She'd spear a single dice of cheese or a lettuce leaf, put it to her mouth, change her mind, and put her fork down. When someone asked her a question, it had to be repeated and she'd apologize. She enjoyed Laddie though. "That boy eats like a hired hand at harvest time," she said. She took it as a personal compliment when Laddie, after his second piece of pie, ate her salad.

The newspaper boy from the courthouse poked his head in the door about five to five. We were the only ones in the restaurant. "Mr. Feinberg said to tell you folks the jury's back." We ran across the street. I felt like we were running for a train that had already left the station. I could only picture the witnesses who'd testified against Wellesley. They'd made the train.

We'd speculated that if the jury came back in less than two hours, they'd taken the easy route and agreed with the state. It took more time to accept the responsibility Mr. Feinberg had asked of them. But when Judge Lally asked the foreman of the jury to deliver the verdict, the man with the string tie and imitation pearl buttons on his shirt announced, "Not guilty!" Mr. Baker finally got his funeral.

32

The sale of the hardware store closed between Christmas and New Year's of my freshman year. Dad went to work for the Sylvanus County School District as Facilities Manager. He became responsible for every furnace, freezer, and school bus in the district. Mom said, "It was the best thing that ever happened to him. I lost a store and gained a husband." Dad didn't take it well at first. He was back in school for the first time in over twenty years.

But the job had hidden benefits. He met people he'd never have seen at the hardware. On Veterans Day in my junior year, as part of his job with the school district, Dad rode with the governor and his wife from the Sylvanus Airport, trading war stories about their Navy duty in the South Pacific. The governor gave a speech from the platform Dad's crew had built next to the Abe Lincoln statue in City Park. It was longer than the Gettysburg address and not nearly as eloquent as Aaron Feinberg's closing argument.

The people in Clearwater knew how to forgive a man who couldn't keep his store alive. They didn't know how to accept a girl who'd shot her dad. The jury's absolution couldn't shake the conviction of Clearwater's storekeepers, butchers, and farmers. While he was cutting my hair, Larry the barber summed it up. "There's something wrong with this generation of kids. Mr. Baker was no saint but he didn't deserve a bullet in the heart!"

People considered the notion of self-defense a poor excuse. Some said it was the work of that fancy out-of-state lawyer, implying he'd imported the principle. Only a few talked openly about the rest of his case, the pattern of physical abuse that Wellesley had suffered. Nobody mentioned what Mr. Baker had done to Tiffany. The town preferred to remember him as the rambunctious driver of the Pink Lady.

Even kids at school avoided Wellesley. Some called her "psychotic." Grant Beller, who Wellesley had once rescued when he was locked in the women's lavatory at the Orpheum Theater, said, "They let her off 'cause she was a girl." But Wellesley never confronted her detractors with the whole truth. Instead, people's whispers fed Wellesley's own doubts. "It pisses me off what they're thinking, Will, but maybe they're right."

By the end of sophomore year, she'd made up for the semester she missed in jail. By senior year, she had a 3.6 grade average and was mad at herself for not doing better. She led two lives. During the day, she operated solo, studying in the library or reading in the football stands at noon hour. At last bell, she went to one of her jobs. She delivered a newspaper route, then got on washing dishes at the hospital and, by the time she was seventeen, waited tables at the Arctic.

"Don't hide, Wellesley," I told her. "If you'd reach out to people, maybe they'd reach back."

"I've never been good at playing games with people," she said.

I tried to reunite our old threesome. Taylor would cooperate to a point.

"She's changed, Will!" he said.

"You're supposed to," I told him. "We're growing up."

"It's not just years, Will, it's that night." He drew back like I was going to slug him. Taylor knew I hated everyone trying to psychoanalyze Wellesley.

On the third anniversary of her acquittal, I had the brainstorm of a reunion in Union Gap, the three of us. Dinner at Maude's Diner. I was buying. Wellesley made arrangements to get off at the Arctic. I dug out the hat I'd worn on the freight train ride that summer and Dad's hunting knife. The idea was to put it on before going in and see if Maude recognized me without the cast.

This time, everything was on the square. I borrowed the family Buick—Dad had a soft spot for cars that drove like ocean liners and bought another one as soon as we could afford it—and I told Mom where we were going. Dad joked about his part in the prior escapade. "Are you sure you're paid up with the railroad?" The yard master hadn't known what to do with the hundred dollars Dad had made me pay them and so he put it into the union's Christmas fund.

Taylor never did pay anything to the railroad. Neither did he show up at my house for the reunion dinner. We checked his house, drove by school and finally went without him.

"Don't let it get you down, Will," Wellesley said, "I'm sure something came up."

"What could be more important?" It wasn't just the celebration of the acquittal. It was a chance for the three of us to recapture something that was fading.

It's not that Taylor ever stopped liking Wellesley. He got distracted by his own hormones. To him, high school was a hunting ground. Taylor was tireless in his pursuit of girls—and careless.

Christmas vacation, our senior year, he told me Lisa Alexander was pregnant. I was stunned. Lisa was the least likely girl in our class to get pregnant. She was a bookish, broad-faced redhead who always knew the answers when she was called on. She didn't smoke, drink, or show much interest in boys.

They married before a district court judge one Saturday. I was best man and Lisa's oldest sister was maid of honor. The parents on both sides agreed that because of the circumstances it should be a family wedding, but Taylor did invite Wellesley. If you had asked me before the pregnancy what kind of wedding Taylor would have, I'd have said extravagant, with reams of imitation silk and lace, live music, and a crowd of ex-girl friends and guys who had to see it to believe it. And I wouldn't have guessed Lisa. But when they were cutting the cake afterwards at the Clark's, I noticed for the first time that Lisa had the same twinkle in her eyes I'd always loved in Taylor.

Most everyone bet he'd quit high school when he started working at his dad's appliance repair shop to pay for his new family, but Taylor insisted on finishing. Even though Lisa was showing, Taylor wanted to go to the Senior Prom and asked me to double-date with them. I'd started going steady with Monica Amberly the previous fall. It probably had something to do with the fact that I'd finally made first-string varsity football. I played end on offense and halfback on defense. Skill positions, my dad called them. At the end of the season, I was voted the Reginald Cunningham trophy by my teammates. Traditionally, the trophy went to someone who played surprisingly better than his raw physical talent warranted.

It had taken Monica and me three years to get back to where we left off on her porch that night after the Labor Day dance. Somehow I'd never been able to quiet the bell that had started ringing inside me at Spirit Lake. But exactly twenty-four hours before I was supposed to pick her up for the prom, she called to say she had the measles.

"That's lousy," I said. "Didn't you have them when you were little?"

Her voice was so soft I could barely hear her over the noise of the clothes dryer. "Mom said apparently not this strain. I told her it was the fault of her being too overprotective."

"Do you want me to come over anyway, to keep you company?"

"No way. It's contagious. Besides, I look horrible."

At first, I was depressed. Then I was relieved. Then I called Wellesley at the Arctic. "Sorry to bother you at work, but I had to reach you."

"Just hurry," she said. "I've got four tables waiting and the boss is glaring at me."

"Let's go out tomorrow night!"

"That's your prom," she said. The clatter of dishes played behind her.

"Not anymore. Monica's sick in bed."

"I'm off at eight." She hung up.

Taylor was more disappointed than me about my not going to the prom. He invited Wellesley and me over to his house for a preprom function. Taylor had rented a tuxedo in Sylvanus and looked like some actor who opened the envelopes on Oscar night in Hollywood. Lisa, with her red hair, had never looked more beautiful in a pale green dress with a high waist that mostly hid her growing stomach.

The Taylor Clarks popped a bottle of champagne that they'd been saving since the wedding and Taylor proposed a toast. "Here's to our good friends, Will and Wellesley. I miss you guys." There was a look of nostalgia in his eyes that told me he meant it.

"And here's to you and Lisa and the baby." I tipped my glass toward Lisa's waist.

"I hope that it's a she," said Wellesley, "and she has the patience to teach her dad to make a decent racing bug." Everyone laughed.

I finished my glass. There was enough for Taylor and Wellesley to each have a second. Everyone was in a hurry so we said good-bye in their front yard and went in our separate cars. Taylor and Lisa were giggling with excitement. I didn't want to spoil it for them by saying anything but I was so glad not to be going to the prom. It was such a supposed-to thing to do, and I was feeling a need for independence. And looking forward to Wellesley. Since going with Monica again, I hadn't seen as much of Wellesley. The measles were a perfect excuse.

I'd made a reservation at Commillini's just outside Nestor. It was far enough away from Clearwater that I figured we wouldn't run into the prom crowd. Mama Commillini was an Italian widow who raised her own chickens and vegetables on a farm right behind the big white farmhouse on the creek that she'd converted into a restaurant. It was elegant but you could go in street clothes and it had the reputation for the best food in four counties. The tables were covered with red-and-white checkered cloths and a candle in a wine bottle caked with melted wax lit each table. A man in a satin vest and a mustache strolled the floor playing the violin during our dinner. I had chicken cacciatore, ladled with Mama's special spaghetti sauce, and heaped with her fresh-ground Parmesan. Wellesley ordered the prosciutto appetizer and baked lasagna. We had spumoni for desert. She kept saying she'd have been just as happy someplace cheaper. "Like Maude's Diner," she laughed. I told her I was just spending the money I'd saved by not going to the prom. We laughed so much talking about pranks the three of us had pulled that my jaws needed a rest by the time we finished eating.

On the way back, we drove through Sylvanus and circled once around the courthouse for old time's sake. I wanted it to be a victory lap. But Wellesley had lived in its basement for almost three months and so it was no wonder that neither one of us could think of anything funny to say. While we were parked there staring at the place, Wellesley took a pint of Jack Daniel's out of her purse. I told her to put it away. "Not here."

"Come on Will, take a nip! It'll take your mind off Monica."

Afterward, we drove to the river and sat on the rock over the swimming hole. The moon illuminated a transparent cloud like the mantle of a lantern. We lay on our backs trading swigs from the bottle.

"Some days I wake up in the morning," she said, "and think it's summer. The old days. Then something clicks inside my head and I'm trapped again."

"Trapped in what?"

"In this . . . fucking town!" She stiff-armed the bottle toward me. "I'm so jealous of you, Will. You're getting out of here." Wellesley scored higher on the Merit Scholarship test than I did, but she didn't bother to apply to a single college. She said it would break her mom's heart if she went away to school. They didn't have the money anyway.

"I won't be that far away. I'm only going to Ellensburg."

"It might as well be on the moon," she said. "It's a town with a college in it. People will worry about something besides how many inches of rain we've had or who owns a TV set."

In spite of the Jack Daniel's, Wellesley's words hurt. I wanted to love this town, but there was a boundary line here as well defined as the bed of the Clearwater River. When she pulled the trigger on her dad, Wellesley had crossed that line. Not Aaron Feinberg's speech or the jury acquittal had let her come back. "They'll have faults we haven't even dreamed of," I said.

"You're always such an optimist, Will. How come?"

"How come?" I chuckled and said the first thing that came to mind. "Fear I guess. I'm afraid to believe that things won't turn out right. Do you think I've got my head in the sand?"

"I think it's got something to do with your family."

"You mean like Dad going broke?"

"I'm serious." Wellesley's face seemed softer in the half light of the moon. As she handed me the bottle, she rested her hand on my thigh. "I'm getting ahead of you."

I took the bottle with one hand and put the other on hers. "You want to know something?"

She didn't pull away. "What?"

"I've underestimated you." I scooted over next to her, not letting go. "It's so obvious, but I've been too stupid to see it. Whenever I looked at these hands before, I thought of how far you could shoot a slingshot or how fast you could shinny a flagpole. I'm going to miss you next year. I wish you were coming with me."

Wellesley tried to pinch my stomach. "Are you going squishy on me, Bradford? Come on. You're going to conquer the world." She let her hand drop where I could catch it again. "I'd just drag you down. You've got better things to do than putting me back together."

"Name one."

"Falling in love with Monica."

"That's just it, I don't think I'm the Amberly type. She's the perfect date but I need a friend."

"Give it time," Wellesley said. "Rome wasn't built in a day."

"Why not do it the easy way, start with a friend?"

"The booze is making you sentimental, Bradford."

"Maybe it's melting my inhibitions . . ."

"Same thing," she said. "If you're going to drink, you've got to keep your wits about you."

"Are you saying no?"

"I didn't hear the question."

I squeezed her hands. "All I'm saying is you snuck up on me. All those times you were beating me arm wrestling and building racing bugs, I acted like you were a guy. And now . . ."

"I'm not rejecting you, Bradford. I guess I'm naturally skeptical about what people say when they've been drinking. Maybe I'm skeptical about myself."

"No way."

"Really. Even this talk about getting out of town." She crossed her legs, letting one knee lie solidly against me. "The thought scares me to pieces. As long as I'm here, I can blame everyone else for my problems . . . they aren't giving me a chance and all that crap. The truth is I feel like the thing with my dad put a big scar down me, forehead to toenail. I'm not talking about what he did. That's stuff for psychologists to worry about. I'm talking about what I did. As soon as I reach for something big, the cords of that scar are going to turn crimson. I'll be found out."

"Wellesley, the jury acquitted you. Look at me." I put my hands against her ears so that her glasses lifted slightly off the bridge of her nose and spoke one word at a time, "You . . . are . . . innocent!"

"I wish. I'm not Catholic, remember. We don't have the confessional." She leaned her head against my shoulder and I wrapped my arm around her. I could smell the kitchen smoke from the Arctic in her hair. "Listen to me. The whiskey makes me feel sorry for myself. I'd rather be sentimental." She laughed and reached out. Sideways to each other, her shoulder against my chest, we hugged. "Of course, I'll be your friend, Bradford. For as long as this damn river runs. Is that sentimental enough?"

"Perfect! One more promise, remember how we used to sit in the tree over my garage and talk about how things were going to be?"

"Kids' dreams," she said.

"Someday we'll own that dude ranch in Wyoming and each have our own Appaloosa and come home dead tired at night from riding and play the harmonica around the campfire. We'll hire Taylor and his kids to bale hay and keep the bunkhouse clean."

We both laughed until we fell over, flat on our backs again, the rushing of the Clearwater echoing off the darkness.

33

My expectations for college were down to earth. The people who said high school would be the best time of my life said the same thing about college. I would have gone without the hyperbole. It was a matter of generational leapfrog. Grandpa Blane had a grade school education. Dad and Mom graduated from high school. I had to finish college.

Central Washington University was part of the state system, a four-year college the state had recently relabeled a university. If I'd saved Grandpa's War Bond, maybe I could have tried for Notre Dame. Ellensburg's major claim to fame was the annual stampede Mom and Dad had taken me to when I was a kid. I saw my first rodeo there. The school was small enough not to get lost in but far enough from home to leave me on my own. And I was on my own again. Monica and I had broken up, by mutual agreement, at the end of the summer. The energy of anticipating new lives at our respective colleges had smothered whatever was left of our flickering romance. The Greyhound ride made it possible to reach Clearwater on a long weekend but I was on a budget that only allowed trips home for major holidays.

That's why in January of my first year, I called Wellesley. Seeing her and Taylor at Christmas had stirred up the feeling that I was missing out on something. Taylor was working regularly and living in a rented house near the cemetery. He'd hired a kid to shovel his walks. Wellesley had converted the Pink Lady from a stock to a street car. She'd blowtorched the doors open, added window glass, and a muffler and, fittingly, painted it pure black. They seemed to be living real lives while I was still studying the possibilities.

But both of them made me feel as if I was at Harvard or Yale the way they bragged about me being in college.

The fact that Wellesley had transportation made it easier to invite her. Because of Lincoln's Birthday, we had a three-day weekend. I'd written up a schedule for myself to study ahead so I wouldn't have to crack a book once she arrived on Friday night. On another sheet of paper, I'd listed friends to meet and things to do, including a Bergman film in the student union, borrowing snowshoes for a hike in the pass, checkers in the coffeehouse, and swimming at the athletic pavilion (unlikely, since Wellesley hated chlorine). The only thing we'd agreed to on the phone was dancing at the local grange, country western. Wellesley said she'd bring her cow-boy hat and stop by my house to get the hunting hat I'd worn in the Junior Rodeo when I broke my arm.

Somehow being away from Wellesley had taught me more about her than I'd learned seeing her almost every day in Clearwater. I'd always thought I'd meet the right person somewhere out there, at Spirit Lake, Union Gap, or even Ellensburg. Never Clearwater. Life was a progression from the home doorstep to the great beyond. But one semester into the game, I started to doubt its premise. The people I'd met so far at college seemed smart enough. Everyone debated books they'd been assigned—*Phenomenon of Man, The Ugly American, The Affluent Society.* The discussions were a form of flirtation.

Rich girls who dressed down to be "beat" seemed like impostors next to Wellesley in her cut-off jeans and sweat-shirt. When they talked about Teilhard de Chardin's forward evolution of the human condition, I thought of Mr. Baker and wondered if the author would have changed his thesis if he knew what Wellesley knew. The more I saw of the out there, the more I was drawn back to my friend in the glasses and the lopsided smile who couldn't pretend if her life depended on it.

When Mom's call reached the third floor phone booth at McMahon Hall I was showering. Phil Wilson hollered at me through the doorway, "Bradford, it's your mom!"

I wrapped a brown terrycloth towel around my waist and went dripping to the phone. The metal tray in the booth had been broken out, so the receiver just hung from the cord, twisting slowly in space.

"Will, there's been a horrible accident," she said. Her voice was on the verge of shattering. "Wellesley's been killed!" A flash of lightning went through my brain. "You remember the rail crossing, at the bottom of the gully. It's been a blizzard here. The train hit her. They think she died instantly."

My insides curdled. "She was driving over here to meet me, Mom. I can't believe it."

"I know. She stopped by yesterday to get your hat."

"Have you talked to Mrs. Baker?"

"Not yet, Will. She'll be destroyed."

"Mom, I'm coming home."

When she hung up, I had to steady myself against the outside of the booth. Wilson stopped me. "What's the matter? You're white as a sheet." I waved him off, weaved my way back to the bottom bunk, and collapsed.

In the shower, I'd been daydreaming about dancing with Wellesley at the grange. She'd always missed out on the dance. Mom's phone call was a hammer blow that smashed our future as well as the past. I couldn't imagine a world without Wellesley. My roommate, Billy Gallagher, couldn't understand how I could be so upset over a girl I hadn't even dated.

I expected to see my body tissue melt onto the crumpled sheets of the bed. I pictured Mr. Baker at the controls of that locomotive, swearing and slapping the instrument panel the way he did the night I listened from the coal bin.

More people attended Wellesley's funeral than Grandpa Blane's. I suspected many were there out of guilt. A Great Northern locomotive finally made Wellesley the victim in public she'd been so long in private. The train that ground her and the Pink Lady into rubble at the State Route 16 crossing had pushed her back over that imaginary line.

Mrs. Baker asked me to sit with her. Nobody could find

Tiffany. I was family. Wellesley would have been so proud to see how handsome her mom looked. Everyone in town treated her with respect that day.

Her mom told me that Wellesley had just sent in her application for admission at Central Washington. There had been life insurance proceeds from Mr. Baker's policy with the union but Wellesley didn't feel right about using them. She'd saved enough on her own to get started though. Most people watched the wind direction and positioned themselves for a free ride. Not Wellesley. "You were her incentive, Will. She knew you believed in her."

We buried her in a part of the cemetery where the graves had plain, flat markers. She was about one hundred and twenty feet downslope from Grandpa Blane. Aaron Feinberg stood at the graveside with his wife and Laddie. I thought of Grandpa's funeral. It had the feeling of celebration, like we'd inducted him into some hall of fame. He'd suffered loss, like Grandma Olive's sudden death, but it came after what Mom called a storybook marriage and her bearing four healthy children. Even though he'd spent half his life looking at her picture next to the bed instead of having her in it, I knew the memory was sweet.

Wellesley's death made a gash in me that resisted healing. She never had the chance to build a normal collection of friendships and experiences. The grandpa she never knew had shot the family dog for pawing at the back door. Tiffany ran away. The only picture of her dad was a collage that haunted her. And Wellesley had to kill him to defend her mom.

With the January snow still covering the ground, the hole seemed darker than Grandpa's. Looking at the coffin, I kept thinking of the car remains I'd seen at A&M Wrecking and how mangled its occupant must have been. Maybe the engine that had hit her was the same one that had carried us away to Union Gap that summer. The only thing that survived unharmed was Dad's size seven-and-a-half hunting hat which the police found wedged between the seats. Walking from the gravesite to our cars, Taylor put his arm around my shoulder and didn't say anything.

After the reception in the basement of the church, I had to get away from the prattle of people who had banished her from this town. Everyone offered their opinion as to why it had happened, trying to manufacture sympathy with their explanations. The car was having starter trouble and must have stalled. They couldn't afford to have it worked on at a real garage. The engineer was drinking. The train had no business passing town that fast in the first place. What a shame, they said.

They'd also found a broken bottle of Jack Daniel's in the wreckage, the same thing we drank the first night I held her at the river. I wished I'd told her then how uneasy it made me to see that single, unfortunate resemblance to her dad. Somehow, his paws had reached up out of his ashes through the floorboards of that cursed car and held her at the crossing.

I took the road to Clearwater Dam. With snow tires, the Buick held firmly. I veered off to the swimming hole. Pine boughs drooped with their loads of snow. The car rocked gently, tracking in and out of the ruts. I was the first one to use the road that morning. The heater burned the dust in the air. I had to duck to see through the porthole cleared on the windshield by the defroster. My headache throbbed with the rub of the wipers as they swiped dry flakes to one side then the other.

When I stepped out, the soles of my oxfords were cold against the snow. A wet spot expanded under the arch of my right foot from powder that had worked its way into my shoe.

From the top of the rocks where we used to jump, I could hear the muffled sounds of the river. Ice and snow bridged the channel. I could see the dark flow of water through melted craters. It looked so secretive.

Then I felt something warm against my cheeks, like I was bleeding. I wiped it with my fingers to be sure.

If Wellesley were here, she'd want to test the strength of those frozen bridges. I could see her lifting her toes and placing them like a young doe. "Come on, Will, let's cross it!"

"The river will paralyze you if you fall," I'd answer.

"But think how good you'll feel if we make it," she'd say, cocking her head, the steam of her words suspended in the air.

19704709R00193

Made in the USA
San Bernardino, CA
08 March 2015